THE ISLAND of LOST GIRLS

Manjula Padmanabhan is a writer, artist and playwright. She grew up in Europe and Southeast Asia, and returned to India as a teenager in the late 1960s. The popular comic strip character, Suki, created by Manjula, appeared in the *Sunday Observer* in Bombay and later in the *Pioneer* in New Delhi through the 1980s and 1990s. In 1997, her play *Harvest* won first prize at the Onassis Prize for Theatre in Greece. She is the author of several critically acclaimed books, including *Getting There, Hot Death, Cold Soup, Kleptomania* and *Three Virgins and Other Stories*, and a number of books for children as author-illustrator, among them *Mouse Attack* and a series of picture puzzle books. Her previous novel, *Escape*, in which the characters Youngest and Meiji were first introduced, has been reissued by Hachette India in 2015.

Praise for the Book

'Manjula Padmanabhan's vivid, sometimes cynically violent, trip through zones, enclaves, islands and water-worlds takes up where Ursula K. Le Guin left off, placing gender at the heart of both dystopia and her protagonists' tentative dreams of utopia. [...] It's wilder, crueller and more hallucinatory than any other novel out there this year.' – Nilanjana S. Roy, *Business Standard*

'Padmanabhan's fictionscape is spooky and her narrative is edgy and fast-moving, hurtling through changing zones that are every bit as ideological as they are geographic.' – *Hindustan Times*

'Padmanabhan has long experimented with the futuristic [...] but the brutality and invention of this new world is on an epic scale. The characters that populate [the novel] range from the demented and irretrievably cruel to ones of complex shades, and command the reader's attention.' – *OPEN*

'The world that Padmanabhan has created...will stir up your imagination.' – *Asian Age*

Also by Manjula Padmanabhan

Visit to the City Market (illustrations)
Hot Death, Cold Soup
Harvest (play)
Getting There
This is Suki! (cartoons)
Mouse Attack
Mouse Invaders
Kleptomania
Hidden Fires
Doubletalk (cartoons)
Unprincess!
Three Virgins and Other Stories
I am Different! (illustrations)
Same & Different (illustrations)
Where's That Cat? (illustrations)
Escape

THE ISLAND *of* LOST GIRLS

Manjula Padmanabhan

hachette INDIA

First published in 2015 by Hachette India
(Registered name: Hachette Book Publishing India Pvt. Ltd)
An Hachette UK company
www.hachetteindia.com

This edition published in 2017

SRD

ISBN 978-93-5195-177-3

Hachette Book Publishing India Pvt. Ltd
4th & 5th Floors, Corporate Centre,
Plot No. 94, Sector 44, Gurgaon 122 003, India

Typeset in Optima LT Std 11/14
by InoSoft Systems, Noida

Printed and bound in India
by Manipal Technologies Limited, Manipal

FSC
www.fsc.org
MIX
Paper | Supporting responsible forestry
FSC™ C043100

PART I YOUNGEST

1

The quickest way across the Poisoned Sea was aboard the Cut-Throat Express. Warriors and assassins, hunters and unattached transies, all travelled on the submarine ferry free of charge, no questions asked. For their own safety, passengers were locked into narrow cages with open drains beneath their feet.

But a cage is also a trap.

So when two mercenaries with steel nails for teeth began needling the silent figure in the enclosure between them, he had nowhere to run. His dark blue hijab marked him as a transie, a transsexual in the pleasure industry. Yet he was tall and broad. His neck was thick. He seemed less a paid slut than a deserting warrior.

The mercenaries sniffed entertainment.

They grunted a question to him in pidgin: *Where fum?*

No response.

They tried other languages.

No response.

Neighbouring inmates began to hoot and whistle.

So the mercenaries pushed their staves through the bars of the transie's cage. They took turns poking and prodding the silent figure until – *Ah!* The transie's hood was thrown aside and his head bared.

Hoo! Hoo! Hoo! howled the other travellers.

His skin was teak brown. His hair was thick and black, hanging down his back in a long ponytail. He wore rings in his nose and ears. He had no facial scars. No tattoos.

Whut team, the mercenaries wanted to know. Their steel teeth threw sparks in the dim-lit passenger hold as they spoke. *Whut master? Two holes? Or three?*

The transie kept his bare head bent, saying nothing.

Egged on by fellow passengers the mercenaries now attached a steel hook to their staves and went to work.

Eventually, the commotion triggered alarms and clouds of numb-gas. By then the tall figure was cowering on the floor of his cage. His jewellery had been ripped off. A dead rat had been plaited into his long hair.

And there he remained, on the floor. Oncc a proud and handsome man called Youngest, he spent the rest of the journey slumped over, covered in blood, fleas and rat-entrails.

2

The ferry terminated at Confluenza Junction, the glittering deep-water port. Passengers disembarked at the lowest of six levels. The air was thick, steamy and vomit-flavoured. Hyenas snickered in the alcoves. Vultures perched in the overhead beams.

Passengers were released one at a time into the ferry's luggage hold to extract their cargo. Then they swarmed out with their enormous loads and up the ramp that would ultimately lead to the Ascensor bays, on Level One far above. They used their luggage like battering rams to force their way forward. They had to hurry. Any traveller too weakened by the journey to leave the dock in a timely fashion was dispatched by the animals.

Youngest had two cases with him. Both were shoulder-height, thick and flat-sided, steel-rimmed and mounted on wheels. He sandwiched himself between them with one on either side. Using their bulk, he thrust himself forward, moving slowly but doggedly one finger-length at a time, until he was buried in the middle of the column of cursing, snarling, brawling men. After that it was just a question of being processed forward along with the rest of the mob.

Announcements were made in three languages following one after the other in strict rotation: Unida, Arabic and Mod¡Kung. As they advanced up from one floor to the next, advertising jingles began squawking from floating speakers: cloning services, prosthetic advice, beast management. Bright holograms flashed on and off offering the latest in swords, spears, double-handed axes and steel-tipped whips. Images from the playing fields of the area known as the Zone flickered on the walls: severed heads, twitching limbs, slimy mounds of gut.

Youngest looked neither left nor right.

The filth in his hair and the wounds in his nose and ears were only a small part of his benumbed state. The much bigger part was the plan he had conceived two years ago. The plan he had set in motion, step by desperate step. The closer he came to its completion, the farther he wanted to be from it; from what he had become; from what he had done to reach this position.

Now that he was at the very threshold of culmination, there was nothing left to feel but a deathly stillness. Nothing left to hear but an audio chip.

Permanently embedded in his upper jaw.

It produced a loop of sound that only he could hear. They were instructions in another man's voice, delivered in a soft, purring monotone. It was not loud so much as it was relentless: *sell-the-girl. find-the-Island. in-the-name-of-all-true-men. do-your-duty.*

On and on, it went. On and on. It never stopped. He could ignore it but there were times when the words filtered up into his consciousness with fresh force.

Tiny robotic cameras buzzed and hummed, weaving above the crowd exactly like flies. He swatted them away or crushed them between his fingers, without noticing that they were machines, not insects.

At the next level up, the ramp became a moving walkway. Promotional messages about the famous terminus blared from loudspeakers.

THREE THOUSAND PASSENGERS PER HOUR!

TWENTY-FOUR-HOUR BROTHEL!

MARINE ANIMAL GLADIATORIUM!

CLONING FACILITIES FOR ONE AND ALL!

Travellers were packed five shoulders abreast now. Some,

in addition to their goods, carried live animals strapped to themselves. Most were goats or sheep, but one man bore, on either shoulder, a pair of horned creatures with spotted skins. Hybrid antelopes or horned cheetah, it was hard to tell.

A traveller carrying stacks of plastic panels on his back blocked Youngest's forward view. On his left was a clone warrior transporting stinking animal pelts. To his right was a leather-goods trader wearing strips of coloured beads instead of clothes. Strapped to the man's front and facing him was a white goat with luminous rosy eyes. Youngest registered something distasteful about the creature, but avoided looking directly at it until a slurping sound caused him to turn his head. He saw the man with his mouth fused to that of the goat. The creature had full soft lips and a long tongue that slithered in and out of the kiss with restless energy. He stared without really intending to until the goat disengaged to focus its glowing eyes upon him.

Shuddering, he looked away at once.

All the while, lithe-bodied vendors had been sidling in and out of the crush, selling compressed meals, sexual services, hand-held toilets and immigration advice. They were all, like Youngest, transies. Some spoke in falsetto voices despite blue-stubbled chins. Others had smooth faces, plucked eyebrows and long false lashes.

It took a while for Youngest to register the persistent tapping that came from behind him. The sensation of someone plucking at his arm continued until he responded by thrusting backwards with the case strapped to his right arm.

'Owwie!' yelped the vendor at once. Then he addressed Youngest in pidgin Unida. 'Hello? Please? I am helping?'

Youngest could understand the language but had never learnt to speak it. He shoved back again, saying nothing.

The man yipped on cue but he didn't give up.

'Listen, Mister – or Miss? Please. I am at your service.'

Youngest said, grinding the words out with difficulty, 'I. Is. Not. *Want*. Service.' His voice was deep. Regardless of his appearance, he still sounded like a man.

'Thank you kind Sir – or Madam?' said the irritating fellow. 'Thank you for speak to unworthy myself! Allow to introduce? My name is Aila.'

He pronounced it: Ah-EE-la.

Youngest was wedged in too tight to free his arms, turn around and swat the creature away. No words of adequate force came to his lips.

'Push on,' he said over his shoulder, knowing that he must sound ridiculously wrong. 'Fall off.'

'Aha! Madam is new to Port? Or is it "Sir"? Well, Sir or Madam – you is super very lucky. Actually, myself is expert in giving the helps.'

'Run off!' said Youngest. 'Die! Shoo!'

'Just listen me *one* time, Sir-Madam! If I is wrong, I is go. Is deal?'

'Go now!'

'You is first-timer in Confluenza. You is far from home. You is transie. All three is correct?'

'Wrong, wrong and wrong. Now go.'

'Really? You is feem, not transie?'

'Feem? What is …?' The words fell out before he could stop them.

'Ha! That is means you *must* be transie! Very good, Madam, now I is happy.'

'No! Go away! Go!'

'Madam, Madam – please. I is one too. Transie. That's why you is needs me. You is needs helps with Immigration. I is give the verygood tips. Then I is meet you on other side, yes? I is give helps to buy licenses, sexing, what-ever-thing, yes? Cheapest and best?'

'No.'

'Reaching to Ascensor Bay is super veryslow. We is have time. Please. Let me helps you. You is thanks me.'

'No.'

'There is many laws in City. I is find easy permissions.'

'No.'

'Just tell me your name. I is find you in City, no problem.'

'No!'

'I is have wash-kit.'

Silence.

'*Two* wash-kit,' said Aila at once. The weakness had been found.

Youngest groaned softly. Port vendors were notorious scoundrels, thieves and con-artists. But his need to clean himself was interfering with his sanity. He heard his mouth say, 'Okay. Yes.'

'No need to turn around, Madam. Showing me hand is enough. It is perfectly fine. You will not regret. But kit is not for use in queue, please! On Ascensor only. Okay, I is have *three* wash-kit.'

The mere sound of the words 'wash' and 'kit' in close proximity had revived Youngest. He breathed in sharply, gagging on the foul air as he cursed himself for his weakness.

'What is Madam's team?'

'Huh? Oh. Uh…nothing. No team,' said Youngest.

'Is not possible, Madam! Is must be team. Is Blue-Blue? Yes? You is wearing Blue-Blue colours. Same to mine. Thanks to Heaven. I will give the best helps. Total. Madam is showing hand to me?' Then he broke off to exclaim, 'Ohhh! Look, look, Madam! Look up—'

Youngest could not turn around on account of his heavy cases, but he managed to peer over his shoulder.

Aila was almost the same height as himself and leaning in

close. He wore the white-and-black chequered cloth of a man's head-cloth, yet his eyebrows were expertly penciled in. The pronounced prow-like nose and narrow face were remarkably smooth, with no evidence of facial hair. The mouth, which was full and precisely shaped, glistened with maroon lip-gloss. There were traces of colour on the undersides of his luxurious eyelashes.

His eyes were turned up, his whole face transfigured.

Youngest followed his gaze.

High above the overhead bars, he could see the glass tubes of sealed-in walkways. Within one of them, he could make out travellers sauntering along at a leisurely pace.

They must be Level One tourists, he thought. Wealthy people. They looked impossibly elegant, clean and orderly.

Then his heart jerked like a puppy on a tight leash.

Slender and languid, dressed in dainty, colourful clothes that swayed alluringly as they walked, these travellers clearly belonged to another species altogether from the sweating, stinking mob around him.

He could hear, as if at a great distance, Aila chittering like an excited squirrel.

'Yes, yes! Madam is seeing? Maybe for first time?'

'Who…?' asked Youngest uncertainly. 'What?'

Aila replied, 'Womanses, Madam! Real womanses!'

Youngest stopped breathing.

Memories dimpled his mind like a shower of white jasmines on the still surface of a pond. Tenderness enveloped his being in a sweet mist.

But…

do-your-duty, whispered the audio chip inside his skull. *sell-the-girl.*

He choked back a cry. Pain and bitterness flooded back into his brain. Steel claws mauled the inner lining of his heart.

find-the-Island. do-your-duty. in-the-name-of-all-true-men. sell-the-girl.

3

Aila had left by the time it was Youngest's turn to board the Ascensor. 'I is see you on other side!' he promised.

Of course you will, thought Youngest cynically. *You've not been paid*. He was grateful, nevertheless, for the various 'helps' provided.

Aila had given him precise instructions for boarding the glass-walled cell of the rapid transport system. 'Is only one cell for each traveller. You is look for overhead handles. If you is use any other handle? Door is not close and alarm is start.' It obviously happened very often, which was why the queue for the Ascensor was so long and slow-moving. 'Catch overhead handles, and atomotic you is swing inside, straight into seat. No problem for luggages. They is follow atomotic also.'

And so it was. The instant Youngest grabbed the overhead handles, the cell's entrance slid open, a mechanical ramp with moving treads extended up from where he stood and he was conveyed effortlessly into the glass-walled travelling chamber. His cases followed suit. Then the door snapped shut and inflation pads puffed out to secure the luggage. His own seat folded up out of the floor around him, positioned so that he faced forward, in the direction of travel.

Meanwhile the entire cell was lifted off its cradle by mechanical arms, raised up towards the continuously moving conveyor belt overhead and locked into place.

Moments later he was off, along with all the other travellers, each in his own individual glass cell.

The conveyor belt travelled within tubes of self-replenishing titanium glass. The tubes led directly towards the Suspended City, 1500 kilometres away.

The port was structured like a gigantic air-filled bell-jar rooted to the sea floor. The glass tubes and the conveyor belts within them radiated up and out of the bell-jar like straws, aimed towards a distant horizon at shallow angles. So for two hours the cells hurtled up out of the lightless depths of the sea, travelling in complete blackness. Gradually, outside the Ascensor's tubes, colours began to appear, formed by the tortured roux of sea and earth. It writhed and churned, creating fantastical patterns now foaming yellow, now emerald green, now black, now cream.

Then the Ascensor tubes breached the sea's surface and the vista passed from primordial chaos to Satanic light show as the surface of the water seethed and the air above it fumed. Plumes of dazzling white steam shot up against a backdrop of purple flame-streaked clouds billowing out of the constantly evolving inferno below the waves and up into the air. Bolts of lightning fizzed and sparkled, igniting further blooms of blinding white, saffron and crimson, punctuated by curving black jets.

Twenty-two years had passed since eco-anarchists had detonated underground nuclear devices at the mouth of the Suez Canal. Their aim had been to hasten the collapse of the petroleum industry. But the explosions punctured the Earth's mantle, spewing molten magma in a furious, untamable geyser that, when it subsided, became the glowering crack now known as the Peace Gorge. In the course of the three years for which the geyser had spewed, the Suez Canal vanished into oblivion and the erstwhile Red Sea was renamed the Poisoned Sea.

Within the cell, an audio-visual presentation played a loop of three languages, detailing the history and physical structure of the region in its current configuration. Youngest tried to follow the Unida as best he could, while scouring his neck and hair, using all four squeeze-paks of compressed water from Aila's kits. He dabbed the wounds on his nose and earlobes with care.

He had to absorb as much information as he could in these few hours. He didn't want to draw attention to the fact that he was an outsider to these parts, that he didn't know the history. Despite the millions of travellers, genuine outsiders were unheard of in this world.

He learnt that the Ascensor system, Confluenza Junction and the glassed-in city perched directly above the Peace Gorge had all been created as memorials to the cultures and populations from the Time Before that had been lost in the detonation. The shores of the Mediterranean had blackened and died. The planet's ice caps had melted. The seas had risen. All but the smallest and hardiest species of wildlife on land and air had perished.

The world's nations had melted away, too, to be reborn as the Whole World Union, the WWU. International travel had trickled to a halt prior to the collapse of the oil industry, but under the WWU the planet was split into four exclusive enclaves. No trade, no travel arrangements, no direct communications, no relocations were possible between the enclaves. Youngest already knew this. Which was why he could not afford to reveal his origin.

The map of the world in its revised configuration was fascinating to him. He knew, in theory, what it was supposed to look like but had not seen one until now. In recognition of changed realities, cartographers had turned the globe sideways. The Equator was the new Zero Meridian. The erstwhile Americas, the Poles and Australia occupied what was called the Ring Enclave. The continents once known as Europe and Asia had become conjoined as the Sunrise Enclave. The Pacific Enclave was a watery dimension all to itself, its island nations having been submerged and all traffic across it halted for lack of fuel.

And in the middle, dominating the planet, was the enclave known simply as The Zone, a giant arena for a continuous, savage and immensely popular cycle of war games.

It appeared as a monstrous, multi-coloured slab filling the centre of the screen. At first glance, Youngest had not recognized the continent he knew as 'Africa' because it had been turned on its side. It was sectioned off into countless divisions and subdivisions, colour-coded for the different teams that occupied them.

There was no script in this age of interactive visuals and three spoken languages. Only numerals were still written, in Arabic. Instead of titles on the map, there were points of light activated by a tap, yielding audio information.

Needless to say, the region to which Youngest belonged was missing altogether.

He had known that would be the case. Nevertheless, to see the result presented on an otherwise highly accurate map was shocking to him. An expanse of blank grey ocean stretched from where the Arabian Peninsula would have been all the way to the promontories of Myanmar and Thailand now shown extending sideways, like tusks. When he tapped the body of water shown in place of the land to which he belonged, the audio identified it only as The Void or The Deadly Ocean. The area had been given this name because, said the audio-prompt, radiation pollution was so extreme in these waters that even birds flying over it would sicken and drop out of the sky.

Nothing more was said.

Youngest continued to listen and to watch as he ate the last of his supplies. He had brought just enough for eight days, wearing the heavy sachets in a belt that encircled his waist, growing steadily lighter. Today was the seventh day.

Having cleaned himself, Youngest turned his attention now to renewing his make-up. In the months since the sex-change surgeries, he had found this to be an activity that calmed and soothed him. He thought of it as an act of meditation that returned his face to a smooth and orderly condition. It was like putting a kitchen in order before starting to cook.

He wore only the minimum, enough to establish what he now was, a man with an anatomically correct woman's body. A touch of gloss augmented the dark plum of his generous lips, mascara lengthened his lashes and a dab of iridescence highlighted his upper lids. He had worn kajal even as a man, but now he used an indigo variety that rimmed both upper and lower lids and didn't leak down onto the cheeks.

When he was done, Youngest surveyed his appearance in the hand-mirrors, of which he now had four, provided with the wash-kits. He certainly wasn't beautiful in the strict sense. But the full-featured good looks he'd enjoyed as a man had survived the gender change. He had a rounded, shapely nose, tall forehead, large, heavy-lidded eyes and strongly marked eyebrows.

His hair had always been thick and long. The man who had demanded that he change his body had also demanded that he dye the natural iron grey of his hair to black.

And so he had.

The creases at the outer corners of his eyes that accounted for the forty-four years of his life, suggested a lively sense of humour, a ready wit. Both of these, he believed, were now lost to him. He didn't think he could ever truly laugh again.

He drew in a deep breath. He would need to repair his wounds before he could wear jewellery once more: a diamond nose-ring, ruby danglers in his ears, perhaps a couple of ornaments in his hair: these were what he liked. When it was all in place and when he could indulge his good taste in brocade silk or organza or filigreed suede, then – yes – he could make heads turn.

He looked at the face reflected in the hand-mirror. He cocked his head to one side and tried to give himself a come-hither look.

Then he flinched and cast the mirror aside.

I'm not free to smile, he thought. *I'm not a man dressed in a woman's body. I'm a pathetic, witless maniac. I should be locked up. I should die.*

Still. It hadn't happened.

He hadn't yet turned against himself.

He marvelled at his own resilience. He had wounds on his conscience, on his heart, on his body. He had the recorded voice whispering in his ears. He had three electronic leashes tying him to the voice that forced him to remain on the path he had created: the twin Satellite Locators, one on his wrist, one over his heart and the pain-radio in his teeth.

Finally, of course, he had the girl. She was the ultimate leash. And talisman. She kept him from losing sight of the mission.

I am throwing her away, he thought. *That's what I'm doing. That's what I set out to do. That's the prize I created for myself. O clever me. What a genius I am. What a pearl amongst men.*

He shook his head, wishing he could scream or cry or rend his hair. But he could not afford any displays of emotion.

4

Fifteen minutes before the Immigration interview was due to begin, the seat began to pulse with light.

'Commencing Prep-Guide,' a nasal, mechanical voice instructed him. 'Sit forward. Relax. Be honest.'

Aila had told him to anticipate the warning sounds and to be sure to be alert. 'Cell is not go slow or stop,' he had said. 'Interview is happen by remote link. Everything is matter: how you is look, how you is speak. If you is look fearing, they is ask too many questions.'

Youngest unwrapped a strand of penga-weed from the stash he wore as a bracelet on his wrist and folded it into his mouth. The root was bitter and tough, but within twenty pulse beats a crystalline alertness coursed through him. The colours swirling beyond the glass ceased to hold his attention but the staccato voice of the Prep-Guide stitched itself upon the fabric of his memory in threads of steel.

He was directed to ready himself for the interview by placing his forearms along the arm-rests with his hands within the depressions created for them. As soon as he had complied, the material of the arm-rests flowed up and became a sheath that enveloped both hands. The tips of each finger were gripped firmly, just within the threshold of pain.

By the time the Immigration Officer – or rather her virtual presence – appeared as a hologram positioned directly in front of him, he was at peak wakefulness.

'Name?' The officer was visibly female, but her voice had a

harsh, rattling edge to it, as if she had a cricket lodged in her throat.

'Yasmine,' said Youngest.

She gave him a choice of languages and he opted for Unida.

'Origin?' The officer was dressed in a body-hugging sheath, dark silver in colour, that left no details of her anatomy to the imagination. Even the hair curling out from under her armpits was visible in tendrils that spread sideways across the tops of her small, tight breasts. She appeared seated within a padded seat positioned upright with writing tablets under each of her palms.

She faced Youngest but it was hard for him to see her eyes. A translucent visor curving right over her head and extending over her eyes provided her with a continuously scrolling display of readouts. The faint light from this display splashed against the taut planes of her face.

'South Relocation Zone,' said Youngest. It was the formulation used by anyone who had been displaced by the Peace Gorge. All survivors who did not live in the Zone or in the City lived in these settlements to the South of the City, in the vast toxic bog spawned by the Cataclysm. His response was met by pressure on his nails and pin pricks on three of his fingers. He assumed that blood samples were being taken.

Between him and the Officer, a digital clock counted down seconds in hundredths and tenths, glowing numbers sliding down an invisible vertical plane. The numbers paused and flowed jerkily. The entire interview was slated to last 180 seconds. According to Aila, any unwarranted extension of the time limit could be a cause for refusing entry.

'Sex?' barked the Officer.

'Transie.'

One second ticked by.

'Complete?'

He wasn't sure what this implied but he nodded and

answered, 'Complete.'

'Profession?'

'Pleasure industry.'

Two seconds ticked by.

'Cargo?'

'Animal parts. Plastrium-ion batteries. And…' He drew in a breath. 'One body.'

'Human or animal?'

'Human.'

'Whole?'

Unblemished, was what he wanted to say. *Perfect. Exquisite.* But he didn't have the vocabulary. 'Whole,' he said.

'Alive or deceased?'

His heart began to pound. The mere thought of the girl, lying coiled up around a life-support system, in deep stasis, caused him to react. 'Yes. Alive.' Was she? Could he be sure? The gel that sustained her had a time limit. If he couldn't get her admitted to the Collectory within the next thirty-six hours, she would slip away forever.

'Male or female?'

'Female.'

The officer's head jerked and he saw the flicker of light on her eyes. It seemed as if for once she had glanced directly towards him. He assumed that for her, wherever her corporeal body was, he too appeared as a hologram. It was a moment's curiosity. Her gaze dropped away once more.

'Age? Of live cargo?'

'Nineteen.'

'Relationship, if any?'

'Dau—' began Youngest, but a fist of pain had jammed itself down his throat and his voice failed. He had to swallow a gulp of air before he could force the word out. 'Daughter.'

Then twenty-one seconds passed during which Youngest

could see the officer's fingers tip-tapping on her separate keypads. His breath squeaked in and out of his nostrils reminding him of nose-flutes from a past so distant he couldn't focus on it any more.

If he didn't get clearance, the cell he was in would be swivelled around and switched to one of the conveyor belts returning to Confluenza. There were no authorities to argue with, no courts of appeal. His only option would be to loop around the way he had come and try again. By which time it would be too late. The girl would either have to be released from stasis and revived or …

'Cleared,' said the Immigration Officer in her cricket-voice.

As abruptly as she had appeared, she winked out of view. He had passed the interview. Dismay and relief fought to gain the upper hand within him. Neither succeeded.

5

The Suspended City appeared on the horizon as a tangle of glass tubes filled with coloured marbles set against the backdrop of purple-blue sky and ebullient white clouds.

That was when the first twinges of nausea began.

As the Ascensor sped closer, the marbles within the tubes resolved themselves as dwellings, stores, restaurants and businesses. Vertical columns contained buildings. Horizontal pipes were transport channels. Clouds drifted between the glass tubes. Radiating away in all directions were the great, glittering arcs of the Ascensor's network, from which the entire City was suspended.

At first Youngest had thought the unease in his belly was motion sickness. Six hours of non-stop hurtling might well produce that result.

Until the appearance of the city there had been no landmarks against which to gauge speed. In the final few seconds of the journey, however, Youngest went from gliding across the open sky to careening through a frantic jumble of planes and voids, horizontal slashes, copper coils, slithering beams, flashes of greenery, windows, beams, jutting ledges, plunging depths. Giant hoardings, posters and banners flew past. Gigantic pennants in all colours of the rainbow, each one representing different teams, regions and alliances, fluttered outside the glass tubes.

Then he was falling, safe within his travelling capsule but falling all the same, as cells were peeled off the travelling belt like peas thumbed out of a pod. As each cell fell, it was caught and cradled by gigantic mechanical arms. Then skimmed away sideways. Then whipped down and into the enclosure of the city's Central Hub.

Youngest didn't watch the final descent as the nausea suddenly expressed itself with greater force. It was no longer mere unease. More like an internal volcano combined with flying trapeze effects. With eyes shut tight and clutching the support straps around him, he bit off the remaining strands of the penga-weed bracelet from his wrist and chewed the whole thing, his mouth filling with saliva. As the cell spun round and round, gradually losing momentum, he swallowed hard, using the fibrous remains of the dried narcotic like a bung, plugging his own gullet.

The cell finally came to a halt, rocking back and forth a few times before the pneumatic padding began deflating with a harsh, snorting whine. The seat detumesced, too, but at a slower pace. The restraining straps and belts snapped away with loud reports.

Youngest opened his eyes. He was crouched on the floor, like a rabbit caught in a snare. His head was whirling and drool was spooling from his mouth. The volcano in his gut had subsided. For the moment.

The wash-kits, he thought. *Trans-dermal drugs. Probably timed to knock him out upon arrival. So he had been conned after all.* It was a dismal realization and an inauspicious introduction to the soaring city.

Glancing at the whirling confusion just beyond the cell walls, he was grateful for the privacy, however slight, that the cell afforded him. In the next instant, the walls snapped away and the clamour of the multi-layered transport station pounded down upon him: screeching announcements in three languages, tinkling advertisement jingles, honks, groaning clanks, pneumatic hisses, sub-audible rumbles and the continuous jangling rattle of arriving cells. Landing stages and cell-tracks slanted away and angled down beneath him. The mechanical cradling arms swooped, swung and delivered.

Cells shot by every few seconds, each headed for its own platform. Coloured patches of light and shards of unintelligible images appeared and disappeared like liquid being poured in and out of invisible containers. Even the platforms, which appeared at first glance to be grey, were alive with monochrome images, scrolling continuously, with photographs, speaking videos and streams of numbers in ornamental fonts.

On the walls, on the pillars, on every surface, Zone Warriors were talking, snarling, strutting, displaying scars, pounding their rivals. Wearing face-paint and feathers, masks and steel jewellery. Bleeding, writhing in pain, dying on the sand.

Within the station, robed and turbaned figures strode to and fro. Some, like giant grasshoppers, appeared to leap between platforms. Youngest couldn't understand by what agency they moved. They appeared to be literally levitating.

'Warning!' a feminoid voice squawked in his ears.

It came from the floor of the cell he was still crouched upon. He scrambled to his feet. 'Warning! Cell clearance in progress. Warning! Cell clearance—'

Then the floor beneath him tipped up and before he could regain his balance he had been dumped onto the narrow ribbon of platform beside the cell. He heard his luggage slide off and land with separate thumps.

He struggled up once more, lurching and unsteady. The combination of drugs in his system were locked in combat. His head felt as thick and heavy as wet dough, while his attention was bright and taut.

His cases lay on the platform like two giant slabs of mahogany in the middle of the heaving pandemonium. As he bent to hoist them upright, a sly whisper rustled through his mind: *Why? Why not just leave everything? Give up. Accept failure. Run away. It would be quite easy, really. Become a vagrant, disappear into the fog of inconsequence*. The same fog that had swallowed so much of his previous life and so many people who had been dear to him. The fog that had beckoned to him on so many occasions in recent months.

He heard a voice call out, 'Madam!'

At the same instant, three black-robed figures dropped down from above, long noses poking out from between the folds of their face-cloths, eyes glittering beneath deep brows as they jabbered in multiple tongues. Before Youngest could react they shimmered and became smoke: holograms. A wraith of sound, in Unida, accompanied their vanishment: 'Beware of unlicensed guides! Look for the City Seal Guides!'

Something was plucking at his sleeve, and the sound of mechanical laughter assaulted his ears. Youngest's left hand swung out, caught the thing and flung it onto the platform. A mechanical toy lay on the skittering images of the floor, smashed but still sounding off in parrot-voice Unida: 'Oh, very nice! Hello! How are you? This is your Courtesy Guide. Thank you! Welcome to the Suspended City. Did you like our Virtual Pirates? Hey!'

'Tch-tch-tch,' said another voice now. Youngest swivelled, furious, fist raised.

It was a man. Solid, not a projection. He was in his mid-thirties. He caught Youngest's wrists as he said, 'Such a shame! Madam has destroyed her City Seal Guide!' With shiny, slicked-back hair that gave him the appearance of a highly polished weasel, the man spoke Unida in soothing, cultured tones. 'How will Madam leave the Hub now? Without a guide?'

Youngest broke the man's hold with a single jerk and raised both arms to strike. The man danced aside even as he produced two more chattering toys like the one lying broken on the twitching floor. 'No, no, my dear Madam! I did nothing – I only offer you a replacement –'

'Go,' said Youngest, in his pidgin Unida. A fresh wave of nausea was starting to ride up his gut. Black spots were beginning to dance before his eyes. 'I am … wait. For friend.' That was a lie, of course. Aila was no friend and Youngest didn't plan to wait for him.

'But no,' persisted the man. 'Madam cannot wait here. All passengers must leave. I am Licensed Guide. I can help you –'

'No,' said Youngest. 'I am not need helps. You is go quick-quick.'

He turned to pick up his cases and find his own way out of the station. But his heart lurched with shock. Two figures dressed all in black, their heads covered, had got there before him and were holding the containers upright, one to each.

Then a familiar voice cut through the fog of confusion and fear that was dropping down upon him. 'Ah – Madam Yasmine? Welcome, welcome! See, here is my brothers. We is find you, no problems! Come – we is give you the helps. Hurry up, please.'

It was Aila.

6

The pedestrian tubes radiating away from the Hub were jammed with departing passengers. The sunlight angling down through the city's transparent walls was magnified and intensified by the crush.

Aila introduced the brothers Dar and Omar as all four pushed their way towards exits.

'I is sick,' said Youngest through clenched teeth. He could feel his body bearing down, thick and leaden, while at the other extreme the penga-weed kept his consciousness soaring like a gas balloon. But he was in no position to regain possession of his cases. 'You is give me kill-drug.' It was maddening for him to be unable to express himself fluently.

'No, no,' said Aila breezily. 'Is very small-nothing drug. Only to make calm.'

'I is must go to … to … Collection—' He had forgotten the correct term. 'Collar—'

'Collectory,' said Aila. 'But no. We is first go my house. Is very near. Then we is eat. Then we is talk.'

'No!'

But he was in no position to make demands and Aila knew it. He shrugged, jerked his head in the direction he intended all four of them to go and began pushing Youngest forward.

The pavements underfoot were not stationary. The entire pedestrian space, narrow as it was, was a travelling surface. Pedestrians had to lean towards the glass walls, jostling along narrow ledges, holding onto straps and handles to prevent themselves from falling towards the centre, which was occupied by passenger cars on speeding conveyor belts. There were no bars or rails: anyone or anything that fell was sucked swiftly down and out of sight by a continuously roaring, whistling current of air on either side of the belts. Dar and Omar trotted fast, cutting a channel through the slower moving throng by using the cases as battering rams.

It was all Youngest could do to keep up with them.

Tiny kiosks tethered to the curving glass walls bloomed into existence every ten paces, selling food, drink and drugs, trinkets and travel aids. Fluttering holographic images of sexual body parts, human and animal, darted in and around the faces of passersby. Mechanical toys clung and screeched, begging to be bought, to be tasted, to be swallowed and consumed.

'Is bad time to be out in city,' Aila bellowed at Youngest leaning towards him, over his shoulder. 'Is safer in home. Big match is ending.'

'What?'

'Bad time …' A plume of blinding red smoke flared out of a kiosk accompanied by a burst of raucous mechanical laughter.

Youngest gave up trying to hear what Aila was saying. The pain in his head had become a scream. He was so unsure of his feet that it seemed to him he was no longer actually moving his legs, but was instead being carried along by the tide around him. He entered a bright delirium, becoming one with the anonymous paste of living particles around him, processed out along a tube of unimaginable length.

He had no idea how long it took before there was a change, a swerving to the side. He could feel Aila's hands behind him, shoving him leftward. There was an alteration in the quality of the heat. A loosening of the air.

They had turned down a tunnel, narrower than the one they had been on. It slanted down sharply, turning, spiralling. Now this way, now that. The number of fellow travellers alongside them fell steadily, too, until it seemed they, just the four of them now, were hurtling through slender corridors lit by intermittent indigo lights.

The two brothers were coasting along using the wheeled cases as a trolley. At some point, the surface underfoot had ceased to be a travellator. Youngest could not recall when they had switched to walking or, as in his case, staggering.

His vision was filled with flashing, twitching, whirling black disks. The final moments of arrival were a blur. He didn't realize they were no longer in motion until Aila gripped him by the arms and told him to stop.

'We is arrive,' he said. 'We is home.'

Youngest's attention snapped taut. The cases?

Yes. There they were. He could see them ahead. The two brothers each had one, and were lifting and shifting them forwards. Over a threshold. Into a space.

Aila's contralto chirp sounded in his ear, 'Thank you, please, for is come to my humble home. You is not be sorry.' His hands were still clamped around Youngest's arms, forcing him to stay upright while also pushing forward.

A curtain of stillness fell like a guillotine over Youngest's senses as he stood just within a covered space. Maybe he recalled a door shutting behind him. Maybe he glanced up and saw his cases vanishing through another opening, into another room.

As if at a great distance, no longer sensible to anything else, he felt himself jerk forward, open his mouth and release a tidal wave of vomit. He roared and gargled for whole minutes, before pausing to catch his breath, wipe his mouth with his sleeve, only to pitch forward again. He could not remember when he had ever emptied himself so thoroughly before.

7

In a vision that seemed startlingly real, Youngest opened his eyes to find a young woman leaning over him. He was on the floor and her hair was touching his face. He realized it was a dream and closed his eyes.

When he opened them again, he saw that the phantom was standing a short distance away now, no longer looking in his direction. She was wearing a flowery silk dress and had long straight hair. He blinked, trying to clear the hallucination, but it refused to go.

find-the-Island, he heard in his head. *do-your-duty.* The droning formula of command was almost comforting. *in-the-name-of-all-true-men.* Like a spider weaving an inexorable web of reality, the words returned him to his purpose and his quest. *sell-the-girl.* He turned over on his side.

find-the-Island.

do-your-duty.

in-the-name-of-all-true-men.

sell-the-girl.

His belly began to growl like a hungry puppy. Or was the sound from outside of him? He couldn't tell. He didn't want to open his eyes again. He was lying on soft furnishings, on a flat surface. At floor level. He could sense rather than hear the throaty rumble that served as a background to the continuous rattling honks, whistling explosions, booms, clangs and thumps in the foreground. He wondered if he had chanced his way into a carnival of some kind. A factory, perhaps?

Certainly a very hot place. Dark, too.

He raised his eyelids once more. Just a slit.

He was lying on his left side, on a rug. Near him was a vertical, flat surface, dark and reflective. There was a light-source behind him that enabled him to see a dim outline of himself reflected in the smooth surface of this wall.

He could hear voices in conversation.

One was Aila's, issuing orders. Maybe to the two boys?

Their voices were too indistinct to follow.

'Don't get distracted,' Aila was saying. 'Don't talk to anyone. Come back at once.'

She was not speaking Unida. Youngest could understand her fluently. He did not even notice this fact right away, but when he did he recognized that Alia was speaking in Farsi. It was not his own language, which was Urdu, but close enough that he could follow it without mental effort.

He raised himself up now, cautiously. Looked around. A tall folding screen decorated with a floral pattern of perforations separated the space in which he lay from the light-source in the adjoining space. He was facing away from it but could see its reflection.

He gathered he was in a narrow, tubular dwelling, divided into sections. He could not tell, from where he was, how long it might be, but he guessed it was one width throughout, from end to end.

His section of it had the screen behind him, and the wall in front of him. The continuous thudding, roaring, pounding sounds that he had heard came from beyond the walls. He estimated that the ceiling was high enough for him to stand up without bumping his head. The width was great enough for him to have lain stretched out straight, his feet reaching perhaps the middle of the space.

He rose to his feet, taking care to move without jerks. The

dwelling was either suspended from cables or resting on flimsy supports because he could feel it shift beneath him as he moved. He steadied himself carefully, not wanting to alert the others to the fact that he was awake. He wondered what lay beyond the black shiny curved surfaces of the tube's outer walls. He could see no windows but the air was not stale.

'No!' he heard Aila say. 'You will wait till you're fifteen! Now go on, *go*! You can eat when you get back. There's plenty of food for everyone.'

At the mere mention of food, the puppy inside Youngest's belly began to whine in earnest. He remained where he was, however, unwilling to engage with his host until he could understand more about his circumstances. He needed to know the extent of the scam that he had been drawn into.

He could see his two cases. They were right beside him. He must have seen them earlier, too, at some moment of twilight wakefulness, because he felt no surprise, or anxiety, at their appearance. They were where he expected them to be.

He shifted his weight carefully, so that he could reach over and touch them without causing the floor to bounce. He ran his hands over the seals on the nearest one. It had not been tampered with. He breathed in deeply, biting his lips. He had been reprieved, yes! But the forest fire he was running from still galloped behind him. He had no idea yet of how much time he had lost. However much it was, it only meant he would have to run faster once he was on his feet again.

That was in the nature of the plan. At each node along his decision-tree he had only one option, each one a high-wire sprint above an abyss. There were no safety lines. No nets.

Then the floor jumped and wobbled. The two boys were obviously moving away, moving out of the dwelling. Aila was following them. Clearly, the entrance and exit was on the other side of the decorated partition.

Youngest wished he could see more of his surroundings. He reached towards the ceiling out of an idle impulse. It was less than a hand's breadth away from the top of his head. The moment he touched it, a clear rectangular window formed in the formerly opaque glass surface, between his fingertips.

He flinched, as if from scalding water. Bright orange light poured in through the aperture thus created. He studied it for a while before reaching up again. He touched the corners of the palm-sized patch: *Yes!* It was a scalable window.

The skin of his cheeks creased in a smile.

He opened three more rectangles, effectively flooding the small spare room with overhead light. He saw now that the floor was covered with a dark woollen rug, woven with elegant geometric patterns. There was no furniture, though the stack of rolled bedding in one corner suggested the presence of multiple occupants. One roll, spread out, was what he had slept on.

The curving walls on either side of the space were bare. What he had taken to be a wall beside which he had slept was in fact the flat side of a glass tank full of water. A shallow recess within that wall suggested the presence of a toilet or a shower.

He felt the floor shake again and heard the sound of a fresh voice enter the tubular home. He reached up at once to close the patches he had opened in the ceiling. Then he crouched down in the darkness, ready to stretch out and feign sleep if he had to.

Aila and another man entered the adjoining space. The newcomer was clearly an older person. 'Wait. What're you telling me?' His accent, in Farsi, had an evolved flavour, as if it had seen many changes, many seasons. 'You *think* you caught a big fish? You don't know?'

A frown formed on Youngest's forehead as he listened. The man had used a belittling form of address as he spoke to Aila. As if speaking to a social inferior. Or to a female child. The tone was harsh, contemptuous.

'Yes,' answered Aila. 'I showed you the shutterfly image …' His own voice was respectful. As if he were addressing a parent or a patriarch. 'Of the tall transie?'

'*One transie!* One tall, lumbering transie stupid enough to fall for your nonsense. That's all you caught?'

'Yes! I … I mean, no, she's not stupid. Or "he", rather. I think he's more of a "he"—'

'What d'you mean "is"?' snarled the other man. 'You must've dumped the fool by now?'

Aila began stammering. 'No … I – that is, no—'

'You're telling me he's still *here*?'

'Yes – because he has to go, you see, himself. To the Collectory. I – I'll go *with* him, of course. Won't let him out of my sight. And they'll pay him full price, you know. More than we'd get. On the black market.' Aila spoke in nervous jerks. 'For whatever he's got in there. In his cases. They're very big you know.'

The silence from the other man was ominous. The floor was still.

'Also, there was something strange about him. He has a kind of metal device in his chest. With a blue light. It could be a booby trap. Embedded—'

Thwap!

The sharp crack of skin on skin was accompanied by a soft yip.

'Enough!' growled the older man. 'Where is she now, your sleeping beauty?' The ground shook. 'Let's not waste any time—'

'No! No, wait—'

'Let go of my arm!'

'It … it won't work. The cases are custom-sealed. They'll only open to his hand-prints.'

Youngest, listening in the darkened room, nodded ruefully to himself. So it was not by chance that his cases had not been tampered with. At least Aila had had the good sense not to try forcing the seal.

'Fine,' said the other voice. 'So we'll cut off his hands before we dump him—'

'*No.*'

'Did you say "no"?'

'Please. Listen to me: whatever's in those cases is worth a lot to this transie. There's something unusual about him. If I help him get them safely to the Collectory, he *will* pay—'

Thwap!

Youngest rose to his feet once more.

'Witless ... spineless ... less than filth ...' The blows rained down, each one accompanied by plaintive chirps. 'Even to beat you dishonours my hands.'

In two steps, Youngest had reached the screen that separated the two rooms. One more stride and he had crossed over to the other side, saying, 'Aila?'

He was nowhere to be seen.

Instead there was a white-haired man in dark robes. He had a beak-like nose and black, shapely eyebrows. Next to him was the woman Youngest had seen in his dream, wearing a flowery print-silk dress. She was half-kneeling on the floor. Her left arm was raised up to protect her head and face.

'Ah!' she cried now, in Aila's contralto voice, speaking in pidgin Unida. 'Madam Yasmine? You is wake up?'

It was, of course, Aila. Without her chequered head cloth and man's robes.

'Here is Amir. He is father of me,' she said now, jumping to her feet. She smoothed back her hair with automatic gestures. Her print-silk dress had a plunging neckline that revealed the taut swell of her breasts. Her face was rouged and eye-shadowed. A bruise was developing below her left cheek.

'Father, this Yasmine.' When she addressed her father

she spoke automatically in Farsi. To Youngest she said, in her childlike pidgin, 'Please. You is come. I is made dinner. We is eat.' Then she turned and left the room, going the other way.

The two men remaining inside this larger room glanced at one another. Youngest could guess the other man's thoughts. He was wondering what Youngest had heard. But when he spoke he used Unida, speaking formally, not in pidgin. He would not know that Youngest could understand Farsi.

'Come,' he said, his voice gruff. 'We may as well eat what my worthless daughter has prepared.'

He didn't wait for Youngest's response but had reached for two rolled-up mats. With two flicks of his wrist he had unrolled them, placing one beside the other at right angles. With the same economy of movement, he snapped open two tiny folding tables and placed one each in front of the mats.

'Sit,' he commanded, indicating to Youngest the position facing towards the door through which Aila had vanished. He folded himself down in the other spot, on what would be the guest's left.

8

Aila returned with meat-stew in two bowls, strips of naan placed across their tops. She placed the bowls on the tables, went back out and returned with another bowl of water. She put it down near her father and washed his hands using a small hand towel, drying them afterwards with another small towel. He accepted her services with curt nods. As soon as she was done with him, he turned his attention to the food in front of him. He ripped the flatbread into small scraps, dug into the stew and began eating with no further ceremony.

Youngest had taken his cue to settle down, but waved away Aila's offer to wash his hands. He scooped the food into his mouth using his scraps of naan, just as Amir did. The stew was salty with an undercurrent of pepper. The meat was chunky, with a stubborn, chewy texture, as if it belonged to an animal that would not normally submit to being domesticated and eaten. Youngest didn't care. He would have eaten it raw, fermented or dry. He was that hungry.

Aila did not join them to eat. Instead, immediately after serving the two men, she knelt on the floor near Youngest but facing her father. She began a nervous one-sided conversation in her pidgin Unida while the other two ate. She spoke in jerks, glancing repeatedly in her father's direction.

'We is must go quickly,' she said. 'Because there is problems. Everywhere in the city. There is much problems. So we is must go. Now. Before morning.'

Youngest indicated his bowl. 'You? Not eat?'

'Not now,' said Aila, hugging her arms to herself, then letting go of them spasmodically. 'I is not have hunger.'

The room was a little longer than the one in which Youngest had been asleep. The same spare aesthetic prevailed: an elegant rug on the floor, and all personal effects in the form of clothes folded into neat stacks, four in all. There was no furniture to speak of, but a black column, flat-sided and opaque, dominated the centre of the space. A gap in the farther wall gave access to the room beyond this one, perhaps a kitchen from which Aila had fetched their food. In the ceiling, two broad rectangles had been opened to admit the dull orange light Youngest had seen earlier.

It was not daylight, Youngest realized now. The light that came in was from the livid glow of the boiling chasm over which the city was suspended. The light was reflected off the canopy of steam-clouds that rose continuously to meet the sky.

Through the two open patches, he could see the glass tubes arching overhead, forming a glittering matrix. Ropes, cables, pulleys and all manner of suspension systems criss-crossed the open air above the enclosed capsule they were in. Wisps of cloud drifted across the field of vision. Figures moved up, down and across the space, on ropes and inside small gondolas.

'After you is eat, you is have shower,' Aila continued. 'You is very stinking,' she said with no trace of insult. 'At the Collectory there is only womanses there. And they is hate the stinking.'

'Shut up,' said Amir in Farsi. 'Your talk is spoiling my appetite. Go away. Bring water.'

Aila stopped, flustered, before getting up to leave the room.

'And you, Transie,' Amir said, addressing Youngest for the first time. 'It is good that you are here. I would talk to you.' The Unida he spoke was more dignified and eloquent than Aila's. Harder for Youngest to follow.

Aila returned with a jug of water in one hand and a glass

tumbler in the other.

'Could you not bring two glasses?' snarled her father, once again in Farsi. 'And what about water for our guest's hands?' Then he patted the floor. 'Anyway, never mind, put it down now – both, yes. Now get lost. Leave us. I wish to talk with our guest.'

Youngest felt embarrassed on Aila's behalf. But now was not the moment to intervene on her behalf. He leaned back, tipping the contents of his bowl into his mouth as a way of buying time to compose his thoughts before speaking with the man. He wiped his mouth with his sleeve, glancing warily in Amir's direction.

Amir's eyes were trained upon him like a pair of precisely focused searchlights. 'Eh,' he began. 'I'll tell you one thing: you're no transie. You're a man. Am I right?'

Youngest put his bowl down. He took a deep breath. This conversation was going to test his language skills to their limit. 'I is have body of a women,' he said, using his hands to indicate the expanse of curving flesh south of his neck.

'—but not the mind,' said Amir, while pouring himself a glass of water, from which he drank. Then he poured another glass and used it to rinse his fingers in his bowl and wipe his mouth before handing the jug to Youngest. 'The way you move, the way you talk – using the masculine voice – the way you stand and hold yourself: it is with pride, with dignity. A man's dignity.'

He nodded as he spoke, self-affirming his statements. He leaned his head back and poured the water in his glass down his throat in a single stream. When he was done, he dabbed at his mouth with a kerchief he drew from the sleeve of his robe and handed the empty glass to Youngest.

He leaned forward now, his eyes digging into Youngest like paired awls. 'So I ask you this: why? A man in full possession of his senses and in the prime of his life, tall, well-built, handsome, a man who might be whatever he chooses – a warrior, a leader, a prince – *why* does such a man change his body to that of a weak, inferior being such as a transie?' The corners of his mouth twitched downwards and a muscle in his cheek jumped as he came to the end of his question. '*Why*?'

Youngest could see the man's dilated pupils and hear his laboured breathing. It was not an idle question and even though he understood only every third word, the passion behind the query pierced his spirit.

He would have liked to answer truthfully. He would have liked to release the burden of his bizarre and complicated story, in its entirety, to the understanding of even one other person. Very few people remained in the world with the necessary perspective and sense of irony to appreciate what he had done. And what remained for him to do. He held Amir's gaze for a long moment.

'I is really want to do it,' he said at last in a petulant voice. 'And so I is do it.'

The light snapped out in Amir's eyes.

'All right, then,' he said. 'Have it your way.' He leaned back. 'The Almighty has delivered you to my hands, and let me tell you: you are lucky indeed to have come to the home of an honourable man. Because no one other than myself would have held himself back from taking advantage of you and your – excuse my harsh words – stupidity. Because it was stupid, my shape-changing friend, to have arrived in this most depraved of cities, where every citizen is either a thief, a scoundrel or a murderer, with so little idea of how to defend yourself as to accept the assistance of a smiling stranger. To come to his home! And, worst of all, to fall asleep on his carpet as if you were in your own private palace!'

He spoke now with the fluent ease of someone reciting a familiar poem, complete with hand gestures and twitchings of the head and neck. 'And you have chosen to come in the shape of one who is a universal figure of ridicule, a transie! *Tch-tch-tch!*

'What can I tell you? You have committed a great folly. Against yourself, your race, your sex. So. So. So. How shall we save you from the error of your ways? What can we do that will be at the same instant a guide to your future behaviour and a cautionary … what shall I call it … reprimand?'

Youngest listened with his neck bent forward. When the time came for him to respond, he kept his eyes lowered and in tones of contrition said, 'All is true. I is not deny. But how is I can make … I is not know the word … correction?'

He glanced up and caught the gleam of greed in Amir's eyes. He continued, 'I is not can take my luggages to home. Because I is not have the money for Deepwater Ferry. So I is must go to the Collectory, yes? And also there is no time. I is must go away quick. I is have much problems in my far away home.'

Amir gave a thin smile.

'That's why I say, my friend, you are *lucky*,' he said. 'Because you are in my home. Because I will help you. All you have to do is two things: first, you must open your cases, so that I can see what you have. The most important thing is to make a correct evaluation. Once we know how much you can expect to get, then … who knows? Maybe I can advance the necessary funds to you, so that you can return to your own land as fast as possible.'

'But it is very much,' said Youngest, blinking rapidly. 'Or I is thinking it is.'

'Let us at least take look. Then we'll know,' purred Amir.

'What is second thing?' asked Youngest. 'You is say two things I must do.'

'Ah. Your hands. Your nails. Show me your nails.'

Youngest cocked his head to one side, frowning. 'My nails? I is not understand.'

'Father?' Aila's voice cut across the room. She spoke in Farsi. 'Do not do this, Father. I beg of you.' She began walking over from where she had obviously been following the conversation all along, in the kitchen.

The white-haired man's head whipped around, snarling in Farsi. 'Shut your mouth, donkey-cunt!' he spat. 'How often must I tell you to not interfere when men are talking?'

Youngest inspected his hands, feigning non-comprehension as he listened.

'I will not let you take his nails—'

'Get back – get back – before I strangle you with my own hands! Can you not see him with your eyes? Such a big man hiding behind a woman's skirts? Why, he could be anything – a viper, a hyena – pretending to be a witless lamb! You made a bad choice, a stupid choice, so now *shut up* while I try to fix your mistakes.'

'No! He has a good heart—'

'I'm warning you,' said Amir, his voice cracking with rage, 'if you don't get lost, I'm going to personally stuff your face into your own stinking, piss-filled glory-hole—'

Youngest sucked in his breath.

'Enough,' he said, in Urdu.

A bolt of energy gripped the room. It was just one word, but he had used a tone of command that was entirely different to the childish quality of his pidgin Unida. 'We are all wasting time. And I don't have any to spare.'

In the silence, the continuous clanking thumps from outside filled the small, hot room.

'Wait,' said Amir. His forehead was heavily creased.

'You speak our tongue?' exclaimed Alia.

'No!' said her father, shaking his head. 'That's not ... that's not *our* tongue. It's different. This man is not one of us. He's ... I don't know. I've not heard that language for a long time. Very long.'

Youngest nodded. 'You are right,' he said, gathering himself to stand up. The relief of being able to express himself fluently was like breathing normally after a week of suffocation. 'It's not Farsi. As I said, I'm a refugee, but from further away. Further east.' He stood. 'I need to get on. And I promise to pay well for your help.'

'Wait,' said the older man in a loud voice. 'Further *east* you say? *East?* No. It cannot be.'

'What does it matter?' asked Youngest. 'I'll pay you good money—'

Amir jumped to his feet with an agility that belied his age. 'Do you not understand ANYTHING?' he screamed. 'We live in times when a man's every heartbeat depends on what place he calls his home! You're no refugee either. You're too well-fed. Too smooth, too polished. And yes, I have seen your kind before, but many years ago.'

He was breathing hard as he stared at Youngest.

Youngest said the words for him. 'Twenty years. Twenty-two, to be exact. Your instinct was correct all along, sir. I am from *beyond* the South Relocation. I am from the tainted land that time forgot. Whose name has been struck off maps. Whose people have been erased from the register of humanity. Yes. But *so what*? Here I am now! I have merchandise that needs selling, like everyone who comes here! I need to reach the Collectory, I need help. And I am willing to pay a very good sum for it.'

Amir's face was creased in a mask of disgust.

'The Forbidden Country!' he growled, his head nodding as if on a spring.

He swung towards Aila, his hands in the air. 'We can do nothing for this man! Even if you can get to the Collectory, once you're there they will – I don't know! I've never heard of such a case! But they won't entertain him, that much I can tell you. No, no! It's a waste! It's all hopeless!'

Aila stared from one to the other, her expression stricken.

'You don't understand,' said Amir, addressing her as if they were alone in the room. 'The land to which this *less than human thing* belongs was burnt out from the memories of all decent people!' A cunning expression had begun to spread across his face as he continued talking. 'For crimes against the entire planet. For shattering the world as we knew it. For poisoning the oceans and sky—'

His left hand had disappeared within the sleeve of his robe, fumbling in his haste to find something in there. A summoning device, perhaps. An alarm.

But Youngest saw the movement.

With one step, he closed the distance between himself and Amir. He picked the man up by his neck and gave him a sharp jerk, severing the connection between neck and spine.

9

From outside, booms, thumps and hissing roars. Inside: nothing.

The limp body was a dead weight, hanging awkwardly between Youngest's hands. He lowered it to the floor without taking his eyes off Aila, who stood immobile, with her hands clutching her face, eyebrows arched up.

Youngest's movements were respectful, even tender, as he lowered the body to the floor. He forced himself to look up at Aila, braced for whatever her reaction might be. There was no point apologizing. 'I've come too far and given up too much to be stopped by ... ' The word 'anyone' remained inside his mouth.

Aila made a slight, strangled sound. She did not look at Youngest. She took two steps forward, then knelt in slow motion, as if falling, with her hands still clinging to her face for support. She was digging at the skin with her fingers. She was on her knees, kneading her face, as if trying to carve expressions onto it. Then she jack-knifed over, burying her face in the still-warm chest of the corpse.

'My father,' she said, her voice muffled, shaking. Her hands, outstretched, plucked at the clothes of the body, looking like five-limbed crabs.

Youngest glanced around the room. Thoughts were careening through his mind. *Should I leave now? Can I manage on my own? What else do I need to know, which, if I don't know, could destroy me?*

Aila's back was heaving as she lay across her father's still form. She was panting and grunting at once. Then with a heaving intake of breath, as much a sob as a scream, she jerked upright, lifted both arms and brought her hands down as fists to pound on the same chest she had lain upon a moment ago.

She looked up at Youngest, mascara streaking down her cheeks. 'Please,' she said, her voice ragged, holding her hand out, flexing the fingers like a child crying for a sweet. 'My handbag. Is behind you. Please ...'

Youngest bent as he turned, locating a leather bag. He handed it to the still-seated figure. She was dry-sobbing now, her breath trapped in her throat as she tore open the two sides of the bag, reaching inside as if excavating a deep pit. Objects began flying out: plastic tokens, lipsticks, a screw-driver set, two spanners, a Summoner in a decorative lace case, red panties, silicone gloves, a pearl necklace, a jar of petroleum jelly.

'I can't—' She was holding the bag upside down, shaking it so that its contents slithered out onto her father's body. She threw the bag aside as she found the item she sought. It was a slender grey cylinder the size and shape of a mechanical pencil. She leaned away from her father's body in an arc, flicking her head far back with her neck painfully exposed. With her right hand poised over her face she attempted to align the end of the tube with her open mouth, the tip of her tongue extended down below her chin. Her fingers were curled around the length of the container, with her little finger raised to depress the plunger at its end. It flailed about miserably, however, like a fat worm sticking up from a straight fishhook.

Youngest jerked forward, knelt and steadied Aila's hand. Held her head.

'Press it,' she gasped from her inverted position. 'Slowly. Onto the top of my mouth. Not the tongue.'

A pale blue drop dangled for an instant at the end of the container, flashing in the livid overhead light before depositing itself on the roof of her mouth.

She remained in her position, curved backwards like an archer's bow but with her mouth shut now. Her oesophagus, enormous and bulging, pumped up and down, once, twice, three times. Abruptly, her eyes, which had been open so far, disappeared into her skull, in the way of someone having a fit, showing only the whites.

There was a pause. Then her long false lashes fluttered. Black butterfly wings.

She blinked, her head still upside down, then straightened up slowly. Rubbed her throat a couple of times.

She raised her head and looked Youngest in the eye. 'Okay. I am fine now. Fine.'

It was true. The hurricane of anguish and emotion that had gripped her had passed so completely that if not for the black streaks of mascara and the tears that continued to course down her cheeks no sign whatsoever of any mishap remained upon her.

Her mouth twitched into a smile as she looked up at Youngest's face. She laughed.

'Huh. You don't know it? We call it the "Eraser". One drop and *phwit!* Everything goes. Sadness, fear, pain, everything. Big help with problems.'

Her head snapped around, taking in the room, taking in the events of the recent ten minutes.

'Come on,' she said, 'we must do it quickly.' Already, she was twisting around, orienting herself in the room before getting to her feet and stepping towards the black column. It was a multifaceted cupboard. She pressed open a drawer and drew out a kit box.

Youngest shook his head. 'What? I don't know what you mean—'

'The nailgrams,' said Aila, as if nothing could be more obvious. 'Come on, you can help me. It is not difficult. I have done it many times, for others.' She was speaking in Farsi as if that was all she ever spoke. The baby-talking pidgin-speaker had vanished completely.

She was kneeling once more, beside the corpse, with the kit-box open. She placed it on the floor and removed a spool of fine wire. She drew out two lengths, attaching each around the wrists of the corpse, but not tightening them. 'My father's nails. We can take them now – just the nails, not the whole skin. Hold up the hands, yes – like that – shake them, slap them, yes, yes, squeeze them hard – let the blood drain so that there will not much clean up to do—'

Youngest stood up. The transformation in Aila shocked and disturbed him. Tears continued trickling down her face, as if her tear-ducts were still stricken with the loss while the rest of her body and her mind had successfully shut down the spigot of grief.

Now she tied off tourniquets, first on one wrist then on the other, talking softly all the while. 'See, it's for the best,' she was saying, 'if we take them, we can use the Travel Cabs. They'll get us across the city like a knife through butter. It's what he would do in my place. *Survive*, he said. *Only survive*. He taught me everything I know. Yes, yes, he was a good man, in his way – he knew what was right and wrong – he knew how to survive – yes – but he was unkind too. Very unkind.'

With the economical movements of long practice, first she marked her father's finger tips with colours, to identify them: blue for the right hand, red for the left. Then, using a device that combined a betel-nut shaver with a brass knuckle-duster, she poked each finger through the five round holes. The apertures each had a gripper similar to a camera's shutter, to hold the digits in place. She took care to align each phalange at the joint. Then she brought down the swinging arm of the fine, steel blade precisely positioned for each hole, and squeezed tight with both hands. There was a crunching *pop!pop!pop!pop!pop!* as the five tips were sliced off and tumbled onto the plastic sheet she had placed down as precaution against any blood-letting that might occur.

'Perfect!' she smiled up at Youngest. 'See? They are almost dry, yes?' She continued to hold the slicer and the dead hand in her own hands. 'I will seal off the ends here, then we'll do the other one. Okay?' She seemed completely unaware of the effect she was having on the tall companion so recently arrived in her life. 'If you don't mind, you can squeeze the ends of these tips out onto this sponge. I'll show you what to do next after I've done the left hand.'

Youngest followed her instructions. 'The nailgrams are … holograms? For identity?'

'Of course,' she said, nodding. 'As a visitor you get them when you first enter the city, on the Ascensor. When they wear off, you have to renew. But we residents have permanent' grams. They are tattooed onto the nailbed in radioactive ink. We can use them in places where visitors cannot go.' Her voice was as unhurried as a nun reading her rosary. 'So you can use my father's nails, you see. Then we can both get inside the private transport. Instead of running on the roads.'

The next twenty minutes were spent in the methodical wrapping up of a man's life. Youngest helped where he could, following the brusque instructions given to him by the other transie. Aila behaved as if she was following well-rehearsed instructions. There was nothing casual or haphazard about her actions.

When they had sealed her father's body into a heavy plastic bag, Aila and Youngest dragged it into the sleep-chamber. She rolled the carpet aside, revealing a rectangular panel in the floor with a seal running down its centre. They placed the body on the panel.

'Stand well back,' she said to Youngest, as she stepped towards the curved wall of the dwelling.

Her hands located a recessed handle. When she pulled on it, the panel on which her father's body lay snapped open. The corpse dropped through. The hatch closed once more. In the space of the instant when the hatch opened, a grinding roar from the chasm beneath them licked up into the room, like the tongue of an insatiably hungry demon. Then it was gone. A wisp of grey smoke remained suspended above the hatch.

Aila looked at Youngest. 'That is called "dumping",' she said. Tears had begun coursing down her cheeks again, yet her expression was absolutely calm.

'We must go,' she said. 'Come.'

10

'You must shower,' repeated Aila. 'There is just enough time. See – I have brought everything.'

They were standing inside the swaying gondola that represented private transport. It had come in response to Aila's summons and docked with the front end of the tubular home.

It was a spacious, furnished receptacle, a vertical tube in contrast to the horizontal one that Aila called home. A memory was triggered in Youngest from his childhood, of a deluxe train compartment, complete with a luggage-hold, upholstered seats, light fittings. He often found it hard to be sure whether these images from the past were dreams or reality.

The separate elements of the structure were placed one on top of the other. Passengers boarded via a booth which had exits above and below. In addition to the quaintly old-fashioned aura of the decor was a stocked pantry, an entertainment console and the bathroom, which Aila assured Youngest was worth the effort and expense of using it.

She had shown him how, at every choice she made within the gondola, she was instructed by a low, robotic female voice of the same sort Youngest had heard on the Ascensor, to press the tips of her fingers to the nail reader that confirmed her account. Then she followed suit with her father's dead nails and the transaction was complete. As soon as she had named the destination, the gondola had begun moving, climbing straight up its cable.

Aila was still insisting, 'If you make a good impression on them,' meaning the women who controlled the Collectory, 'they pay better.'

'But I don't have a change of clothes,' protested Youngest.

'You is lie,' Aila said, switching now to her pidgin Unida. 'I is pulled it out from outside of case.' She held up a black item, with flashing lights in the shape of tiny blue stars winking on and off. '*This* is good one. Is perfect one.' Evidently she had been through the outer pockets of his luggage, and now her mouth was twisted sideways in an amused smirk.

There was nothing more for Youngest to protest. He allowed Aila to lead him down, via a stairway set into the walls of the unit, to the bath area.

'This is bath,' said Aila. 'You have see before? One like this?'

It was a cube-shaped room. The corner farthest from the point of entry had a triangular patch on the floor that was lighter than the rest of the space. Youngest, mystified, shook his head. There was no sign anywhere of fixtures. The two walls across from the corner with the triangular patch were furnished with shelves, each one displaying products and services in a video-loop. The two walls directly alongside the triangle contained a video montage of images from the Zone.

Aila crossed over to the triangle. One panel of a folding screen emerged from her right-hand side. She tapped its forward edge, saying, now in Farsi, 'When you are inside the triangle, you can pull the screen across. At once, hot water will flow from all sides. Plus soap. Two minutes only. When the screen closes, you'll see controls appear on it – for changing the temperature and speed.'

She beckoned to him to approach her, to take her place, 'Come now, stand here before I move away. Or else it will charge us for two showers.'

Youngest began unbuttoning the front of his robe as he walked towards the triangle. He was feeling awkward.

As Aila exchanged places with him, she did not move away. Instead, she looked expectantly at his hands, clearly wanting to see what he looked like under his clothes.

He felt his skin prickling with discomfort. He would have preferred to turn his back on his transgender companion. He guessed that would seem unfriendly. He couldn't know what was considered typical amongst men who had had body-altering surgery. Or perhaps even unaltered women? Did women get together to discuss and compare one another's bodies, in an atmosphere of friendly appraisal?

He had no idea.

He delayed the moment of disclosure by pulling his boots off one by one, using the wall beside him for balance. He stripped away his socks, undid the drawstring on his salwar and let them drop away. Then, feeling extraordinarily awkward, he lifted the hem of his calf-length robe up and over his head, shaking his hair free as he pulled the garment away.

Youngest had always had broad, muscular shoulders, a generous belly and limbs like tree-trunks. The reconstructive surgery had not given him a waist, but had built on the natural fullness of his chest to provide plump, generous breasts. A matching, voluptuous bottom had been achieved by rearranging the adipose around his hips. He stepped out of his frilly black briefs first, then peeled away the pale mauve chemise over his head, exposing the faintly glistening aureoles of his bruise-brown nipples. He wore no bra.

'Ah, yes,' said Aila immediately, nodding appreciatively. 'It is a good job.' She meant the surgeon's handiwork. She leaned in close. 'Expensive. No scar.' She lightly patted the sides of Youngest's breasts, testing for firmness. 'They are quite strong. Very attractive.'

He glanced down at himself, feeling an embarrassment that had become his norm. Looking down at the twin bulges on his own chest he felt as though he were outraging the modesty of a woman. It was true, they looked good. Plump and well-balanced, each with its thickened tip, plum-dark and shaped like a paddy farmer's straw hat.

Beyond them, he saw the glossy double-tiered expanse of his own generous belly, but even this was unfamiliar now. He had once had a strip of hair that ran down the middle and over his navel. He had never consciously thought of this narrow frontal mane as a sexual feature until it was no longer there for him to run his fingers through, to tug at now and then, feeling a thousand tiny prickles of pain.

He felt like a stranger to his own body. It was his and yet it was completely unfamiliar. It was attractive to him, but as a stranger's body; not his own. He felt in awe of it. Afraid almost. Saddened.

He looked up to see that Aila had undone the single clasp that held the front of her frock together, revealing her own pair, quivering upright and bra-less on her narrow chest. 'But mine are better, yes?' She looked up, her eyes shining with unaffected immodesty. With her hands, she cupped the shapely flesh, pushing the pearl-pink peaks out in a pout. 'I am choose nipples from catalogue.'

A twang of phantom desire passed through Youngest's body like a frisky eel. It took his breath away. 'Uh,' he said, not wanting to pant. He was overcome. It had been so long since he'd experienced anything bordering on desire. He felt completely unravelled.

'Yours is real? You is feel *this*?' She reached out and tweaked the dark points on Youngest's breasts.

'Ouch,' he said, flinching and pushing her hands away. 'Don't. Yes – I can feel, but not in a nice way.' He had not been wired for erotic pleasure. He had chosen to accept the losses that came from the removal of his original sexual organs as a form of penance for all the crimes he had already committed and for those that lay ahead.

'Feel mines! They is got touch-sensitive,' said Aila, taking Youngest's hands and placing them on her breasts. 'See? They is gone tight and I is feel wet flush downstairs! Just like real womanses.'

When she chose, she could maintain her voice at the higher end of her register by speaking in a breathy whisper, sounding girlish. She was close to Youngest in height and stood now with her face tilted up towards him, staring into his eyes.

'*Wah!*' she exclaimed, her breath faintly scented with the cumin from her meat-stew. He could feel the flush on his face and guessed that his pupils were dilated. She would know, from looking at his eyes that she had kindled genuine desire within him. 'You is still *want* womanses?'

Leaning in closer, pressing herself to him, she said in an attempt at a husky drawl, 'You is want … me?'

But her voice zigzagged and broke just then. The illusion of femininity was shattered.

Youngest pulled his hands away.

'N-No,' he stammered, adding, 'not now.' To protect Aila's feelings, assuming she had any, he added, 'Please. We must remember the time.'

He didn't look at her face, but stepped back into the stall and pulled the two sides of the enclosure shut, forming a hydro-tight seal. Immediately, warm water began spurting from the sides of the triangular cabin, followed by liquid soap. It had an artificial scent that, to Youngest, smelt of burning rope and mango. He didn't believe it was a great improvement upon the personal 'stinks' he was supposed to remove. But he was reassured that whatever fleas remained on him would surely be nauseated enough to drop off.

11

Six precious hours had passed by the time Aila and Youngest were standing on a wheeled pallet within the main concourse of the Collectory. It was circular and the floor was electrified in order to prevent any visitors from moving around unsupervised.

Overhead, through the tall glass dome, the night-sky was visible. Inside, running the entire curving length of the corridor was a 360-degree projection from the Zone.

Youngest glanced around.

Some fifteen pallets were sailing at an identical stately pace, each one with its crew of importer, agent, agent's helpers and stack of goods. Like Youngest, every importer present was dressed in his most formal clothes. There were breast-plates made of leopard skulls. One man sported a tall crown of peacock feathers. Some men wore shimmering silks and looked obviously feminine. Others expressed their masculinity with leather hides, belts of fur and wristbands made of bone.

But all these costumes, howsoever gaudy or elegant, were eclipsed by the video projection on the curving outer wall of the Collectory: currently, one hundred bronzed and naked warriors were whipping themselves into a frenzy by leaping rhythmically between two rows of bright flame. Scarlet-feathered headdresses framed faces painted white, mouths rimmed with indigo paint and gaping wide as they simultaneously pumped two-metre-long spears in the air. Behind the warriors, a tangerine moonrise was in progress.

Aila watched Youngest's face for several minutes before she

said, 'You have really no idea about the Zone? You don't know what it is?'

She spoke in Unida now, but not in pidgin. Before they left the gondola, she had bought a speech-aid for Youngest, a voice disk. According to her it was a common gadget, universally used in the City to help disentangle the Babel of tongues that would otherwise be spoken.

Youngest shrugged. 'Not really. No.' He spoke through the flexible membrane that fitted over his vocal cords and bonded with the skin of his neck. He needed to use it, said Aila, in order to communicate effectively with the Examining Officers at the Collectory. It produced a version of his own voice, modified so that his original speech came out in translation. The resulting hybrid sound was utterly unnatural to his ears.

She shook her head slowly, though it was not clear whether she was expressing amazement or disapproval. 'It may not be safe to admit such a thing.' She inclined her head towards the interior of the building. 'They are always looking. Listening. Waiting to hear if someone is telling the truth or not.'

'Will they ask me about the Zone at the interview?' It was very odd for him to hear his own voice producing complete sentences and thoughts in another language.

Aila glanced reflexively over her shoulder. 'If they hear me explain, it's the same thing as telling them you don't know,' she whispered.

'Sooo …' said Youngest, rolling his eyes. 'In that case they already know!'

Aila had no sense of irony. She gave him a puzzled look and dropped her voice. 'See. There are teams. They fight. They can win or they can lose. They can get taken prisoners, or become champions. Whatever happens, the teams go on fighting. Unless they are destroyed. But that rarely happens.' She broke off, clicking her tongue. 'It's hard to explain.'

'It's a game, then? Not a war?'

Aila cocked her head. 'Is there a difference?' She shrugged. 'Well, it's a war, of course. Many small wars. Men are fighting and dying.' She jerked her head towards the screens. 'Each team has colours. So there we can see the team of Dzing!-*Ben* and they're getting ready to fight the Dzing!-Dzing!' She made a clicking sound in the back of her throat as she spoke. 'Actually this match has already been played. We are watching a replay and the *Ben* have already lost. Now they will all die.'

She stopped and corrected herself. 'Not at once, you know. That is not allowed. To kill prisoners is not allowed. But the—' She stopped abruptly and looked around, her expression fearful, and her voice dropped even lower as she slipped into her pidgin Unida. 'We call the Dzing!-Dzing! the cannibal team, the Red Team. Because they is very bad, very horrible.' She grimaced, as if she were speaking to a child. 'When they is win, is BIG losing for everyone else. All teams is lose.'

Youngest frowned, trying to make sense of the description. Earlier, when he had asked Aila why she persisted in speaking pidgin, she had smirked: research had shown that clients preferred transies who baby-talked, she explained. It was an affectation that had become a habit she slipped in and out of without conscious effort.

'If today Dzing!-Dzing! is win, then tomorrow they is get big prizes. They can buy many womanses—'

'Wait,' said Youngest. 'When you say "buy women" do you mean from here? Or in the Zone?'

'Heh!' snorted Aila, a chuckle breaking from her at the very thought. 'Women from *here* don't go in the Zone! Here they are all Free Women. Born free, living free. In the Zone they are … I mean, yes they're born-women, but they're not …'

She faltered, realizing that her explanation was not holding up to scrutiny. She tried again.

'Maybe for you all women are the same, the ones in the Zone and the ones here. But we make a difference between them. Like we say of men, This one is a Warrior, that one is an Importer. So. The women in the Zone? We call them "feems". All born-women there are feems.' She waited to see if comprehension had settled into place.

Youngest nodded. 'You mean feems are born-women who offer sexual services?'

'No, no,' said Aila shaking her head emphatically. 'Making sex is the pleasure industry. Transies make sex. You, me, all transies – we are in the pleasure industry. We make sex and that's all we do, nothing more. It's only pleasure. Feems are different. They make sex, yes, of course. Obviously. But they are also … well …' she cast around for a suitable analogy. 'They are like Doctors. Engineers. They are part of the Zone. They are resources of the warriors. Without them, the warriors cannot find their courage.'

She was growing increasingly incoherent. 'Can you understand me? It's very hard to explain. Maybe it's just something you have to *feel*, inside your head, like the basic meanings of words. And maybe if you don't already know, it can't be explained. Do you understand?'

Youngest shook his head. 'No.' He could place his finger on the translator disk, in order to suppress it, so that his comment came out in Urdu. But he felt too altered from his norm to bother. *My own voice is no longer my own,* he thought. One more nail in the coffin of his identity. Only the maddening whisper circulating in his head reminded him of his mission, of who he was and what he was doing: *find-the-Island. do-your-duty. in-the-name-of-all-true-men. sell-the-girl.*

A single thread of continuity in the disorderly confusion of his life.

12

The Examining Officer had red hair coiffed in shining loops around the translucent whiteness of her bony face. Her eyes were pale aquamarine. Her pupils were like onyx needles with which she impaled the objects of her interest. She wore a stiff brocade garment that covered her from her collar bones to her ankles, while leaving the central plane of her taut alabaster torso fully exposed. She wore a red jewel in her navel and, curving up from between the plump folds of her labia, an ornate silver ornament in the shape of a peacock's head. She sat high up on a raised platform, in a seat that resembled an antique throne, carved out of precious woods. It was heavily cushioned as well as mechanized so that she could swivel around in it, move around the room or make it recline.

She had laughed out loud when Youngest extended his hands towards her, with Amir's fingertips affixed over his own. 'What did you think – that we would not notice your fingertips are not your own?' she asked, throwing her head back and exposing the long silken expanse of her throat. She had snapped her fingers at an aide, a younger woman in a neatly styled grey jumpsuit who stood just behind her, her face mask-like in attentive expressionlessness. 'The hands,' she said, and the aide sped away.

Then she returned her attention to Youngest. 'All right. Mr … Yasmine? Are those your cases on the side? Have they been in your sole possession from the time you packed them? Do you have any reason to believe their contents have been tampered with?'

'Good,' she said, when Youngest responded satisfactorily to her queries.

The aide returned with a basin, a container of water and a pouch in which she carried a selection of instruments similar to a manicurist's tools.

Aila remained mute and fidgeting on a wooden bench half a metre lower than the Examining Officer's seat. When they had first entered the Examination Room, she had attempted to act as Youngest's intermediary. But her manner had irritated the Officer so much that she was ordered to maintain absolute silence if she didn't want to be escorted out.

To Youngest the Examiner said, 'We cannot proceed until your ludicrous "tips" have been removed so that you can unpack your items for viewing. You will be charged for wasting our time. Lucky for you, it is also my lunch break, or I would send you away.'

The aide knelt by Youngest, and silently snipped away the now gray and fraying skin from around the dead man's nails. They had been cemented firmly in place but the aide had clearly faced the situation before. She was able to pare the fake ones down to match the contours of Youngest's nails. Then she led him over to a booth in the corner of the room in order to re-install his identity holograms.

The procedure took half an hour, but the officer seemed in no hurry to finish her lunch. Her food was brought to her by more aides, who murmured the names of each dish as they served it to her: cherries flambéed in gold foil, olives stuffed with hummingbird hearts, bees curried in chocolate sauce served on a bed of steamed seaweed. She ate with gusto, drank three thimbles of wine and ended the meal with coffee and a hookah, while watching a performance of *The Nutcracker Suite* as a desktop 3D projection. At no time did she pay any attention to the two importers in her chambers, hide herself from their view or offer them any refreshments.

The room was decorated in a minimalist-opulent style, with carpets on the ceiling, but no furniture aside from the bench and the cushioned seat on which the officer sat. Access to her chamber had been effected through panels that opened in the floor of the waiting area, leading to a sunken stairwell and corridor. There were no windows or doors to be seen, but the glass out of which the entire chamber was constructed could, of course, at a moment's notice be converted into a projection surface that simulated windows opening onto panoramic vistas or any other desired visual effects.

When at last her meal was done, the officer snapped her fingers at the aide. The wall to her right shimmered and grew translucent. Youngest saw his cases displayed there, where he'd been asked to deposit them at the time that the interview began. The aide led him through a partition then locked him in on the other side, while she returned to the officer's chamber.

'Open them,' commanded the Officer, her voice as clear as if she had been standing right next to Youngest. 'Choose the order of your preference. Move slowly and follow my instructions exactly. If you must turn your back to me, ask my permission. I can hear you, but raise your hand to ask permission before you say anything.' She had swung her throne around to face the glass partition.

Youngest moved with the unhurried actions of an underwater dancer. He opened the inanimate case first, the one of containing batteries and animal pelts. Anticipating the moment when he'd have to show his merchandise to an Examining Officer, he'd had the case constructed to function as a portable shelf, the two halves coming apart to look like a kiosk.

It was an impressive haul and he knew it: the plastrium-ion batteries looked like fingers of solidified rainbow, each in its customized cradle, capable of providing enough energy to power a one-man hoverjet for two years of continuous flight. 'Six hundred of these,' he murmured, holding one up for her inspection. The glass between the two rooms was zoom-enabled from where she sat.

The pelts were from Siamese cats, spotted hyenas and king cobras, six each. There was also one clouded leopard complete with claws and teeth.

'Interesting selection,' was the Officer's comment when she had inspected all the merchandise to her satisfaction. 'You chose well.'

The value of the haul was represented as bars displayed on the pane between the two rooms. Youngest did not understand the notation or the value it represented but from Aila's awestruck expression he assumed that the price being offered was a good one.

He turned now to the second case. Sweat began trickling down his back. He had no way of being sure what he was about to reveal.

Like the first case, this one was rectangular, with rounded sides. However it did not open in the same manner. He stood it up on one of its shorter ends and began by puncturing the seal along its the front edge. He peeled away the outer layer, laying it down flat on the floor and repeated the procedure twice. Underneath the third layer was a firm matte metallic surface, slate grey in colour. There was a seam down the middle and seven broad overlapping latches.

In the silence, Youngest could hear his own breath whistling in and out of his nose. He had followed the officer's instructions, had requested her permission for all his actions and had no reason to be nervous. Nevertheless, he could hear himself beginning to pant. There was a weakness in his fingers that was hard to overcome. He had been kneeling while setting up the case for display and now he paused, flexing his fingers, with his head bowed.

'What's the matter?' asked the Examining Officer.

'Nothing,' said Youngest and returned to his task.

One by one he undid the fasteners. They gave way with a slight click and a hum. The last one was in the middle. He drew it aside and then, after seeking permission to turn his back towards the officer, pressed his thumbs into two depressions on either side of the joint.

Pinpoints of blue light twinkled along the length of the seal, signifying that the unit's power supply was healthy. Youngest moved aside, still on his knees, shifting to the left of the half-opened case. The lights strengthened and merged, becoming one continuous line of blue light. Then, with a sucking sound, the two edges came undone and the air-seal was broken.

Immediately, a sky-blue gas began to escape from the lit-up interior, fading to white before vanishing altogether as they merged with the surrounding atmosphere. The taut skin of the cover began to crease as it pulled itself away from the centre, shrinking towards either side. The escaping gas became a storm of snowy curls accompanied by hissing jets of air that rimmed the interior of the case and were now dispersing the waving tendrils.

Youngest covered his face with his sleeve to protect himself from the gas, but as the hissing reached a crescendo he raised his head and made himself look within the now fully opened case.

There she was.

Embedded within the glowing gel that sustained her life, she looked like a fossil bird, her hips and shoulders flat, her head turned to the side, legs curled sideways and her arms arranged so that her hands rested free of any other parts of her body. A magician's assistant had helped place her diagonally within the flattened, confined space, choosing angles that were the least stressful for a human frame to assume over a period of days. She was emaciated down to the final vestiges of skin and muscle. Her head was as shaven as when she went in, accentuating the pure lines of her nose, her forehead, her shapely ears. And the mouth: dark and full like his own, carved from a single plum.

There was no quickening of life. She was in suspended stasis. It was a technique synthesized from little brown bats which freeze solid in winter only to revive in summer. There were no blackened spots on her skin and her joints did not appear to be swollen or out of alignment. He could not know for sure whether her mind was intact until she had been revived. Which would take several hours. Perhaps days.

Nor would he be present to see it.

So he might never know.

The Examining Officer's voice sliced through his thoughts.

'Huh. A bag of bones. Doesn't look alive, if you ask me. Still. It's certainly got all its limbs in mint condition. That's unusual. Recycling potential, if nothing else.' She raked him with her steely eyes. 'Well? Tell me something about your precious merchandise, then. We'll be auctioning it, you know. They don't often come to us alive. But when they do, that's the procedure.'

Youngest faltered, his mouth open, his heart hammering in his chest.

'Oh, stand up, *stand up*!' said the Officer. 'For you to behave like a rag-doll won't improve her price. You have to tell me what I should tell the Island Mentors. Try to understand: I will do the bargaining, while you remain silent. At the end, we will split the proceeds sixty–forty–sixty to me, of course. Is it understood? So it's to your advantage to tell me what you can that will make her attractive to the buyers.'

Youngest got to his feet, moving as if his limbs were filled with lead. 'Madam,' he began. 'What can I say? She's my *daughter*—'

'Oh my!' exclaimed the Officer, hands clutched to her breast.

'I faint with pity!' Then she jerked her chin in a gesture of contempt. 'Sentimental fool. What are we – professional mourners? Do we have nothing better to do with our time but weep for your loss? I need information that'll be of some use to the bidders. I need to know her age, her mental condition, what resources an Island will require to make her functional …'

She turned to her aide, who was already pushing buttons on a lighted locator. 'Round up the Mentors, will you? They know we have a decision to make.'

She turned back to Youngest. 'Well? Have you thought of anything useful to tell me?'

'I know nothing about the Island. Or … Islands? More than one?' said Youngest. 'I have no idea what they would find worth acquiring. I have heard only that they take in girls who can go nowhere else.'

'In that case,' said the Examining Officer, 'you are misinformed. *We* take in girls here at the Collectory. *We* assess their condition. Then, and only then, do we send them out to the Islands. They're usually partially or completely dead when they get here. Some are missing limbs, some are missing internal body parts, most are unable to eat or sit or stand. We recycle the body parts of the dead ones. And those that are partially alive? Well, we stitch their bodies together, tack on the missing bits and send them out to the Islands. But, as you can imagine, they all need psychological and social rehabilitation before they are released into the world once more. Which is what the Islands are for—'

'My daughter is sane,' cut in Youngest. 'She is nineteen. Intelligent. Well-read.' *Headstrong, independent, willful,* he thought, though he did not utter the words. *She is the jewel at the centre of my existence. Yet I cannot afford to keep her. My heart is breaking.* 'Beautiful,' is what he finally said out loud.

'Useless information. What I need to know is what kind of

damage she has sustained. The Islands have to budget their resources. If she's going to require extensive reconstruction her cost to the Islands may exceed what they can afford.' She shrugged. 'It happens.'

'But she is *not* damaged,' said Youngest. 'Not in any way.' He paused, his heart thudding in his throat, in his ears. 'She is completely … intact.'

His tone made the Officer sit forward. 'Oh?' Her eyes narrowed to slits. 'Meaning what, exactly?'

Youngest could see, peripherally, that Aila was leaning forward too. She was frowning. Perhaps shaking her head.

'Meaning …' said Youngest, struggling to keep his voice steady and unemotional. 'Meaning that she has not been exposed to sexual activity. That she is a … a … *virgin*.'

The Officer sucked in her breath hard, as if hissing.

'Now *that's* a word we haven't heard in this building for a while. Maybe in this entire hemisphere.' Her expression hardened. 'It can't be true, of course. There are no virgins left in our world. We are all ritually deflowered immediately after birth. To demystify the cult of purity. How can you not know that?' She held up her hand. 'No, do NOT interrupt. Your reasons are of no interest to me. Only one thing matters: is it true? Because if it is, then … yes. Your bony little larva will fetch a good price.' Her arctic face was lit by a faint flame. 'A very good price indeed.'

'It *is* true,' said Youngest. He clenched his teeth, to keep his mouth from trembling. 'And a physical examination will prove it. But it won't be necessary. It's the reason that matters. You'll understand when you hear it.'

There was a pulse of silence. Youngest could see that Aila was very agitated. She was silent, but her entire body was shouting at him, telling him not to say what he was going to say.

The Examining Officer's eyebrows rose.

'Well? I'm listening.'

'Because,' said Youngest, his traitor's head bent while he bled inside, 'we are from beyond the South Zone. From the land you call the Forbidden Country. She was raised as a boy. She wears prosthetics to hide her sexual parts. She does not know what it means to be a woman. And she has never been …' He paused, looking for an appropriate word. 'Penetrated.'

13

They came in like a team of lionesses setting off on a communal hunt, eight Senior Mentors. They were not physically present but virtual, life-size holograms. Each woman was the leader of a different Island as well as a Council Member at the Collectory.

They greeted one another with the ease of long-term comrades, smiling and sharing anecdotes, speaking in several languages at once, their voices soft and musical. They arranged themselves on either side of the Examining Officer, who was a Council Member herself. They gazed into the room where Youngest stood, looked at the opened case with the still figure of the girl in it, fidgeted with their clothing, added comments to previous conversations, leaned forward with their jewellery flashing, laughed.

None of them, even by mistake, glanced in the direction of either Youngest or Aila.

I am invisible, thought Youngest, remaining beside the case he had opened.

Aila had not budged from the bench she had been told to sit on. It was behind the row of Council Members. Youngest could see her, framed between two holograms, hands folded in her lap. She looked tawdry, he realized. A pathetic cardboard cut-out with her gaudy clothes and her fake breasts. A female clown in a room full of spectral Free Women.

Women. Free Women. Any women.

He repeated the words to himself in his head, trying to rekindle the tenderness he had felt when he looked up while standing in the Ascensor queue. The sensation refused to return however. These were older women and would most likely not have been attractive to him, even if he had remained intact as a man. But that was not the whole story.

The Examining Officer, for instance, with her smooth body, her highly manicured appearance, her gorgeous clothes, perhaps even the grotesque silver ornament rising up from her groin was meant, in some way, to be alluring or arousing. Yet he found her utterly repulsive. It was the same with the others. For all their soft contours, the hairless faces, the delicate build, they frightened him.

He had never in his life seen women interacting with one another in this way before. It wasn't just that they were carefree and relaxed. It was that they were completely unconscious of being women in the way in which he was accustomed.

In the distant past, when he had still been a young child, he had known all the women of his family – his mother, her sisters, the sorority of cousins. But when they met and even when they were alone with him as a small child, they were always conscious of themselves as women, as entities distinct from men. In the way they stood and sat, in the way they might glance over their shoulders to see if a window was open or if a curtain had been shifted aside, they were always fearful of being watched.

They would sit with their feet and arms folded in graceful positions. They would remain covered even when there was no adult male gaze within miles of them. They behaved as if they were thin-skinned balloons, so fragile that merely to think of a pin in their presence would deflate them. They laughed with their mouths covered and sneezed, coughed or cried in the same manner. They would never raise their voices too loud or draw attention to themselves in public places. All the events of their mysterious bodies were conducted in silence and with their eyes averted, as if they too believed that their hidden parts were unclean, not worthy of sight. They would not so much as break wind in the presence of another. Not even him, not even a child.

So to see a group of women who met together as colleagues, exchanging pleasantries and conducting themselves as if they had no personal chores in the world – in particular, no chores involving husbands, parents, children – stirred layers of darkness within him. Currents of memory were set in motion. Pain. Fear. He was looking directly at them, but in his heart he looked away.

The Examining Officer drew the meeting to order. 'We are gathered here, etcetera, etcetera,' she said, her mouth curving in a feral smile. 'We see before us, in the examination room, one body, complete and alive. A rare situation. The subject is …' she listened to the tiny voice of the data recorder in her hand '… nineteen years of age … female … healthy … and—' Her eyebrows arched high on her forehead, creating a moment of suspense. '*Intact*,' she finished, the needle-points of her eyes flashing in and out of the tapestry of her colleagues. 'A virgin.'

An audible gasp rustled throughout the company.

The first to speak was a tall ebony-skinned woman with a cap of tiny mirrors upon her shaven head. 'Interesting!' was all she said. She wore white robes that billowed slightly, as if she were standing in the open air, being buffeted by a fresh breeze while facing the holo-camera from which her image was received at the Collectory.

'Do we know it for a fact?' came another remark. 'Has she been examined?'

'I thought all girls these days were systematically deflowered at birth—'

'No! In some communities they wait till the fifth day—'

'Where I grew up, they used a beautiful silver instrument, called a *peen*, to effect the first penetration.'

'Yes, but at what *age*?'

'It looked just like a fish leaping out of the water—'

'Ahhh – I don't believe it. No one can last till nineteen without *some* contact.'

'Or else there's a congenital defect. Can you see? There's some deformity there …'

One woman said, in a soft, thoughtful voice, 'Poor thing. If it's true, I feel sorry for her.' She was almost as tall as she was broad, wearing a voluminous baby-pink shift. Her silver hair flowed down her shoulders in the way of a snow-covered peak above the spreading mass of the mountain below. She was barefoot and pale-skinned, with a blue gecko tattooed above her left ankle.

'It's not a deformity,' said the Examiner. 'It's a prosthetic. Look carefully and you'll see a faint colour differential along the hips. But from another perspective now, consider the shape of the nose, the head, the eyes. Ask yourself to which continent those shapes belong. Then ask yourselves: if there could be a girl who looks like this and who has escaped the ritual deflowering that is common in our world … where would she be born?'

There was a moment's silence.

'In a place where no other girls have been born for twenty years,' said another member who had not said a word so far. She spoke in a slow, wondering tone, as if she were seeing her answer form in her mind letter by letter. She wore a strip of white raw silk wrapped tightly around her torso, covering every part of her except her breasts and ending just above the crest of her pubic hair. 'Am I right, Marisa?' She addressed the Examining Officer, and began shaking her head even as she spoke. 'Which means we cannot accept her, of course. No one can accept her. She must go back.'

'Nonsense, Q'alifa.' This was the Examining Officer. 'Her origin does not concern us. We ask no questions at the Collectory—'

'You're the one who mentioned it!'

'To establish her bonafides as a virgin, that is all. She grew up hidden behind the identity of a boy. Elsewhere in our world, girls are relieved of the burden of intactitude to save them from being objectified as immaculati. Whereas *she*, brought up as a boy, retained hers! Is that not an irony?'

Q'alifa spoke again. 'Irony? Not at all. I call it an affront.'

'What, her entire existence?' This was a woman with thick grey curls on her head, wearing a red tunic embroidered in black whorls over grey shorts and bare feet.

'No, Sarro, not her existence,' said Q'alifa, 'but her presence here, in the free world. It's an insult to all that we have endured as a result of her culture's abominations.'

'Oh, is it a free world you're living in, Q'alifa?' Marisa said sharply. 'As a custodian of hundreds of girls mangled by the Zone?'

'Do not belittle the sacrifices made by our mothers, and their mothers before them!' snapped Q'alifa. 'If this girl is here, in this building, it can only be because terrible deeds were done in her name in order to convey her here. The culture to which she belongs was disbarred from the common weal of humanity for what its people did twenty, twenty-two years ago. They have never approached the Whole World Union for a change of status. They have never apologized for their unspeakable crimes. Why should we lift our sanctions against them?' Her holographic image scanned the room. 'Why should we dishonour the history of our planet by admitting her, innocent though she is, to our ranks?'

'Before I answer your question, I want to ask Vane why she pitied the girl,' Marisa said, turning towards the monumental woman in pink.

The silver-haired mentor had been standing with the tips of her fingers together just under her nose, in the attitude of someone in deep thought.

'It seemed obvious to me,' she said, choosing her words carefully. 'And it should be obvious to any one of us. For a girl to be a virgin at nineteen? In our world? It has to mean utter and complete loneliness. I am not concerned about her provenance. Her skin colour and features no longer tell me anything. We see all types on our Island. I'm with Marisa on this subject: wherever she was before, she's part of our world now – and profoundly alone. Our commitment is to girls who need us. Not to the ghouls that created them. If we turn her away, we become one with them. And I will not do that.'

Marisa gave a brisk smile. 'Vane has better words at her command than I do. Her answer is my answer.' She addressed the other members in the room. 'Let us open the bids. The discussion is bound to continue but I think we have the information we need. Q'alifa?'

'Excuse me, Marisa, Vane, Council Members, I will no longer participate in this auction. I am deeply offended by this outcome. Vane, your words are clever but I fear for you. I fear for all of us. Even asleep in her casket this girl has driven a rift between us! What will she do when she awakens? Mark my words: we will regret this day's proceedings.'

'Q'alifa—'

'No! The roots of this folly go deep. But of course as long as even one of us remains to bid, it means the damage is already done and there's nothing I or anyone else can do to stamp it out.' Her chest was heaving with emotion. 'With all respect to the Members, I'm sorry, but I must take my leave.'

Her hologram blinked out of view.

Two more members raised their hands and asked to be excused, one with the mirrored cap and another one with glass beads cascading down her shoulders.

'Five of you remain,' said Marisa. 'Good. Vane? Would you like to begin?'

Youngest glanced across the room at Aila. She was staring at him, a smile on her face. When she saw him look at her, she nodded and gave him a thumbs-up sign.

He did not smile back.

14

Some hours later, Youngest and Aila were escorted away by a silent attendant to a pay-out register, where the transaction was entered into the Collectory's records. The value assigned to Youngest's possessions was embedded into the nails of both his hands. In case he lost control over this record by the physical removal of his fingertips, he had twenty-one solar days in which to return to the Collectory, sans his fingertips, to be identified by means of his voice-print. If his voice-print did not match the claim he made against the loss of his nailgrams, then the loss would become unrecoverable.

Aila's commission was added to her lifetime account as an agent of the Collectory.

As they made their way out of the building, Youngest told Aila she could buy any one thing – clothes, shoes, perfume or jewellery – as a gift from him, over and above the tip he had originally agreed to give her. She was levitating with pleasure by the time they arrived at the shopping district, a glass tower with chutes circling around the merchandise.

Youngest waited in a narrow strip of park at the foot of the structure, watching the parade of men, the word is used here for the first time and beasts circulating in the sharp, flavoured air. Restlessness plucked at him like flocks of tiny vultures, gnawing at his skin, his bowels, his eyes, his heart, his soul. He had promised Aila that he would allow her to show him around the city. He wished now that he had not been so generous. All he wanted was to get away.

But he knew, too, that he needed Aila's advice to depart in the shortest possible time and by the most comfortable transport. He should be able to justify the expense of time as necessary wastage, but it took all the resources of his waning will power to wait patiently.

While he waited, he fiddled with Aila's shutterfly viewer. Shutterflies, tiny flying machines, closely matched the behaviour of annoying flying insects. The viewer was a strip of metal meant to be worn on the wrist that picked up and displayed the video images recorded by random shutterflies as they buzzed around. Aila had given the viewer to Youngest, saying she would pick up another one for herself.

Its tiny, shimmering screen, about 20 centimetres in width, streamed surprisingly sharp images. A few simple controls enabled tuning and audio. Youngest amused himself for several minutes tuning in to images of strangers, looking up hairy nostrils or listening in to conversations in unfamiliar languages. According to Aila, the wrist-viewer had a range of 50 metres, always choosing the nearest available fly as a first reference point. It could be locked to one particular fly or it could receive streams from any flies within a chosen range. More advanced models could be controlled and used as mobile video devices.

Aila took an hour to choose a slinky brocade gown, blood red in colour. She wore it before leaving the shop. It had a high collar and see-through beaded panels outlined with tiny blinking lights over the crotch and breasts.

'Come,' she said. 'I is take you to View Point.'

'Is it far?' asked Youngest.

'You is promise you is come everywhere I is want to go!' said Aila, pouting.

'Well I …'

'I is want to ask you something important.'

'And you can't ask me here?'

'I is want to be safe from shutterflies,' she whispered, leaning in close. 'Sometimes they is recording too much. Is better to be safe from them.'

Youngest shrugged. 'Okay,' he said.

The View Point was a ring of crystalline glass that permitted a 360° view of the seething abyss over which the City was poised. A transparent gondola moving along predetermined tracks took passengers on a trip that could stretch over six hours, but could also be speeded up or slowed down at will. Passengers were not required to return to their starting point in order to disembark.

'So,' said Aila.

The gondola had a rail against which to lean on the side facing down into the gaping wound in the planet's mantle beneath them. They were both leaning against this railing, sealed in by the glass. Youngest stared at the black and orange clouds flaring far below, his face expressionless.

'First I is ask the question,' said Aila.

Youngest did not look at her. The baby talk was getting on his nerves.

'You is become very rich man now. But you is not happy. Why?'

'I've done what I came to do,' he said. 'And now I must go.' He wondered in what way such a question might be a security risk.

'You is go back to … your home?' Even though there were just the two of them and the location was secure, she looked around herself reflexively. 'In Forbidden Country?'

'No, no,' he said. 'Not so far. I'll go to a small ship. A yacht.' He didn't have the energy to lie.

'Ship!' chirped Aila. '*Whau!* I is like ship! Why you is not be happy then? Is you not go back to your man? Is you not want to meet him?'

Youngest clenched his teeth. Aila's expression was that of a dog staring expectantly into its master's face, waiting for a ball to be thrown. His instinct was to kick her away.

'No,' said Youngest. 'I don't want to meet him. But I still have to get back as soon as possible. I know he's waiting.'

'Ah!' she said, her warm brown eyes opened wide with guilelessness. 'So he is love you but your heart is wander?' she asked, slipping her arm around his.

Youngest recoiled, thrusting hard against her as he snarled, 'No!'

He heard the pained gasp. His mind registered an image of her face crumpling.

It made him want to hit her all the more.

The absurdity of the question!

'No,' he repeated, as he forced himself to calm down. 'It's not like that.' He drew in his breath. 'He uses me and I have no choice but to let myself be used. There's no love. It's pure dependence. And I must go. Now. Right away.'

'Ah,' said Aila, her voice wobbling. 'I see.'

No, thought Youngest. *You see nothing.*

'It – it is like … contract marriage?'

Youngest did not answer.

'Is only for jig-jig?'

Worse than that, thought Youngest. *Much worse.* 'You won't understand,' he said out loud. 'And I can't explain.'

Aila paused now. She wasn't done. She dropped her voice to the level of a child's whisper and leaned towards him. 'No. I am understand. That is why I is have the idea. I is see you is not happy. So. You is take me with you?'

Youngest swallowed hard before saying, 'What?'

'You is hear me, I know. I is ask you to take me with you. As … as co-wife,' said Aila. She turned away from him and was staring into the inferno too, now. 'And you is want to scream *no! no! no!*'

She paused, and when she continued it was in Farsi.

'I am not stupid, Yasmine. But I am a transie. Maybe that's why I have feelings. More than you, because you are really a man, not a transie. Even at this moment, with the Eraser circulating inside me, I still have feelings. And I want to come. With you.'

She was staring at him once more, with that expression of unreasoning trust.

'I like you, Yasmine,' she was saying. 'Maybe you think it is strange. Maybe you ask yourself, how can she like a stranger who comes into her home as a guest and then kills her father? But I can answer you. The answer is that my father hated me. You saw a little bit of it. I saw a lot. From the time I was very young, he kicked me, beat me, spat on me. When I changed my body, he would fuck me like a dog. Every day. Twice a day. Then he would kick me senseless. Why? Because he knew that unlike other boys who became transies for money, I was a transie deep in my heart. In my blood, in my soul. And he hated me for *that*.'

She paused, staring into the abyss. Youngest said nothing.

'When he was a boy, men ruled over women. Then the world changed under his feet. He refused to change with it. I was his first-born and he was happy he had a son. But then, little by little, he began to see that I was not the son he wanted me to be. And for that he felt a hate that had no mouth to scream with.'

She sighed.

'I hated him too. Or maybe I hated him so much it became the same as loving him. I don't know. What I can say is this: there's no reason any more for me to stay in the City. No reason at all.'

Youngest frowned. 'Your half-brothers?'

She turned her face up towards Youngest. 'They are clone-brothers, not half. Maybe not even anything-brothers. My father had them made when I was already fourteen and my mother was dead. They are fifteen years old in body-years, but in time-years? Eight.'

Tongues of flame licked up now and then, followed by blinding flashes of lightning, fuming purple clouds and flaring black blossoms.

'They signed up for the Zone Warrior programme two years ago. They don't care about anything else – they were created to be warriors, nothing else. They live only for that.'

'Aila,' said Youngest, as he watched the demonic forces unchained far below them, 'you don't know what you're asking of me.'

'Please, you is *not* say "no",' said Aila, reverting to her baby-voice pidgin. 'Please.'

15

Aila took him to the Thunder Palace for lunch. It was a Zone-themed restaurant where fans could celebrate their teams' latest victories to the accompaniment of realistic-sounding weather effects. According to her, the noise levels caused shutterflies to drop senseless to the floor. So it too was safe for conversation.

Youngest felt like a shutterfly himself as they entered the place. There were two dozen news screens, three hundred boisterous patrons and ear-shattering artificial thunderclaps sounding simultaneously.

Audio-holograms twittered and swerved overhead, simulating bird-life. Poison-green streamers of artificial leaves swayed and twirled in the chaos. The walls were ringed with video images of sports commentators bellowing the latest results. Sweat-slicked victors held up the still-dripping heads of their most recent adversaries while on cutaway screens the shredded corpses of losing teams were hauled away by staggering, bloodied teammates. New recruits practised their screeching anthems alongside the keening howls of professional rape victims submitting to victorious warriors.

There was no space on the main floor, but Aila and Youngest got seats on either side of a pole that boosted them high in the air as soon as they sat down. A system of pulleys and steam-driven winches enabled the restaurant to accommodate scores of diners perched at varying heights.

Aila reached towards the steel jar embedded in the surface of the circular table that rimmed their section of pole. 'Try this,' she said. 'Delicacy of the Suspended City. Very sweet! Very good.'

White fumes from the dry ice within the container seethed down its sides. She held up what looked like a diseased blue marble. 'We call them Sheep's Ice,' she said, essaying a little joke. 'You get it? Sheep's eyes. Filled with honey. Frozen.'

'Aila,' said Youngest, ignoring the dessert offering. 'You must give up this idea of coming with me.'

'I will not give up,' said Aila as she popped the Sheep's Ice into her mouth.

A waiter rose, travelling up a service pole and locked himself in place beside their table. His skin was blue-black and the whites of his eyes were dyed silver-indigo so that they alternately flashed and darkened depending on where he directed his gaze. When he smiled he displayed a keyboard of perfectly white and even teeth and his costume consisted of belts and chains that displayed his wiry torso to best effect. He chirruped at Aila in Mod¡Kung, and Aila chirruped back, glancing now and then in Youngest's direction, while placing the order.

As soon as the waiter had gone, Aila leaned towards Youngest, so that he could hear her above the pandemonium. '*You* don't understand,' she said. 'There's nothing for me here. Even if you show me the entrance to Hell, at least it will be something different to what I have here.'

Youngest tried and failed to imagine the chasm between her understanding of his reality and his own knowledge of it. Out loud he said, 'If you don't want to hear "no" then don't ask me questions to which that is the only answer.'

'I have control over my father's account. So I am rich, too, now. I can do whatever I want. I can buy my own ticket on the Ascensor. We can travel on deluxe tubes. And even after that I don't need you to look after me. But I want to get away from the City. Before it is too late.'

'Too late for what?'

'No one here dies of old age, Yasmine,' said Aila. 'I want to grow old. I want to have wrinkles. I want to be heavy with years.' She stared at him. 'Can you not understand that? You are older than me. You must understand what I'm saying. You must know what I mean!'

Youngest turned his face towards her. He wasn't smiling. 'The only thing I can promise you, Aila,' he said, 'is the terrible regret you will feel if you come with me.'

She stared back at him, uncomprehending.

'Let me show you something.' He was sitting within easy reach of her. Supporting himself on the footrests around the pole, he leaned towards her and drew her head towards him. Her expression cycled through wild hope and sudden fear before he said, 'No, no, I won't hurt you. Don't struggle.' He turned her face away from him. 'Listen,' he said. Then he covered her right ear with his mouth.

Despite the uproar around them, he felt her go still between his hands. The purring voice that echoed softly and ceaselessly within his head, threaded its way out of the cavern of his mouth and into Aila's ear. After a few seconds, she drew away.

Youngest gave her his handkerchief and she wiped her ear with it, looking at him. The simple features of her face were stretched to their limit, expressing something between alarm and amazement.

'He is ... in your mouth? Your man?' she asked. 'Is that *him*?'

Youngest nodded.

'He speaks in your head? All the time?'

'This is a recording,' said Youngest. 'It plays inside my head all the time. I'm out of range of his radio transmitter right now. But when I'm in range, then I hear not just this recording but his living voice as well. Inside my head. All the time. And he can hear mine.'

Aila was silent for a beat. 'Right now? Can he hear you now?

Everything you say?'

Youngest shrugged and shook his head. 'I don't think so. But I don't know. Maybe.' He gave her a hard stare. 'It's not just sound. Sometimes he sends what he calls punishments. A fine wire that connects directly to the nerves in my teeth. When he hits that button, I shit myself. I can't help it. My brain shuts down. Then he does it again, just to hear me scream.'

Aila's eyes were wide. She was impressed, Youngest realized. In her value system, a cruel and despotic man was automatically attention-worthy. Powerful. 'What is his name?' asked Aila. 'What do you call him?'

'He has only a title,' said Youngest. 'No name. He's … the General. That's all.'

'*Whau*. A General!' said Aila. 'What army, which …'

But Youngest was already shaking his head.

'You know what clones are – of course you do,' said Youngest. 'Your brothers are clones. All right. But the Generals aren't ordinary clones. They're a team of maybe five hundred men, maybe more, created to be leaders. They're extremely intelligent, physically powerful and highly competitive. They also think with one mind. Not because they're clones, but because they all have the radios embedded in their jaws. From the moment they are … well, from the moment they can breathe outside their incubators, they are connected to one another by the radio implants.'

Around them, in the restaurant, a rhythmic drumming had begun.

'They think of themselves as sculptors, carving reality to suit their ideas. For instance, they believe that women are inferior versions of men. So the first thing they did when they came to power was to force all the men to destroy all the women of our region. *All the women*. The women who resisted were hunted down, dragged into the streets and butchered. Grenades were inserted into their private parts. Their entrails were hung from the trees like garlands. Unborn babies were torn out of their wombs.' He paused. 'Any men who resisted were treated in similar ways.'

The frown on Aila's face had been growing. She was distracted by the disturbance around them. She cupped her hands around her mouth and shouted towards him. 'But the girl you took today? She is a real girl? A born girl?'

'Yes,' said Youngest. 'The last one left alive in the Forbidden Country, my world. She was born in secret after the purge of women began.' His throat constricted with emotion. 'Then her mother killed herself. And we … my brothers and I … raised the girl without telling her anything about what she was and why—'

At that very moment a triumphant roar ripped through the room. Diners began jumping to their feet, howling, ululating, thumping the tables. The air began to shimmer with holographic projections of fireworks and fire-fountains in red and white. Virtual confetti began to rain through the air.

'What's going on?' asked Youngest.

Aila indicated the rest of the room. 'Can you not see how many people here are dressed in *red*?' She clutched at her arms, hugging herself tight. 'It means that their team has won – the Dzing*!*-Dzing*!* The Cannibals! Ohhh … this is bad, very bad for everyone.'

A transie wearing glittering red feathers had started a conga line on the main floor. The music shifted gear to suit her exuberance. Their own waiter came sailing up along his pole. He was beaming so broadly his teeth bisected his face in a line of solid ivory.

'Whaooo!' he whooped, as he delivered crisp seaweed, giant crab-claws and turtle-meat kebabs in steel bowls that were magnetized to the surface of their table. He plunked two tankards of bright red beer in front of them and set down individual squeeze-jars of glistening orange sea-urchin sauce before vanishing downwards once more.

He returned a moment later, bearing aloft a flaming iron spike. He rammed this down into a notch on their pole, just above the surface of the table top. 'Compliments of the management!' he sang out, his indigo eyes flashing as he slid away once more.

The spike bobbed back and forth at a jaunty angle. It was stuck through with a dozen or so irregular disks, red and white in colour, still fizzing with heat.

Alia's face registered disgust. 'You see what they are?' she asked, pulling one of the disks loose and handing it Youngest. He saw it was a potato crisp in the shape of a human ear, deep-fried and covered in scarlet goo.

'These are only fake,' she said. 'But in the Zone, they are the Red team's specialty. There they are real. Ears. Their team champions boast that they eat whole people after a victory. They say it makes the Reds strong. And, for sure, at least for now, they *are* winning.'

16

Aila paid for the food and suggested leaving the restaurant. The level of sound had risen beyond tolerance.

Outside, shutterflies buzzed around them once more, so Youngest spoke guardedly, using evasive terms. 'It's a long story,' he said. 'I believed there was no way to get my girl out without making compromises.' He indicated himself, his body. 'One of the, uh, Top Men I met was interested in me. I gained his confidence. I realized that he and his clone-brothers were starting to turn their attention to the world beyond my … uh … my home land.'

He paused, looking away. Only a lunatic would have devised the plan he set in motion. And he was that lunatic.

'They had heard about these … uh … safe-places for damaged girls. But they understood that in order to locate one of these places and to infiltrate it they would need an actual female. And they didn't have any.' He glanced at Aila. 'So.' He indicated his body once more. 'My body. Plus one living girl. That was the bargain I made. To get my girl out of my country.'

Aila nodded.

He tapped his wrist and then pointed at his chest, just below his breast bone. 'You've seen these?'

'Sat-Locs,' said Aila. 'Satellite Locators. But they are—' She shrugged. 'Old-style.'

There was no time to explore what she meant by that. He tapped his wrist. 'One is for me to track my … my shipment. The other is for the Top Man to track *me*.' He tapped his chest. 'They both have poison-sacs inside. Any time he wants to send me off on my final journey, he can. The same is true for the … for my shipment. That was the deal.'

Aila made a face. 'It was not a good deal,' she said. 'And it's not so easy to find those *safe-places*.' She had brought away a take-away container from the restaurant, filled with kebabs and the ear-shaped potato crisps. She opened it now.

'Maybe,' said Youngest. Once the girl was on an Island, he could track her. Once he could track the girl, he could enter the Island. 'But let's say we succeed,' he said. 'Then the Man will have got what he wants.'

'But why he wants to go there?' Aila asked, reverting to pidgin. 'Is nothing in those places. Only girlses. And womanses who is look after girlses. Is like jail. Girlses is go to other safe-places. Never to home again.' She picked up a kebab and bit into it; spicy red grease spurted down her chin. 'What anyone can get from them?'

A toe-hold, thought Youngest. *A toe-hold in this world that wanted to erase the Generals from its memory.* 'I can't explain,' he said out loud. 'I don't know. I'm not one of the Top Men.'

He reached for a kebab from the container.

'Tell me about your Cannibal Reds,' he said to Aila. 'They have won today, yes? But you said earlier today, no team is ever allowed to truly conquer the whole Zone—'

Aila's head was bobbing, her mouth full. 'Yes,' she said, when she could speak, 'is very bad day for other teams. Many, many warriors is die, is get killed. Maybe eaten. We is not know how much is true of that story.'

Youngest sampled his kebab.

He knew from what his General had told him that the wealthy and peaceable nations that created the Zone used the blood-tide of the battles for their own purpose. By nurturing the ding-dong of victories and defeat, they had created a dynamic lottery with which to keep the pendulums of their own wealth swinging, now this way, now that.

It was a method of syncretizing all the centuries preceding the cataclysm, all the bloodshed and strife of history into a single gigantic sports-cum-battlefield. A gory spectacle on which money and power depended, contained within the Zone.

Youngest guessed that there were subtle mechanisms in place to prevent any teams from winning "too much". Today's victorious Reds, for instance, would be encouraged to extend themselves too far. Their victories would diminish and they would eventually slink back down to the middle or the bottom of the pile.

But what if they were to be supplied with firearms?

Chemical weapons?

Nuclear missiles?

The Generals had all these toys.

Out loud he said, 'Still, if they *could* win every game in the season …'

Aila reached for her next kebab. 'Is cannot happen. Is never happened.'

Youngest shrugged and changed the subject.

At his request, she took him to the Clone Palace with its display cases of see-through incubators. The next generation of citizens and fighters could be viewed developing behind thick layers of titanium Glaz. The structure was circular with a continuously circulating belt of the most advanced foetuses presented for viewing by the public.

'Still,' said Aila, as they gazed at the gleaming ovoid cases, with their tiny sleeping occupants variously turning, covering their faces or yawning in their pre-natal cocoons. 'I is want to come with you.'

'I won't let you,' said Youngest.

'I is come any way.'

17

Three days later, Aila and Youngest were teetering upon a narrow wooden ledge. They had travelled via the Ascensor to Confluenza and from there, on a more comfortable version of the Cutthroat Express, to Sokotra Deepwater. Located at the base of this outcropping of ancient rock, the submerged port was the gateway to the Poisoned Sea for all travellers pouring in from along the southern coast of the Zone.

The majority were gatherer-traders bringing in the loot that was being continuously cast off from the fields of battle. But there were tourists too, from villages in the Zone; young men hoping to improve their lives by becoming warriors; transies visiting their homes in the Zone before returning to ply their trade in the City.

Rearing up above the deepwater port was a tangle of soaring lattice-work towers called the Iron Cliffs. They had been built onto the rock of Sokotra, and were all that remained of the tiny island, now drowned by the ocean. From the Iron Cliffs, flimsy jetties and piers gave access to water-taxi services.

Directly in front of where Youngest and Aila stood, stretching in all directions towards the horizon, was the Giants' Graveyard. Soaring blackened structures, streaked with rust and paint, like the giant jagged tusks of long dead behemoths poked up from the black toxic waters of the Poisoned Sea. They were the upended carcasses of hundreds of ships – tankers, cruise-liners, warships, cargo containers. The twenty-two-year-old catastrophe that had spawned the modern world remained memorialized in these enormous rusting hulks with the water slopping and slapping cheerily at their sides. Even the worst of human excesses, the water seemed to say, is just another junkyard of playthings for me.

Seagulls swerved and shrieked in the stinking mist that rose continuously off the water, reducing the tropical sun to a harmless white disk in the sky.

The gulls' cries were echoed by the calls of the water-taxi men bobbing in the black scum, their wiry arms waving like a forest of animated ebony toothpicks. The men belonged to a race of mariners who had been specifically bred by the Deepwater Port Authority to live amongst these gaunt ruins. Their leathery skin was impervious to radiation. Their bones and teeth, it was rumoured, glowed in the dark. They were given licenses to ply their trade, ferrying passengers to and from the Zone across the open sea in flimsy skimmers, pulled by the marine creatures they called Goliaths.

'Madam, Madam! See! My skimmer is have cushion seats!'

'No, come to *me* Madam – I is take you to the faaar away – half-price only!'

'See! Goliath is pulling at harness! He will take you by light-jump speed!'

'Where to, Madam? How is much?'

'Best price, Madam! Cheapest and best—'

Aila and Youngest were dressed in billowing black robes that snapped and fluttered in the light breeze. Beneath their robes they wore bright blue skin-tight costumes with goggles, face-masks and boots. The blue suit was to protect them from the little yellow crabs that famously infested this western limit of the Deepwater Port Line. The frisky crustaceans, each one the size of a single apple-slice, skittered over their clothes like flightless mosquitoes, searching for warm flesh to feast on. The seagulls, wheeling and swooping, lunged for the crabs, plucking them off with sharp nips.

Youngest turned to Aila. They had been arguing for all the three days of the journey so far. 'You don't understand,' he said. 'Once we get to the General's yacht, you won't be able to leave. And you will want to. Believe me. Take my advice. Go back, go home, right now.'

'No!' exclaimed Aila, waving her hands at the seagulls. 'There is nothing for me to go back to.'

'You are making a terrible mistake.'

'I don't understand what we're waiting for! Are you going to choose a taxi or not? Or else we'll both be eaten alive before we go anywhere.'

Youngest didn't answer. He turned to peer between the looming wrecks of the Graveyard, ignoring the howling mob of drivers at his feet, as if trying to catch sight of something.

The drivers, sensing a decision about to be made, redoubled their efforts to capture Youngest's attention, their limbs flailing in the air, their cries indistinguishable from those of the gulls now.

Each ramshackle craft was fashioned out of a single satellite dish, about three metres in diameter, its sides built up with sea-weed fibre and tortoise-shell. The floor was crisscrossed with strips of shark skin leather to create a taut, springy surface.

The skimmers were attached with ropes to bolts driven into the shell of the Goliath, a giant marine turtle. A bridle held its head up and controlled its front flippers to prevent the creature from diving beneath the surface of the water. Reins connected to the bridle were held by the driver who sat up on the very front edge of the skimmer, directing the creature by hauling on the reins and giving it the occasional kick on the head with his feet.

For all that they were made from identical materials, each saucer-shaped vessel was decorated in its own unique and individual way. One had images of palm-trees etched white on black, another was covered in geometric arrangements of sea-shells, yet another had a shark's gaping maw painted onto it. All of them were positioned in a bobbing arc, with their backs towards the boarding platform.

'You,' said Youngest, pointing to a man with a bright yellow cloth wrapped around his head. His vessel's rear-panel featured a leaping shark snatching a seagull from the air. 'We take you. How much?'

But the question was rhetorical and the answer was swallowed up in the blur of activity immediately following the choice. Half-a-dozen hands reached out to Aila and Youngest, gripping them and tugging them forward before dropping them into the bucking, swaying, interior of the skimmer they had chosen.

Seagulls dive-bombed at that very moment, snatching crabs off the distracted passengers as they boarded the tiny craft, clutching one hold-all each. In the same instant, the driver sprinted nimbly along the edge of his craft and sprang into his perch, facing away from the Iron Cliffs. He jerked up on the reins that had been secured to the pommel there, hauling up while hieing and whistling. The saucer tilted back and then, with a silky, fluid motion, began to move forward.

The mob of fellow water-taxis melted away on either side to let them through before surging back to fill the void created by their passage.

18

The driver called over his shoulder, 'Where to, Madams? South Relocation Zone Three? Four? New Gyppi? Trans Janji?' His voice had a gabbling quality, as if he were attempting to speak several tongues at once. 'East Madaga?'

Youngest was kneeling on the floor of the skimmer, leaning towards the driver.

'Go west,' he said, pointing to one of the several paths available to them through the thrusting hulls and upturned decks that formed a puzzle-course leading eventually to the open sea. 'I'll show you where I want to go.'

'West?' screamed the driver over his shoulder. 'There is too far to go west – wait, you is mean New West or Old West? I is go to Old West.'

'New West,' said Youngest, pointing in the direction that for him would have been South, ninety degrees away from where the sun would set.

'What? No! I is not go beyond the Horn of Su'lili. Is nothing there. Rubbish places only – no return fare.'

'Don't worry,' said Youngest, unperturbed. 'We are only going to the boundary of the Graveyard.'

'But—' squawked the driver.

'Don't *worry*,' repeated Youngest, patting the man on his arm. 'Tell me about Goliath. I have never seen or heard of this animal before. What is it?'

The driver hawked and spat as he prepared to deliver his standard lecture about the sea-creature that was pulling them.

'This beast is go by name of Goliath Chellion. He be hybrid marine turtle. Superfine beast of pulling, having very big size and very fine mood. He be never got angry. His life-long be twenty years. His ladies be making many eggs, which all Mariners be eating for yumyum food. Also keeping back few for to make breed the h'animal.'

Aila left Youngest to his deliberations. She settled back into the damp lumpy cushions placed along the rear of the skimming saucer. She watched as the craft wove in and out between the steep shadows leaning down from the ruined hulls poking up from the water.

Thick growths of greenweed, bell vine and marine orchids trailed down to the water's surface. They shifted this way and that with the movement of the waves. It was an eerie, life-like motion, augmented by the sudden shrieks and startled flights of birds that had made their homes in the derelict vessels. There were pelicans, cormorants and gulls as well as hybrid species such as the skreet with fish-scales on its head and functioning gills that enabled it to breathe underwater. There were also countless creatures with no names or identity. Hybridization was at its most active along the shoreline. Many new life forms came into being, flourished and died out unnoticed and unnamed.

Here and there, she could see something more substantial than a bird or a vine moving amidst the abandoned ruins. A person: head and shoulders, a flash of clothing, a curious glance, disappearing from view almost as soon as she had spotted him or her. She had heard about them, these Mariners, these marine peasants, who made their living on the water. They never came up to the city, even though that's where they were created. They were licensed only to act as ferrymen, but if they were pirates and foragers, hunters and gatherers as well, no one paid much attention.

Becalmed by the rocking motion of the small craft, Alia

continued to watch until she fell asleep.

Youngest sat up beside the driver. He faced front and asked questions about the Goliath. He could see its head, a great domed thing covered with circular scales and with a pronounced beak, parting the black water ahead of the skimmer. He wanted to know what it ate, how easy or difficult it was to train, how long it took to grow from hatchling to working adult.

'We is take too much long-time,' complained the driver about the route. 'I is go die before Madam is find location!' But he continued answering the questions, perhaps enjoying the exchange.

Two hours passed.

When Aila awoke, the shadows had lengthened into dense stripes laid across the black, swelling water. From between the towering black profiles of the sunken ships the orange rays of the setting sun flashed directly into her eyes. She had a momentary impression of what it might feel like to be a mouse moving through thickets of tall grass. The intervals of light between each stalk were more harsh and more narrow than at the peak of day. Now and then there came a bright flash, where the slanting rays struck sparks on portholes or shards of mirror on the old vessels.

Daylight sounds had given way to the muted booms and sloshes of evening, the slap-slap-slap of waves on decaying metal, creaking joints, the soughing of night breezes through hanging vegetation. All around, a symphony of unknown peeping.

She was about to say that they seemed to be going more slowly than before when she saw that the driver was lying on his side on the floor of the skimmer.

Yasmine was sitting up in his seat, apparently holding the reins.

'Ahh!' cried Aila, jerking upright.

Youngest turned his body slightly, just enough to acknowledge her. He held up a hand. At that instant, they passed through a stripe of orange light and she saw him limned in gold before the next shadow swallowed him once more.

With no warning, dangling vines brushed her face. 'Oh!' she exclaimed, clapping her hand over her mouth even as the cry left her, not wanting to call attention to herself. They had entered a space so dark that she felt suddenly blinded. A moment later, Youngest had switched on a torch and was holding it up above his head.

They were in a cavern that may have once been a container on an oil-tanker. It was upended now, half full of water. The entrance to the space was curtained with vines. By the light of the torch, she saw the languid profusion of white, sunless vegetation carpeting the surface of the water. Staccato movements snagged her attention: crabs that had been lounging on top of the pale leaves scuttled away from the skimmer, pausing to look at them with what seemed like curiosity before scurrying out of sight.

At the forward end of the skimmer the Goliath began jerking as it lunged after the crabs.

'Look there,' said Youngest in a low voice. He directed Aila's gaze to the far corner of the cavern with the beam of his torch. The light did not extend quite that far, and she was on the point of asking him to tell her what there was to see when she saw it too.

A ruby, blinking in the darkness. A small red light.

It was a transport, he explained. A submersible.

'The light was steady when I left it here,' said Youngest. 'That was two weeks ago. The battery is at its limit. We must leave at once.'

'*Two weeks?*'

Youngest turned to look at her, his face in shadow. 'I come from far away. I told you that already.'

'Yes, but when I met you at Confluenza you had just arrived ...'

'When I left the General's yacht, I came in two submersibles. I rode in one and brought the other with me. I looked for a hiding place and left this one here. Then I returned to the yacht in the other one, secured my cargo and got dropped off at New Janji Deepwater. It took me five days to get all my permits. From there I went to Sokotra Deepwater …' He paused. 'A complicated journey.'

Aila said, '*Whao!* I didn't know that.'

Youngest glanced in her direction, then away again.

'This man you are with,' said Aila, 'the man you call General. He must be … I mean … is *he* paying for this all?' She made a gesture of inclusion to take in the submersible, the trip, Youngest's expenses over the entire period of time. 'What kind of reason is big enough to be worth this?'

Youngest fixed the torch onto the side of the skimmer.

'Big enough,' he said, as he began pulling up on the Goliath's harness. 'Come on. The submersible wasn't built for two. It'll be a tight squeeze.'

'What about this driver?'

'Sleeping,' said Youngest, 'not dead. I've put slumber-patches on his skin. He'll be awake by morning. We'd better get moving.'

19

Forty-eight hours later, a few minutes before dawn, a tall, whip-like man stood at a square wooden table on the foredeck of his pristine white yacht.

He had pale skin beneath which the unborn stubble of his smooth chin showed blue-black. His head was close-shaven, steel blue, oiled and polished till it shone. In the place of eyebrows, he had a tattoo of a dotted line. Where it ended, on the left, he had tiny silver piercing in the form of a pair of scissors.

Two figures sat by him, Aila on his right and Youngest on his left. Both were dressed in white, in women's clothes that were tight and revealing, with flounces, eyelet lace and silk bows. Aila's hair was open while Youngest wore his in a single thick plait down his back.

The General faced towards the rising sun. 'I am not often surprised,' he said, leaning with his clenched fists knuckle-down on the table. 'It is a novelty.'

He too was dressed all in white, in a loose cotton tunic and white silk boxers, his feet in cotton-lined straw sandals. 'I am intrigued.' Then, unable to remain still for a second longer, he swivelled and swung away towards his left, to the narrow prow of the deck, reached it and swivelled around again, propelling himself forward till he was back by the table. The circuit took him less than five seconds.

'Whose idea was it?' He looked at Youngest. 'Not yours, I suspect, my rare dove.' He nodded before Youngest could respond. 'No, no. I thought not. It wouldn't be. You know me well enough. I don't like surprises. So it must be you.'

He shot a glance towards Aila before swivelling off towards the prow once more. 'The unexpected intruder. The femaloid corruption – or *feem*, as I believe you people call yourselves? Am I right?'

Aila shook her head and said, 'No, I am a transie. A feem is—'

But the General paid no attention to her as he continued with his rat-a-tat staccato speech. 'You're a man who was born perfectly normal but had himself altered for purely emotional reasons. I find that beyond pathetic. You disgust me. You should have been melted down and reconstituted at birth.'

Aila had initially raised her head in the attitude of a schoolgirl answering questions in class, but as the General's missiles found their mark, she flinched, her mouth opening and closing a couple of times. She glanced at Youngest, but he had lowered his eyes to the table.

'You must have forced yourself on my handsome jewel, because you found him irresistible. That's it, isn't it? It must be. No other explanation. He is, after all, irresistible. Not a feem, such as you are, but a genuine reversi. It's a term I coined myself: a man who, against his will, against his nature, is forced to change his body into that of a … well, I call them Vermin. Non-men. Those who are born in nature yet are unfit to belong to the ranks of men.

'Yasmine is my own private creation, my personal sex-machine. His private parts were restructured to suit *my* needs. He was perfect as a man, gorgeously muscled, tall, dense, powerful. But now he is a man who, while retaining his masculine nature, nevertheless has the body-parts of a Vermin and – ah! – now he is beyond superb.

'After all, there is no question that a Vermin's genitals evolved to be the counterpart for a man's. However, in order to have access to those verminous body parts, men were forced to embrace despicable, slimy beings with weak minds and intolerable emotions. For me and all those others who form my unique tribe in the country we call the Brotherland that compromise was always abominable. We had no option but to enjoy other men as our intimate companions. Even so, I always found there was something … what shall I call it … incomplete in these connections.

'You, who are merely a feem and worthless in my estimation, you cannot know the first part of what I mean. Because you know nothing of what it means to be a Man. A lord-like being whose need to flatten the imperfections of the world, to bend reality to his vision is like a burning, untameable passion. You cannot know what delight it brings to me to be able to bend another being such as myself – my equal in physique, in performance, in intellect – to bend such a being to perform as a Vermin, *within the body of a Vermin.*'

The General had been marching back and forth across the deck of the small ship all through his speech. As he marched, he rang bells placed strategically along his path, in order to bring his crew of subordinates up from below deck, until six of them stood to attention on either side of the table, a respectful distance from it, their backs to the water.

They were not full-sized beings, but Drones: diminutive albino clones, created with low-functioning intellects and as mutes for the sole purpose of being slaves to the Generals.

They had hairless skulls and their digestive systems had been reconfigured so that they could only process a specialized liquid diet, making them wholly dependent upon their masters for nutrition. They were physically strong, but constitutionally delicate and short-lived. They wore singlets and loose shorts, and though they appeared to be male they had, in fact, no sexual organs of any kind. A single orifice served for all excretory eliminations.

'The fact that he suffers, that his personality remains intact and that he submits to my will not out of emotional weakness or lust, but out of the nobility of his own, unconquerable desperation – *this* is what makes him a pearl without price.'

He came to a halt once more at the head of the table. 'Time for a small demonstration, don't you think, my peerless jewel? Yes, you've been away for longer than we agreed. Too long. I missed you.'

He gestured as he spoke, to the drones behind him. To Youngest he said, 'Stand up.'

The General stripped himself naked as two drones snapped forward, ready to receive his clothes before they touched the deck. Then another pair approached. One held a bowl of hot almond oil, the other wore chamois gloves.

Without his clothes on, the General looked more than ever like a mechanical construct. His body was composed of hard, straight lines, a sheath of muscle stretched in elastic planes over the uncompromising rigidity of his bones. He had no navel. His chest and concave belly were covered in a pelt of dense black fuzz, sculpted to form an arrow pointing towards his groin, which had been plucked bare. The pallor of his skin gave way there: his organ was bruise-purple with thick blue veins clasped around its shaft. The head was deep crimson, glistening and rounded like a nectarine. His scrotal sac was tattooed midnight blue and weighted down with silver piercings, star-shaped.

Youngest faced away from him and bent over the table, supporting his torso on one forearm. With his free hand, he reached behind to undo the ties on the back of his dress. It was constructed so that the ruffled and whale-boned skirt fell open once the drawstring holding it together was undone, exposing his naked buttocks, rounded and succulent as a pair of giant, smooth, teak-brown melons.

The drone with the gloves oiled the General before turning its attention to Youngest.

The General continued to speak, addressing Aila, his voice breathy.

'Yes, you see ... yes ... this is what I miss. He hates me, you see? Can you see his face? He hates me. That is what charges my engine with indescribable joy. He hates me and yet he submits. Because he must. He has no choice. *Hhah.*' He broke off to address Youngest. 'Are you holding yourself tight? Shall I test you with my finger? Yes! Yes. That is tight. That is perfect.'

He drove himself in then, with a falsetto grunt, his head back, his teeth bared, 'Good! That is GOOD! Good!'

Aila had remained seated. Youngest's arms were spread now so that his hands gripped the edges of the table and his head was level with hers, but neither looked at the other. She heard his muted exhalations and the scraping of the table's legs on the deck, but her attention was riveted on the General.

He had stopped and was panting, his entire angular frame vibrating visibly. 'You see ... you see—' he said, addressing Aila once more, 'I must stop, I must arrange myself now – this is another reason that I need a Vermin's body, why a mere man's body is not enough. To enjoy the full range of my needs, I need to ...'

He was bobbing up and down, panting with his mouth open, balancing on the balls of his feet, one hand on the rump in front of him, one hand hidden from view. The gloved drone was busy too, assisting. 'Because you see – even though you *can't* from where you sit – I need to block up both apertures. The rear is suitable for my primary engine – *yes!* – while that filthy slit receives my—' His voice warbled and broke, as he performed the difficult manoeuvre '—star-studded pouch – *angghhh!*'

He panted, half-swooning where he stood. 'You cannot imagine, either of you, you cannot dream of what I feel at this moment.' He stood, leaning back, his face raised up towards the powder blue sky and sweat dripping off him onto the polished deck.

He began to move once more, neighing and whinnying with each stroke. His eyes were shut. A crimson flush enveloped his face, his earlobes, the sides of his nose and front of his neck.

Aila rose to her feet. No one saw her except perhaps the drones, who paid her no attention. In one stride she was beside the labouring General. Then she knelt, pushing aside the drone who stood between her and the shuddering piston-like motion of the standing man's hips. She timed herself with precision: at the exact moment, she reached in, gripped the General's member with her right hand, a man's hand, and blocked his crisis for a split second. In that instant, she had pulled out the engorged member, turned it towards herself then released her grip so that the full force of his spurt fell on her face, her neck and down between her plump breasts.

The silence that fell was like a thunderclap.

Aila had shut her eyes. She could hear the General breathing hard, chuffing like an antique engine. She could hear the faint slap of waves against the side of the vessel. She felt one of the drones remove her hand from the organ that she still held in her grip. She opened her eyes.

The General towered over her, his face in silhouette against the brightening sky. He was standing still, staring down, his expression unreadable. The drones had closed in now, with steaming, scented wash-cloths. They were dabbing at him, dabbing at Youngest's exposed rear. One stood right by Aila and she could see it hesitating, a wash-cloth in its hands. This was an unfamiliar situation for the drone, with three performers rather than two. The little mannikin did not have instructions to follow. Youngest was stirring, straightening up.

The General said, looking down at Aila, 'You … surprise me.'

Then he motioned the drone who stood beside Aila to get on with its task, to aid her.

She closed her eyes once more as she felt the small hands wiping her face and neck down with the impersonal solicitude of a professional servant.

She smiled. *The General is just another man*, she thought. *Yasmine was wrong. There is nothing for me to fear here. Pleasuring men is what I am used to.*

20

Youngest took Aila on a tour of the vessel after lunch. It was 20 metres in length with space on the lower deck for three bedrooms and accommodation for two permanent crew members. It had been modified, however, so that there was only one bedroom, for the General. It had a queen-size bed, cupboards and shelves, a dressing table and desk, but the décor was strictly utilitarian, all straight lines and discrete bright lighting, polished black surfaces, khakhi grey carpet on the floor.

The crew, consisting entirely of drones, took turns occupying six hammocks in the cramped closet-sized space that had been allotted to them beside the kitchen.

'We needed to set aside as much space as possible for storing food,' said Youngest, as they stepped into the larder, which occupied one of the two unused bedrooms.

'Wah,' said Aila, her eyes wide as she stared at the neat stacks of sealed packages. 'But is all same like lunch, today?' She made a face. 'Dry biscuit is no good. I is want to choke but you is look *stop!* at me. So I is stop. But I is eat only the meat.'

Youngest said, 'We were just lucky today, with the turtle.' The creature, a female, had been snared in nets trailing from the ship. Its body yielded a bounty of soft-shelled eggs, perhaps as many as sixty. There would be fried eggs for at least ten days ahead, including for the drones, for whom eggs of any kind were an unexpected treat. They ate them raw, being unable to process any solid food.

The vessel had a mirror-shield which made it virtually

invisible during daytime. Even at night, the wheelhouse was not lit up, having been fitted with night-vision glass in all its windows. But no sea-faring vessels crossed the open ocean. No flights passed overhead. So the elaborate camouflage was a minor amusement for the General. He enjoyed stealth for its own sake.

The ship ran on a fusion-powered engine that used desalinated sea water as fuel. It needed no maintenance and could run near-indefinitely for as long as the ship remained on the water. It could not be switched off, however, which meant that the vessel circled around its location when it needed to be at anchor. The front of its hull was fitted with a submerged hatch for launching and retrieving its submersibles.

Youngest was avoiding eye-contact with Aila. She probably thought it was out of embarrassment. He could sense her desire to tell him that she would never think poorly of him for allowing the General to humiliate him in her presence. He preferred to let her believe that.

He wanted at all costs to avoid conversations with her. He had no way of predicting how she would react to the General. So he could not warn her in advance to be discrete. He could not afford to depend upon her loyalty to him. The radio-link was live now. The General would hear everything that Youngest said as well as muffled versions of Aila's voice.

And he would certainly be listening. He would be very interested in anything Youngest might have said to Aila about his plans for the future. Plans that were in any way different to what he'd agreed to with the General.

'What is here?' Aila wanted to know, tapping the floor with her foot. Inside the larder, there was a locked trap-door in the floor.

'I don't know,' said Youngest. He was telling the truth. 'The General only tells me what I need to know.'

He heard the General's hissing snicker in his ears. *Well said, my precious! How honest we are.*

'Hmm,' said Aila, unconvinced, looking down at the padlocked bolt in the floor.

'Don't underestimate him,' said Youngest. 'You may think you know him because he doesn't bother with being friendly or polite. It's easy to mistake his rudeness for truth. But it isn't, really. It's an absolute disinterest in your feelings, my feelings, anyone's feelings. He'll surprise you because he never feels the need to be predictable.'

Aila looked up and caught his eye. 'You is not curious? You is not try to find out?'

'No,' said Youngest, shifting his gaze before she could ask him any more questions. 'If he didn't want me to know what's in there, finding out won't help me.'

21

Later that day, after the sun had set, the General called Youngest into the bedroom.

'Massage me,' he said, sitting down on the stool reserved for this purpose, positioned in front of the full-length mirror of the dressing table. 'We need to talk before you set off again.'

Youngest brought a steel dish, placed it on a portable hot plate and brought them both with him, pouring almond oil into the dish as he walked. He wore a loose garment made of black lace that clung to his damp skin. He had pinned his hair up behind his head and wore a small gold hoop in each ear. In his nose, a tiny flat gold sun flashed with every movement of his face.

'Yes,' he said, looking at the oil in the dish he was holding. He anticipated the fragrance that would rise up to tickle his nose, as he watched the tell-tale swirls of heat forming in the liquid.

'If you had asked me, I would never have agreed to let you bring someone back with you,' began the General. His tone was friendly and conversational. He was dressed in a white cotton terry robe, but he had slipped its sash so that he could admire himself in the mirror, naked, with his legs splayed apart and Youngest behind him, about to commence oiling the blue dome of his skull. 'Which just goes to show that I can occasionally be wrong.'

Youngest put the bowl on a gimballed stand. Looking up, his mouth curved slightly as he said, 'So … you approve then?'

Testing the oil with two fingers, he allowed himself to enjoy the moment of heat, on the borderline of pain. He turned the heater off and dipped the tips of all ten fingers in.

'Tell me how you found him,' said the General.

Youngest began the slow rotary motion of his fingertips against the other man's skull, gradually increasing pressure as he talked. He described the chance encounter at Confluenza Junction, the drugging, the crisis in the glass-tube home.

'Ah! So his father was abusive, yet he loved his father? More and more interesting. There is much I would like to know. And perhaps I shall! Now that I am to have him all to myself in your absence.'

He stared at Youngest's face in the mirror.

'You know, I missed you terribly. It was unprecedented. I cursed you for every minute you were away. It was the strangest thing. That has never happened to me before.'

Youngest kept his eyes lowered to his task.

'I'm guessing you did not miss me one bit. Hey? Go on, tell me. Did you?'

Youngest glanced up, met the other man's eyes in the mirror. 'No,' he said, before looking down once more.

The General's mouth twitched. 'Yes,' he said, 'that's what I prize about you. You stand up to me. But … that's not why I missed you. It's not your physical presence – well, of course it's also that – the drones are worthless for the purpose of the rut… But anyway: the thing I missed, to the point of madness is the … the sound of your voice. In my ears as well as in my head.'

Youngest glanced up again.

'You see, you cannot understand what it's like for me. Not to hear the others.' He was talking about his clone brothers and the shared radio network of their voices. 'Not to hear that entire glorious gang of others. In my head. Whispering. All the time. When even you went out of range it was like going deaf.' He paused. 'I am glad to have you back.'

He cleared his throat. 'So. Let's talk about what lies ahead.' His tone changed. 'You've got some plot up your sleeve, I suppose. Am I right? Don't answer, because you will only lie and that will annoy me. I'm sure I'm right because it's in your character to be insanely, psychotically hopeful. But you know it's futile, don't you? Of course you do.' He tapped his own chest. 'Because of our little electronic friends. The satellite locators. Because of what they'll release into you – you and your Vermin brat – should you happen to disobey. You'd not forgotten, had you, that I can cause catastrophic death by neurotoxin any time I want?'

Youngest shook his head. 'No. I had not forgotten.'

'Still,' insisted the General, 'my guess is that the only reason you went along with this plan from the very start was that you hoped you would find a loophole that you could exploit. Did you think I didn't know that? Of course I did. I think of everything. No interest like self-interest, as they say. But it won't work in your case. You know why?'

He gazed at the man massaging his head before continuing.

'Because you have no self any more. From the moment you tied your fate to mine, you lost your right to have a self. That's how it is amongst us Generals. That's the whole direction of our way of life. No self, except the Greater Self. Nothing we do is for ourselves alone – because we are *not* alone. That's how we want everyone to be. In philosophical terms it is the Ideal State, the Merging of Consciousness, the Liquidation of Self, the end of Selfishness ...'

He talked on, growing more heated and animated as he went. It was a favourite theme.

Youngest listened, never pausing in the slow rotary motion of his finger tips. The pitiless, ranting voice poured into his ears as well as deep into his skull via the radio link. The overload of sound pushed all rational thought to the outermost periphery of his mind.

Even so, at the very edge of his sanity, one private thought continued flickering: *So! You're missing the network, are you, General? You've never known what it is to function as an individual. But that's what you are right now. Single. Alone. Weak. Good. Excellent. It's not much, I know. But it's better than nothing.*

22

Youngest stood on the darkened foredeck, leaning against the rail, looking out into the impenetrable darkness below. Six hours from now, before dawn, he would slip into that lightless depth and leave, to fulfil the final part of his complicated mission.

Inside his head, he could hear the General talking to Aila. It was as loud as if it were his own voice. It caused his tongue to shift uneasily within his mouth, struggling to make sense of this paradox of speech that did not require its engagement.

To have that voice within him, to hear it day in and day out – the General slept only four hours – and to have endured it for over sixteen months had been like keeping a live scorpion lodged under the roof of his mouth. The respite, slight though it had been, of hearing only the recording for the ten days he'd been away, had been wiped away within the first moments of re-entering the range of the transmitter.

He heard as it ranted now.

'... why, you ask? *Why* do I have such a low opinion of Vermin? Oh foolish, oh ridiculous feem! The question goes the other way. Indeed, there was a time when no one, anywhere, wondered *if*. Men were understood to be superior to Vermin. They knew they were lower than us and they accepted their place. Men went out hunting, fought off other men and brought life-sustaining meat to the community hearth. Vermin strained and grunted to bring forth fresh generations of men and the effort was so great that they could do little else to justify their existence. And they didn't have to. The world was a simple place.

'Then came agriculture. Then came animals to till the fields and to provide milk and domesticated food. Little by little, Vermin began to take a hand in the maintenance of dwellings, in the provision of food, in the creation of that space called home. The storing of food meant that they had more time to ask themselves dangerous questions. Such as, *Why must we work our fingers to the bone, when men do not?* Such as, *Would it be so wrong to demand a greater portion of respect in our day-to-day lives for the work that we do? What difference is there between men and ourselves, once we augment our strength with the labour of animals and machines? If there is no difference, then why should we accept our subordinate position?*'

Youngest gazed down at the softly lapping black water, listening. He had heard it all before, of course. Many times. The novelty was hearing it said to someone for whom such ideas were a revelation.

Aila was close enough to the General that her voice was audible to Youngest. 'It is true, what you say. My father always told me—'

'No, no, I told you not to stop. You must continue at a regular, unvarying pace or else I cannot sit still, I will need to move around,' said the General. 'Slower. Yes. Where was I? Yes. When two groups compete for the same resources, there can be only one outcome: conflict. From the moment that Vermin began to challenge their lowly position, they entered the arena of conflict.'

He paused to bring his breathing under control.

'Do I need to spell it out? From that moment onwards, Vermin lost their right to maintain any position at all. In a conflict between men and themselves, Vermin are bound to lose – never mind that even today there are millions of men who do not accept what I say, men who believe it's possible to live in harmony with Vermin. Never mind that Vermin have been cunning enough to gain control of reproduction to the extent that they think they no longer need us.

'Do you see where this is going, feem? Do you have enough of your masculine reasoning to understand the point I'm making? We men lost our bearings. We allowed ourselves to be beguiled. To be swayed by the Vermins' slithering words. Once they wriggled free of our constraints, they could not be beaten back into servitude. Which left us with only one alternative: removing them altogether.

'So that's what we did in my part of the world. We removed them altogether. And what did we get in thanks for that? We were struck off the map! People of your generation haven't even heard of us. Have you? No, of course not. You didn't even know we existed. It was an enormous price. So what? Everything that's worth doing is going to seem too expensive – until someone pays up.'

There was a long pause then, during which the General's breathing became erratic, before breaking apart into short panting yelps.

Youngest straightened up.

He had thought he understood Aila. But she was changing. Becoming more complex. More opaque. He couldn't tell, for instance, whether she was genuinely attracted to the General. His powerful personality, the confidence he projected, his wealth: she came from such desolate circumstances that it would be easy understand that she would be dazzled. Or was she, in some inarticulate way, supporting him, Youngest, by distracting the General?

If so, she may also know that she could not convey this fact to him. She may understand that they could not afford to say anything that could be interpreted as criticism or a sign that Youngest had any ambitions beyond the orders he was supposed to follow.

He had always lived in dread of betraying himself by talking in his sleep. He had to assume that he hadn't done so yet. Or, if he had, that the General had chosen to keep the knowledge hidden.

The air was humid, the night was still. The mass of restless water beneath the boat was not entirely opaque. It contained blips and flashes, discernible indirectly, from the outer margin of consciousness. Unknown, unknowable life forms, lit by their own mysterious energies, moved continuously this way and that. He heard the reassuring *clop-clop, clop-clop* of the water against the sides of the boat.

His thoughts were interrupted by the General clearing his throat like a whinnying horse before he resumed his conversation. 'Where was I? Yes. Vermin. The price we paid. It was worth it. It was a mistake on the part of the outer world's nations to make us invisible. To underestimate us. We did *not* disappear, after all. We rebuilt ourselves. Re-invented ourselves. In secrecy. In confidence. We grew in power. And now we are ready.'

Youngest felt his spine tingling.

'To infiltrate the greater world. To return all True Men to their senses. To snatch the rug of power from under the filthy feet of Vermin hordes and stand upon it ourselves! Once more unchallenged.'

PART II

WELCOME

1

The girl surveyed the recovery room through slitted eyes, pretending to be asleep. If she owned up to being awake, someone or the other would come by to irritate her. Then she would start to throw things. Following which, she would be immobilized for an hour or two, unable to scream or cry or sleep.

I must leave, she told herself. *Now. Right away.*

Except it wasn't possible. Her bones were filled with lead, her skin was armour-plated. Her head was solid clay.

She knew it was only how she felt, not how she looked. When they had held a mirror up to her on the first day, she was quite surprised to see that she recognized herself: the full dark lips, clear forehead, straight nose with plump nostrils. The shaven head. Only her skin seemed markedly different. It was normally as dark and polished as oiled teak but was now the colour of milky tea and painfully stretched. She could see her bones just under the surface.

Definitely me, she had thought.

Initially she hadn't been able to remember her name. That had been horrifying. They had tried palming off a fake name on her. That was horrifying too.

Joo Li, they called her. *Juli.*

Juuuu. Liiii.

Wrong! Incorrect!

But she couldn't tell them the correct one.

There was a wall within her brain that made it impossible for her to know the simplest of things. What's happened to my memory? Why can I remember some things but not others? *Why am I in this place, alone and weak? In the company of strangers?*

The lack of a name had been worse than anything else. When it came back, the lack of other memories became even more mysterious.

The lack of memories wasn't her only problem, however.

She shifted her eyes from side to side without moving her head. She had a good view, because she was on an inclined surface. Soft and padded.

There were others in the recovery room with her. At least five, though sometimes less. These others were also lying limp and helpless, within padded, contoured sleeping pallets.

The pallets were extensions of the walls. They could be retracted when required, for instance, when the body within them was removed. She had seen the beds fold up and slip back into the wall with a soft clicking sound and a smooth motion. Once folded, it was difficult to see any trace of them. It was as if they had vanished altogether.

As for these other bodies: the girl found them deeply disturbing. To begin with, they were naked. That was bad enough. So was she – and that was hateful, beyond hateful, that was abominable. But at least she didn't have to look at herself. These others, she could see.

She could see they were deformed.

Normal people, that is to say *men*, had tufts of wiry hair down below, at their crotch. Between their legs, they had soft puffy danglers and dark pouches. These danglers sometimes grew into taut twitchy tusks that stood right up at astonishing angles.

One reason she knew men's bodies were the norm was that she herself was *not* normal. She knew that. She was not a man. She had a dangler and pouch too, but they were fake. It was part of some very important secret that for the life of her she could not remember just now. All she knew was that it was vitally, crucially important.

She had a hairy patch too, but it was invisible. It was hidden behind the fake dangler and pouch. Also invisible were the folds of skin and the impenetrably deep slit she had within her lower body, the slit that sometimes oozed. These were all terrible secrets, and if she were to reveal them, for any reason at all, she would die. What she could no longer remember was *why*.

Nothing made any sense. She couldn't remember who had forbidden her to be naked in the company of strangers. Yet here she was, naked, and alive, in the company of strangers. Indeed, no one here was the least concerned about the nakedness. As for the secrets of her body, no one noticed those either. Neither the fake dangler nor the hidden secrets.

The other recliners in the room, by contrast, were not merely hairless at the crotch, but the area between their legs was completely bare. There were no folds there such as she had. Just a plain, bare slit. It was as if they had been surgically altered and their secret parts cut away, leaving only that pathetic, flat slit.

They were also crisscrossed with black stitches, these fellow-recliners. Some of them were like ragdolls that had been sewn together from a collection of spare parts. Their bodies were covered in tattoos and skin decorations such as rings, studs and tiny coloured blinkers that flashed on and off like pulse beats. One of them had a ring of tiny lights around her nipples, and another's twinkling adornment spiralled down their legs. The girl had seen decorations on the skin before, but never in such profusion and never lit up like this. They looked painful. Bizarre.

As for the growths on their chests … they were enormous. The girl had a pair of her own but she had been taught to bind them tight and to keep them hidden. Either for that reason or because that was how she was built, her own were almost flat. These other people had attachments they sagged like soggy sandbags, sliding this way and that. The decorations seemed especially dense on these growths, embellished with piercings of bone and metal. It hurt her just to look at them.

She wished she didn't have to.

She wished she could leave the room.

But there were no visible entrances or exits.

She had scoured the room countless times with her eyes, trying to spot a door, a window, a ventilator. Nothing. It was true, though, that she was often semi-conscious. Perhaps she had never been awake at the time when the exits and ventilators were opened.

The walls, too, were dark, curving up towards the narrow ceiling with not a single straight line to be seen anywhere. Every surface was rounded, knobbly with projections, cables, protrusions and unfamiliar hanging structures.

Jointed tendrils extended down from the ceiling, some of them bearing instruments, others with bright points of light at their ends. Besides the lighted tendrils there was a bluish-green background illumination that seemed to well out of the walls, as if the room was made of luminescent materials. She didn't allow herself to focus on the more peculiar aspects of the room. There was no point exploring things that could not be explained, and it was hard to locate the contours of openings under these circumstances.

There were sounds for her to think about as well. The constant gurgling of water for one thing. Down tubes or sloshing through narrow spaces, or flushing violently, as if the entire room was actually under water or perhaps immersed in a swimming pool.

There were booms and thumps that had no obvious origin. Mechanical groaning sounds, whoops and bellows, creaks and scraping chirps. Every so often, a furious clicking-rattling would break out, growing louder and then fading away. None of it was familiar or identifiable.

The air was thick and steamy, with medicinal scents that

poked into her nose and hurt her throat and lungs. Behind these smells was another one, softer and more familiar. A trace of memory might return briefly before vanishing again. Of being by the sea, of the tide coming in, of the sand scattered with the crushed and lifeless remains of thousands of nameless creatures.

The memory was just a fragment, like finding one corner of a photograph, with no way of telling how much more of it there was or whether it was one of a series or who else was in the frame.

Frustrating. Everything was frustrating.

The attendants, for instance, who occupied the room along with her and her fellow recliners.

They too had weird lumpy bodies, though at least they had the good sense to keep themselves covered. They wore pale tunics and moved around with brisk, angular movements. Their tunics glowed white and bluish-green, reflecting the lighting in the room. They had masks across their mouths and noses, clear visors over their eyes, shiny gloves on their hands.

Indeed, one of them was approaching her right now. The girl shut her eyes tight, hoping to avoid attention. Too late. The assistant was by her side and gently tapping her on the shoulder. It was making those sounds that signified speech in this place.

The girl turned to see the attendant opening and closing its mouth. The sounds were like speech bubbles in a comic, such as the girl had read as a child, but with no speech within them.

She opened her own mouth, intending to say yet again that she understood nothing, when an odd thing happened: attendant's speech bubble floated into her mind, intact.

Now, for the first time, she saw the words spoken by the attendant appear on the inner screen within her head where meanings were displayed.

'Joo Li?' the attendant was asking her in its odd voice. High. Squeaky. 'Why are you crying?'

CRYING?!

The girl wanted to scream.

I'm not crying, I'm vomiting!

I'm vomiting tearsshitpisspusblood …

What she actually said was, 'This. Place. Is.' After a pause, she added, 'Wrong.'

The voice she used, the one that exited her mouth, and the words on which that voice rolled out, as if on the wheels of an ungainly cart, were all utterly and completely *wrong*. Her speech felt as if it were made of uncooked dough.

Immediately, she attempted to re-express this thought, but her mind kept jamming.

'Every. Thing. Is roo … rog …' She searched for a better word than the one she had used, even as her mind scrambled to understand why it was necessary to search. *How can words slither away, out of reach, just when I need them?* 'Wrong. WRONG!'

She jerked her head around, this way and that, her breath coming in short grunts. The attendant was speaking to her again. It was asking again what was wrong.

'I … I …' stammered the girl.

Now a second attendant joined the first one. They wore identical clothes but the first one had long hair, restrained under a headband and tied back, out of sight. The second one had short brown curls that bounced on either side of its head. They were both of a similar skin colour, but the long-haired one had strangely shaped eyes, angular and sharply pointed at either end. The new one was slender with a pronounced nose. Neither of them had the least trace of facial hair.

The girl repeated her statement in the queer, shapeless sounds which were nevertheless all that she had at her command at the moment. 'There … is … SOMETHING … *WRONG*,' she exclaimed, unable to control the force with which the voice fell out of her mouth. Her eyes were bleeding tears. 'With my words. And my name. Also. You is say my name WRONG.'

'I told you what your name is,' said the slim attendant. Its voice was even higher than the other one's. 'It is JULI. Juli. JOO-lee. Nice name.'

'No! NO!' cried the girl. 'Not that. NOT!'

'Then what is it?' The attendant paused.

The girl shook her head, panting, her face knotted with fury. 'I told you that already,' she cried. 'I told you earlier today. It's Meiji … Meiji! MEIJI!'

But the brown-haired attendant had already reached into her pocket and brought out the slender tube that would bring down the curtain on one more drama.

2

The next time Meiji woke up, she was alone. In a different room. She was on the floor, sitting up, with her back against the wall. Her knees were raised in front of her chest and she had locked her wrists around her knees.

She didn't know or couldn't recall exactly when she had left the recliner room.

She was no longer naked. That was a relief. She inspected the loose, sleeveless shift that reached down to mid-thigh. It was joined underneath and had slits on either side. It was a pale colour, like a leaf that's been bleached by the sun. The material was so light and insubstantial that it seemed to float on her skin, not quite touching it.

She was still weak, but she knew she could walk now. She had walked to this room. She could flex her ankles and wrists, she had almost complete control over her limbs. She had her name. That was wonderful.

Best of all, she was alone.

Her mind was still blank. Restless, seething and blank. There was still that partition inside her head, behind which mute phantoms surged and struggled, a crowd of shapes thrusting against a stretched white curtain. She could sense them churning, throwing their weight against the curtain, as if desperate to be released. Yet she could hear only the faintest of sighs and whispers from their side of the divide. She could do nothing to invite them over to her side.

She had to find a way. To get out, to break free of the restricting veils surrounding her. Her mind as well as her body.

How to begin? Where to start? What manner of weapon or tool did she need to employ?

She hugged her knees closer to her chest and looked around. The memory of walking to this room was more like a dream than reality. She had been flanked by two attendants. They had told her not to run along the corridors because the floor was in some way fragile. It could not support the weight of more than four people at a time, along one length of passage.

She hadn't tried to understand what that meant.

The room she had been brought to had a curved, irregular shape. It contained no furniture. She could lie flat inside it if she wanted, with her arms and legs stretched out, and stand up straight on tip-toe with her arms extended upwards. That was about it: the room conformed to her dimensions with very little space to spare. The walls were knobbly, like the recovery room, and curved inwards at the ceiling. All visible surfaces in the room, including the floor, were a shiny sea-green in colour, giving off a slight luminescence. From the ceiling, a single tentacular light had been pulled down, its white tip dangling above her head, just within reach.

It was quite bright, this light. It shone uncomfortably close to her face. She put up her hand to push it aside and was shocked when it flinched away from her finger.

Wait! I didn't even touch you, she thought.

She reached up towards it again. Had she imagined the movement? No: it flinched again.

That shouldn't happen. She looked reflexively over her shoulder, as if expecting to find someone else there, watching her. There couldn't be, of course. She was leaning against the wall. There was no space for anyone to sit behind her. But the sense of being observed persisted. She looked back at the lighted tip of the tendril that hung down from the dark ceiling.

Can I turn you off, she wondered. There was no other light in the room. If she could turn this one off, then even if there were hidden cameras she would be in darkness.

She extended her finger once again towards the light, without touching it. *Okay. So you move away even before I touch you. But what if I—*

She snatched at the light, tugging sharply.

Immediately, the tendril retracted, slithering with surprising force out of her grip, straight up into the ceiling. There it blinked twice and went out, leaving a faint after-image of itself against the surrounding blackness. The luminescence in the walls provided the only light now.

Oh! she thought. *Oh! You move fast, don't you?* Though it was embedded in the ceiling, the tip of the light was still just visible. It did not look all that far away. She believed she could reach it if she stood up.

Her joints creaked as she got to her feet. She was extremely stiff. With one hand against the wall, she reached with the other hand towards the ceiling. It was quite a stretch. For a while, she wasn't sure she could make it. Standing on the balls of her feet, she paused, then bounced up, and with the tips of her fingers bumped the still-glowing light-tip.

Instantly, across the ceiling and then more gradually extending down the wall surfaces of the room, a breathtaking projection bloomed.

The night-sky, in all its velvet blackness, sprinkled with diamonds, cold and magnificent, spread its unfathomable wings over her head. She knew it was only an illusion yet her skin prickled with delicious awe. She was standing alone in the Universe, with only the dark green floor beneath her feet to anchor her to the Earth.

She turned her head from side to side, finding – yes, she remembered these names – Cassiopeia, Orion, the Big Dipper.

Her old friends, her favourites. The Pole Star. The Andromeda Galaxy. Sirius.

She raised her arms in gladness, embracing the vast expanse, her spirit soaring. These names had not vanished behind the curtain of oblivion.

For long minutes she drank in the sensation of being out-of-doors. She breathed in deeply, even as she chided herself for imagining that the air smelt different, that she could hear the sound of the ocean lapping at invisible rocks in the distance, because of course she could not. Then she lowered herself to the floor, her face still turned up towards the illusion of sky, smiling.

She did not even know that she had fallen asleep until she was awake again. She looked up at once to see if the constellations had shifted to accommodate the change of time.

Yes. She could no longer see Orion.

By her reckoning, that meant she had slept three hours, maybe four. She wondered why she could smell food. Then she looked around and saw that the floor was no longer bare. There were two covered dishes near her, plus a pair of hinged spoons and a napkin.

3

Youngest had come up to the surface. According to the signal on his locator, he was within range of the girl. But there was no sign of land. No birds overhead.

The sky was overcast. The sea was choppy.

He had left behind the submersible some hours ago. All he had now was his Whole-Body Mask or BoMa. It was watertight, jointed in the way of a fish and capable of generating its own supply of air so long as he kept moving. In this way, he had been propelling himself underwater for a day and a half. He employed the slow, undulating movement that minimized oxygen consumption while making the most efficient use of the suit's friction-cells. When he needed to, he could raise a pipe up above the water's surface and suck air into a pair of flotation bladders to bring himself to the surface. Once there, he could rest, breathe normally and nap.

It was just after midday. He had told himself that if he hadn't found the Island by nightfall, he would have to abandon this attempt. That would mean returning to the submersible, replenishing his supplies and trying again.

He could not tell whether it was his imagination or his hunger that was causing him to feel that the quality of air provided by the suit had gradually decreased over the past five hours. He had a supply of liquid food that would sustain him for another twelve hours. It provided him with vital energy rather than satisfaction: he felt hungry even though he knew he did not need more food.

But the air quality was more troubling. While underwater,

for the same output of effort, he was feeling more fatigued and less able to maintain his speed, than he had at the beginning. He had been doing an easy four to six knots per hour, the speed of a medium-sized shark, when he left the submersible. Now he was crawling along at barely two. The only explanation he could think of was oxygen-depletion.

Beneath the surface, the water had the consistency of grey gruel, swarming with new, unnamed creatures. The end of transcontinental traffic from the Time Before combined with toxic pollution following the Cataclysm had resulted in a chaotic and unnatural explosion of marine life.

The BoMa had a visor that, aside from providing logistical read-outs such as speed and distance, also gave him vision-filters, magnifiers and information about the living things that entered within its sensory field. The database had its limitations. When a whale shark had loomed out of the murk directly across his path, the visor had produced nothing more than a flashing red dot suggesting a general alert. The creature was a placid, slow-moving filter-feeder but so immense that just one whack from its massive tail could have disabled Youngest if he had bumped into it. Once it had drifted past, the visor had helpfully informed him of an 'unidentified massive presence' in the water before correctly naming a small school of silver scouts off to his left.

When he was not gazing at the visor's read-out he was following the girl's transmitter. He had nothing to guide him except the waning or waxing of the signal. Currently, it was strong. Which should mean that he was getting closer. It could also mean that only the transmitter was alive, not the girl. He did not allow himself to pursue that line of unproductive thought.

The ocean was not a silent place. The hiss of his breathing apparatus and the thudding of his pulse were constants. Behind these sounds was a continuous formless murmur. Clicks and hoots, feathery sighs, distant booms: they might come from entirely ordinary sources such as whales or sea turtles or ... from an artificial Island.

He had no way of telling. Tangled knots of sound echoed back and forth across the deep, trailing who-knew-what of meaning and chaos.

Periodically, he would hear the General's voice via the radio link.

So long as he could hear that voice yammering away either at Aila or the drones, it meant the yacht was within range, less than 11 kilometres away.

4

Two women in their thirties were standing in the Council Chamber of the submerged structure known as Vane's Island.

It was a broad, bare room, brightly lit, with folding chairs stacked along one wall and a pile of rolled mats along the other. Both mentors were dressed in cotton tees and shorts, and wore sandals. Emmi was lean, taut and blonde; Kesh was softer, shorter and brunette. Both had identical buzz cuts and were pale-skinned with sun-pinked accents at their noses, elbows and knees.

On the wall-sized monitor that filled the third wall of the room, as they watched, six young Candidates walked across the smooth green expanse of the Welcome Field. Waiting to greet them was the tall white-haired figure of Mentor Vane. Her arms were held out in a gesture of greeting and her loose pink robe fluttered in the breeze. A murmur of sound accompanied the video.

Kesh sucked in her breath. 'Which one?' she said.

Emmi shrugged. 'Second from right. I think.' She did a slow, methodical forward stretch. Her movements had an elastic, feline quality. 'With the clean-shaven head but without tattoos. It bounces light, like a marble.'

'Oh, right,' said Kesh. 'I see her.'

Emmi paused a moment. Then she shook her head, saying, 'You know, I used to really believe in this place. These Islands.' She had straightened up. 'Even until two weeks ago, I was willing to be hopeful. But once the decision was made to accept that girl … '

'Shh—'

'Oh, it doesn't matter any more,' said Emmi. She began a series of side-stretches. 'I don't care who hears what.'

'Look, it was a shameful decision,' said Kesh, 'no question. But that doesn't have to mean you've got to give up.'

'I don't know how you say that,' said Emmi. 'I signed up for the Islands because I wanted to dedicate my life to something *real*. However hopeless it might be. However thankless. But this?' She made a disgusted sound, dry-spitting. 'It sickens me.'

Kesh turned away from the screen. 'What are you thinking of doing?'

Emmi continued to shake her head, her eyes looking nowhere. Then she made a gesture instead of speech. She twirled the forefinger of her right hand near the side of her head, made a fist and pantomimed pulling something out. She wasn't smiling.

'Oh Emmi, *no*. No!' Kesh looked stricken.

Emmi shrugged. 'It's the most likely outcome. If I want to leave, they'll erase my memories. I don't think they offer choices.'

'No …'

'And what's it all for?' She didn't wait for an answer. 'For being an idealistic fool. For wanting to save the world from becoming even more witless than it already is. Haha. Losing my wits in order to save the world!'

There was a rustling crackle as the entrance panel, on the side opposite the wall-monitor, split down the middle and snapped open. Two more mentors stepped through the gap.

Zara and Maia were both small and rounded, but their similarities ended there. Zara was in her late thirties, broad and thick waisted, with small, pointed breasts and a posterior so hugely developed that it looked artificial, even though it was not. She wore beads rather than clothes, her skin was glossy black, and the palms of her hands and the soles of her bare feet were salmon pink. She wore her hair cropped close, in a dense cap. Her face was unornamented, but she had enormous, expressive eyes and an almost perfectly circular mouth. The rims of both her ears were pierced with bright brass rings.

Maia's skin was bone-white, her silver hair was drawn up in a topknot and her eyes were flat grey, with no highlights or softness. She wore a tight white halter-top, a pair of loose white shorts and transparent plastic sandals on her feet. Her belly was distended by advanced pregnancy. Her face was lined and the silver in her hair was from age, not bleach.

Having entered together, the women immediately moved apart and took up positions on opposites sides of the room, Zara to the right and Maia to the left. Kesh and Emmi said 'Hi,' after glancing around when they heard the entrance creaking open.

'Anything interesting happen so far?' asked Zara glancing at the screen as she pulled out a chair. She had a notepad and pencil in her hand.

'It's a loop,' said Kesh. 'Not fresh footage.'

'Oh?' said Zara, looking surprised. 'I thought it was a standard screening.'

'It's a special session,' said Maia, a sneer embedded in her voice. She reached for a mat from the stack in the corner. She moved with cautious care. There were chairs against the wall, but the central space of the room was bare of furniture. 'If you lot bothered to listen to the circulars you'd know that.' She rolled out the mat.

'Cha was meditating when I saw her,' said Zara. 'Brahi has a migraine. Asma is coming, but said she'd be late. She's doing the rounds today. I'm not sure about the others.'

'Hmmh!' snorted Maia. 'Shirkers!'

There was another silence.

On the screen, the tall woman's white shoulder-length hair hung open in the breeze. She was barefoot in the grass, standing beside a rectangular slab of grey stone. It was too low to deserve being called a platform, but anyone standing on it would be raised up by a hand's width.

Kesh said, 'I'm turning up the sound.'

5

The morning after Youngest had left, the General invited Aila to sit with him on the front deck. Two places were set for breakfast, but the General could not remain seated for more than a few of minutes, so Aila sat mostly by herself. Four drones stood with their backs to the wheelhouse, watching their master's every move.

'Well now,' he said, as he strode back and forth across the deck. 'Here we are. Alone again. It's very annoying.' He sat down. 'I am grateful that you're here. I told Yasmine that. But I will miss him all the same. You don't have much conversation.'

Aila was wearing one of Youngest's robes, a pink and black chiffon piece, cut so low as to leave both breasts entirely exposed, with ruffles at the wrists, at the waist and at the ankles. Around her neck, she wore a delicately wrought necklace made of tiny winking lights that extended halfway down her chest. She looked up at the man with whom she had spent much of the previous night, though he insisted that she sleep on the rug in his bedroom, not on his bed. He said such intimacies had to be earned.

'Yes. I miss him too,' she said, unsure whether or not to essay a smile. It was difficult to predict the General's moods. He could switch from friendly to vicious within seconds. Smiling irritated him.

'So. What do you think of this,' he indicated their surroundings. 'The whole set-up here?'

'I is like,' Aila said, in her pidgin Unida. Experience had

shown her that, more often than not, to seem slow-witted was an asset. Also, to offer opinions that matched the expectations of the audience. Her father had always railed at her for daring to express her own views. 'Is different.'

The General made a peculiar hissing sound and leapt to his feet once more. He swung back and forth across the deck, his knuckles held hard against his bared teeth, as if he were suppressing a reaction. '*Different?*' he exclaimed, finally. 'Of course it's different. It's something completely foreign to you, isn't it? Yes? You haven't known anything outside your own miserable City, so far. Isn't that true? Yes?'

She didn't suppose he included the Zone when he used the words 'your own miserable City'.

'Yes,' she said. 'But I—'

'You're not eating,' cut in the General, sitting down. 'Come on, come on – you've got to eat.' The food was an unappetizing mixture of stored goods, such as tea, powdered milk and canned fruit, alongside items that had been recently harvested from the sea, such as boiled seaweed and jellyfish that had been evaporated and flattened, then deep fried. In a glass container, there were biscuits of concentrated flavour that Youngest had shown her could be eaten directly as whole meals.

'I ... is like this,' said Aila, timidly, tapping the cylinder.

Once again the pale man leapt up with a stifled snarl and swung away from the table, jogging back and forth across the deck like a mechanical toy. It took him several minutes to return to the table and to Aila's mystified expression.

Leaning down at her, he said, 'Do you realize, when you stare at me with those beaten-dog eyes, you make me want to smash your face in?'

His tone was calm.

'You've got to behave less like a Vermin and more like a Man. Or else I'll start kicking you, the way I kick the drones, and I don't want to do that. Not because you don't deserve it but because I need you to remain sentient until Yasmine returns. Or else I'll go mad. And I can't afford that. I've got to last until either he gets back or we are once more within range of my brothers. Tell me—' the conversation made an abrupt U-turn '—tell me about your life. In the City. Have you ever been somewhere else?'

'The Zone,' said Aila, in pidgin. 'I is grow up there. In the Time Before. I is have childhood there. With mother, sisters, father—'

'*WILL YOU STOP THAT?*' screamed the General. His voice was as piercing as an air-raid siren. 'Can't you speak normally?'

Aila had jerked back in her chair, her eyes wide.

Then he was calm once more.

'All right! The Zone. Tell me about it. How many teams are there? How are they recruited? What do they do between engagements?'

6

The Council Chamber had gradually filled up with its full complement of mentors. On the wall monitor, in the replay of that morning's Welcome Ritual, Vane spoke Unida slowly and precisely. She scanned the young faces before her. 'Some of you know what to expect at this morning's Ritual. You've been to the Welcome Field before.'

The six young women stared back, their faces impassive, eyes narrowed against the glare. The sky arching over their heads was already blinding blue, even though the sun had only been up a couple of hours. There were no clouds in sight and the air was thick with salty heat.

Shutterflies darted this way and that with their characteristic musical whine. They were the source of the video footage that was screened periodically in the Council Chamber.

'For the benefit of those who are here for the first time,' said Vane, 'I will take a few minutes to describe what we are about to do and to give a brief explanation as to why.'

Indicating the patch of bare stone in the grass beside her, she said, 'Each of you will come up to this stone slab here, face around and ... remove your clothes.' She paused. 'If you can remove your jewellery and piercings as well we would appreciate it, but we won't insist.'

The point of view was turned towards the girls as Vane spoke. Three stared back, expressionless: the one with the bright halo of orange hair, the one with the prosthetic arm and the one with the misshapen head, all her hair bunched to one side. The burkha-clad girl, whose face was uncovered, opened her mouth wide in alarm, arching her eyebrows. Of the two with shaven heads, the one with swirling tattoos that reached down to her cheeks, narrowed her eyes and flexed the corners of her mouth: unimpressed. The remaining girl jerked now as if a string had been pulled in her neck. Her eyes opened wide, as if in panic and her eyebrows arched high.

Vane continued as if she had not noticed the reactions. 'There are two reasons we believe in nudity here. The first is that we consider our bodies to be instruments of social change. By opening our bodies to air and sunlight, we cleanse our spirit. The sun's light returns us to the condition in which we enter this world. It brings every member of a group within the circle of sameness. Flattens the curve of deceit. Discourages vanity.

'Now I come to the second reason. It is more complex. You are perhaps aware that your presence on the Island has a specific cause. Whatever you might call it, allow me for the moment to refer to it as a Trauma. A Wounding. An Assault. Some of you – most of you, I should say – have known enormous damage.

'Even though most of you no longer know exactly what the cause of the damage was, you can see the effects upon your bodies. In your lives before you came here, these once-perfect bodies were turned into prisons for your spirit. Whatever you yearned to achieve in your lives, you could not, on account of social attitudes regarding the container in which your spirit resided: your bodies. Some of you have scars, some of you have missing limbs. But all of you, along with the physical traces of wounds, have invisible wounds, too.

'Here on the Islands, we follow a policy regarding invisible wounds. We have a process called "Memrase" by which we can heal them.' Vane paused, as if carefully considering her next words. 'Some of you know what it is and some of you resent our methods. It is no surprise: there are losses and damage that result from our process too.

'It is on account of this secondary loss, the losses connected to the Memrase process, that I say: you need to accept your body with all its wounds, scars, weakness and infirmities. You need to *own your bodies* before you can heal completely. It is the first step you will take towards recovering whatever was lost to you in the course of the experiences that brought you here.

'So. With this reason held firmly in your minds, each of you will come forward, stand on this platform and bare your bodies to the group that is now your family.

'I can see, looking into your faces, that for two of you in particular the very idea of being naked in public is humiliating. Degrading. Yet you will each do this as a mark of belonging and respect to each of your companions. In order to inspire and encourage you and to show you that we at the Islands take our own beliefs seriously, I will join you in being disrobed. I will begin.'

Saying which, she slipped her shapeless robe from her shoulders. One moment she was clothed and in the next the garment lay crumpled around her feet, a garland of pink faded cotton. There she stood, a great mountain of naked, sagging flesh, puckered and dimpled with a life-time's worth of experiences. From the shoulders down to her calves, she was the colour of boiled sago, with moles and blemishes scattered across her body like paint-spatters. Her belly was a billowing expanse, slung from the broad and powerful superstructure of her bones beneath. Her breasts were small, with huge flat nipples raised up like a pair of pale mismatched eyes staring out from her chest, while her navel was a punched-in nose. The grizzled triangle of her pubic hair dangled incongruously from under the vast belly, like a grey goatee beard.

As if an invisible giant's hand had ruffled a collection of life-sized clothes pegs standing stiff and wooden in the grass, all six young women flinched and murmured. Those who had attended a Welcome before averted their eyes out of politeness. But the girl with the smooth unmarked head clapped her hands to her eyes and let out a fluting squawk. She sank to her knees, bent over double, while emitting short sharp chirps. The girl with the orange hair turned away, curling her lip up at the nakedness of the other's distress.

Vane smiled.

'You have all just witnessed the power of nudity,' she said. 'It affects some of us more obviously than others. But in the end we are all altered by it. Just as we are influenced, and sometimes diminished, by the layers of clothing we customarily hide behind, we are altered by the act of baring our bodies. Come now. Let us begin.'

7

The previous night, when Youngest had surfaced and set his suit to float, he had remained awake for some time. With his face toward the ocean bed, he had tuned his visor to night-vision. Immediately, the space beneath him had sprung open and he felt as though he were suspended from the glass ceiling of an infinite hangar.

Thousands of gelatinous globes drifted beneath him. They had been invisible in the darkness, but the night-vision revealed them, pulsing with a mystical grey-green light. They were swarming jellyfish, semi-sentient carnivores, which killed and consumed without needing to make any conscious effort. Their glassine tentacles contained vicious poisons. The slightest touch from these seemingly delicate vines was enough to immobilize the tiny fish that darted amongst them. The fish, unaware of the danger they flirted with, were attracted to the scraps of food thrown off by the jellies. Meanwhile their less fortunate companions could be seen being digested, immobilized within the transparent bodies of the predators.

Youngest watched, mesmerized, until sleep called to him. He turned himself over so that he could doze on the surface, breathing normally.

In the morning, when he returned underwater he turned his night-vision filter on once more.

The swarming jellies paid no attention to him. He was of as little consequence to them as a spur of rock or floating wooden log. Being non-sentient, the curve of their motivations was easily plotted: a steady food source balanced against the temperature of the ocean. At that moment, the bright little fish they consumed as food were their only concern.

Youngest had scanned one of the little fish through his suit's sensors. It belonged to a species that the scanner identified only as Not Yet Named.

Nor will it be, he thought. The age of knowledge-gathering belonged to the Time Before. In this post-Cataclysmic world, there was no place for scientific curiosity or intellectual pursuit. There were no books, no scholars, no Universities. No paper. No written scripts.

Not in the Zone, anyway.

He glanced again at the fish for which the scanner had no name. According to the information scrolling in his visor's text-window, the creature was a relative of the clownfish, a popular aquarium resident in middle-class homes of a century ago.

Youngest looked around once more at the clouds of jellyfish drifting in the water. An idea was forming in his mind.

Was it possible that the descendants of clownfish were reef-dwellers as well? If so, should he consider the possibility that there was a reef in the vicinity?

An artificial reef, perhaps?

Masquerading as an Island?

8

On the wall monitor in the Council Chamber, the first of the Candidates was being called to stand on the platform. A voice-over read out her name and some details of her life. 'Rahmato'u, seventeen at the time of collection, performer with a travelling sex circus in the Zone ...'

Maia said, in a loud voice that carried over the voice-over, 'Why do we have to listen to this again? We've all heard it once already.'

Zara said, 'Oh, please! I missed it the first time around.'

'Some of us don't take our duties here very seriously, do we?' sniffed Maia.

Emmi glanced over her shoulder towards the older woman. 'Just because you're the Sacred Bearer in our midst, Maia, doesn't automatically give you the right to be the resident scourge as well.'

'All I know,' said Maia, 'is that time is precious and some of us choose to waste it.' She shrugged, flexing the corners of her mouth. 'Those who missed previous sessions should catch up with them in their spare time instead of wasting a whole new session watching the same thing all over.'

'Oh, give it up!' snapped Emmi. 'You and your CONSTANT harping—'

The door opened and Asma strolled in. 'Has it begun?' she asked. She was of medium height, pleasant-faced, in her forties. Her hair was drawn back into a plait that ended in a fat stub of unruly hair. She wore a striped floor-length garment and sandals that she removed at the door. The toes of her feet were covered in small agate rings, a different colour for each toe, so that at first glance she seemed to be wearing toe-socks.

'Of course,' said Maia.

'Oh wait,' said Asma, squinting at the monitor. 'Isn't that this morning's session?' No one answered her. She bit her lower lip, as if suppressing a smile, and looked around. 'My goodness, Maia, you do look huge!' she remarked.

Her words fell to the ground with a clang. 'Sneer all you like,' said Maia, staring straight ahead. 'The antidote to your rudeness and ignorance is kicking within me.'

'Good for you!' said Asma. 'We are all grateful that you bear the burden the rest of us cannot or will not face. We thank you.' She smiled as she settled onto a mat that she rolled out with a quick flick of her wrists.

Maia did not deign to reply.

On the screen, the big-haired girl was stripping off her meager clothing. As she revealed more of herself, the piercings across her breasts and her distinctive white rice-grain tattoos gave her the appearance of being sheathed in a skin-tight costume.

'See how comfortable she is with her nudity,' observed Kesh.

'What else can you expect?' snapped Maia at once. 'She was born into slavery. Sold by her mother to a circus. Hasn't known one minute of natural life.' She turned her head towards the others. 'If you want my opinion, though of course I know you don't, *this* is the kind of Candidate who has no place amongst us. She is a waste of time. Human scum.'

'I'm sorry, Maia,' riposted Asma, 'but it was for just such *scum* that our island communities were set up. Without her and all the others like her, we, these Islands, this community of mentors, caretakers and healers – would not exist.'

'More's the pity,' murmured Maia, stroking her belly.

'Oh, wait!' exclaimed Emmi. 'I've just understood what you're getting at, Maia! Of course, in your view the only Candidate worth our time is the one who should never have come here in the first place, right?'

She meant the girl with the shiny marble head.

'What are you *saying*, Emmi?' said Zara. She had a soft voice, all its consonants rounded and dimpled, but she raised it now, in concern. 'It is we who were so lucky to get her – a rare and precious jewel—'

Maia answered before Emmi could. 'Huh! You always were such a soft-hearted fool, Zara. That is not the reason we should be glad to have her.'

'*Rare and precious*?' interjected Kesh. 'My goodness, Zara. We're supposed to be free of bias, blind to race, disability, social status ... where does *rare and precious* come into it?'

Zara pushed her chin out as if offering a target to be punched. 'I admit it then: in this case I *am* biased. I'm biased in this girl's favour. And in my opinion, we should all be. Why? Let me just bring it out in the open: because of where she's from. In my opinion, that's not just one of the reasons for taking her on, it's surely the *best* reason.

'The women of that country – no, that whole region – were systematically *destroyed*. Initially, only the unborn were being killed. Then it was newborns. Then it was the young married women. Then those who tried to stand up to the abuse were ritually humiliated by being raped by the whole community or stoned to death. Eventually it was decided that women as a class were no longer necessary to the human race because reproduction could be managed through cloning and the use of animal surrogates such as cows and apes.

'And so it came to pass: women were hunted down and exterminated like animals. Those men who tried to protect them were also tortured and killed. In two generations they ceased to be.'

Zara's voice was heavy with emotion. 'Maybe you, Kesh, like anyone else from the Sunrise Enclave, were too sheltered to be aware of all this—'

'Of course we knew!' said Kesh, interrupting. 'Why d'you think Emmi and I are here at all?'

Three more mentors, Brahi, Pearl and Tasha, entered the room.

'Well then,' said Zara. 'If you really understood the implications of what you knew, surely you must recognize that to get even one such Candidate from such a background, and have the chance to nurture her ...' Her voice melted and warbled. 'It is a *miracle*.' She blinked and bit her lip, to stop it from trembling.

'Yes, but I – I ...' stammered Kesh, turning towards Emmi for support. 'We heard that the circumstances concerning her escape were questionable. I mean, she was smuggled out of her birth-country under false pretenses, possibly by a man who killed and murdered women himself, in order to save just this special one—'

'No, no, we don't actually know any of that,' cut in Emmi. 'All we can say for certain is that getting her out of the Forbidden Country would have required the cooperation of the regime that's had absolute control over its borders all these years. We have to assume that. For twenty years, the outside world has eliminated that culture from our discourse. We wiped its presence from all our charts and maps. At the time that decision was taken, the international councils believed it was an appropriate punishment for their crimes against our home planet. Instead, it left them free to do whatever they liked, however they liked, with no oversight, no external control.'

Zara looked away, not speaking.

Behind Emmi, on the screen, the burkha-clad girl was now removing her black garments.

'As for "nurturing" this girl? Saving her? I don't know. I

mean, what we have here is someone who has been dragged across the borders of time. From the black night of the past in which she lived for nineteen years into … well? I'll call it the complicated daylight of our present world. Can we truly call that "saving"? Won't the shock of displacement cancel out any benefits we might bestow? Is this what *she* would want if she could truly understand her choices? And, last but not least, does she have anything of value to offer *us*?'

Emmi paused to scan the room.

Maia had assumed the lotus position. She sat with her eyes closed and a faint, superior smile on her lips throughout Emmi's speech. She spoke up now, in the brief silence, without opening her eyes. 'It does not matter,' she said.

'Oh, but it does,' countered Emmi. 'You see, I know what you're interested in Maia – we all do – and I can assure you this Candidate will *not* provide you with the pay-off you're looking for. So maybe I should sympathize with you? I don't know. What I do know is this: I was the Witnesser at the time of this Candidate's awakening and I can tell you that from the very first breath she drew, I *knew*. I knew that to accept her here was a terrible mistake.'

9

Out on the Welcome Field, Meiji had turned towards Vane. 'I can't do it,' she said. 'I *can't*. I won't.'

'The feeling of discomfort passes very quickly,' said Vane. 'Nakedness is our natural state, but we are taught to feel ashamed or defenseless when our skin is bare—' She did not betray the fact that she knew the reason for Meiji's reluctance.

'That is NOT why I can't do it!' said Meiji, her voice rising.

One of the other Candidates called out, 'Whatever you have, we've got it too!'

'Then tell me what the reason is,' said Vane, as she held up a hand for silence.

'If I tell you, may I keep my clothes on?'

'No,' said Vane. 'I am surprised you feel so strongly about this. You were naked in the recovery room.'

'That was different,' said Meiji. 'I was weak. I had no choice—'

'Mentor Vane,' cut in Rahmato'u. 'Why not allow her to put her clothes back on after she has dropped them?'

Vane turned to Meiji. 'Well? Would you agree?'

Meiji's face began to crumple. 'Why!' she cried, 'Why does it matter so much?'

Vane said, 'Meiji, listen to me: it's just *clothes*! They're only a covering. They're not you, they're not even a part of you. And anyway, whatever it is you think you're hiding, believe me, it cannot be something that will cause anyone to harm you or hate you.'

Meiji turned her wet face towards Vane. She was breathing hard. Keeping her head turned in that direction, the girl removed first her upper garment and then, moving as slowly as if she were under water, she undid the cord that held up her pajamas. Underneath them, she wore a pair of loose shorts. She paused a moment with her thumbs hooked in the elastic waist band. Then she pulled it loose from her body and let the garment drop down to her ankles.

Dangling from the girl's groin was a limp and pathetic package of masculine parts. It was of a size and shape suitable to a young pre-pubertal boy. The device perfectly matched her skin and the method of its attachment to her pelvic region was so expertly achieved that it looked entirely at home on her body.

Exclamations burst from the other girls.

'Aaah!' said Rahmato'u. 'You IS different! You is got man-parts! I is not know that is possible in a girlses.'

Meiji kept her face turned towards Vane, her eyes burning with accusation.

The Mentor looked back, her expression cool and unmoved. 'You see?' she said. 'Everyone knows your secret now. But has anything changed? Are you worse off than you were before?'

Meiji dropped her gaze. She tightened her mouth and said nothing.

10

In the Council Chamber, the screening continued to play, but someone lowered the volume.

'This,' said Emmi, waving her hand at the wall-monitor, 'is only the curtain raiser to what we are likely to see. Or anyway, that's what I believe. This Candidate's experiences are too unique for her to be of any use to us. It's not just that she was born within the borders of the Forbidden Country. It's that she was distorted by her Custodians, the so-called uncles. Or biological parents. The person who accompanied her was apparently a transie but referred to her as "daughter". The note accompanying her was unusually garbled so I don't know what part of it was accurate.

'All I want to say is that I had my misgivings even when I read the notes. But when she woke up, that's when my doubts were erased altogether. She is a broken, mangled toy. Even her ability to speak is compromised because the translator disk is calibrated for Farsi, not Urdu, which is what she speaks. In my opinion, she cannot and will not, *ever* be made whole again.'

She paused, looking around the room at all her fellow mentors with a steady, challenging gaze.

'And another thing,' Emmi was looking directly at Maia now. 'I'm talking to you Maia, though you're pretending to be lost in meditation. You believe she's that rare jewel, a "perfect, unblemished *virginal* girl". Meanwhile the reality of her psychological abuse escapes you completely. Let me tell you: she is exactly as scarred as any of our more typical girls. At least they know what they are. She doesn't. When she began to speak after her recovery, she didn't even know how to use female pronouns. She kept using "it" instead of "she".

'So in terms of your Grand Design – oh, come on! We all know you dream of nothing else – forget it! She's not the One.'

'Keep ranting,' said Maia. 'You alone will waste your energy.'

'You are wrong, Emmi,' said Zara, raising her eyebrows and opening her eyes wide. 'Just because you have no understanding of what it means to be a True Virgin—'

'Oh my *god*,' exclaimed Emmi, clutching her head. 'Here we go! Hymen worship of the most traditional, superstitious kind!'

On the monitor, the fifth girl had begun removing her clothes.

'I notice that you do not mind invoking the name of the Good Lord when it suits you,' murmured Zara.

Emmi said, 'Ah! Why do I bother talking to primitives? There's nothing further I want to say here.' She folded her body down onto the floor and began twisting her body into the pretzel-shaped posture that would end with her balanced on the palms of both hands.

Maia said, 'Her purity will be something to celebrate, something rare. She could turn into an example and a beacon of hope to all the Candidates.'

'Indeed, to all of us,' said Zara, in her rounded, melodic tones.

'With all due respect, I think we are all looking in the wrong direction, as concerns this Candidate.' The voice belonged to Folia. She was short and muscular, completely naked but covered in a dense pattern of extremely realistic green swirling leaves, including her face and shaven head. Her nipples and navel had been surgically removed and smoothed over so that the taut, seamless contours of her body were effectively camouflaged in full view. 'The reason she's with us has little to do with the condition of her private parts.'

The attention of the whole room, now comprising all fourteen mentors, short of Vane, swung towards her. 'Full disclosure: what I'm about to say is based entirely on conjecture. A lifetime of conjecture, I might add.'

'Get to the point, Folia,' growled Maia.

'Thank you, Maia, I will get to the point *and* I'll take my own time at it. As everyone here knows, vegetation is the focus of my life. Roots, trunks, photosynthesis: these are what power our planet. But just as plants need water and sunlight to stay alive we humans need money. You want the short version, Maia? Okay, it's simple: I followed the money. The bid involved in procuring this Candidate is staggering. We might have secured twenty other Candidates within that amount.'

Mentor Pearl raised a hand, signalling a desire to interject. 'Which only means that a special circumstance exists to explain why this Candidate was accepted.'

Pearl was middle-aged, dark-skinned and tall, with her hair arranged in thick braids that tumbled around her head in an unruly thicket of short bronze ropes. She wore a pair of plain white shorts and nothing else.

Mentor Tasha looked up from where she sat. 'We are wasting time,' she said. 'This Candidate is here now. We have no choice but to go forward with her.' Tasha was in her sixties and spoke in the rasping whisper of someone fitted with an artificial larynx. She wore her hair as if it were a grey shroud, in a loose-knotted macramé pattern, embellished with beads and flowers, reaching down to her knees. Beneath the hair-cape she wore a black body-hugging outfit. 'Why do any of us feel the need to continue debating it?'

'I agree with Tasha,' said Mentor Cha. She was short and slight, her thick grey hair molded like a helmet over her head. She wore a high-collared shirt, almond green, over loose white pajamas. 'Our mission was conceived as one which would patch the oozing sores of the world we inherited after the Cataclysm,' she said. She used the careful intonation of one who would never adjust to speaking a foreign tongue, which in this case was Unida. 'But we have gone beyond patching up. Now we also preserve. We augment. We take crushed flowers and make them … into birds.' She raised her hands as she spoke, to pantomime the transformation of a flower into a bird taking flight.

Several voices spoke but Kesh prevailed. 'Yes, yes – we all acknowledge that it's too late and that we're meant to welcome all who come to us, regardless of the nature of their wounds. But I believe, and I'm *not* alone, I believe the thing we should be concerned about is *contamination*.'

She had the room's attention.

'This is a girl who was born and raised within the poisons of a culture in which women were treated like vermin and eventually destroyed altogether. Surely she has internalized a view of womanhood that we cannot afford to bring within our fold? Surely we owe it to our other girls to keep them from being infected with ideas and principles that we abhor?'

She paused, scanning the room. Mentor Gosami put up her hand, but Kesh raised a finger in her direction, requesting more time.

'Zara and Maia believe that this girl's lack of sexual experience is an absolute virtue. But looked at from another direction, is it not a liability? Doesn't this girl's ignorance of the sexual sphere make her totally unfit to face the debauched world in which we live in? And what about the sight of her unblemished body? Will it not be a subtle rebuke to the other Candidates? A reminder that they have been disadvantaged by comparison to her? Will they not be tainted by body-envy?'

Gosami stood up to speak. She was in her late thirties, wearing a loose thin tunic, petal pink in colour and scattered with tiny mirrors. 'You make valid points, Kesh,' she said. 'But I have a special interest in this Candidate and for reasons very different to Zara and Maia. Let me state it clearly: the original birthplace of my family was the Forbidden Country—'

'Bias!' yelled Emmi from where she sat. '*Racial bias!*'

'Yes,' acknowledged Gosami, nodding in Emmi's direction. 'Yes. I have deliberately opened myself to that charge. I accept it. But that does not alter my interest in this Candidate; my desire to feel hope for her; my need to protect her.' Gosami's eyes were glistening. 'To refer back to what Cha told us, our mandate goes beyond mere patching. Our mandate surely permits us, when an opportunity comes our way, to preserve and protect a young person who may be the last of her kind. Yes, I acknowledge the danger of origin-worship and yes, I admit that nostalgia and sentiment play a role in *my* interest in this young woman. Yet here she is, a lone survivor. It's not just one twig or one branch that has been mercilessly sawn off the family tree to which she belongs, but the *entire biosphere* that she represents! If ever we must find it in ourselves to make an exception, is this not such a time?'

Kesh made an exasperated sound under her breath. '*Tcheh*,' she said.

Mentor Asma muttered, 'Sentimentality.'

But Folia said, 'Ahh … good analogy, the branch and biosphere. You got me there, Gosami.' Then she turned towards the entrance. 'Here comes Vane now.'

11

'I have a question,' said Aila. 'I don't know what to call you. I don't know your name.'

She and the pale man were on the rear deck, where a white-and-blue striped awning had been set up to provide shade from the sun. The General was striding back and forth across the width of the deck, pausing on either side, to do sit-ups while gripping the rails.

'My brothers and I don't bother with names,' he said. 'We all know who we are.'

Four drones were standing, as usual, facing towards their master. The rounded flaps decorating the edges of the awning were hanging down, motionless. The ocean was inert. The air felt like an invisible blanket of hot jelly.

'But you can't hear your brothers now,' said Aila.

'Are you making a point?'

'Does that mean, when you can't hear your brothers, that you don't know who you are?'

The General wheeled around, took one step in the transie's direction, slapped her hard, then wheeled away again, returning to pacing and exercise. The sound of his hand on her skin was like a gunshot report.

Aila rubbed her face, seeing if she could convert the stinging sensation into something pleasurable. It was one of her minor amusements: translating misfortune into fortune. Now, for instance, she could tell herself that being slapped was good for … circulation?

She was on the verge of smiling, which was the ultimate aim of her private amusement, when she realized she could hear an odd snuffling. It could only come from the drones. She turned, and saw that they were standing as before, still, with their hands folded behind them. Their expressions were unchanged, but two of them had their mouths open and their small chests were heaving slightly. The sound came from them. They were laughing, it seemed.

At her. At her discomfiture.

She turned back towards the pacing General. Standing up, she undid the buttons that extended down the front of her robe, exposing herself to him. 'Come on,' she said, 'it's time for your next dose.'

'What are you doing?' he said, his voice furious. But he came striding towards her anyway, already tugging at the fastenings of his white shorts. 'You don't have the right to demand anything from me. What do you think you are?'

She raised her right foot and placed it on the wooden table that was bolted to the deck. She wore no underwear. She tilted her hips up and spread herself so that the General could ram himself in with his characteristic lack of ceremony.

He obliged her. 'A dominatrix?' he said, grunting, '*—uhh!* – A hyena bitch? *Uhh*!' He shuddered with the energy of his rut, sweat pouring off him in rivulets.

Aila could hear the drones snuffling, all of them now. She turned her body slightly, so that they could have a better view. She wondered if they were capable of enjoyment. She was used to performing for an audience and it allowed her to feel some pleasure in her predicament if she thought she was offering herself as entertainment for more than just one man.

The General grunted and bellowed, lifting her clear off her feet in the final moments of his crisis. Then he stood still, swaying and panting. Small bare feet pattered on the deck. A drone hurried up, holding out hot cloths and a bowl of water. The mannikin reached for the General's detumescing member, slipping it out of the transie's surgically created purse with a combination of delicacy and speed. It behaved as if it were handling a precious artifact that must be reconditioned, oiled and tucked away in a fresh velvet pouch the very instant it has been used.

Aila felt a tapping on her buttock.

She was surprised to find a second drone beside her, offering a hot towel for her use. It was not looking directly at her and its expression was as bland and unchanged as ever. Yet this was the first time that one of them had acted this way, entirely on its own initiative.

'Thank you,' she said, feeling oddly touched.

12

Vane went up towards the lectern. She had asked for the screening to be rewound, and paused with Meiji's tear-stained face filling it.

'As you can see,' said the white-haired Mentor, now facing towards the room, 'she *did* have something to hide. It's a prosthetic attachment that she wears. The reason she wears it is that she was brought up in an all-male environment in which she needed to pass for a boy.'

'I thought you said she was hidden from the world around her?' asked a voice. It was Kesh.

'Throughout her childhood, yes,' said Vane. 'Or at least that's my understanding. Then around her sixteenth year, she apparently aged dramatically over a very brief period of time. "Arrested childhood" is the term used to describe her circumstances before the sudden growth spurt. At the end of this process, she was introduced to an all-male urban culture as a young man with feminine tendencies. She began to wear the prosthetic device only in that sixteenth year, when she was making the transition from her life underground to the one she was being conveyed towards.'

Vane drew in a breath.

'I am glad to find that you are all deep in discussion already. Good! That is what I had hoped.' She glanced over her shoulder to the face on the screen before returning to the others. 'As you may have guessed, the girl whose face is on the screen behind me is very much on my mind. I wanted you to air your disagreements amongst yourselves and I will address some of your concerns during this session.

'To begin with, though, I would like to focus on two quite different matters. One is extremely urgent and will affect all of us directly.'

She paused and looked around.

'It concerns our Island home. Some of you will recall that four weeks ago I mentioned the need to relocate in the course of the next twelve-month, in order for this Island to rejuvenate. Well, it turns out that my estimate was wrong.' She drew in another breath before continuing. 'Instead, it needs to happen any time in the next couple of weeks. Maybe sooner.'

There were several gasps.

Vane raised her hand.

'Yes, yes, it's not going to be easy for any of us, believe me. I'll give everyone her chance to speak. Before that, in order that our discussion can take place within a meaningful context, I need to say a few things.

'All of you know that I was amongst the original designers of these artificial floating environments. Before they were called "Islands" and became places of refuge, they were places where alternative thinkers such as my friends and I could get away from what we thought of then as a toxic world.'

She gave a rueful chuckle. 'Huh. Well. I have been living on this particular Island from the time when it was a single ring of chambers anchored to the ocean bed, dependent on supplies from the mainland for everything except water and air. So, for me to abandon this particular facility, which was named for me, is no small matter. It is a wrench, every time it happens. This is the fifth.

'In the next few days, we will scale down, reduce and thin out our ranks. Those of our girls who are ready will be redistributed to other Islands at once. I have already been in touch with some of my sister Senior Mentors. They have all agreed to accept our overflow.

'Those who are still in process will be taken through to completion before being sent away to other Islands, along with their attendants. The aim will be to reduce our numbers here until only our core of fifteen Mentors—' she indicated the whole room '—and a handful of Candidates remain. After which we will all relocate to Base Vane on the mainland.'

Hands began going up, but she paused them.

'Wait. I mentioned there were two matters I wanted to discuss. The second one is equally urgent but has broader implications.'

She paused again, composing her words. 'We all know that these Island communities came into being as a reaction against the Zone. As noncombatant healers operating off-land we allowed ourselves to imagine we were providing a service that benefited the most needy.

'It turns out we were wrong. It turns out that all we've been doing for these past fifteen, twenty years is patching tyres. Human tyres. Soft-bodied wheels that have kept the Juggernaut of destruction and degradation rolling forward unchallenged.'

She glanced in Emmi's direction.

'We have always thought of ourselves as non-combatants. But by our actions, by doing nothing to oppose the horror around which we live, by being absolute pacifists, in effect, we DO support it.'

She looked now at Folia, then at Gosami. Then at Pearl.

'It is all with the best of intentions. Yes. Our intentions have been outstanding. Our compassion is peerless. Our results superlative, when judged by the quality of life we restore to the girls. Meanwhile, all unhindered, the Juggernaut lumbers on.

'I am talking, as you know, about the Zone. The Zone lumbers on and with it thrives the economy it supports. The nations and the people who live in comfort because of it.'

She stopped, closing her eyes, steepling her fingers in front of her face before continuing.

'So. Some years ago, my sister Senior Mentors and I came to the conclusion that the time would come to go beyond mending tyres.' She opened her eyes. 'Time to make our presence felt.'

13

'How many little men are there?' asked Aila. She had rarely seen more than four above deck. But the food came from below-stairs and the ship's maintenance was carried out, she knew, by them.

'Eight now, I think,' said the General. 'When we left, there were sixteen.'

'Oh! What is ...' she checked herself from slipping into pidgin. 'What happened to the others?'

'They're weak,' said the General. 'They don't live long. The heat affects them.'

He and Aila were on the rear deck. Aila was sitting at the table set out there, watching the setting sun, while the General stood by the rail that pointed towards, the old South, twiddling the dial on his radio while looking nowhere in particular. It was a small, hand-held device that duplicated some of the functions of the bigger machine downstairs in the bedroom.

The General lapsed into silence. This had a happened a couple of times since Youngest had left. Even in the short span of time that she had known him, Aila recognized it was unusual behaviour for the General. What was more typical was for him to spend the entire day pacing the deck, eating and drinking even as he moved ceaselessly back and forth. She wondered if he might be suffering from some physical disorder. Such as heatstroke. Or plain fatigue.

The thought had come to Aila that she might find herself alone on the ship, with an ailing or dying General and a crew of mute dwarves. What would she do in such a circumstance?

'Also, I deconstructed a couple of them,' said the General, starting up again. He had returned to the subject of drones. 'While Yasmine was away in that Verminopolis you belong to. I pegged them down onto the deck and carved them up in small increments, with the idea of seeing how long it would take for them to stop struggling, first, and stop breathing, second. It was quite entertaining. It gave me something to think about for at least three days.'

'They ... they took that long?'

'Oh yes,' said the General. 'I was quite surprised. I didn't think they had the stamina. One of them survived almost twice as long as the other one. But it turned out there was a reason for that.' He looked up now, animated by the memory.

'Why?' she asked, knowing that he expected it.

'Because his fellow-drones had been feeding water to him,' said the General. 'They actually conspired to do it! Imagine. I had not thought they were sentient enough to care about one of their own – or even to have enough space inside their heads to think of themselves as belonging to a group.'

Aila kept her expression neutral. There would be no point doing otherwise. 'How are they created? Do they know what they are? Do they grow in family groups?'

The General glanced in her direction, then away again. 'They're one more asset that your world lacks,' he said. 'They're what we created in the Brotherland to replace the service functions of Vermin. We tinker with their DNA in order to suit our needs exactly. As embryos, they're implanted in sows, then extracted at one month and speed-grown in incubators until they're mobile and can feed themselves. Some of them reach full height in less than one year. They are easy to train, but they have no emotions, no conversation. They're ideal slave units. Very strong when it comes to physical labour, dependable because they don't have real thoughts and easy to replace because they're so similar to one another. Short-lived, too: they don't last longer than five or six years. We designed them that way, like batteries that cannot be recharged. Once their life-processes wear out, they just stop where they are, lie down and die.'

Aila struggled to remain silent. She wanted to ask questions such as: *How is it possible to be so cruel? Are all the Generals equally cruel? And if so, why?*

She knew that such questions would only provoke a vicious response. She did not make the attempt to prove herself right.

14

Rahmato'u nodded her approval, making the big halo of her hair bounce back and forth. She and the other girls were in their newly assigned sleep chamber. The room was hexagonal, with the rounded corners and uneven surfaces that were typical of Island construction. A virtual window filled one of the six walls. There appeared to be no furniture whatsoever.

Shaya, with honey-gold skin, moved her smooth-shaven tattooed head from side to side, her expression blank. She kept her arms tightly wrapped across her chest.

Alarie's scalp was bare on the left side of her head while on the right she had a thick woolly cap of amber-brown hair. She remained in the middle of the room, staring at the floor. Aside from her eyes, which were both intact, the left side of her face had been replaced with shiny pink scar tissue.

Dani, smiling in small nervous jerks, tried to make small talk. 'It's a nice room, isn't it?' she said. 'Better than the clinic! I really like it.' No one responded to her remarks. Her skin was criss-crossed with tiny zig-zag markings like a suit sewn by a hasty tailor.

Messina had a mechanical prosthesis in place of her left arm. Both her feet were transplants, mismatched from one another and pale brown by contrast to the dull mahogany of the rest of her skin. When she opened her mouth, the pair of metal plates she had instead of teeth flashed in the artificial sunlight shining in through the virtual window.

Meiji was huddled beside the window, her shoulders

hunched, her whole emaciated body pulled into itself, giving her the appearance of a bent pole, leaning away from the rest of all humanity.

All six girls were unclothed. For five of them, tattoos and piercings made up for the clothes they had removed. All except for Rahmato'u also wore an implant that looked like a metallic ornament embedded under the skin of their throats. This was an artificial voice generator, which translated their natural languages into Unida.

Rahmato'u, who spoke in her own voice in heavily accented pidgin, had the assertiveness of a natural leader. She began showing the others that the room's emptiness was deceptive.

'See?' she said, to no one in particular. 'Here is lights. Here is … oh! Is table. And seat.'

The fittings were all recessed and could be pulled up from the floor or down out of the ceiling by finding the slight depressions that indicated their presence. Everything was made of the same shiny, nonmetallic textured material that the walls were formed out of. The construction and design of the objects was such that they could be folded away, but were stable once deployed. Strong elastic bonds held jointed members in place. Slight variations in colour, pattern and shape distinguished each one, so that there was a pleasing organic symmetry to each new item as it came into being.

Rahmato'u looked around. 'Come on – you two? You is been on Island before? You is know what I mean? You is help set up room.'

Alarie and Dani responded, knowing that she meant them, but Messina raised her right hand. 'Me too.'

Shaya was looking around, her eyes wide and uncertain, as if unable to take in what she saw. On her chest were shiny pink circles of scar tissue that were all that remained of her breasts. Her skin was covered in welts. Her tattoos were in the form of

Arabic numbers.

'You!' Rahmato'u said. 'You is Shay … Sha-ya? You is first time in Island?'

Shaya nodded before saying 'yes' in the artificial voice that emerged from her throat. She blinked rapidly, before adding, 'Oh! I … I … sound so different …' She touched the front of her neck.

'Is fake-voice,' said Rahmato'u, nodding, 'but is useful.' She patted her own bare throat. 'I is not have. I is not need. I is speak anyway.'

Finally she turned towards the still figure by the window. 'Aho! You! Why is you not speak? You is name … Mee-Dja? Mi'dju?'

Meiji hunched her shoulders higher, turning her face to the window, squeezing her eyes shut against the light.

Alarie whispered to Dani, her hand against the translator disk to muffle its sound, 'You saw? That thing – the thing she has between her legs?'

'It is weird. No wonder she wanted to hide it …'

'You is shut it, both,' said Rahmato'u, her manner brusque. 'She is new. Not like us. Not understanding how to be here.'

'Shaya is new too,' said Messina.

But Rahmato'u had crossed towards the silent figure. 'You is not be apart,' she said. 'Come. We is team now. We is work as a team.' Then she tapped the girl on her shoulder. 'Mid-Ji?'

Meiji gasped and flinched.

She covered her face with her hands. 'No! I will NOT stay! NOT!' The force of her distress gave her the energy to lift her face to Rahmato'u. They were of the same height. 'I am *not* on your team. Or any team. I must not be here!'

The sound came from her throat disk, but her eyes spat venom at the girl with the big orange halo about her head.

The others clicked their tongues in disapproval.

But Rahmato'u squared her shoulders and held her ground. She had an angular face, her skin drawn tight as stretched canvas, indigo black in colour. She was tattooed in white ink, in the luminescent rice-grain pattern that glowed in the dark. Her mouth was as dark and as lush as a pair of purple peach-halves. She everted her upper lip now, revealing its deep crimson inner edge. 'Pooh! You is not make me fright! I is long-time Islander. I is never have fear. Tell me: why is you have so much problems?'

One of the others called out, 'Ask her about the *thing*! Between her legs!'

Meiji breathed in, breathed out in order to stop herself from panting.

'There is a mistake,' she said, speaking in a calmer tone. 'I must not be here. I must be somewhere … else. Elsewhere.'

'So is what?' asked Rahmato'u. 'We is all from other places. We is all come from otherwhere.'

'I cannot speak in my own language. I do not recognize anyone here as my own … my own … *people*.' She tapped her throat. 'This is not my speech. Not my words. Nothing I have is my own.' She was starting to breathe hard once more. Her head was jerking from side to side. 'I can't – I won't—'

'No, no,' said Rahmato'u, her voice slicing through the panic rising in Meiji's voice. 'You is stop. You is listen me. Just listen.'

Meiji clenched her teeth, her chest heaving.

'You is know best, what is true, what is not-true, about the before-life of you. Still, but. Now you is here. In Island. And Rahm – that is me, that is my short name – Rahm is know much-many things about Island. Rahm has return six times. Same Island. So Rahm is can help. Is can help to you. You is agree?'

Meiji stared into the impenetrable blackness of the other girl's eyes. Something in the quality of Rahm's conviction caused her own despair to ease. The effect was very slight, hardly a nail-paring's worth of relief. Yet it was enough to allow her to incline her head and nod.

Once. Twice.

Her voice remained locked within her throat, behind the translation disk. But her breath slowed down.

'Good,' said Rahm, nodding as she turned her body to include the others now. 'Because first rule in Island is: Candidates is have no time. Ever. We is have to learn many-much things, before tomorrow. Then we must sleep, because we is learn in sleep too. So quickly now. We is set up the room and choose our sleeping places.'

'What?' asked Shaya.

'I is explain,' said Rahm. 'We is set up the room during my explain. Then we is eat.'

15

'About your objections, Emmi,' said Vane, turning towards the slender younger woman who returned her gaze unblinkingly. 'I am aware of your concerns. You may think that your words have fallen on deaf ears. Not just today, not just yesterday, but over the long course of the … nine? … nine years you've been here. I sympathize with your objections regarding the Candidate whose image is on the screen behind me.

'Some of you others, I have heard your arguments, too. Gosami, yours is, as you yourself admit, race-biased and therefore disappointing. On the other hand, who can fault you for stating your case? Any one of us in a similar position would do likewise.

'And back to you, Folia, yes: the acceptance of this Candidate did involve an exorbitant price in the auction. Plus a bribe. There was no other way that she would have been delivered here, unharmed. She was unblemished, after all and her body-parts might so easily have been harvested for further use. Instead, she arrived here absolutely pristine. I saw to that … by paying a "special handling fee" to bring her back myself.

'So the question that has to be answered is: Why? Why did we do so much to bring this girl to our Island?'

Vane paused with her eyes closed, as if she were collecting her energies.

'Because,' she said, 'there may be a connection between these two subjects,' she said. 'Between the change in the course of our mission on these Islands. And this particular girl.'

She raised her head and looked up once more, her gaze passing over each of the women in front of her, one at a time, as she spoke.

'Thousands of young women have passed through our hands. Many have been exceptional. All, as we know, have known terrible suffering. That is their badge of belonging, that is what brought them here. This girl, too, has suffered. She has been subjected to an extreme form of self-denial. She was brought up as a boy in a world that did not acknowledge the existence of women. In her confusion and ignorance about what she is, she is pathetic, malformed and mentally scarred. And yet ...' Vane paused. 'She has a quality of absolute innocence. It is like a titanium shield, that innocence.'

Vane looked at Zara and then at Maia.

'You may call it virginity if you want, Zara. Or moral purity, Maia. But I maintain that it's something beyond either of these. Something unknown in our world. I believe her unique quality is a complete lack of fear.

'This is a girl who, until her sixteenth year, was never told that being a victim was her biological destiny as a woman. She knew that harm could come to her in the form of death or physical pain but she was never taught that her body itself marked her out as a victim.

'And so *she is not one*.'

Vane paused, lips pursed together in what might have been a smile or a grimace.

'Even I, whose consciousness is covered in calluses, even I am moved by the sheer improbability of her existence. That is my first reason for believing we owe it to our diseased world to find a place for her on our Island – on my Island. To shelter her and to mend her as we have sheltered and mended others.'

Then she shook her head. Her voice hardened.

'But we cannot afford to be sentimentalists either. And I do not believe in chance. This girl's appearance in our world is a sign that something has changed in the impenetrable pit from which she has emerged. It's not enough for me to say that I am moved by her condition. I owe it to everything we stand for to see beyond the pathos of her life. To understand what her presence in our midst might mean. For all of us and for our fractured world.

'So my second reason for bidding for her is that I believe the poisons she has supposedly escaped may instead have followed her out.

'If I am right, then our Island will be the first to meet this challenge, whatever it might be, just because of our geographical position. If someone or something has been tracking her, then whatever it is will come first to us. We will sound the alarm. We will share news of this development with our sister Islands. And if we go down as a result, then so be it. At least, by our example, we will have saved others from making our mistake.

'Gosami, do not despair. Either way, this Candidate will get her chance to prove herself. But Emmi and Kesh, do not despair either: she will not be *princessed.* She is intelligent, but lacks mental discipline. If she cannot improve her attitude, she will succumb to the challenges we set her. And we will bob our heads towards the gods of evolution and accept that her bloodline was no longer fit for the world we live in.'

'But. If she succeeds … then you, Maia, will have your chance.'

The white-haired woman, still seated on her mat in the lotus position, smiled and raised both hands above her head, palms together, in a gesture of exultation.

'She will go into training to be a Sacred Bearer. She will be schooled in the classical tradition of giving birth, including the full, nine-month gestation. Her body will be adjusted accordingly. And she will, with the blessings of our entire community of Islands, enjoy the experience of true, natural motherhood.'

16

The six girls were seated at the hexagonal table that occupied the centre of the room. Rahm had shown them that each of the six segments of the table had recessed compartments.

'When is open,' said Rahm, 'there is food.' She leaned towards the centre and pressed at the narrowest point of the segment. It gave under the pressure of her fingers and then, with a twinkling movement too fast for the eye to follow, a section of the segment flipped up, with a steaming container presented to view. 'See? Is lunch,' said Rahm.

As each of the girls reached to follow suit, the team leader showed them a feature in the form of a press-up spout, from which they could get water, for the cup that folded out alongside the spout.

'Oh!' exclaimed Shaya, as she held her container of food as yet unopened in front of her. A newcomer to the Island, the hot meals and tasty preparations were a novelty for her. 'It smells so good!'

'Food on Island is always good,' said Rahm shortly. She had snapped open the lid on her portion, broken off two shallow-bowled spoons that were part of the lid and begun to dig into the dish of crab soup and baby squid tentacles that occupied the central well of the container. In one of the two side receptacles there were crisp lettuce leaves and slices of white radish. In the other, there were tight rolls of cured seal meat, dark red and chilled. Along the top edge of the container was a smaller pocket in which nestled three triangular containers, each shaped like tiger-claws, each with a snap-off tip.

'Where is it made?' Meiji asked, looking with interest at her bowl. The one thing she approved of on the Island was its food. The first meal she'd had on her own, in the Night Sky room, had been delicious. She reached for one of the tiger-claws, knowing what she would find in there.

'In kitchen,' said Rahm. 'Level Six—'

'*Six?*' said Shaya. 'Up?'

'No, no,' said Rahm. 'Down. Candidates is on Level Three and then also Four. Mentors is on Levels One and Two. Below us is all attendants and helpers. Then down, and down and down, is many levels of work spaces.'

The others looked impressed. Dani said, 'I didn't know it was *that* big ...'

'Oh yes. Island is big-big place. Kitchen Level is only for make food. Below is for grow green plants in water. Below that is for grow meats in—' She shrugged, inclining her head as if the open sea were actually outside the virtual window. 'I is not know how to explain. Is like farm, but is in sea.'

Alarie asked, 'How do they do that?'

Dani said, 'I know. I did my first Task there.' She tried to describe what she had seen, but began to falter, as she lost confidence in her ability to provide an accurate picture. 'It's a big room, but like everything here it's ... it's underwater, yes? So they can open the gate – in the outer wall, there's a kind of gate – when they open it, they can let sea water in. So they can keep the animals inside, but also ... let them swim outside, too.' She stopped with an uncertain smile on her face. 'I think.'

'Is correct,' said Rahm, her mouth full. 'They is look after many animals. Lady seal is use for milking. Meating is from shell-animals or fish. Also shark, also turtle. And man-seal. Also eggs from turtles. Milk-animals is never use for meating.'

Meiji broke off the tip of her first tiger-claw. Inside it was a single drop of a clear fluid that added sharp, stinging accents to the food. The least trace lit up Meiji's whole mouth with a flash of bright, momentary pain, then just as quickly vanished. Leaving a sparkling aftertaste.

She looked up, her eyes smarting with pleasure and asked, 'What is *this* made from?'

Rahm smiled, her full mouth stretched wide, 'Ha, you is liking! Is good. Is healthing. Is jellyfish poison!'

'Really?' said Meiji, looking at the now-empty pouch in her fingers with fresh respect.

'They is make-safe by cooking. Maybe changing also the chemixtry. I is not know for sure. But is good for you. Make's clean the tummy. Now come on quick-quick. Then we is go down for Task Lesson One.'

Rahm explained the basics of a Candidate's life. 'We is here to learn,' she said, in her brusque, telegraphic speech. 'We is have five days only. So we is have to learn at night. By sleep. Then in the morning, early-early, we is know what we is do, where we is go. We is get the Tasks to do. When is we do the Tasks correctly, we is get credits and go on to higher lesson. Maybe we is go to new Team.'

'There are other teams?' Shaya's eyes were opened wide in surprise.

'Many-much teams,' said Rahm. 'Just like same to we. After many days, when we is ready, some of us is find work on Islands and some of us is go back.'

Meiji's head had snapped up then. ' "Back"! Where is "back"?'

Rahm whinnied. 'Haha! You is joke?' Then she shrugged, 'I is say already once. We is all come from other places, you know. So some feems is go back to that place after training is finish.'

Meiji subsided into silence. The turmoil that was constantly boiling within her made coherent speech difficult.

The others had questions. Supposing they could not learn fast enough? What would happen if they failed? Could they choose their tasks? Messina wanted to know how to avoid a lesson if she knew she would fail at it.

'You is cannot know,' said Rahm matter-of-factly as she tipped her head back, picked up her bowl of soup and drained its contents. 'Even if you is know once that you is not like the Task, you is cannot know next time.' She wiped her mouth with the back of her hand.

'Why?' asked Shaya, frowning in puzzlement.

Messina and Alarie snorted softly, like those who share an important secret. Dani scowled, unamused.

Rahm made a gesture across her forehead as if she were drawing a zipper. 'Because!' she said.

Meiji had missed the gesture, concentrating as she was on her dinner. She looked up, realizing she had missed something. Her eyes were still sparkling with pleasure from her second tiger-claw. 'What?' she asked.

Rahm said, with an exasperated sigh, 'Ohh! Is nothing. They is do brain-wipe. That is all.' She shrugged. 'Some people is not like. Like Dani.'

Brain-wipe.

All the breath left Meiji's lungs as those two words went plunging into the depths of her mind, striking flames as they went. Here, then, was the explanation for her confusion! Her memories had been destroyed. Her mouth opened, but she couldn't scrape a single syllable of sense out of herself.

BRAIN-WIPE.

Her mind's store of thoughts, knowledge and consciousness was empty. No wonder she could not think. All that she had were the ghosts of what she once knew: shifting, shapeless thoughts that shrieked wordlessly within her head, reminding her of the enormity of her loss.

Her entire gut began to tremble, as if she had nothing inside her but a collection of violin strings vibrating at high speed. She pushed her bowl away, all appetite gone. She wrapped her arms tight around herself, to prevent herself from spinning apart, out of control.

The others continued with their chattering conversation, oblivious to her distress.

17

Exhaustion and tedium were conspiring to make Youngest light-headed.

What sounds does an island make, he asked himself. *Does it sing? Does it snore in sleep? Does it curse when it's angry,* he wondered. *Does it know pleasure and pain?*

It should be within sight. The locator's signal was now a steady pulse. Which meant that its source had to be within a radius of 200 metres of him. Yet there was no visible structure in which a girl wearing the transmitter might reasonably exist.

He had concluded she wasn't dead. The locator's battery was dependent on her unique pulse. If she no longer supplied it with current, it would continue functioning for a while, but would eventually fade out, even if someone else tried to wear it. Enough time had passed now to allow him to assume she had to be breathing. Somewhere. Somewhere big enough to house not only her but all the others with whom she would now be living. He reckoned, based on the fragments of evidence scraped out of Aila, the number was at least six hundred people. Six hundred women. Plus all the facilities required to keep such a large number of people healthy and productive.

So: it had to be a structure at least five or six storeys tall. Maybe more.

From what he had understood, the Islands were not natural rock formations, rooted to the ocean floor. Instead, they were artificially created environments, maintained with funds from the Whole World Union.

He had assumed they would be cloaked to shield them from satellite view. That is, from above. But he had been scanning the ocean wearing his underwater goggles and, still, he had seen nothing.

What would be the point of deploying underwater shields? The Islands did not need to defend themselves against assaults. The underwater ferry network was staffed exclusively with women. Even transies were not accepted as crew. No travel took place except via the deep-water networks. No one aside from the Islanders monitored these networks. Plus: the Islands' resources were valuable only to themselves. Their only concern was to maintain their integrity as independent, functioning units.

So why bother being invisible underwater? What was there to hide?

It did not make sense.

18

'But it was *wrong*!' protested Meiji. Rahm had noticed Meiji's silence and needled her until she was forced to confess the source of her anguish. 'They took our memories without asking! Now I have nothing but my name. I don't know who I am, I don't know where I am, I don't know where I came from!'

'And that is *good thing*,' said Rahm, forcefully. 'Ask Shaya – ask Alarie – ask ANYONE! Ask Mentor Vane. She is mention Memrase at Welcome speech but she is not explain fully. What is inside old memory is useless stuff. Burning, stinking sick-sick. If we is know that memory, we is not sleep, we is not work, we is do nothing but scream. Why is Shaya not have the chest bumps? She is not know. Why is Alarie have blank-face on left side? What is happen to foots of Messina? They is not know. So they is not care.'

'Yes,' said Meiji, 'but—'

'There is no *but*. You is here now. You is part of team. You is safe.'

' "Safe"!' said Meiji bitterly. 'What is "safe"? When strangers can reach inside my brain and take away whatever they want?'

'It's for your own good,' said Alarie. 'Can you not see that? Whatever they do is for our good. We are lucky to be here. Lots of other girls are not so lucky.'

Meiji's brow creased slightly and she opened her mouth. Then shut it again.

'What is your thought?' asked Rahm. 'Speak now. We is have time. Later, is not.'

'I just …' said Meiji. She shrugged. 'Well. I am not the same as you. All of you.'

The light from the virtual window was bright with afternoon sunshine.

'Look,' she said, extending her arms in front of her. 'I have no scars. No tattoos. No decorations. My feet and hands are my own.'

'What about your little *thing*?' cut in Messina, pointing.

Meiji shrugged, not looking down. 'All right. I have that, yes. But it's not the same. It's not like …' She glanced around. The other team members stared back at her with closed expressions. 'It's not the same, because it's only on the outside. It's … it's like a piece of clothing. Everyone else here has *real scars*.' Surgery, amputations, implants. She couldn't find the words. 'Your bodies are cut and changed. Added to or taken out from. Everyone except me.'

'So?' Alarie's voice came from her implant and the scar tissue on her face skewed her expressions so that she seemed to be smiling, though she was not. 'What do you think? That you are better than us?'

'Not better,' insisted Meiji. 'Just *different*.'

'Anyway, it doesn't matter,' said Messina. 'If you're here, it means something very bad happened to you in the past. Why do you want to know? It's over now.'

'No! If I don't know what happened to me it's the same thing as …' Meiji struggled to find words. 'Losing my arms or …' She stopped, glancing at Messina, realizing that her words might sound unkind. 'I mean, like you, for instance. Don't you want to know what happened? Don't you care that parts of your own body have been taken away?'

Messina shook her head and shoulders in vehement denial. 'No! I don't care. Why do you?'

'Just by being here, you *are* the same as us,' said Alarie.

'What's gone wrong with you can't be seen, that's all. It's inside. But it must be horrible, or else you wouldn't be here. You should be glad you don't know what it is.'

Rahm remained silent, biting her lips. The corners of her mouth were flexed downwards. She leaned on the table, arms folded, listening.

'That's my point! How can I know if it was horrible or *not*-horrible,' asked Meiji, 'if I don't know what it was? Why can't *I* choose?'

'Because you is must have the trust,' said Rahm now. She straightened her back, asserting her position as leader. 'Trust in the Mentors. They is know what is good for you – for all of us. We is on Island now. We is Candidate. We is grow strong, We is grow in power. If you is do good, maybe you is even grow into Mentor! But out there?' She pointed in the direction of the window. 'In Zone? You is have nothing. No protections. No helps. You is only lone feem. Lone womans. And womans alone in Zone is need big-time protections.'

A frown creased Meiji's forehead.

'What?' asked Rahm.

Meiji shook her head, unable to talk. A powerful tremor was building up inside her.

'I said, womans alone is need—'

'No, not that.' Meiji was breathing hard, unable to continue. A kaleidoscope of images was careening through her brain, triggered by what Rahm had just said. The images winked on and off so rapidly she couldn't make sense of them. The other girls had trained their gaze on her like laser torches. She had to complete her remark or risk being scorched. 'You called me a … a … *woman*!'

Rahm looked surprised. 'Ya. So is what?'

Meiji said, her slender frame quivering, 'I'm … I'm …' She realized she was about to jump into a pool of molten shame, but she had no choice. She was poised at the edge of a diving board from which there was no going back. 'I'm not a *woman*. I'm a … a … *person*!'

There was a fraction of silence. Then the others began to neigh and snort.

Shaya said, 'Huh! No wonder you don't feel afraid to know what's happened to you! You don't know what you *are*!'

Messina gave out a harsh cackle, 'Oh! It's that funny little sausage dangling between her legs! She thinks she's a *man*!'

'A man! A MAN!' The team gave in to hoots and barking shrieks of laughter.

Meiji blinked rapidly in confusion.

'No,' she said. 'No! Of course I'm not.' She knew exactly what men were and she was perfectly aware that she wasn't one. But how was she so sure? Who had brought her to that knowledge?

In that instant, a bolt of lightning cracked through her mind and she felt the presence of that man, a tall man, who had … who had …

Gone. The memory or shadow or wisp of smoke, whatever it was, snapped off.

'If you're *not* a man and you're *not* a woman,' shrieked Messina, '*what are you?*' She rocked from side to side, howling with laughter so hard that her seat folded up abruptly beneath her. She was deposited on the floor with a bump, which caused the others to collapse in another round of hilarity.

Meiji did not share in the laughter. In answer to the question, she heard the medallion in her throat issue the words, 'I'm a … person.' Her inner self was crumbling, liquefying, ceasing to hold up her exterior.

'A person,' she said again, in desperation and misery, clinging to the bare syllables, as if to a flimsy lifeline in a blizzard of uncertainty.

PART III

NOOR

1

Folia was already seated on a cushion in Mentor Vane's sun-lit apartment when Maia stepped out of the elevator car.

'Oh no,' she said at once, taking a step back, 'I'm not—'

'Come in, Maia. This audience is for both of you,' said Vane, who was also seated on the floor. She held out a hand. 'Take this seat. You'll find it more comfortable to settle into.'

The pale-skinned woman came forward, walking carefully, supporting her belly with both hands. 'I have no need for special help,' she said, her voice stiff, though she accepted the suggested seat. It had been positioned under a pair of hanging supports that she could use to ease herself down.

'Very soon now?' asked Vane, nodding at Maia's rounded belly.

She and Maia were dressed in white garments. Vane's was flowing, while Maia's was a sleeveless silk tunic that ended just above her knees. She wore a bright red hibiscus in her hair and her forearms were clad from wrist to elbow in tinkling clear-glass bracelets.

Maia nodded. 'As you know, I can choose the day. I was thinking, perhaps, tomorrow? Or the day after?'

'Ah. I had not realized you were that close.'

'I was hoping to perform for the new Candidate.'

Folia breathed in deeply and swung her head in a slow circle, as if flexing her neck.

Maia ignored her. 'In fact, I was hoping to beg a concession from you, Vane. I wondered if it would be possible for me to arrange a private viewing for this new girl, without the others around.' Vane had begun to shake her head. 'Please! Hear me through: I believe, this girl, with all that is unique about her, needs to be helped towards her destiny—'

Vane cut in. 'Maia, you do not understand how far from acceptance this girl is of anything you might want to reveal to her.'

'But she is a blank slate! She can become anything we choose to make her!'

'All our girls are blank slates in that sense,' said Vane. 'Whatever they knew of their earlier lives, only the barest minimum remains. But Meiji's minimum includes a great burden of negativity. Towards her feminine self. Though I have promised her to you, I will be surprised if she accepts your direction gladly.'

Maia's upper lip was raised in scorn. 'Ohh! You are all wantonly ignorant, all of you – even you, Vane, I am sorry to say. Ignorant of the mystic powers that dwell within Womankind in her uncorrupted state!'

'Let it go, Maia,' said Vane, firmly. 'The reason I have asked Folia to join this discussion is that we need to anticipate how to manage the girl in case she does not, in fact, fall in with our plans.'

'What are you saying?' cried Maia. 'Surely you cannot go back on your promise!'

Vane leaned forward till she could cradle both feet in her hands. She spoke slowly and thoughtfully. 'This girl represents something so unlikely and so unique, that no one in our version of the world has the experience to understand what it is. She is, you could say, the first crack in twenty-two years to appear in the opaque shield that has obscured the region to which she belongs. In all this time we have had less than a trickle of information from that direction. There are many who say that our punishment was counter-productive. That by cutting them out of our reality, we gave them the license to become whatever they wished, with no oversight. Be that as it may. In twenty years, nothing of any significance has emerged from that pit. Now, with no warning, this: a girl.'

She turned towards her right. 'Folia, about the price we paid for her. You have a keenly political mind, so I am sorry you could not work it out for yourself. The simple fact of this girl's existence here, sprung from that hidden world, suggests that something has shifted and it *must be responded to*!'

She was breathing heavily.

She paused, with her eyes shut, to calm herself. She turned once more to Folia.

'So do you get it, Folia? At the auction, my fellow Senior Mentors, those who stayed to bid for her – we all understood this thing and responded to it in the best way we could – by showering money upon her, hoping to be the ones who might get the chance to throw our weight upon the die rolling unexpectedly in our direction. We did it because we believed it had to be done. One of us would get the prize. It turned out to be me. But it could have been any one of the others. We didn't have time to confer, we were using our intuition and we all had the same thought: this girl is a call to arms. We must respond.'

She turned now to Maia.

'As for you, Maia? I need you to understand that even though I have bankrupted our Island by acquiring this "pearl without price", it is NOT for the reasons you may have dreamed about. I don't want you to get your hopes up. Even if she survives the challenges we set her, there is a high likelihood that she will destroy herself before she will allow herself to be used or indeed be useful at all, in any social sense.'

Maia's forehead was creased in agitation. 'I thought you agreed with those of us who recognize her value not to discard her! Ah, how can you do that? Why, you might as well execute her right here, on the Island! It would be kinder, less cruel—' She was shifting off her seat as she spoke, reaching for the hanging supports.

'Oh, calm yourself, Maia. I am not discarding her,' said Vane. 'Not by any means. At the same time, I will not be soft on her. She will have to prove herself worthy of the resources we will spend on her.'

Maia had pulled herself upright. 'But she should not be risked *at all*!' she exclaimed. 'Why should she be tested, like all the other common scum? She will have no chance – I know it already – I can see it happening. First we acquire something of unimaginable value only to toss it out again, pretending to be careless millionaires who can have whatever we want for the asking!'

She waved her palms in the air, as if fending off any comments that Vane might make. 'No, no – leave me be. I will need to calm myself in preparation for the birthing. I believe, when she comes to it, she will surprise us all.'

Then she pulled herself up and onto her feet, turned and stalked away, moving at her characteristic slow pace.

Vane sighed.

Folia waited till Maia had exited completely before saying, 'Vane, let me be clear about what you're saying. You think the girl's a decoy?'

Vane grimaced slightly, but nodded.

'Really? You have proof?'

Vane said, 'Oh yes. She has a locator chip embedded within her. The kind that bounces a signal off a satellite and dies if she dies.' She glanced towards Folia. 'Someone is following that signal and will soon appear in our midst. That's why we've got to evacuate the Island. There are too many lives at risk if we allow ourselves to be boarded.'

'Can't the chip be switched off?' asked Folia.

'Yes, but we need to know who went to such lengths to plant this living beacon in our midst. And why. Folia, I need someone to keep an eye on the girl. I'd like that person to be you. She represents an investment that we can't afford to lose.' Then she smiled. 'And also: I just like her. There. My bias. I want the best for her, even though I have no idea what that might be.'

Folia cocked her head to one side. 'Why me?'

'Because you love and admire the force of nature,' said Vane. 'You, more than any of the others, will protect this tough little seedling sent our way on the back of a black wind. You will respect her just for herself. That, more than anything else, is what she so desperately needs, whether she knows it or not.'

2

The new Candidates' first Task Lesson was held below, at Level Seven, in a Training Dock. Eight other teams were also present, each with its own pair of trainers. Overhead lights and tall ceilings created a bright but shadow-laden atmosphere. The startled howls of the young women, combined with the booming commands of their trainers, echoed and ricocheted within the confined space.

Meiji began gagging just watching the other girls in her team training to use the Trak. 'It's like a face mask,' explained Trainer Engen, a heavy-set woman in a slick black skin-suit. 'Except, it's got the Trak poking up from its centre and it's filled with Ooze.' The Trak was a mucous-coated artificial trachea. Ooze was the name given to the gel that cushioned the user's face. 'Empty your lungs, open your mouth and just fall forward onto the Trak, as if you were going to swallow it whole. Don't fight it – it's semi-sentient – all you have to do is let it slide all the way in. It will do the rest.'

The other girls seemed to find nothing especially difficult about the task. This only made it worse for Meiji. She was the last to go up to the basin where the practice-mask had been set up and therefore had plenty of time to watch the others retch and struggle even before it was her turn to approach the raised platform on which each trainee lay prone. The fleshy gel was cleared out and refilled for each student rider. Even so, it gave off a powerful stench of putrefaction and looked like nothing more than a dish of clotted, blood-flecked phlegm. From the middle of this glutinous mass, the obscenely glistening nozzle of the Trak poked up like an enquiring snake, twitching slightly.

'Come on up,' said Trainer Engen to Meiji, holding out her hand. She was smiling in the tired way of someone who was looking forward to taking a break immediately after the session was over.

Meiji lay front-forward on the platform. The basin was directly before her, while the Trainer stood beside her. The Trak was made out of porcine cartilage and wired with neuro-electronic circuits which gave it a type of blind consciousness. Its task was to lock onto a user's trachea and remain bonded until released by the user peeling the gel-filled mask away from her face, unclipping her nose. If the Trak could not form an efficient bond, the user would suffocate and drown. But the muscular pipe had a lewd, uncanny presence and when the Trainer reached forward to wipe it down with a sterile swab it wriggled as if with pleasurable anticipation.

Then it coughed up a trickle of yellowish drool.

'Aaaaaargh!' Meiji flung her head sideways. 'I can't – I'm going to be sick!' she wailed. 'Auuughh!' She clamped her teeth tight, but the fountain of half-digested food from lunch surged up her throat and spewed from her mouth with explosive force. Straight onto the Trak.

Hoots and jeers rang out. Meiji was beyond caring. She tried to wriggle off the platform.

But Trainer Engen would have nothing of it.

'Come on, come on!' she insisted. With one hand she held Meiji in place, lying prone on the platform, while with the other hand she hosed down the Trak and the face-mask with warm, salty water. 'I'm sorry my dear, but you're going to complete your training if we have to spend the whole week at it.'

Then she played the stream of water on the girl's face, forcing her to open her mouth, before pushing her down onto the panting and quivering nozzle.

Four, five, six, ten times, Meiji had to submit to the assault before the trainer was convinced that the girl would be able to use the equipment correctly without drowning.

Finally, it was over. 'All right, take a break,' said the trainer. 'Meiji, double dose of the sterile soother for your throat. You won't be able to talk for half an hour, but it'll flatten the pain. Back here in fifteen. As soon as you're here, begin spreading yourselves with grease – it's in this vat, there's plenty for everyone – cover the front of your neck, entire torso, belly and down till just above the crotch. I'll bring your wets with me. We'll suit up and go to the next practice dock, where you'll meet the Harness Dummy.'

3

'It's nothing,' said the General. 'Your question is as meaningless as a dry raindrop.' He was standing up, his hands on his hips, wearing only a white linen shirt open to the wind. Aila was positioned in front of him, kneeling on a mattress with her rump raised up while he slid his engorged member at a leisurely, measured pace, in and out of her anus. He could keep this action up for half an hour or more. Occasionally he might steady himself with a hand on the small of her back. The sea was choppy and the deck swayed as if in response to his sawing motion.

Two drones stood by on either side, applying warmed almond oil as required.

Aila panted as she supported herself against the thrusting actions behind her. Sweat was pouring off her face and the rest of her body, streaming down towards her shoulders and down her arms. She wore a light cotton lace gown that was flipped up, with the hem over her head.

It was at the General's command that her head was covered. 'I have always found it tedious to think of my rut-partners as people,' he had said. 'You, for instance: when I can see your face I cannot help but be aware of your specific name and with your name goes your pathetic history, the fact that you chose to become a Vermin and all the rest of it. When you are reduced to an anonymous body I am spared the distraction of rational thought.'

He panted, softly, in time with his movements.

'Except for Yasmine,' he had resumed speaking in the pauses

between each stroke. 'Yasmine is special. It's because I know what he was before he changed his body. I know what it took to break him to my purpose. He suffers my attentions with an intensity and an intelligence that I find' – he broke off to grunt, to stand still and twitching, and to bring his breath under control before resuming his regular thrusting – 'that I find more intoxicating than anything else I have known.'

That was when Aila had asked, 'So – you love him?'

The question had fallen out of her mouth before she'd had time to consider it carefully. The General was not a man to lose an opportunity to punish her for lapses into what he termed 'verminous' impulses, behaviours that were weaknessess he associated with the Other Gender. The cramping in her thighs caused by her uncomfortable posture and the mental effort of resisting the clench-reflex of her sphincter had distracted her.

But he answered her calmly enough, with an amused snort. 'Love? Huh. You think we of the Brotherland have any use for something so bland and ridiculous?'

Aila asked now, emboldened, 'Still. You know the word? You know what it means to other people?'

'Yes,' said the General. His breath was starting to lose its rhythm. He ceased moving once more. In the silence of their joined bodies, she could feel his pulse in her anus. It was a profoundly intimate communication, as if their circulatory systems were a pair of solo drummers picking their way towards synchrony.

Aila clenched her teeth.

'Of course I know,' continued the General. 'I have heard it many times from others. Those who don't understand their own emptiness or what their so-called "need for love" reveals about their own emotional starvation! That's what it is, you see. Those who have no idea of a higher purpose are eaten away from within by ridiculous and degenerate yearnings. By contrast we who are born into the brotherhood, experience a sense of ultimate belonging from the first moment of awareness. We are born into absolute connection. We are continuously present for one another. We *are* one another.'

He began to jerk back and forth now, repeating himself. 'We *are* one another. We *are* one another—'

Aila felt her face melting with heat as he grunted and pounded in pursuit of his climax.

4

'My name is Vahabis,' said the short plump woman with dark brown hair braided and tied back behind her head. 'I am your trainer for the Whale Rider Challenge.'

All eight teams from the previous training were once more present. The new venue was nine storeys below the surface. The overhead lights were bright as day but the girls were shivering. Their breath was visible even though they were wearing shiny black wetsuits that covered them from neck to toe leaving the hands bare.

Each team occupied its own rectangular space, separated by low wooden ridges. In the centre of each space, a tall ridge of black rubber rose out of a shallow trough filled with water. Arcing over the black hump was a laddered semi-circular hoop. Alongside the trough were sections of what looked like a massive leather harness, with buckles and linking rings.

'This,' said Trainer Vahabis, patting the right side of the inert rubber hump, 'is your basic Whale Dummy. Now then, Candidates! Which of you is going to tell me what she knows about whales?' She scanned the six young faces in front of her with the practised eye of a professional teacher.

The girls had formed a curving line, facing her. Meiji was at the edge of the Trainer's vision. Whether by design or chance, the other girls had bunched themselves close together, leaving her separate, on their left. Her hand shot up at once. 'Whales are marine mammals,' she said. 'They live in the sea, but they breathe air. Just like us.' The words spewed from her mouth like marbles spilling from a burst paper bag. She couldn't help herself. 'There used to be several species. Most have been hunted to extinction. They're very large. The Blue Sperm Whale, for instance, is the largest animal that has ever lived on earth…'

She faltered to a stop.

The Trainer was staring at her. It was clear now that she had asked her question rhetorically, never expecting that her audience would attempt an answer. The other girls were silent too.

'S–sorry!' stammered Meiji. 'I thought you wanted us to answer.'

Trainer Vahabis clucked her tongue and said, 'No need to be sorry – and you're right, of course – that's just what I was going to say,' she smiled her encouragement at the girl, '… though it seems I don't have to any more, eh?'

'No!' snapped Rahm, leaning forward. 'We is *need* to hear what Trainer must say for our challenge. We is sorry we is interrupt, very sorry—'

Meiji bit her lips and looked at the floor.

Trainer Vahabis nodded at Rahm and continued with her instructions, her voice rising and falling in a rhythm that was clearly a habit with her. 'Like I said, this thing here is only a dummy. It represents the back of the whale's neck – but that's the only part of the whale you'll be in contact with. The neck. Now: can anyone tell me why we're only showing you the top of the spine and the neck? Not the whole body?' She paused a moment, before answering her own question, '—because of course it's a *very big body*!' She glanced over at the girl who had already revealed this fact, but Meiji was concentrating on the floor.

The training proceeded from then on without interruption. Trainer Vahabis demonstrated the two methods of mounting the whale and how to use the harness for guiding the animal. 'You'll all get a chance to train on the dummy,' she said, 'but before that we'll return to your morning's lesson, where you will learn how to breathe *using the whale's air supply...*'

The animals had been reverse-engineered, she explained, and fitted with the flexible semi-sentient Trak that the girls had learned to use earlier that day. 'It's connected to the whale's wind-pipe.' She gestured to her throat. A sturdy one-way valve would protect the girls against differences in pressure, 'but if the whale doesn't like you he can hold his breath. If he sneezes he can rupture your lungs!' She chuckled, as the girls gasped on cue. 'Okay, okay! No need to look so terrified! That's what this training is all about – teaching you how to use the equipment safely.'

Meiji listened with her head hanging low. The way the words had spurted from her mouth had taken her by surprise. They were a reminder of what lay hidden within her, the storehouse of knowledge as well as memories from her past. The idea that it was no longer available to her was intolerable. She couldn't settle into acceptance the way the other girls on her team had, yet there was no source of help or guidance. No one who would understand.

5

Youngest had spent the morning trying to follow the idea, if it could be called that, of watching the jellies. Trying to discern directionality in their drifting movements, trying to assess them for variations from the natural currents pulsing through the water.

Now, once more, he turned on the night-vision. The gently undulating jellies were as dense as ever. It was like being surrounded by living clouds of gelatin. It was late in the afternoon. He sank low in the water, hoping that the greater depth would create greater contrasts between light and dark, density and opacity.

It was only then, immersed within the swarm, that he realized what an excellent cloak the jellies provided for anything behind them.

For there, behind the curtains of their soft shifting bodies, loomed a monstrous structure that he might have never seen had he not plunged in amongst the jellyfish.

It was an artificial object, not a natural rock formation. Heavily textured even in the livid glow of the night vision filter, it had bulges and contours, protruding spurs, ripples and pleats besides being encrusted in a carapace of barnacles. It was impossible to gauge the scale of the thing, though it curved away from him in both directions, suggesting that it was cylindrical. No light escaped it and when he turned off the night-vision filter the sea was once more opaque. He may have been looking directly at it before, but would have failed to see it.

Youngest had to remind himself to breathe.

Perhaps the quality of the water supporting such a gigantic unnatural formation became oxygen-depleted or so polluted with cast-off surface chemicals that fish did not thrive near it. Certainly, the air he was breathing, which was microlysed out of the water around him, had deteriorated still further from the day before. He would have to hurry to avoid having to replenish his oxygen by surfacing.

Keeping his night-vision filter on, he moved cautiously around the structure. It was certainly not built for ingress. There was nothing to indicate openings of any kind. He could attempt to grope his way to the top and look for some form of entrance there. Going the other way, towards the ocean-floor, wasn't an option. The BoMa was not equipped for depths greater than fifteen metres.

He flippered around the immensity of the thing, trying to get a sense of it. *How was it anchored to the ocean's floor?* he wondered. *Are there underwater air-locks for divers to come and go unseen? Garbage chutes? Sewage pipes?*

He approached closer, to give himself an understanding of construction and design. The outer surface was far from smooth. Not only was it textured but there were seams and joints that revealed themselves to his gaze the nearer he came. The surface did not appear to be made of metal, because there was no trace whatsoever of bolts, clamps or jointing.

He was still puzzling over this issue when, from around the curving surface to his right, there came the sound of a muffled eructation. Simultaneously, he felt the water around him bump and warble. Then a great shimmering bubble of gas, at least the size of five adult elephants clumped together, burst from a hatch in the side of the structure. Trailing after it was an equally giant comma of fizzing bubbles. He didn't exactly see the hatch so much as guess at its position, because it had opened and closed with the winking speed of a camera's shutter.

Then with no warning, a second hatch opened right beside him and he was sucked into the body of the Island.

6

The afternoon had waned into evening and thence to night before the girls returned to their room. They were exhausted, silent within the cocoons of their private thoughts, their bodies thudding with heat and exertion.

Rahm showed them how to pull down their sleepers. The room had six long narrow bunks that folded out of the ceiling, shaped like the petals of a giant flower. They tilted towards the hexagonal table that defined the central point. Thin screens surrounded each petal, with an entrance at the lower end. Each unit was lined with a cool, spongy material that moulded itself to its user like a velvet cloud.

Meiji got hers down and clambered into it without joining the others at the table for the night's meal. No one stopped her or suggested that she needed to eat as much as they did. In the course of the long day, the separation between herself and the others had grown gradually more pronounced. Meiji believed that it was the fallout of her blurted confession at the table. About not thinking of herself as a woman.

If only she'd been able to hold her tongue! It was impractical to be an outcast within the close confines of team-life. During the training, she was always the last to be taken into a simulation or use of the model. Occasionally this resulted in her losing her turn altogether. If there was an instruction given to one member of the group which had to be communicated to the rest, then Meiji was left out. Twice this had resulted in her slipping off a model because she had not been correctly strapped in. The situation only improved when Trainer Vahabis began to entrust Rahm with instructions. The team leader made an effort to watch out for Meiji, to include her. But towards the end of the day, even she ran out of energy and Meiji was left to struggle on her own.

By night-time the pattern of excommunication was so clearly established that Meiji could not face sitting down at the table. She had saved a boiled turtle-egg from the late-afternoon break and she ate the egg unobserved, in her bunk. It did not quench her thirst but she didn't feel confident enough to go back down, to claim her space at the table and take a drink.

Inside the bunk it was cool and the lining material had a sleep-inducing quality. But Meiji lay in it with her mind and body on fire.

She had not even noticed how hot it was until she was within her private cell. It was as if the accumulated stresses of the day expressed themselves in a private monsoon of sweat combined with sharp spasms of trembling. The voices of her teammates were feathery whispers swirling outside the semi-opaque screen around the bunk as she gave free reign to her anguish. She gasped, sobbing and panting, within the privacy of her womb-like enclosure.

The day's experiences had been a continuous elaboration of the very first one: whenever their trainer had told them something that the other girls had not known, Meiji could sense the shadow-thoughts in her mind, twitching and reacting, reminding her that she was different, that she had a fund of knowledge these others did not, that she was deeper and richer than they. But these thoughts were not comforting because they could only remind her of the miscarriage of fate that had taken place without offering her any method of escape from it.

Her thoughts kept circling around that moment at the mid-morning meal when Rahm had referred to her as a woman.

Meiji tried to conjure up the feelings that erupted within her at the time. The word 'woman' had been the trigger, yes, but what mechanism was it connected to?

It was not an unfamiliar word, yet the associations she felt with it went well beyond any verbal definition. It meant something much more than a particular collection of body parts, distinct and separate from those that defined a man. It included social and psychological dimensions that were profoundly distressing to her. When she heard that word it was as if a very powerful force, acting invisibly, caused her thoughts to scatter like iron filings in the presence of a magnetic field. Why should that be so?

She understood, intellectually, that Rahm had been correct to refer to her as a woman. She had the breasts, the double-folded slit between her legs and the internal organs. Nevertheless, she did not consciously use that word to describe herself. The fact had to be dragged out into the open as a statement made by others, and her internal reaction was much sharper and more painful than she had revealed to them.

As for the curious item that dangled from her crotch? What could she say about it that would make sense to anyone? She used it in the way that she knew men used theirs. She knew with absolute certainty that there was a perfectly rational explanation for her unique appendage, but she couldn't say what it was. She couldn't provide any answers that could satisfy the curiosity or at least stop the flow of questions.

Lying up in her bunk, she could hear the other team members playing the memory game with Rahm. Each girl took a turn describing one item from her memories belonging to a time before she had arrived at the Island. Listening to them, Meiji told herself that she was at least the same as them in that she too could remember a happy childhood. She was astonished to realize how warm and pleasant those memories were. For several minutes she was lost in reverie. But when she returned to eavesdrop again, her heart began to thump once more in the awkward labouring manner as in the morning, when Rahm had said the word 'woman'.

There were several triggers this time around.

'Mother' was one. Also 'Parents'. And 'Father'.

It wasn't simply that she couldn't remember her parents but that she couldn't remember ever having had any. Instead, in the place where parents should have been, there were other figures: tall, swathed in robes, shadowy. Figures whose faces she could not see, yet beaming out such a powerful message of devotion that even now, confused and distanced from these extremely abstract impressions, the force of their profound and unquestioning love enveloped her in warmth.

She felt a cry developing in her throat.

Who? When? Where? Why?

Why was there so much she did not know?

Meiji's thoughts careened within her head.

She imagined herself diving into a swimming pool filled with clear acid. She imagined how it might feel to be stripped of the entire outer sheath of her skin, her body tracing a streak of bloody redness through the pool. All artifice, all disguises, burnt away entirely, transforming her into a clean, shining thing. Pure muscle, pure bone, pure intention. The pain would be glorious, a hard, bright shock that would knock all confusion out of her mind. That's what she needed. A jolt of such violence that distraction became impossible. The shifting madness and confusion within her mind would cease to exist. Be obliterated.

The lights in the room dimmed to darkness, as the stillness of shared sleep took over the room.

The questions remained in Meiji's head like a bed of stinging nettles but eventually she fell asleep over them, exhausted by the sheer volume of her frustration.

Some hours later, she woke with her stomach knotted with hunger.

She heard a sound.

There was a fingernail scraping against the underside of the bunk.

She raised her head, not sitting up. Just outside the screen she could see a denser darkness silhouetted against the surrounding gloom, a huge round halo of hair.

It could only be Rahm.

'I know you is awake,' whispered the team leader. 'Come. I is want to show you something. You will like.'

7

Unable to avoid hurtling down the slimy chute in pitch-darkness, Youngest concentrated on trying to avoid a bone-crushing impact upon landing. He couldn't curl himself up in a foetal position. The suit was too stiff for that. But it would also act as a buffer.

He could smell rotting fish guts, seaweed and the sweet-sickening stench of wet, clotted blood even through the BoMa face mask. If he didn't remove it very soon, he'd suffocate. He needed to be fully immersed in water in order to receive breathable air. He was moving fast, chaotically, now upside down, now sideways, around corners and tumbling through open junctions. He could do nothing to halt his descent and didn't want to risk damaging his hands by attempting to use them as brakes.

As abruptly as he'd been swallowed, he crashed into a flimsy barrier and landed with a jarring thump on a flat surface not low enough to be a floor. Blinded by the light because his night-vision visor was still on, he tore at the clasps on the mask that obscured his whole head, his fingers already growing numb as he sucked in on the now-empty reservoir of air. Dimly, as if at a great distance, he could hear high-pitched shrieks around him and gabbling voices calling out in alarm.

Then the mask was off and he flung it away from his face with a violent gesture, careless of who or what was watching him. His body arched up, as he gasped, choked, retched, his mouth opening and close spasmodically. His fingers wrenched the metal stays away from his suit so that his lungs could fill with air, while his naked body spilled out into the open like a basket of warm, brown fruit released from too-tight packaging on a hot day.

When he finally became aware of his surroundings, it was as if he'd had his eyes shut for the entire duration of his turmoil.

He'd been disgorged from the chute into a shallow trough raised up on a low platform. Alongside him in the tub were the flopping, wriggling bodies of other marine creatures. A ring of women wearing white tunics huddled a short distance away from him, staring in silence, a combination of fear and disbelief on their faces. His ruined suit, open to the waist, still enfolded his legs in a sheath of glittering metallic scales. He was forced to lean heavily to his left, like a beached mermaid too obese to find her way back to the sea. His own long black hair hung down over his face, framing his vision on either side.

A plaintive two-tone bleat suggested that an alarm had been set off. He felt an irrational urge to laugh at the sound, more a frantic sheep than an alarm!

A woman with an angular body and lined, leathery skin stepped forward from the huddled group. 'Who are you?' she demanded to know. 'What do you want?' She spoke Unida with softly rounded consonants. She had an air of authority and held a bamboo-handled gaffing hook in front of her in the manner of a shield.

Youngest pushed the hair out of his eyes, then covered his bare breasts with his forearm, in an attempt at modesty.

'My name is Yasmine,' he said, also speaking in Unida. He could, to some extent, modify the sound from his translator to achieve a more feminine register. 'Is … is this the Island?' He glanced down at his legs, still immobilized in the sheath of the suit. 'Please, I need help – I cannot move in this position.' A painful cramp developed in his hip right then and he winced in pain, automatically stretching his limbs.

The hard-faced woman yelled, 'Stop! You will be still!' as she swung the gaffing hook around with its business end towards him.

'I'm sorry,' said Youngest, 'I can't help it—'

The heavy tool swung towards him anyway. He ducked out of its reach, but allowed the rounded end of the curved steel hook to catch him in a glancing blow. He let himself fall over sideways to make it seem as if he'd been felled. He slid into the squishy mess of entrails at the bottom of the trough and rolled over onto his back as he straightened out his legs, pretending to have fainted.

8

Rahm showed Meiji how to operate the entrances and exits within the Island. 'Back of nails, four fingers. Like *this*,' whispered Rahm. She demonstrated, lightly scraping the sixth wall of the room. It was the one on which the virtual window appeared but was now blank. When she scraped it with the back of her fingertips, the flat, hard surface parted along invisible seams and drew back with a rustling creak.

'Is easy.'

She stepped through and Meiji followed.

The darkened corridor curved around to the right and left, following the contours of the room they had just left. Meiji had not attempted to understand by what mechanism anything on the Island worked. Indeed, she had not felt even the slightest curiosity about it.

The walls of the passage were illuminated in the same way as inside the room, with a faint luminescence. Rahm knew her way around and moved confidently. Meiji followed at a more cautious pace. She could hear the sounds of the corridor expanding ahead of her, knowing that eventually it would lead to a mobile compartment. This was how the team routinely entered and exited their living quarters: they walked along a corridor till it reached a little cubicle that moved around.

Her stomach clenched and unclenched with hunger.

Sounds filtered in from all sides: rumbles, thumps, clickings, rattlings, scrapings, snatches of conversations. A love-song in plaintive semi-tones. Always, behind everything, the soft, continuous *ratcheting-clicketing, ratcheting-clicketing*, of scores of smooth levers in motion.

Rahm strode without hesitation, first right, then left, where the corridor branched in two directions. Patches of light shone through the walls here and there, indicating rooms in which other Island inmates were talking, eating or working. The curving, non-linear structures made it hard to anticipate the dimensions of the place.

They arrived at a junction of three corridors at the centre of which was a vertical shaft. Rahm scratched on its side, opening a gap to reveal one of the moving compartments. The moment they were inside the tiny space, its entrance snicked shut and they were off, rattling upwards with a jerk.

The car was narrow and tall. Meiji was pressed up against Rahm, forced into contact by the bumping and swaying of the transport. She could smell the musky odour coming off the other girl's skin. She could see the intricacy of the rice-grain facial tattoo, picked out in white luminescent ink, against the team leader's skin. She felt acute discomfort, being so close to a virtual stranger.

A *female* stranger.

Here and now, up close to Rahm, it was hard to ignore the distaste she felt at the thought of touching the other girl's body. There was nothing neutral about the distaste. It arose out of the recognizable sameness, the fact that they had similar bumps and dips.

Her whole being throbbed with discomfort until, suddenly, a memory slipped through the iron curtain in her mind: the memory of a man's body. She remembered knowing the sensation of being pressed up next to a man, a particular man. She had felt him, the hardness of him, against her back.

Who?!

Then he was gone, as quickly as he had appeared. She made

a gulping sound inside her throat, stricken by the vividness of the memory.

Rahm turned at once, the huge mass of her hair brushing against Meiji's face. 'What?' she asked. 'You is say something?'

'N-no,' stammered Meiji, as she struggled to maintain the distance between them. 'It's just that I … had a … I mean, I remembered something.' Without really meaning to, she squirmed away from the other girl, tucking herself tight into the side of the elevator car.

She saw the silhouette of Rahm's face twitch. 'You is not worry. I is not touch you.'

'I'm not worried,' said Meiji.

Rahm laughed softly. '*Kheh*! Well, you is *should* be. Some feems is make force-touch. You is lucky I is not that feem.'

Meiji frowned, not sure how much she understood, but before she could ask, the elevator car had come to a halt and the entrance panel wrinkled aside once more.

Stepping out, she recognized the vestibule that preceded the stairwell up to the Welcome Field. There was a refreshment stand here. She remembered it from the time of the ritual.

'You is hungry, I am think,' said Rahm. She reached the narrow stand and its spout before Meiji. Pressing the base of the spout resulted in a precisely measured spurt of hot viscous liquid filling into the bowl positioned directly below.

Meiji's stomach growled with pleasure.

She accepted the bowl, lifting it to her face to breathe in the scent of seaweed and crab meat, before following the team leader up the stairs. The soup was hot but not scalding and she drank it gratefully even as she climbed the stairs. The combination of heat and flavour and nourishment percolated down her throat like a silken magic spell, smoothing out her anxieties and loneliness as it went.

She had finished the soup before she reached the roof of the

Island, climbing directly onto the grassy field where the Welcome Ritual had been held, and into the open night.

'See?' said Rahm, who was standing a few paces away. 'Is beautiful. You is like.'

The great dome of stars winked and blazed above the two of them, while the warm ocean air soughed through the grass at their feet.

Meiji's skin rippled with pleasure. Her mouth hung open: whatever she had experienced in that room with the virtual sky, it was nothing compared to this.

She didn't realize she was holding her breath until Rahm touched her shoulder.

'You is like?'

Meiji could not answer. Her spirit had vaulted up too high. She was weightless. Words were too heavy for her just now.

Rahm chuckled and turned, sprinting aimlessly away from the centre of the circular field.

Meiji felt giddy, her senses spinning with limitlessness. She put the bowl down and jogged a few steps, feeling hesitant and unsteady at first. Then she raised her knees, lifted her elbows up behind her and paced into a run. Her heart began to lift. Nothing could stop her. She felt the air against her face, the grass beneath her feet and the tiny pinpoints of light prickling down upon her from above. Bolts of energy came fizzing through her, dimpling her skin, striking sparks across her whole being.

She glanced around, not seeing Rahm anywhere. It did not matter. Nothing mattered. She was still a long distance from the edge. She wondered what it would be like to run all the way up to it. To run beyond it. To soar away into the night.

She could hear the sea in the distance.

She felt wild and free.

She ran until her throat hurt with panting, then circled back around to the bare patch in the grass which revealed the presence of the entrance hatch. Rahm was already lying down there, flat on her back.

Meiji joined her, lying a short distance away, resting in companionable silence until it was time to go back down into the Island.

9

An older woman had come down into the fresh-catch hold to inspect the day's unexpected haul.

She was tall and stately, her grey hair framing the smooth, sculptured planes of her face. The other women in the room clearly deferred to her, calling her by the title 'Mentor' rather than a name.

Youngest affected the disorientated movements of someone recovering from a blow to the head. He sat on a stool, leaning sideways against the trough into which he had fallen. He was completely naked except for the Locators embedded in his wrist and on his chest. He sat in the way of someone who found this condition intolerably humiliating. He had been hunched over with his arms crossed over his chest and his knees together, staring vacantly at the floor, when the woman came in. He glanced up to look at her.

She did not introduce herself or look directly at him. Instead, she moved around behind him, asking the woman with the gaffing hook to show where she'd struck the interloper.

Youngest sat still as the older woman probed his head, wincing on cue when she found the swelling. But her fingers moved with the assurance of an experienced medical practitioner. She must have realized right away that the damage was minor. His skin had not been broken. As soon as she'd seen that, she released his head and turned to the two deputies who had accompanied her in. She was already walking out as she gave them instructions.

It was these two women who escorted Youngest out. They

were young, dressed in simple tunics and long pajamas and wore their hair in low ponytails, with no adornments of any kind. Their expressions were completely neutral, as if they avoided any thoughts that were not strictly functional. Before they left the room, they covered his face with an opaque mask they had brought with them. He was led away without ceremony or anything beyond the bare minimum of words. He was helped to his feet, after which he was directed to move forward with only a touch here, a pat there.

The mask obscured his vision very effectively. However, he could tell from the feel of the surface underfoot that they had passed from the slick floor of the hold to perhaps a carpeted stretch. It was hard to tell precisely what it was. He assumed they were in a corridor. Even so ... a carpet? In an underwater facility?

A moment later, they were entering another smooth-floored area. The smoothness was not the result of tiles. He had noticed that in the previous room, too, while he waited with his eyes directed towards his feet. The floor was bone-grey in colour and smooth to the touch, with a slight texture. Like solidified cream. There were seams, but spread so far apart that he had to assume what lay between the undulating joints were not so much tiles as layers of moulded material set into place. But what material? And why were there no straight lines, only soft corners?

Then he felt hot water at his feet and a spasm of fear shivered through him before he relaxed: his two attendants were preparing to sluice him down. Inside his mask, he smiled. Was this, then, the ultimate sign that the domain he had entered was distinctly and specifically feminine? A famously opaque and secretive citadel where, nevertheless, even an intruder arriving with no warning and no credentials, is first treated to a hot shower?

Whatever the reason, he was profoundly grateful. The congealed juices and body parts of the macerated fish that had shared the stinking trough with him had remained on his skin in disgustingly sticky clots. Not for the first time, he found himself wondering whether the fastidiousness that had always been innate to him had become even more pronounced as a result of the womanly body he now possessed.

When he had been thoroughly hosed down, one of the attendants handed him a rough material with which to dry himself. Then he was handed a loose tunic. Cotton perhaps? Though it seemed a little stronger and more elastic than that. The garment had the general dimensions of a caftan but ended just below his knees. He couldn't see it, but guessed it was a soft, natural colour. Pale salmon. Muted beige. He smiled to himself.

They walked on now, passing quickly through a variety of different spaces. Youngest had only his feet, his ears and to a lesser extent his nose to help him make sense of his surroundings. Since leaving the sluice-stall, he had not encountered smooth floors again. The rough-textured rug, mat or carpet, whatever it was, persisted throughout, though there were subtle changes in the weave and density of the fibres beneath his feet.

Most intriguing were the sounds. He noticed a number of instances when a hand on his shoulder would indicate a halt, followed by an unfamiliar creaking swish before they moved forward again. Sometimes the sound was accompanied by a distinct change in the quality of air, texture, temperature and scent. He had enjoyed the strong citrus flavour in one place followed by the heady fragrance of hot syrup in the next, and the sound of bottles being stacked as they approached another area. There was a brief pause as they passed through each space, then behind them, once more, he would hear the regular clacking and dull clinks. There had been bakery, too, and a blast of heat as they passed an oven or maybe a steaming cauldron of soup.

But these sensations had occurred early in the transit through the Island. Following one of the creaking swishes, they had entered a confined space which required both his attendants to stand sideways, facing him and holding him by his arms before the small chamber they were in began to rise up a shaft. An elevator! But this one was unusual. It moved sideways too. And its motion was jerky, accompanied by a continuous shuffling and clicking sound. It rocked forward, rather than rolling smoothly. At nodal points it swayed, as the shuffling sound marginally increased, before resuming its headlong motion.

It had gone straight up, jerking between what may have been five separate floors before pausing, then shifting, then dashing sideways along what felt like a curving path. Then it paused again before shifting once more to a vertical shaft.

In this way, Youngest estimated, they may have travelled perhaps eight floors above his initial location and several hundred metres to the right before changing direction once more, moving forward and then to the left. Then a brief halt and the creaking swish that indicated a doorway. Then they were walking again, along a corridor. Now there were no smells and the air was cool. There seemed to be no people about any more. Even mechanical sounds were greatly reduced, but the creaking swish had become more noticeable and didn't seem to be accompanied by the sense of passing through an entrance.

Throughout the journey, neither of the attendants had spoken. But when they reached their destination, the one who had been walking in front of Youngest stopped and turned, putting both her hands on his arms. 'Here you must go in,' she said, as she swivelled him a half turn to his right before giving him a sharp shove forward so that he stumbled as he caught his balance.

He hadn't had enough warning to realize that they would not be accompanying him any further. 'No, wait—' he cried, swinging around at once. But it was too late. He heard the creaking swish even before he remembered that he was free to use his hands to whip the mask off his face.

All that remained of the entrance through which he had been pushed was a perfectly bland and featureless panel, stretched between two struts that curved up to meet the ceiling. Around him was a small, bare cell, lit by a single light dangling down from the ceiling on a jointed stalk.

10

When his eyes had adjusted to the dim lighting Youngest was surprised to realize that he was not alone. There was a young woman in the room. She was leaning against the wall beside the entrance at a very odd angle. It was only as he opened his mouth to greet her that Youngest noticed her closed eyes and the peaceful, regular breathing. She was apparently asleep. He couldn't understand what was keeping her from falling over.

She wore a different tunic to what the two assistants who had brought him to the room had worn. Hers was shorter and more sheer, ending at her hips. She appeared to be wearing nothing else.

Are the clothes a sign of rank, he wondered. A uniform?

This woman was youthful, in her twenties, perhaps. Her hair was pale brown with lighter streaks, drawn back in a ponytail secured at the nape of her neck. Her features achieved a middle-path of attractiveness not quite amounting to beauty: a small nose, a straight mouth, a moderate chin. She might have been manufactured in a doll-house. Her skin was lightly freckled, with beige rather than white as its foundation. Her hands were at her sides. She gave off a faint scent, not artificial.

Youngest found himself breathing harder than usual. He leaned away now, the corners of his mouth raised in an involuntarily salute. To himself. To her.

It's been a long time, he thought, *since he'd been alone in a room with a ...*

With a grown woman.

Why had he been assigned a room which already had a tenant? A woman at that?

It was only then that he checked his thoughts.

Ah. *He* was a woman too.

So it was not really so extraordinary that he should be partnered with another one.

Taking a deep breath, he looked away.

The room was an irregular shape. It had five sides, three of approximately the same width and height, while the other two were significantly longer and tapered towards one another, forming a shallow apex. The entrance was situated in the middle of the three shorter sides. The mysterious young woman was asleep to the right of the entrance.

The ceiling was uncomfortably low. Youngest could touch it without even trying. He assumed it had not been designed with his height in mind. There was no furniture whatsoever. The floor was covered with a dark brown rug. He guessed this was what his feet had registered along the way to the cell. It looked rather more like coarse fur than a rug, with no particular pattern or grain.

He looked around, wondering how to increase the available light in the room.

A single tendril, dark ivory in colour and as thick as his index finger, extended downward from the ceiling. Its tip was brightly illuminated, yet it gave off no heat. Youngest looked around. Yes. Discrete dimples in the ceiling suggested possible locations of further tendrils. When he reached up and tentatively pushed into one of these depressions, he was rewarded with a sensation of burgeoning growth pushing back against his questing fingertip. When he let go, a sepia-coloured polyp stretched downward at a languorous pace, changing colour until, having reached a foot in length and the same shade of ivory as the other tendril, its tip quickened and grew bright.

His forehead puckered with feverish curiosity in his desire to understand the principles governing this technology. But there was another and more urgent question pushing its way towards the forefront of his attention: Where was the toilet?

He had not voided his bowels since the morning.

He looked around, though he already knew there was no toilet in sight.

Immediately, the pressure to find an outlet intensified a thousand-fold.

He gave himself a half-amused, half-anxious shake.

There had to be a logical solution. *Everyone's got to use the toilet,* he thought to himself. *So either there's one for me to use in here or I'll need to go outside. If I needed to go outside, those escorts would've told me how to leave my room.*

Everything Youngest had seen of the Island so far suggested an ultra-fastidious mentality of the kind that would place bodily functions at the centre of all design considerations.

Then again: perhaps social habits had changed a very great deal in the world outside the closed culture that he had been living in for twenty-two years. Perhaps it was no longer considered disgusting to relieve oneself whenever and wherever the urge came on.

He bit his lips, frowning. Was it possible that the fur on the floor was absorbent? Was there any type of variation in the texture that suggested drainage? Was there a hidden drain?

He looked around again, trying to convince himself that it was possible for norms to change so much that using the floor could be achieved nonchalantly. He pawed idly at the coarse, stringy material with his bare feet. The fibres were not separate from the floor, he realized with surprise, having assumed it was a rug. Was it a type of ceramic with the fibre embedded in it? If so, he could not discern any seam-lines. Between the fibres, the material was not cold enough to be ceramic, nor was it slick or synthetic enough to be plastic.

He looked up and around: the entire project of his presence on this Island, and what he hoped to achieve while he was here, could ultimately depend upon understanding what type of material it was made of. Whether it could be cut or carved or burned. By what means entrances and exits were formed. By which type of power the countless devices he had already seen were powered.

Then a powerful spasm from within reminded him of his immediate priority.

He glanced over at the other occupant in the room. He could always wake her up, he assumed, and ask for her help. But to be reduced to this pathetic, childish condition, of having to ask for directions to the toilet from a complete stranger – and a young woman at that! – caused the inner lining of his stomach to bristle with thorns.

He wanted to laugh at himself. To cry. To groan.

This was ridiculous! He was literally squirming with discomfort yet he'd have to find his way back into his Yasmine identity before he would permit himself to wake the sleeper.

Realizing that the struggle was going to be resolved very soon with or without his conscious consent, he decided his best option was to squat down in the narrowest section of the tiny room. Two strides got him there. As he was pulling up the hem of his loose tunic, he touched the narrow strip that connected the two long walls, in order to steady himself before squatting.

That was all he had to do.

An elegantly shaped object swung out and down.

It was as broad as his forearm, twice as long and tapered from back to front. Its inner surface was flattened and the whole object curved gracefully upward and outward, like a giant talon protruding from the wall. A broad groove ran along the middle of it, leading back towards the interior. A hollow, booming sound that did not immediately make sense was newly audible.

In the recess created by the gadget's deployment, Youngest now saw a simple graphic that showed the fixture was made to be straddled in a standing position, facing towards the room rather than away from it.

Youngest backed himself into position, relief mixing with intense curiosity.

Immediately, the echoing sound was explained: it was caused by vacuum suction. The moment his bare skin made contact with the wedge-shaped seat, the spongy material that lined its interior adjusted to his shape, creating a snug, airtight fit.

He relaxed control then, over his suffering sphincter. The rush of pleasure he felt embarrassed him, it was so intense. His skin pimpled over with gooseflesh.

When he was done, he found he was held tight. Rather than panic, however, he waited. Sure enough, after ten seconds of inactivity, he felt the cavity underneath him fill with warm liquid. This was followed by a sensation that bordered on the surreal, of something scouring his anus. It felt literally as if some living thing were performing an extremely thorough cleansing of his nether regions. The experience was borderline unpleasant, though it did not actually hurt. This was followed by a second sluicing and then by a final blast of hot air which broke the vacuum seal and released him.

The moment he got up, the panel snapped back into position and vanished from sight.

He stood looking around at the barely perceptible dent which was all that remained of the astonishing device, feeling a combination of pleasure and amazement. He had never before encountered a piece of plumbing designed exclusively for a woman's body.

The novelty of it amused him.

He asked himself whether or not it would have worked

equally well for a man.

Then his smile faded as the thread of recorded sound that was always circulating in his skull swam back up to conscious awareness: *in-the-name-of-all-true-men.* Oh yes. There was still all of that to deal with. *do-your-duty.* Not that there was a choice. Yes. He would have to. He could not relax. Nothing had changed.

11

The undersea dock was as bright as daylight even though it was nine floors down. The cavernous space boomed and echoed with shrieking squeals, the sharp reports of water striking wood and stone, the hollered instructions of trainers as six teams were introduced to their mounts for the day.

No more models. Today, they would be straddling live mounts.

The whale-bays were organized in sets of six, a fan-shaped arrangement with a platform for the trainer at the narrow end of each fan. For as long as it took for riders to get settled on board their mounts, they could look around and see other members of their team in adjacent bays. Their trainers were behind them, raised up on the central platform, and each girl had, in addition, a mounting assistant, dressed in a full wetsuit, with her breathing mask lifted up on top of her head.

Meiji's nose and throat tingled with a phantom soreness that rose above the double dose of the antiseptic pain-killer she had swallowed on her way to the training today. There wasn't much to see of her mount. Just its back, as it wallowed in its trough, sloshing water onto the floor of the Island's undersea dock. More than three-quarters of its bulk was underwater. Even so, what was visible was three times longer than Meiji's height, with a dorsal fin that would have reached her chin if she were to stand right next to it. From where she stood, it looked like nothing so much as the topside of a submarine.

The creature had a killer-whale's distinctive black and white colouring but the elongated body and bumpy carbuncled skin of a humpback. It was a hybrid, created from three different species. Its exterior had been gene-sculpted to include a contoured prone-saddle on its back and the apparatus that enabled co-breathing: when the whale inhaled air, a portion of what it drew in was siphoned off into a specialized sac, connected to the Trak that stuck up out of the top end of the saddle. A sturdy harness made of bright orange shark-leather encircled the creature's lateral limbs, so that physical commands could be conveyed under water. Each rider also had a sonar device that she could operate by hand in order to convey communications in rudimentary whale-clicks.

All around the dock, participating teams were being introduced to their mounts. Prior to the session, they were given an orientation lecture by Mentor Brahi. She was the Island's marine mammal specialist. She was tall, with olive brown skin and tawny, luminous eyes. A mane of grey hair framed her face. She wore a sleeveless white garment that extended down to mid-calf.

'The reason we cannot provide trial sessions with these creatures is that each of them is unique,' she said. 'Much as we are. They are, as you already know, warm-blooded mammals. Some are docile, some are not. Some have powerful temperaments, others are dull or unresponsive. The ones we use are not in any sense wild. They've been bred by us and trained by us. But it's important to understand very clearly that they are *partners*. Not pets. Not slaves. We can hope that they will cooperate with us. We cannot force them to.' Whatever their particularities, the Mentor explained, it was entirely the rider's responsibility to direct the narrative of their cooperation.

Meiji gazed with dismay at the rubbery black form she could see in the water. She tried to imagine straddling the thing in the way they'd practised, and her imagination failed her. It was completely impossible. The notion of climbing on board a gigantic slab of black, living whale-flesh had seemed absurd enough the previous day while training with models. Today, confronted by the living animal it was beyond absurd. It was insane.

At that moment, the creature rolled on to its side and looked up at her with its giant right eye.

In a single piercing instant, the confusion of the past several days was swept aside. The excited howls and yelps of her teammates and of the other teams, the shouted instructions of the handful of training staff circulating amongst the teams and the loudspeaker announcements echoing through the dock faded to a background rumble.

It was exactly as if the creature had reached up out of the water and enfolded Meiji in its vast salt-scented embrace. Whatever she had known or read or recently been told about whales, nothing had prepared her for this: that an animal could, with one single glance from its enormous eye, drench her with the full twenty-ton force of its personality.

Then it shifted its bulk and the eye slipped from view once more.

A moment later, it gave its dorsal fin a shake that sent a wave of water sloshing over her feet.

A smile flooded Meiji's entire body. *It's saying hello!* she thought. She knelt on the damp planks that edged the trough, looking down at the enormous animal that was to be her companion. The great whale filled her attention from horizon to horizon.

'What is your name?' she whispered to the creature. They were trained to respond to their individual names. 'Who are you *really*?'

She wanted to leap into the water there and then, align herself along its back in the way they had been shown, sink her face into the Trak's face-mask and glide away.

Away, away, away.

Into the limitless deep.

Into infinity.

12

The General sat on the front deck, a tea-table spread with a tray, two cups, two plates and the crumbs of biscuits past. He was holding the end of a rope. Aila sat beside him on his right, facing the left side of the deck, over which the rope was looped, pulled tight by a weight at its other end.

It was early in the morning and the man with his polished bullet-blue skull was facing in the direction of the setting sun. 'So,' he said, his tone uncharacteristically mild, 'what do you think, Atilla?' He did not wait for an answer. 'Do you think he is dead? Or merely avoiding us?' He was referring to Youngest.

Aila was wearing a black lace caftan over a pink satin sheath that left her breasts exposed. She had french-braided her hair and wore drop-pearls in her ears. Her eyes were lowered. 'I … I … don't know,' she said in a nervous whisper.

'Of course you don't *know*,' said the General. 'Slit-wit. Cunt-brain. I asked you to tell me what you *thought*. Which is expecting too much, I know, given what I've just said about your mental abilities. But still. Give it a try. I'm bored. I'm tired. I am sick of this waiting. *SAY SOMETHING!*' His expression had not changed, but his voice briefly reached the pitch and volume of a pneumatic siren.

'Is not dead,' said Aila, slipping into pidgin. 'Is alive. But maybe … maybe …'

'Avoiding us then,' said the General. 'If you speak pidgin again, I will repeat the sea-water enema.'

'He is not avoiding us. He cannot signal, because he …' Aila's voice began to falter. Tears rolled down her cheeks.

There was a brief silence.

'The fact is, he cannot turn off his radio link,' said the General, 'not without an accomplice. Even if he were dead, that link would continue at least for a day or two. But the satellite connection has been switched off. Or muffled. That is what disturbs me. And his voice fades in and out, as it would if he were buried deep in a building. He might be held captive. Or he might be betraying us.'

Then the General smiled, stretching the lipless slit that was his mouth to right and left in a straight line.

'Not that he will succeed. I planned ahead, of course. For this eventuality. The fact is, Alladin, everyone betrays us in the end. You will, too – that is, you will try. But you won't succeed. Because you can't succeed. Because no one can succeed against us.' He stood up. 'The line is twitching. Shall we see what we have caught?'

In two strides he was at the rail, looking over it. 'Ah! Outstanding! Come – come quickly – oh *such* a sight –'

Aila remained where she was. She didn't want to see what he would show her.

'You will come *now*,' said the General.

She rose and followed the rope to where the man stood leaning over the rail, his face lit up with excitement. She heard the sound of violent splashing and slapping, and the thuds of the boat's hull being struck. And a panting, voiceless snuffling. She had never heard a more brutal and pathetic sound in her life before. She, who had heard so much.

One of the drones had been lowered over the side of the boat, in a harness. Gashes had been cut into its sides in order to attract sharks.

The General was grunting with pleasure. 'Ah!' he said. 'Ah! That is magnificent. Two glorious brutes! Twenty foot apiece. A sublime vision! Both extremes of the struggle for existence – the eaters and the eaten. Are you looking? I insist that you look – come on, come on! Or I'll throw you in next.'

Aila stood with her hands clutching the rail, eyes shut. That would never be enough for the General, however. A moment later she felt the man's strong hands at her neck and shoulders, forcing her to bend over the rail, to look straight down.

He couldn't make her open her eyes, however, and she struggled, mutely, in his grip. She knew it was futile. He would gouge out her eyes before he would permit her to resist him. So she looked.

There in the water was thc round white button of the drone's face. Around that focal point, were the pale, lunging shapes of two great fish as they struck repeatedly at their meal, their eyes bulging yet deadpan, the great jaws extending obscenely out from under their snouts. The water frothed white and pink.

The drone's mouth was parted in agony, but it could produce no scream. Its eyes were open. Open and fixed on her. In that moment of ultimate self-awareness, on the threshold of death, its gaze was no longer dull. It knew the sweetness of existence and the horror of its approaching loss.

Aila felt her heart split open with pain. At that moment she remembered what Yasmine had said to her. About regretting her decision to follow him.

She stopped struggling against the General's hands, and went limp. The immediate result was the hard pressure of the iron rail, pushing against her ribs. Then she straightened up, by pushing back with her arms. She surprised the man as she snapped herself out of his grip. She swung away, heading for the lower deck. She did not run, but was at the hatch in two strides.

As she plunged downwards, she saw the remaining drones. Five of them were standing in their customary positions, their backs against the wheelhouse, their bodies turned in the direction of the General. But their faces followed her as she descended. Stony-eyed.

13

Youngest dreamt that he was lying under a softly humming generator before opening his eyes to realize it was the girl. She had fallen asleep leaning on him.

He had no idea how long he'd been unconscious. He was desperate to start looking around. He needed to understand the mechanics of the place before he could even begin to think of strategies for unfolding the complicated plan that he had set in motion so many months ago. But there was no way he could stir from his vertical sleeping pad without waking up his unexpected companion. The moment she was awake, he guessed, she would start talking.

He shifted his eyes around, careful not to move his head. The tendrils with lighted tips had retracted into the ceiling but he realized there must be some other source of illumination because the room wasn't in total darkness. There was still nothing in the way of an entrance. He looked at the head of the sleeping girl whose name he did not yet know, trying to understand what exactly she was. A security guard in the form of a seductress? Or really just an assistant?

After all, it was extremely clear that the Islanders did not expect intruders. The women in the Fresh Catch hold could not have been more flabbergasted than if they'd caught a two-headed mermaid. Being hard to find and impossible to break into was clearly part of the Island's core definition.

If that's the case, thought Youngest, *it means I'm being treated as a guest until someone higher up the command can decide what to do with me.*

Maybe the girl's presence wasn't intended to stop him from exploring. Maybe it was just routine for an attractive young woman to offer pleasure to a woman guest in this all-female establishment. Maybe that was how hospitality was being defined these days, a sharing of familiar pleasures – in the same way that, in the past to which he belonged, people had offered a cup of tea or a meal.

What do I know of the world as it now is, he asked himself. Almost nothing. For twenty-two years, he'd had no contact with the world outside his birth-culture. The changes he knew about were cataclysmic. The pandemic cement-rot disease. The collapse of urbanism that followed it. The annihilation of the oil-fields. The disintegration of the oil oligarchies. The partition of the planet. But of the social equations that must have formed in the wake of these grand general themes he had caught only the merest fragments.

He glanced again at the sleeping girl. He could see only the back of her head. *I can do this*, he thought, quelling the wriggling worm of doubt in his mind. *I can allow myself to be seduced by her.* It was more than doubt. There was fear there, too.

He brought his left hand up and lightly stroked the girl's head. His right arm went around her back. She stirred sleepily. He leaned forward now, bending his neck, nuzzling the soft tickling abundance of her hair, reaching to release the catch that held her ponytail together. He found her ear just as the tie came loose. He pushed himself away from the niche of the bed behind him, his feet seeking the floor. She began to straighten up as she caught her balance. Then he bent over, gathering her weight in his arms, and nipped her ear.

'Aaah!' she said, springing to full consciousness. Her arms had been folded in front of her, between the two of them, and now they wriggled loose and encircled him with crushing vigour.

'Ohh good! You are awake!'

Her face whipped around to meet his and her mouth sought his. For a single, electric moment, Youngest felt flashes of lighting around the two of them, as she parted her lips.

Then the moment ended.

Her tongue entered his mouth, frantic with energy, darting, stabbing, probing. His own tongue tried in vain to parry her thrusts. Their teeth jarred against one another, bringing to mind unhappy associations with fencing. Simultaneously, her hands reached for his body, squeezing him in places which meant nothing or very little to him: his full firm breasts, his unresponsive nipples. He could feel sensation in these areas, but no pleasure. He knew where the girl was touching him, but had no greater response to it than he would if she had been massaging his forearm.

'Come on!' she panted, releasing his mouth to speak before plunging back in again. She grabbed his hands. 'Me, too!' she said, as she placed them on her own breasts. 'H-uhh!' She moaned, sounding disturbingly like a bicycle pump. 'Hha-*AH*! Hha-*AH!*'

Then she pulled away and half-fell towards the floor, drawing him down on her. It was all he could do avoid crushing her with his weight. She flung off her short tunic and pushed him over, making little whinnying shrieks as she peeled away his loose, shapeless shift.

She descended upon him with her mouth open and her legs parted, demanding the same of him. He tried to keep up, but she was always ahead of him, her tongue voracious, her fingers insatiable, her thighs muscular. She knew what she wanted and she got it from his hands, his knees, his nose, his mouth, each time breaking off to lean back and whoop. Her whole body quaked as each crisis took her. Then she would be still for a few minutes before starting up again.

Youngest did not attempt to protest or to explain his situation. He did what he could to cooperate, though for the most part he felt like a blind spectator at a fireworks display. He could feel the excitement of the crowds around him without being able to participate. He was becoming sore from her attentions before he understood that the only way to ring down the curtain was to pretend that he was satisfied.

So with her fingers digging into his anus, her tongue deep in his ersatz vagina, he began to yodel and honk in an imitation of what he'd heard several times in the past hour from her. His vocal cords could only manage a mournful contralto bleat, like a love-lorn steam locomotive from days gone by.

He wanted to laugh but was too out of breath.

When it was finally over they lay entwined, exhausted, their bodies moist in the companionable twilight of the room, the rough fur of the floor beneath them.

In the silence, Youngest allowed himself a wry smile. Whining complaints were trickling in from various sites around his body: *we're tired!* said his hands, *we're bruised!* said his mouth. Points further south were even more vociferous. *But it was fun too*, he protested in response, *in its own weird way. We didn't mind. Not really. In a short while, we'll get up, have a shower and then …*

Then his scalp rippled with gooseflesh and the smile froze on his face.

Inside his head, he heard a familiar voice, not his own.

'Very interesting,' said General. The radio reception was scratchy. 'Was that what I think it was? No need to answer, since you're certainly not alone. Who was your companion, I wonder? That was quite a virtuoso display you put on, I must say. I should like to hear it in person some day. Soon, I hope.'

Youngest's mouth went dry.

'No doubt,' continued the voice, 'you've missed hearing my voice in your ears. Maybe you realized that the radio signal isn't steady?

Or maybe you just thought that the yacht is out of range. But we're not. I assume the structure you are in is at fault. It blocks the signal intermittently. Anyway. I hope you didn't think I had forgotten you. Quite the contrary. I think of you all the time. And of everything that remains to be done. Tick-tock, my pretty. Tick-tock. Here's a little keepsake now.'

A bolt of pain screamed out across Youngest's skull. It ended in a second, yet his body arced up and he gave a short anguished yelp.

'What's the matter!' cried the girl, jerking awake.

'Nothing,' mumbled Youngest, his lips numb and twitching. He pressed her head back onto his shoulder, so that she wouldn't see the involuntary tears streaming from his eyes.

In his ears he heard the General's soft chuckle. 'That was delicious, my darling,' he said. 'I miss you so.'

14

The Trainer, whose name was Tamar, knelt beside Meiji. 'His name is Noor,' she said. 'He is four years old.'

Meiji glanced around. 'He *looked* at me,' she whispered.

Tamar smiled. Responses to the whales came in only two speeds: abject terror or total adoration. 'Yes, he's a friendly boy. Are you ready to begin?'

She helped Meiji into the wetsuit made from rubberized seal-skin which covered the wearer from head to foot leaving the front bare. 'Now grab hold of the hoop – and align yourself by his blow-hole – '

Meiji knew exactly what to do. Holding on to the tall iron hoops set into the sides of the trough in which the whale lay, she leaned out and over its knobbled form. She held her hand directly over the flap beneath which was a v-shaped depression with two huge nostrils, each one larger than her hand, etched deep into the onyx flesh. She said his name, as she did this. 'Noor,' she said, 'Noor … Noor … Noor …'

She saw the puckered edge of the flap lift up, like a door opening into another world, and a fierce jet of blood-warmed air struck her hand. *Breathing out*, she thought. Then she heard a sibilant rustle as he inspired and she saw the nostrils dilate, just like a person purposefully inhaling a fragrance. In the next instant, the huge body arched and bounced in the water, causing a minor tsunami to leap up and out of the trough, entirely drenching Meiji in warm, salty water. She gasped, coughing and spluttering, but even as she did so, she looked down – and there was that immense eye staring up at her again, eyelids parted wide, as if in amazement. The dark pupil had swivelled around to where she stood, still leaning out towards the blow-hole.

'Ahhh!' laughed Tamar, as she sprang back. 'That's his sign that he's caught your scent. I think he likes you!'

Meiji was overcome, speechless and trembling.

The water had half-drowned her but it felt like a blessing straight from the soul of the creature, as if he had licked her, covering her with his body heat. She was burning and shivering, both at once. She turned to Tamar, wordlessly, her face so naked with emotion she wondered if her thoughts were seeping out of her brain, directly into the air around her head.

'I'm ready,' she said, her voice husky. 'I know what to do, I know how to do it. All I'd like is for you to centre him for me.' In order to enable a rider to position herself on the whale, an assistant had to prevent the whale from rolling and accidentally crushing the girl against the sides of the trough. The whales were trained to clamp down on a rubber ring which the assistant held out for them at the centre of the front end of their bays.

Tamar shook her head. 'No, no, not yet. You've got to confer with your team before you mount,' she said. 'You won't be able to communicate with them once you're on the whale so each team has to work out a—'

Meiji turned at once and began climbing down into the water using the short metal ladder that hung by the side of the trough. 'I'm sorry,' she said, 'I just want to get on.' She was perfectly aware that Rahm and the others were paying her no heed. She too had not bent a thought in their direction from the moment she had made her connection with Noor.

'Wait!' wailed Tamar, but her voice was easily drowned out by the clamour all around them. 'Wait – I have to hold his head!'

15

The girl had introduced herself as Anita but went on to explain that it was a type of designation. When Youngest asked for explanations she looked pained and shook her head.

'Do you mean you're not allowed?'

'No,' said Anita. Then she shrugged and said, 'I cannot explain. These are ordinary things. Everyone knows them.'

She showed him how to find the shower, where fresh clothes were stored and how to summon food by tapping open a niche in the wall on her side of the room. Anything beyond simple physical necessities, however, were outside her domain. Either she didn't know or she wasn't allowed to tell.

'Let us talk about other things,' she said, sitting down cross-legged on the floor. She was wearing a tunic over shorts now, in two shades of natural pink cotton.

Youngest was restless and tense. He could no longer hear the General. He folded himself down, forcing himself to relax as he sat on the floor, facing Anita. 'Look,' he said out loud, 'if you can't answer questions then what's there to talk about?'

Anita opened her eyes wide, looking up at him. 'Ohh! *So* much! You can tell me all about your life – where you came from – what you do – where your family is.' Her voice dropped to a conspiratorial whisper. 'You can tell me your secret dreams. I can tell you mine.'

'Suppose I don't have dreams?' asked Youngest. 'Suppose I'm here by mistake?'

Anita smiled pityingly. 'Everyone has dreams! And there are

no mistakes. Whatever happens in the world, there's a reason for it.'

'Really? You believe that?'

'Of course. It's part of a philosophy called Self-Determinism. It was very popular in the Time Before. Have you never heard of it?'

'Anita, let's talk about philosophy tomorrow. Today, I really want to understand more about this place we are in.'

'Then let's talk about romance. I think you do not know very much about love, Yasmine. That is the feeling I get. You are not very good at sex. If you don't mind my saying this? I mean, it took a very long time for you to reach climax. That is not good for you. It is not good for the community. You must really consider taking lessons.'

Youngest stared at the woman before him, wondering how to characterize her behaviour. It was as if she were missing whole chunks of what might be called a personality. Yet she seemed to be perfectly content with who and what she was.

'When you say "community", what do you mean, Anita? I don't think I understand.'

The girl gave Youngest a considering look. 'I meant this Island community.'

'In what way does it affect the community if I … ' Youngest shrugged, finding it hard to concentrate on a conversation which did not, in his opinion, deserve serious attention. 'I don't know. Surely it's my personal business, whether or not I'm a good lover? Isn't it just between me and whoever I am intimate with?'

Anita gasped. 'Hah! No wonder you're so clumsy at sex! You think it's not important! Is it because you're from the Time Before?'

Youngest felt his consciousness being stretched thin between what he wanted to think about and what was being said in the room. 'Anita, believe me, these things really don't matter that much. It's got nothing to do with which era I belong to ...'

Anita's face was awash with derision. 'You don't know what you're talking about, Yasmine! You're so old-fashioned that you don't even know you're old-fashioned!' Colour had risen in her cheeks. She seemed genuinely aroused for once. 'Meeting you has given me a chance to understand what it was really like in the past – why it was possible for women to remain backward and ignorant for so long – because even when you're shown the truth, you don't accept it!'

Youngest was leaning back, with his hands locked around his knees. He shut his eyes and dropped his head back, as if taking a moment to think through his response. Then he opened his eyes again, his forehead creased in a puzzled frown. He was looking up at the ceiling. The lighted tendril: something about it had caught his attention.

'What is the matter?' asked Anita. 'You are not behaving normal.'

Youngest got to his feet. There were three tendrils extended and brightly lit, directly above the two occupants of the room. 'This light fixture,' said Youngest, reaching up towards the one closest to him. He examined it carefully, the tip level with his eyes. He turned it this way and that. It was flexible but he could feel resistance when he tried to force it into a tight loop. 'Is it possible that it ... ?'

He looked at Anita. She returned his gaze, her face devoid of expression.

'I think I saw it move,' he said. 'It's not just a light, is it? It's also a camera recorder?'

It must be powered remotely: he could feel it twitching, as if trying to pull away from his hand. Whoever was operating the gadget did not like it being manhandled.

He stood there, looking down at Anita from his height, continuing to bend the tendril back and forth in his hand. Anita no longer returned his gaze. 'You can tell me. Or I can pull this thing out. It's your choice.'

At that, the girl turned towards the panel between the room's two shorter sides and touched it with one of her hands. A moment later, the seemingly rigid partition melted away to either side with a soft creaking sound. The movement was like the nictitating membrane on a bird's eye, too quick to follow. One moment there was a flat opaque surface and the next an aperture had yawned open, revealing a passage beyond it, curving to the left.

Anita looked up at him. 'You must leave now,' she said. 'Mentor Vane will see you.'

'What—' began Youngest.

'I can't explain anything more. That's what I was told to say if you … if you … behaved unreasonably. The corridors will take you to her,' said Anita. 'Go quickly. The entrance does not stay open for long.'

He stepped through the opening. The corridor curved around on either side. He turned towards the left.

16

Meiji had only a few seconds at her command. The whale couldn't see her once she was astride his massive neck, but he would feel her movements in the water and was trained to respond when his harness was manipulated. Like any young animal, he would startle or buck until he had adjusted to her presence and he could pulverize her merely by turning his head in her direction, if she was in the water of his trough. But in a single fluid movement, she had caught the arm-strap that was floating free and pushed herself away from the ladder with her feet.

Down she slid, holding her breath in water that was soupy with the heat pouring off from the whale's body. But her feet struck sideways and down, seeking the great trailing flipper she knew she would find there, and with her arms she kept herself upright by hauling on the harness. Even as her feet touched the upper edge of his pectoral fin, Noor obliged her by raising it. In the next moment, she was being lifted smoothly out of the water, her feet supported, while with both hands she held on to the harness. She was perfectly positioned now to find foot-holds in the deep creases along the whale's back and sides. One – two – three – and she had crested the proud neck of the leviathan.

Her heart was pounding with the exertion, but she felt light as a feather riding a current of bright air up into a limitless sky. Nothing and no one existed for her now but the great heaving creature beneath her, upon whose tall back she sat as comfortably as if it had been a saddle made of clouds. Directly in front of her was the white four-point star that the whales had been genetically modified to possess on their upper surfaces, precisely so that a rider could lie prone upon it, skin to skin. There, at the apex of the star was the oval indentation of the Trak apparatus.

Meiji slid forward on her belly with both arms spread wide, her hands pulling on the double reins of the harness. At a great distance, she could hear high squeaking sounds, like a chorus of mice: Tamar and perhaps Rahm, too.

She was well past caring.

No doubt there would be consequences, but she had no attention to spare on anxieties. The previous day's training had done its job only too well and, now, as she slipped her feet into the looped stirrups of the harness and pulled on the reins on either side of the whale's head, it was with the assurance of someone performing in her sleep. She slipped into position and then, without a second's hesitation, she engulfed the quivering noodle of the Trak in her mouth, plunging her face in the connective jelly as she did so.

Immediately, a vast thudding darkness received her.

She had entered an enormous sensory cave, where taste, touch and sound merged so completely that she barely noticed that sight, the one sense she was utterly dependent upon as an air-breather, was now entirely missing. Smell was lost to her as well, since the trachea-tube bypassed her nose, but ghost sensations washed back to her via her throat and tongue.

The Trak was equipped to provide her with a filtered ration of air from the whale's own stock, while protecting her against the pressure difference which would otherwise rupture her lungs. She could breathe at her own pace, but the air entering her body had been inhaled by Noor, warmed by him, vibrating subtly with the thundering beat of his giant heart.

She would not be able to say, later, whether she actually

gave him any commands or whether his own impatience and exuberance compelled him to surge forward, pushing against the flimsy barrier that had so far kept him contained within his bay.

She may have pulled up her legs, yes, and dug down with her knees, yes, and she had known or should have, anyway, that these were commands to go forward, to charge ahead, to be reckless. But from her perspective the act of swallowing the mouth-mask had caused her to merge her mind and body with the creature. She became, for all practical purposes, a semi-conscious polyp of flesh and blood, attached to a titanic force over which she had not a single ounce of control. With a booming sound that she felt rather than heard, Noor broke through the barrier, swung down into the channel that led beneath the undersea dock and *out*. Out from under the Island's confines and into the open ocean.

Time was suspended for Meiji as she and the great whale exploded through the water like a gigantic missile of muscle and bone. She could no longer feel the water around her, but there were moments when Noor grazed the surface so that she could feel a thrumming sensation against her back before he dove again, deep enough that she could feel the screaming chill of water pressure. He wove, rolled, bounced and corkscrewed through the water.

And as he went, she could feel his voice, a rumbling tumult of sound that pulsed through her body rather than through her ears, in whooping, fluting groans and sharp staccato squawks that numbed and dazzled her. His voice became her voice. She could no more tell the difference between what came from him and from within herself. Though she could not understand a syllable of the language he spoke, it became hers for the period they were together. So she howled and roared and rumbled with him, merging with him, gamboling through the ocean like a beam of pure energy, losing all boundaries.

Noor was trained to follow a certain path, looping around a submerged spur of rock, some three kilometres from the Island in the direction of the rising sun, before turning back. Whether he did or not, Meiji did not know. She had no idea where he went, or how far or how wide he had strayed from the beaten track. All she knew was that after a time of boundless momentum he came to a halt.

The change was abrupt.

The first indication came when, with a sudden hiccupping yelp, he ceased vocalizing altogether. The silence was deafening. Even as she struggled to adjust to it, his forward movement ceased. He did not merely stop; it was as if he had slammed into a physical wall, though without any actual physical effects. The silence then became a vacuum that sucked other sounds towards it. Powerful forces were moving through the water, expressing themselves as harsh changes in pressure.

She realized, though with delayed awareness, that she could hear the voices of other whales. Other whales in the water. If she had been asked, she could not have said how she was so certain that these approaching animals were whales. All she knew, from the faint bellows and clicks she could feel and hear, was that they were coming. They were moving very fast, closing in with frightening speed.

Meiji felt the trembling terror that overtook Noor, the thudding of his heart speeding up, the tremors that ran up and down his spine. She was helpless. She had no idea where she was or how she could find out. As her mind gradually returned to its normal position within her own head, she began to wonder how she would release herself from the situation she had got herself into.

Noor did not attempt to evade his fate.

The first blow came from the right, a brutal ramming bump, matched immediately by a blow from the left, so that it was unclear whether the second was the result of the first or an action in its own right. Then a thump from underneath. He was being corralled between the bodies of other whales. The last sound Meiji heard directly from him was a piteous wail that travelled all the way to his tail flukes, like a shiver, until it faded out. Then he went silent again but in a more profound manner. Previously, it was only his voice that had quietened but now it was all of his body's responses. Even his heart appeared to have slowed down.

The other whales remained close around him, shoving and jostling, as they turned him around to escort him back towards the Island. When he dove down to access the gate to the undersea dock, Meiji felt the water pressure first increase and then subside as he rose once more, this time to nose himself into position inside one of the bays.

Then she felt the dry air above her back, and beneath her only stillness.

17

Youngest ran forward, taking note of his surroundings as he went. He could hear all manner of creaks, whistles, distant poundings and thumpings, the smooth trickling of water and the violent hiss of steam, muffled conversations. But there was very little to see. The floors, walls and ceiling of the corridor he was in were unornamented.

The lighting was set at twilight, as in his cell when the tendrils were switched off. No window panels. There were occasional nodes, marked by round-cornered frames, like man-sized portholes, beyond which the passage would turn in one or the other direction.

He could hear voices directly around him, on the other side of the passage walls. The one sound he heard above all others was the continuous clicking he'd heard when he'd been brought up from the hold. What kind of mechanism would produce such an effect? Not gears, not springs. More like pairs of scissors operating at great speed.

A node appeared, beyond which was a narrow cabinet. Youngest stepped in, immediately wondering how he would decide where to go. But as soon as he was in, the entrance closed and it moved off. His head grazed the ceiling of the little booth and he noticed the dark dimples that marked the presence of the tendril-bulbs. Or cameras? Even as he reached to push one in, the travelling chamber stopped and its aperture sprang open.

A corridor stretched away, curving to the left.

Youngest hurried through even as the thought crossed his

mind that it seemed very like the corridor he had been in previously. But how could it be? The chamber had certainly moved some distance, going sideways. Glancing over his shoulder he saw that the entrance had already shuttered itself up.

On he went, his footsteps less certain now. Once more, the same routine: lengths of corridor, all vaguely familiar, ending in a small cabinet. Was it the same one?

Youngest stepped inside, and this time, he reached immediately to switch on one of the tendrils. The entrance aperture blinked shut and with no warning the booth whooshed downwards, jerking between floors as it had when he was being escorted blindfolded.

Had he misunderstood the instructions? Anita had told him to follow the corridors. Well, he'd done that. Of course, it was possible that Vane, who had summoned him, was buried deep in some underground vault! But he was finding this hard to believe. The bright-tipped tendril hanging down beside his face was turned towards him. Was it recording his reactions, noting his heavy breathing, his mystified expression?

He reached for it, wondering if dismantling the fixture would help him understand the mechanics of the structure he was in. But he must have gripped the tendril too hard. Barely had he caught it than the light switched off and the flexible tube shot back into its housing in the ceiling. However much he dug and prodded at it and its fellow dimples, they remained stubbornly unresponsive.

The booth had, in the meanwhile, halted perhaps six floors down and was standing still with its aperture open. Youngest paused on the threshold, looking around. He felt along the edges of the aperture on which he stood, trying to pry around the margins, searching for some sign of yielding, some indication of what type of material was used to make the rigid panel that appeared. The only information his fingers brought him was that there were fine pleats folded into the seam of the aperture and that they were slightly tacky. He walked backwards as he stepped through, determined to catch a glimpse of the closure as it happened. The aperture, however, remained open.

He stood there for long minutes, refusing to believe that a mechanical hatch could successfully thwart his curiosity until he began to feel it was even more ridiculous to play this game of catch-me-if-you-can. The moment he turned his back, the aperture snapped shut.

It was hard not to feel he was being toyed with.

Once more, a corridor stretched away before him. This time he was sure it was a different one. It had a distinct smell, salty and damp. The floor was different too: the rug had a chequerboard pattern woven into it. And the walls had a texture stamped into them. The lighting was too dim to see what it was.

The fourth travelling booth was of a different shape from the one he'd been in the first time and, yet, when he pushed on the tendril lights they refused to descend. It was as if one booth had remembered what he'd done the last time he was inside it, and told all the other booths. In the next booth he entered, he didn't try the lights. Yet, just as he exited the little chamber, two of the lights descended simultaneously, of their own accord. As if to mock him.

He exited without trying to reach for them.

As he walked along the corridor he was currently on, he considered his options. He could lose his temper and flail at the walls, pounding on the ceiling with his fists. Or he could lie on the floor, waiting for however long it took for someone to find him. Either way, he guessed, he would not be satisfied with the response. That was not the way here. There was a very particular intelligence at work and it was waiting for the single appropriate response that would result in his moving on to the next stage.

He continued moving through the corridors. According to his reasoning, this meant that, at the very least, he had some idea of what kinds of different environments were housed within the structure. Even if he could not catch a glimpse of its overall mechanism, at least he was gaining insights into its massive dimensions.

Some of the corridors were hotter than others. He passed alongside rooms full of voices without seeing anyone. He crossed over spaces that echoed with his footsteps. He heard pumps and engines at work. In one place he could hear the sound of chickens clucking. He entered and exited half a dozen travelling booths. Some corridors were familiar, others were not. At no time did he find the entrance to a room.

When he eventually came to a halt it was because of ordinary fatigue. He had no idea how long he'd been on the move, but his legs told him he may have walked two kilometres or more. He was sweating and needed a drink. A booth yawned open, and when he had entered it he slid down onto its floor, his back against the wall and his legs sprawled apart.

The little mobile compartment jerked its way upward and then, pausing in its path, swivelled slowly around its own axis. It moved forward a few metres, paused and swivelled once more before rising straight up. When it halted now and opened, he saw a lighted aperture leading ahead to what appeared to be a chamber rather than a travelling booth.

He jerked upright and hurried across the short distance to the inviting doorway only to realize that it was his own room. He had spent several hours being led around in a circle. Anita was gone; he could not even question her about her instructions.

Youngest sucked in his breath, holding his fist to his mouth. There would be no point in giving vent to his frustration. If indeed there were surveillance cameras, whoever was watching him surely knew that, for the moment, he was defeated. Their message to him was very clear: 'We will see you when we're ready. Not before.'

He stepped through the entrance, not bothering to watch it snick shut behind him. One of the tendrils was hanging down, already lit. He pulled down two more and looked around, just to confirm that he was alone in the room. He saw now that a table had been enabled, with a flexible spout sticking up from its middle. He leaned down and, tugging lightly on it, directed a stream of water into his mouth. He drank for several minutes before releasing the nozzle. Then he subsided onto the floor. No doubt there was some method of pulling up a seat, but he could not be bothered to discover what it was.

Right then, the cricket-chirping voice of the General sounded in his head. 'Ah. There you are.'

Youngest choked back a curse. How could he have forgotten the General?

'Silent for at least two hours! Where have you been? I was beginning to wonder whether it was time to shut you down.'

'Back in my room,' said Youngest. 'I got out of it for a while, but ...' He must have been out of range again. He glanced at his surroundings with renewed interest, as he continued a stammering conversation, 'but the ... the ... structure is labyrinthine. The construction is unconventional. Unfamiliar.' If anyone was watching him, they'd think he was talking to himself.

The walls and corridors must have signal-blocking properties, he thought, which shielded him from the General's radio intermittently. The Island's structure was cylindrical which meant that the closer he got to its centre, the greater the shield. Even within the room, there had been periods of silence. He didn't have time to work out the mechanics, but it was an unexpected boon.

'You're wasting time!' screeched the General's voice in his ears. 'I'm not interested in engineering details.'

It was only then, when Youngest looked down at his wrist that he realized, for the first time, that Meiji's locator was dark. No light pulsed from it. His mouth went dry. Then he dragged down the neckline of his tunic and saw that his own locator was dark too.

The devices had been switched off. Both of them.

The General must know that the locator's off, thought Youngest. *He must have thought I'd been killed. He must have been beside himself with fury. Or anxiety. Or both.*

His skin prickled with inexpressible emotion.

'The Island must have a cloaking device,' said the General in his ears. 'I'll do the rest.'

So he had been bluffing just now, when he threatened to 'shut down' Youngest. There could be no shut downs without the locator.

Out loud, he answered the crackling voice in his head, 'Yes, of course. You're right. I … I'm sorry, I'll have to try harder. I will. I promise.'

He refused to think about how he'd find Meiji without a locator.

18

Meiji awoke feeling rested and calm. She had only a sheet wrapped around herself. The wetsuit was gone.

She didn't know how long she had been asleep, or where she was. She lay in the dark, waiting for her thoughts to form into whole sentences. The previous day's events filled slowly into her mind, scene by scene, as if she were watching a display of still pictures.

She guessed there would be some punishment for taking off from the whale-dock without consulting her team. She could face anything now, however. She felt no regret. She had found an anchor around which she could build her life. Whatever lay broken or unknown inside her did not matter, because she had met a being who could contain her, all that she was, all that she would be, in his immensity. And keep her safe.

She returned repeatedly to that moment when she had looked into Noor's great eye. Her skin prickled anew with pleasure. She could not remember feeling anything similar ever before. It was like drowning, but gladly. A happy death. He had been so vast in the beauty of his spirit, as she lay on his back, skin to skin, wetness to wetness. Sensing the majestic, slow pounding of his immense heart. Feeling his warm, living breath inside her lungs.

Then she gasped aloud, sitting up.

All around her, in a single blink, the walls, floor and ceiling of the room switched from darkness to dim light. They were not ordinary walls at all, but screens.

On the screens was a projected view from beneath the ocean's surface. It could not have been very deep, because sunlight stabbed down from above. Except for the fact that she could not feel any movement, she might have been in a glass-walled capsule, gliding at a leisurely pace through the grainy marine murk. There was no furniture in the room. She might have been a speck of seaweed, floating aimlessly within the infinite waters.

She lay back down, watching passively for several minutes. She couldn't tell right away whether or not she was watching a loop. She waited to see whether the shifting light and the continuously drifting flotsam repeated in any way, but the panorama was too shapeless to make out.

She sat up once more, whereupon the vista gave a jerk. The sensation of movement was heightened.

So they are watching me, she thought. *They waited for me to sit up.*

Knowing that she was expected to watch the presentation helped prepare her for the scene that gradually unfolded in three-dimensions all around her.

Over the regular Island noises in the room she was in, she began to hear the brassy groans and rubbery bellows that heralded the approach of large whales. She turned her head and saw them moving in from behind her position. Remotely controlled underwater cameras filming in three-dimensions must have been positioned ahead of the whales to record the action. As the massive streamlined shapes rumbled into view on either side of her, accompanying themselves with boisterous vocalizations, events began to speed up.

On the panel directly in front, in the distance, she saw three dim, cylindrical shapes. They were suspended motionless but it was clear that they were also whales. She and the animals directly around her speeded towards the stationary figures. When they were within a few hundred metres, the video device stopped moving while on either side the escort powered on towards their target, with bubbling, exuberant honks.

One of the three stationary figures was most likely Noor, while the other two were guardians.

At a distance, he looked like any other whale.

So she watched without reaction as the initial blows were struck. She felt an abstract, elliptical sorrow. She knew he was suffering, but she felt sure he was strong enough to withstand a beating. *He is being punished*, she thought. *Eventually he will be released. And soon enough it will be time for my next training.* If anyone was watching her reaction in the room, she would not give them the satisfaction of seeing her cry out or react.

But then plumes of blood began to seep lazily from that distant whale-body, the one she thought was Noor. Into the surrounding depths leaked that dark and viscous liquid. Like smoke billowing from the furnace of a bright and joyous young life.

Meiji began to gasp.

This was not going to be a mere beating, she realized. She squeezed her eyes shut. But she could not shut out the sounds. A medley of trumpeting honks and booms grew in intensity and frequency. They became a blood-curdling chorus of cetacean violence. She was glad that she couldn't distinguish any specific words or phrases in their cries, nor could she tell which part of what she heard came, perhaps, from Noor.

She continued sitting as she was, with her eyes shut, her knees raised and her wrists locked around them, rocking slightly from side to side. She waited for the sounds of the attacking whales to recede. Then she waited some more. And for a long time after that, too. She felt sure the scene would be a ghastly one.

Even so, when she opened her eyes, the sight was a hammer-blow to her heart: all the screens were deep maroon. Then, as her eyes adjusted, she saw on the panel directly in front of her the dark and broken bulk of Noor's dying body drifting within a reticulated curtain of his own blood. With intuitive cruelty the video-recorder had focused in on his right eye. It was still open and, through the sorcery of optical effects, looking straight at her.

Meiji felt rather than heard the unearthly shriek that emerged from her throat. She flung herself at the screen, now screaming, now wailing, now howling as if her throat would burst apart. She hated herself for her lack of control and she hated the watchers who had undoubtedly calculated this disintegration of her spirit. She lashed out at the panel with her fists, her arms, pounding and screaming. She wished she had something to throw at it, something with which to shatter it. Something to blot out the obscene horror of that huge sad eye staring at her from across the unfathomable chasm of death.

19

Youngest looked around the room without moving his head. He had been shifted to a new room and had been provided with a new attendant. Her name was Bella. She had informed him politely but firmly that he must lean back into his vertical sleeping pallet and succumb to slumber. That was some hours ago.

Bella was dressed in a sensible tunic and pajamas. There was no hint of seduction either in the style of her clothes or in her manner. She appeared to be in her early thirties, with a calm, serious demeanour, smooth coffee-brown skin and dark hair tied back in a ponytail. She had been sent as a replacement for Anita. She was seated at the table in the centre of the room, facing towards him, but looking down at a tablet in her hand.

Not wanting her to know that he was awake, Youngest clicked his tongue softly against the roof of his mouth three times. It was the agreed-upon signal to the General to show that he was awake but not alone. He did not know yet whether the new room was within range of the radio signal.

The Genereal responded at once. 'You took your time, my precious. I've been signalling every half-hour. I thought you might be in a coma. You've been in a drug-induced sleep. It's got to be that. You never slept so much before. Are you alone? All right. You can't talk. Perhaps you've got your Vermin watchdog hanging around your neck? Or is it vacuuming up your nether juices? Haha.'

Youngest clicked twice, 'No.'

'This is taking too long. I am growing dangerously bored.'

Youngest clicked three times.

'And you need to get up now. Get up. I'm within range. You need to be able to tell me how to board your … wherever you are. Get up now. Get up. Are you up?'

Youngest clicked three times.

'Speak to the Vermin guard. That's how I'll know for sure you're awake.'

Youngest opened his eyes fully. 'Hello, Bella,' he said, then immediately cleared his throat. He had spoken in the natural register of his voice, a man's voice.

Her head had whipped up, a shocked expression on her face. 'Oh!' she said, her hand to her mouth. 'Is there something wrong? Are you unwell?'

'Tell it that in your natural state, when you were a fully endowed Man, you could disembowel three Vermin with a single thrust of your flaming lance.'

'It's just my … uhh … the translator disk,' said Youngest, tapping his throat. 'Needs adjusting now and then.'

'Ah,' she nodded, looking slightly puzzled. 'Really? I thought they matched the sound of the wearer…'

'Well,' said Youngest, 'mine is variable.'

'Shut it up. You've lost two days already. Make it show you how to move around outside the room.'

He detached himself from the wall-bed and looked around uncertainly. 'This room is different to the last one I was in.' He tapped the panel between the vertical sleeping pad he'd been in and its partner on the other side. 'Where will I find the …'

'That's the entrance port,' said Bella quickly. 'What are you looking for?'

But Youngest remained by the flat, featureless panel that the woman had called an entrance port. He tapped it again. 'A washcloth,' he said, lying. 'This is where it was in the last room.'

Bella shook her head, 'Oh no, you're mistaken.' She pointed

towards the three panels on the opposite side of the room. 'That's the shower area there. Washcloths are always stored beside it. Were you on some other Island?'

'You're wasting time. Force the Vermin to show you.'

'How does this port open, Bella?'

She looked puzzled. 'If you can't open it then … well … I don't know.'

'Force it.'

'I'm not sure I understand what you mean. You don't know the mechanism? Or you're not allowed to show me?'

Looking very uncomfortable, the girl said, 'I can't explain. Usually we can all just do it.'

'Use force!'

Youngest said, out loud, 'No, I won't.'

The girl raised her eyebrows in confusion. 'What?'

'Sorry, I … I can't make sense of what you're saying. When you say "we" for instance, who do you mean?'

'Anyone here,' said Bella, though she was frowning now. 'From the time we're accepted here, we can do it.'

'Make it show you then.'

'Well. Would you mind showing me?'

'It's not what I was asked to do,' said Bella. She was standing up, a sturdily built woman though clearly not muscular. It would be easy to overwhelm her. As with the other girl, Youngest registered a curious blankness in her expression. He wondered if this was the effect of memory loss. A chronic lack of context. 'We have certain tasks and we're trained to remain within the boundary of those tasks.'

'Ask it what the boundary of its task towards you is. Go on. Ask.'

Youngest drew in a breath. 'Bella, I'm going to make a suggestion, all right? And if it doesn't suit what you've been told to do, you can tell me—'

'All right.'

'I believe that you've been told to keep me imprisoned here. But I need to get out of this room.'

'Oh no, I'm not allowed—'

'Yes,' he cut in, 'I assumed that. My guess is, whatever you do to open the port, it's likely to involve a gesture with your head. I saw one of the Mentors do that, down in the Fresh Catch hold. She moved her chin in an odd way. So I'm guessing that's what you'll need to do too—'

The girl was shaking her head. 'No, no, that would have been a *Mentor*. They do things differently from the rest of us. We use our hands.' She stopped abruptly, her hand to her mouth.

'All right, grab it then. Get behind it and wave its arms around.'

'All right, Bella, then here's what we'll do—'

Before she had time to react, Youngest reached out, gripped the girl's shoulders and swung her around, so that they were both facing the panel with him behind her. He gripped her wrists in his hands

'No!' she cried, immediately starting to struggle. 'You don't understand – it's not that simple—'

She began to kick backwards, but Youngest wrapped both his arms around her and lifted her clear off the floor. She immediately braced her feet against the panel and tried to push herself away from it. 'Stop! Stop – let me go – you don't understand! If we struggle, it won't open at all!'

Youngest shifted his weight forward so that Bella lost her balance. Her knees buckled automatically and her feet dragged on the floor while he supported her entire weight, with her forearms held tight in his hands. It was an awkward position and she was gasping and sobbing as he forced her palms into contact with the panel.

But she'd spoken the truth. The panel remained obstinately unresponsive and the tendril lights had dimmed altogether. Now the only source of light was from the luminescent walls.

Youngest stepped back, lifting the girl to her feet before letting her go. She swivelled around at once.

'Wh-why did you do that!' she screamed, her cheeks wet and her mouth quivering. She stood with her back flat against the panel. 'You're mad, you're crazy. You don't know what can happen if you try to force the ports!'

'Bella, just tell me what I need to know and I'll be on my way.' He dropped the feminine register and spoke normally.

'And your *voice*! You have a … a … man's voice!'

'Yes, there's nothing wrong with my translator disk. I was a man before. I'm not one now. Are you going to tell me?'

'I can't! It's not allowed!'

Youngest took two steps back and said, 'All right then. Move aside.'

'I won't! It's dangerous—'

'Move aside, I said!'

'No! You don't understand! It's – AAAHH!'

Youngest had rocked forward, swung the woman aside and with the same momentum dealt the panel a powerful kick with his right foot.

The panel cracked with a sharp report like a gun shot.

'We're going to drown!' Bella screamed, as a white plume of water came spurting into the cell from the broken panel.

20

Much later, Meiji found herself on the floor of the room, wrapped in her sheet and curled up in the semi-darkness. All but one of the screens had been turned off. She stirred and raised her head, wondering whether she had heard a sound. Then she heard it again. Someone had said her name.

'Meiji?'

It was the white-haired Mentor, Vane.

She too was on the floor, seated in what looked like a neighbouring room. In reality, her image was just another projection, on the one panel that was currently lit.

'If you're ready to listen, there's something you need to know.'

Meiji flipped herself over, facing away from the lit screen, remaining on the floor.

'If you're not ready, you can tell me. If you refuse to speak, I'll take that as a "yes" and will continue. Are you ready?'

Meiji breathed slowly in and out. She felt as if she would never be able to speak again in her life.

'So that's a "yes" then,' said Vane.

Meiji said nothing.

'You need to understand why it happened,' said Vane. 'And what part of it was your fault. Or else you'll never go forward, beyond this situation.'

Meiji said nothing.

'There's a lot that you do not understand,' said Vane.

Meiji said nothing.

'The main thing to understand is that the world we're in is

broken. Smashed.' She paused. 'It wasn't especially fixed in the Time Before either. Not for young women, not for girls. But at least there used to be some comfort from traditional roles. Now that's gone too. Now there's actually nothing. Girls like you are either in Hell. Or you're dead. Those are the only choices.'

Meiji said nothing.

'Except here. On this Island. This Island is your only choice.'

Meiji said nothing.

'I know you can hear me. In fact, I know what you're thinking too.'

No, thought Meiji. *You do not.*

'I'm sorry my dear. This will come as a shock. I *can* read your thoughts.'

That's impossible, thought Meiji. *She's lying.*

'It's possible, Meiji,' said Vane. 'I am not lying.'

Meiji began to tremble. She felt the laces within her innermost self unravelling.

'You're right,' continued Vane in a gentler tone. 'It used to be impossible. But now it's commonplace. Well. To those who have the technology.'

I won't listen, thought Meiji. *I won't.*

'Don't be childish,' said Vane. Her voice was like an axe covered in lamb's fleece. 'I know you're listening. So, yes. We can translate the language of thought. In front of me here, I have a screen on which I get a read-out of your wave-patterns accompanied by an interpretation, in ordinary words, of what those patterns mean.'

Meiji became a tiny mouse, frozen in front of an enormous white-haired cat. It was purring. It knew that it had, for all practical purposes, already caught and eaten her.

'That was clever, Meiji. Yes, it's true that we cannot read images. You were thinking in pictures just then. But believe me when I tell you that we know a great deal about you. We know, for instance, that you think you're different to the other girls. Yes, in some ways you *are*. But in every other way, you're exactly the same as them: you know nothing about the world, you have no idea what your place in it is. Unlike them, however, you're not merely ignorant but arrogant too. The fact that you know so little allows you to imagine there's not much to know.

'Meiji, so long as you believe there's a special fate awaiting you because of your false idea that you're special, you'll *never* be in control of your life. It's not your fault. It's just the way you were brought up: to think you were a princess. The other girls were brought up to be obedient, to be patient and to be proud of their stupidity. Both ways are a burden. What we do here, what we *try* to do, is to help you break out of these kinds of habits. To teach you ways of gaining control.'

A mental image appeared in Meiji's mind of herself as an empty skin, from which her real self had been sucked out whole, then replaced. By a smooth, clean, bland-faced doll. Ready to follow orders and be resourceful and responsible. All hours of the day, every day of the year, every year of her life, for the rest of eternity.

'I need you to sit up straight now. I need you to turn around.'

Meiji bit her lip, wanting to remain as she was. But she forced herself to move. She sat up, facing the lighted panel. She sat up with her legs folded to one side, neck bent, her weight supported on one arm, looking away from the screen.

'So,' said Vane. 'I need you to understand that however much you might think the opposite, your presence here is the best thing possible for you.'

No, thought Meiji.

She could smell urine. She realized it must be hers.

She decided she didn't care.

Nothing mattered any more.

'The fact is you chose to come here.'

No, I did not, thought Meiji. She thought the words deliberately, wanting them to register.

There was a smile in Vane's voice as she spoke to Meiji's bowed head. 'That's not actually true, my dear.' She paused before continuing, 'We know for a fact that you made a tremendous effort to get here.' She paused again. 'Of course, I realize that you can't know what that effort was. Or what you thought or said or did before you made it. Because, as you know, we erase memories here.'

Meiji wondered if murderous rage had its own specialized wave-pattern. It was so wrong, so unfair. To be so helpless as to lose the privacy of her own mind. To be deprived of her own memories. She could no longer form complete thoughts. Fragments of words tumbled through her brain like water-beads skittering on a scalding hot griddle. She aimed inarticulate bolts of pure violence at the image of the Mentor on the screen.

'Of course, if you want, we can give your memories back to you,' continued Vane, in her gentle, unhurried voice.

Meiji went still.

'You heard me,' said Vane. 'We can return your memories to you. But you've got to give us something in return.'

Meiji clenched her teeth. *You should die,* she thought. Her breathing became ragged. She was gasping in anger. *People like you should DIE.*

Vane mouth curved up slightly. 'Thoughts like that are not helpful, child.'

Tell me who I am. Tell me why I'm here. Tell me!

'You're going to have to open your mouth, Meiji, if you want to communicate with me.'

You say you can read my thoughts.

'Part of your training on this Island is to understand the extent to which you are truly powerless – and then to move onwards from that point. You think that I have needlessly humiliated you?

I would say, no, I have only forced you to face the consequences of your princess-ways. You need to move beyond the prison of your private self. We don't care whether or not you like us. In fact, we don't want you to become attached to us or to your time here. Our concern is to heal the wounds of the girls who come to us. Only then can any of you move forward.'

Meiji's face and mouth were quivering with the force of her anger. She could barely speak. But she forced herself to. 'Yes. I want to know. Tell me. I … *must* know. I need to know. Who I am.'

Vane inclined her head. She had won the round. 'We usually wait till a girl has come to the end of her training. Then we give her the choice to recover her memories.'

Pause.

'But we make exceptions now and then.'

Meiji struggled to bring her breath under control. 'What,' she panted. 'How. When.'

'Spell it out, Meiji. Ask me to tell you what we need you to do in order to have your memories returned to you ahead of time.'

You'll want me to rip that smile off your face with my teeth, thought Meiji. *You'll ask me to poke your eyes out with my fingernails. You'll ask me to feed you pig-entrails.*

'We can also make the loss permanent,' murmured Vane, half-closing her eyes.

Then she drew in a deep breath.

'Meiji: I'm going to leave you now. Go back to your team room. Think through your choices. I can either restore your memories to you first or I can send you out on a new challenge. One that's better suited to the violence you're currently expressing with your thoughts. In my opinion, it will be better if you go out on the challenge first.'

Meiji was shaking again. She couldn't control her muscles. She pressed her face into her hands in order to conceal her anguish as Vane's voice flowed over her in an oily, treacherous tide, searching for any remaining cracks in her consciousness that might yet be explored and vandalized. In her mind, she writhed this way and that, struggling to keep herself from drowning in that slimy ooze.

Then, as she squirmed, the image of Noor's battered body hanging lifeless in the blood-darkened water returned to her.

The memory pierced right through her soul, a spear of absolute pain.

She embraced it, hungrily. It was clean, it was pure. And Vane could not read it, because it was an image.

Why? She thought the question as a statement at Vane. *Noor. You didn't need to kill him.*

Pat came Vane's voice. 'We did nothing, Meiji. You're the one who killed him.'

It was a slippery thing, that pain. It sliced and skewered and punctured every tender nerve Meiji possessed. Yet the closer she held it to herself, the stronger she felt. The pain was a shield against the mind-altering poison of Vane's words.

'You let him race away, without commands, without control. You allowed him to have his way with you. You allowed him to do what he, a mere animal, wanted to do. Instead of the other way around! Once a creature of that size knows he can have his way, he becomes useless to us. He will fight his harness and refuse to be hitched to the underwater shuttles for which he was being trained as a draught animal. He would become a liability, because all he'd want to do is play. And if no one played with him or fed him, he'd become aggressive. We had no choice except to destroy him at once.'

The remembrance of Noor's being filled slowly within Meiji's brain.

A deep, rich, echoing immensity.

Impenetrably alien.

Yet *radiant.*

She would never know him again, but at least she had known him once.

'Try to see that your actions resulted in the tragedy of his loss. Five years of his life including two years of our time training him, snuffed out in one afternoon. And for what? One foolish young woman's idle pleasure.'

Meiji removed her hands from her face. In her mind, she held the image of Noor's lifeless body, she heard his voice in her ears and her skin recalled the heat of his body.

She had touched the thundering heart of Nature.

She was calm.

21

Youngest couldn't make sense of what he saw beyond the smashed panel of the portal: giant bulging surfaces curved away in three directions, covered in knobs and protuberances. Clusters of jointed limbs shaped like crab-legs, complete with claws at the ends, stabbed out of the glowing darkness, jittering with a ceaseless rhythmic motion. Light came from patches of bio-luminescent moss and the voice of the ocean boomed and echoed, amplified within this interior lattice-work of hidden spaces.

'The water, the water!' shrieked Bella, her voice tipping into hysteria. She was standing on the service table and holding on to two darkened light-tentacles as if they were straps on a commuter bus.

'It's not going to flood,' said Youngest. They had been lucky: the tide was low and the Island had buoyancy. But the whole room was shaking and twisting, as if trying to rid itself of its occupants.

In the shimmering light beyond the portal Youngest saw that the shattered panel was rimmed by a thick flange of tight-folded material. Along the outer edge of this flange were smaller versions of the hanging crab-limbs, each one as thick as one of his fingers. They were also jerking back and forth with manic energy, the claws flinging themselves outward, then curling back in, again and again, as if seeking purchase.

An idea formed in his head.

'Come on,' he called to Bella. 'If we're going to get out of here, we'll have to do it fast!' He reached out as he spoke and, gripping one of the gyrating claws, snapped it off where it joined the outer frame of the portal. It came away with a satisfying pop.

'No!' wailed Bella. 'There are jellyfish in the water – box jellyfish! We keep the seas around the Island infested with them on purpose—'

There was no time to think. Youngest held the still struggling claw in his hand and folded it over. It instantly formed a tight loop, hooking onto its own torn end. He immediately snatched up a second claw and did the same with it. Now armed with two thick loops of twitching crab-limb he took a single stride in the knee-deep water toward the table on which Bella was standing. The light barely penetrated the room but he knew she could see him, silhouetted against the portal. 'Reach for me,' he said, 'because I can't see much.'

He had to estimate her position by reaching out with his left arm and was relieved when he connected with her waist immediately. She turned at once, with no fuss and limpeted onto his shoulder. He felt her hot breath on his back, no longer screaming.

'Hold on tight,' said Youngest.

As he turned to move back across the threshold his entire right foot was engulfed in flames. He might have stepped into a bucket of acid; it would have had exactly the same effect. 'Ahhh!' he roared, in shock and pain.

'What happened?' cried Bella in alarm.

'Nothing!' gasped Youngest. His foot was an inferno but he forced his attention away from it. There was no choice. He had to assume it was a jellyfish. Holding the hastily devised loops in either hand, he reached up towards the jittering mass of claws hanging from the bulging walls around him and … Yes! With a soft, snickering click, one of the bigger claws hooked into the rudimentary loop he had created. In a smooth, waving motion, it passed that loop on to its neighbouring claw, easily supporting his and Bella's weight.

He understood now how the corridors operated. Matched sets of claws operated as living zippers, drawing out or collapsing the passages, like rectangular tubes. The tubes were formed from membranes. When not in use they folded themselves tight outside the portals of rooms or travelling booths. Each of the rooms was an individual, separate cell, sealed against the water in which it was immersed.

'Bella! Slip over in front of me – that's right! Face me – wrap your legs tight—' Youngest panted, as the woman slid into position around his front, like a baby monkey cleaving to its mother. He thought his right arm would be ripped out of its shoulder-joint, but it held long enough for him to raise his left arm and engage the second claw-loop. There! Done. Now they were supported on both sides. With a jerk, first one side then the other, they began to move forward down the passage.

Youngest allowed himself to bellow in pain, trying to make it sound as if it was the effort of exertion. His foot was melting, it was a fire-ball of agony but the exhilaration of smashing his way out of the claustrophobic room partially made up for it.

He struck out sideways with his legs, finding slippery footholds above the water line, on the knobbled sides of the passages. His mind scrambled to make sense of what he was experiencing: a mechanism that was at least in part organic. The claw-loop in his hands had reacted in the way of a primitive nervous system when separated from its parent body. Its muscles had contracted and locked into position. The hook-and-eye system by which the corridors expanded and contracted was mechanical, but the functioning parts – the claws – were organic.

A thudding sensation on his back made him aware that Bella was trying to communicate with him. She was pounding him with her fists.

'Stop screaming!' she said, screaming herself. 'There will be a vertical shaft very soon. There won't be a cabinet there. When we reach it, be sure to move UPwards—'

22

Meiji left the room she had been in still wrapped in the sheet. She negotiated the curving corridors on her way back to the team-room without conscious thought. She knew that if she moved inwards, away from concave surfaces, she would eventually turn a corner that would lead to one of the elevator shafts. Then she needed to go up six levels and follow Rahm's instructions from the previous night to find the correct cell.

She had just entered a fresh corridor when it began to quiver. She had been walking slowly, not running or jumping. So it was definitely not her doing. The floor gave a couple of gentle jerks at first, then abruptly the entire corridor, walls, floor and ceiling, began shuddering violently.

Meiji was too surprised to be afraid. She stopped moving at once, wondering if that would make a difference.

For a moment, she thought perhaps it had.

In the next instant, there was a loud boom, a crash, and a powerful tremor shook the entire passage. Meiji was thrown off her feet. The blue-green lights that seeped out of the walls were pulsing on and off.

She had no idea what was going on. Nothing of this kind had happened so far nor had anyone ever hinted at the possibility. Her first thought was to turn around and return to the Screen Room. Every moment, the shocks were getting worse. She could hear the sound of water gushing, muffled shouts and screams from what seemed far away. She had no idea what any of it meant.

Staggering to her feet, with the floor beneath her bucking like the back of a galloping horse, she turned around only to discover that the corridor had closed in on itself. There was nowhere for her to go, either forward or back. She was trapped in an elongated capsule about four metres long, with no idea as to how it came to be that way. There was no reason, for instance, to hope that it would not continue to collapse inwards. The entire notion of a solid corridor shrinking in on itself with no warning was impossible to comprehend. There was no way to imagine what might happen next.

As the floor continued to twist, and the walls to shake from side to side, Meiji felt that her best option would be, at the very least, to move away from the direction in which she'd been going. Sliding to the right, along the convex wall of the corridor, she soon reached its terminus. It looked like a flat panel of the kind that most of the entrances and exits were made from. More out of habit than thought-out reaction, she scraped it with the backs of her nails as she would any other exit panel.

To her immense relief, the panel gave a slight shake, then slid away from her, affording several more metres of corridor. She moved forward gratefully and cautiously. Even at the depth of her panic she doubted that she was the source of the problem. Whatever the crisis was, it had apparently started elsewhere within the Island's structure.

When she reached the end once more, she scraped it again and it obliged her again, by sliding away even further. This time it slipped around a corner to the right. She knew that the elevator shafts were located along the inward corridors, so as long as she moved radially, leading inwards, she guessed that she would eventually arrive at a vertical shaft.

The shuddering movements began to reduce even before she turned the corner. She could walk upright now, without needing to lean against a wall. She continued to keep her right hand out, just in case. The corridor ahead was not blocked in any direction that she could see. There was no shuddering at all any more. In a couple of turns, she saw the familiar vertical pillar and an open cell within it. The sound of pouring water was still a bit louder than normal, but there were no more voices or booms. She stepped inside the cell. Her heart was thumping as she got the door panel to close and tapped out the number of her level.

There was nothing unusual about the remainder of her journey. She got off at her level and began looking for the faint decorative symbols that distinguished rooms and levels from one another.

23

By the time Youngest and Bella had found a vertical shaft, the pain in his foot had become a fiery demon. The clawing hooks of the transport system did not discriminate between his feet and the loops in his hands, giving him painful nips as they passed him upwards.

Three floors went by before Bella told him to stop. They were facing a portal. Bella's back was to it. Still clinging to him with one arm, she twisted around and scraped at the membrane with her fingernails. It snicked back at once and Youngest was processed out by the claws.

He staggered forward, still mindful of the woman slung across his front, until he had set her down. Then he toppled over, first on his knees and then on his side, knowing only that he had once more arrived at a quiet hallway with stairs leading up … somewhere.

He could no longer afford to think about anything but the flaming curtain of pain that had fallen over his senses, blotting out all reason and dignity.

He could hear himself trying to speak intelligibly, but he wasn't making sense even to himself. He felt hands hauling him up, then bodies all around him, as he was lifted onto a horizontal surface and his clothes were stripped off. For a short while he didn't know whether or not he was still in the landing area outside the elevator entrance. Then, without losing consciousness, but with his eyes shut, he felt a sensation as if a cloud had been shifted under him.

A moment later, he realized that he could no longer feel his right foot.

He could not move it. He had no toes. It was not there.

His head and torso jerked up as if on a spring, his heart hammering. He looked down the length of his body to where he expected to see his foot. But there was nothing there.

Then he blinked.

In the place of the foot was a misshapen wad of grey jelly.

'Don't worry,' said a voice, 'it will heal.'

An immense presence was standing beside him, a tall, wide woman with a tide of white hair flowing down to her shoulders and back. He recognized her from the Collectory.

'I am Mentor Vane,' she said now. 'You may call me Mentor, or Vane, or both.'

He was lying on a raised platform, with his upper body curled up in panic.

'Try to lie flat and relax. Can you tell us your name?'

'I am Yasmine,' he said, straightening his body carefully as he rolled onto his back. He wondered whether she remembered him from the session in the Suspended City. Of course, she had been a virtual presence there and had been focused on the auction. She may not even have seen him.

'All right, Yasmine. You're lucky that we still have the antidote for jellyfish stings,' she said now. 'It hasn't happened to any one of us in a very long while.' She had a mellow voice, with a slight yodel on certain words.

He was in a light-filled chamber. On the ceiling over him was a projection of sunlight filtering through rippling palm leaves. Then he looked around and saw that the walls of the cell or chamber or wherever he was were also displaying beach imagery, with blue sky and dazzling white clouds scudding over golden dunes of sand.

'I had no idea,' he said, 'about the ... the ... ' He remembered belatedly that he had little right to expect hospitality. 'About the rooms being cells. The water. I wouldn't have tried to break out if I'd known.'

Vane nodded without smiling. 'We have much to talk about.'

Youngest looked around, taking in his surroundings.

'You're in my apartments,' she said.

Youngest looked down, realizing only now that he was completely naked. He tried not to feel anything about this, but failed. His hands fluttered ineffectually in the air above his breasts.

'I'm sorry, but I—'

'We're wholly unconcerned with nudity here,' said Vane.

'Yes, but I'm not used to … to …' stammered Youngest.

Vane shook her head slightly as she moved out of his range of vision.

24

Aila climbed up the short flight of stairs to the deck, taking care to avoid making a sound. The General was asleep. She wanted to ensure that he remained that way. She needed to be away from him, to think.

She had never before needed to be in the open to do her thinking.

Then again, there was nothing about her situation that was familiar. Every waking moment brought unique experiences. Even her dreams were different to any she'd had before: there were times when she couldn't tell the difference between waking and sleeping, good dreams and bad ones. The simplest terms, such as 'good' and 'bad', were no longer clear to her. There were times when she found herself looking at her hands, wondering when she would no longer be able to tell left from right.

She wore a thin wrap that covered her shoulders and upper body, ending just above the swell of her rounded bottom. The General had said he wanted her in a state of continuous readiness to accept his attentions. Particularly when they were in his room. Two nights after Youngest's departure, he had permitted her to lie on his bed. Only at the foot of it. He liked to be able to kick her in his sleep, he said.

The night air was hot, thick and moist, like the breath of a drunken giant. She stood at the polished brass rail, looking out into the darkness in the direction in which the sun set, that to her was called the North. The unquiet depths of the ocean merged in the distance with the spangled blackness overhead. Somewhere into that distance was where Youngest had disappeared.

Are you there, she asked him in the silence of her mind. *The General says he thinks you are 'lost'. But he has your coordinates. We are moving in your direction.*

There was, of course, no reply.

I came with you to be with you, she continued. *But you are no longer here. Maybe you never will be, again. When you tried to stop me from coming, you never mentioned this: that you would vanish. Maybe you didn't know? Maybe you knew but feared that if you told me I would tell the General? Perhaps in my sleep? After all, the General gets what he wants, one way or another.*

Still. I don't care. Even without you, I'm glad I came.

She looked down towards the sound made by waves lapping at the sides of the boat. She regarded the black waters with dread. She could not imagine how Youngest, whom she continued to think of as Yasmine, could have immersed himself in that impenetrable otherness, knowing that it might be days before he would emerge into the air once more.

There's so much I don't understand, she thought. *Sometimes I think this man, this General, is growing a little bit kinder. Then he does some new thing that makes me see the claws within him. The way he treats the manlings, for instance. He treats them like … no, there's no comparison. If they were animals, he could not treat them worse. An animal cannot suffer with such concentrated awareness – the manlings can suffer because they have awareness. They know that they're being harmed, but they can do nothing to save themselves. And that is what he likes.*

He has a mouth with poisoned fangs in the place where other men have hearts.

When you tried to warn me, I could not believe there was more to know about the world. I thought I had already seen everything that could be seen. I know now I was wrong.

Greatly so.

And it makes me happy.

Happiness can grow in strange places. This is one of them: this knowledge of my stupidity, my ignorance. It pleases me to see the vastness of my ignorance before I met you. Why? Because it allows me to hope that knowledge is rushing in to fill the places that were empty till now.

She heard a slight sound behind her. Small bare feet were padding at a measured pace across the polished deck. She didn't turn to look, because she knew it could only be one of the drones. The General would never approach with such a light footfall.

The short pale figure entered her field of vision now, no higher than her elbow, to her right. It stood at the rail, also looking out towards the North.

Aila shivered slightly, though the air was just as hot and thick as before.

The manling did not look at her, did not acknowledge her presence, did nothing to reveal that it knew she was there. Yet its very presence by her side was a sign that it had come out with the purpose of being near her.

What type of consciousness could such a being possess, wondered Aila. *Created without a voice, yet able to understand language; proportioned like an adult human male yet with no organs of generation; equipped with the muscles and the ability to perform complex and repetitive tasks yet lacking a sufficient sense of self to protect itself from harm.*

What did that amount to?

She could not imagine. She shivered once more.

25

Youngest was about to turn his head to follow the white-haired woman with his eyes, when a familiar voice stabbed into his mind.

'So. You're within range once more. Are you alone? You keep going blank.'

Youngest breathed in sharply. He clicked his tongue once.

'You can't talk. All right. But you've been inside the Vermitorium for over two days. Tick-tock. We have to decide how to proceed. Either you get out with whatever I need to know or you tell me how to get in and find out for myself.'

Youngest clicked twice, signalling a negative.

'No. No what? No you can't do either?'

Youngest clicked three times.

'Why can't you just talk? Are you telling me you're never left alone?'

Youngest clicked three times.

'Does that mean the Vermin know? Why you're there? Are they watching you?'

Youngest held his breath. He didn't know what answer to give. On the one hand, he truly didn't know, but on the other hand he had no idea how long he could afford to stall the General.

He clicked twice. Then, after a pause, clicked three times.

'You're not sure.'

Three clicks.

There was a pause. Then: 'That's not good enough,' said the General. 'You need to recall the point of this entire operation. Do you need a little primer?'

Two clicks.

Youngest raised his head, looking around. What would happen if he screamed now? Would Vane try to investigate? Would she be concerned or just suspicious?

'Ah! So you don't want one. Strange. I had hoped you might start to enjoy your excursions into the pleasures of pain. Like your little friend here. She tells me that she actively invites pain. Of course, as you can imagine, this causes me some annoyance. Inspiring pleasure in others is not my game. But I digress. For the moment, you're in luck. I am guessing that there's more than one person around you. In which case a scream from you might draw too much attention. Am I right?'

Three clicks. Youngest lay back once more, his eyes shut. He wished he had time to think.

'We are perhaps ten kilometres from your position. We should be able to see the Vermitorium. I am assuming there's a shield?'

Three clicks.

'All right. In that case you will have to guide us in. What kind of entry point is there?'

One click.

'All right you can't tell me. But you're in there, so there must be one. Several. Underwater then?'

Three clicks.

'Wet docks? Undersea?'

One click.

'How did you get in then? Not from above. And not from below. So that leaves only the sides. But that has to mean air-locks. An air-locked vent. Yes?'

Three clicks.

'So … you broke in? No, unlikely. You had no tools for breaking and entering. They will have camouflaged the vents. Some other method then. Chance. Chance?'

Three clicks.

'Well, that's no help to me. Can't depend on chance. It'll have to be from above. The shield. You'll have to turn it off. It'll take time. To access the mechanism. Whatever it is.'

Youngest opened his eyes.

Vane was standing beside him, looking down. She was not smiling. On the other side of him was a new figure, a young woman with the unadorned appearance of a Bella, but dressed in the plain white shift of a nurse or a clinician's assitant. 'I heard a clicking sound,' said this person. 'I came over to investigate.'

'What's the matter?' The General sounded petulant. 'Why aren't you answering? I know you're not out of range. Have you been intercepted?'

Youngest looked Vane straight in the eye. He clicked twice. He stared up at her, willing her to understand.

Vane was silent for a beat, staring at him, a crease between her brows.

Then, 'It's a signal,' she said. 'You're signaling.'

'Then what's the problem? Someone's talking to you. Yes?'

Youngest drew himself up in a seated position.

He clicked three times now, but brought a finger to his mouth, still staring at Vane.

Her frown deepened, her eyes narrowing.

One click. Youngest pointed to the side of his face, to his jaw. Then tapped his ear.

'If you open your mouth, I'll be able to hear what's being said,' said the General.

Youngest opened his mouth and with his hands gestured to Vane to bring her ear to his mouth.

'I don't hear anything. No one's talking. And you're not clicking.'

She didn't seem to understand and drew in a breath as if to say something. But Youngest opened his eyes wide to signal alarm, shook his head then …

Once again he tapped his ear, tapped his mouth and pointed

to Vane.

Vane bent down and put her ear to Youngest's open mouth.

'Yes or no,' she heard. 'Can you signal?'

Vane jerked upright, her expression riddled with complexity. She may not have understood the language in which the General spoke, but she knew now that there was a channel of communication within her unexpected visitor's head.

Youngest clicked three times. Pouring the full force of his intention at Vane, he used his hands to suggest talking mouths, then pointed between her and the white-clad assistant.

'Open your mouth! I want to hear what's being said.'

Vane raised her head to look at the other girl. Youngest had his mouth open, but he was holding his breath. This was the moment of truth: either the white-haired woman had understood enough to say something neutral or she would say out loud that she knew Youngest was sending information out of the Island to an unknown entity.

She had no way of knowing whether or not it was an invading force, an approaching armada, bristling with hostile intent.

Why should she be sympathetic? She had everything to lose.

'See if you can find something for our guest to wear,' said Vane in a loud voice, to the assistant. 'It seems she is overcome with embarrassment. And call Asma to me. Perhaps Brahi, too. We need to understand our guest's skills in order to find a place for her amongst us.'

PART IV

ISLAND

1

When the entrance panel to the team-room snicked back, Meiji found Rahm sitting at the table, alone.

'*Wah*!' exclaimed Rahm, jumping to her feet, throwing her hands up in the air with impatience. She was wearing a light, sleeveless cotton shift, beige in colour, that covered her to mid-thigh. 'I is think you is never come back.'

Meiji shrugged and said, 'Oh.'

She felt completely cold within. She wanted to lie very still, thinking through the options that lay before her. Such as they were. Had the white-haired Mentor made any firm promises at all? It was hard to tell.

'Come on,' said Rahm. 'We is must go.'

'I'm staying here,' said Meiji. 'I want to think.' She wondered where the other members of the team were but was glad they weren't present. Their mute hostility would have been one more burden upon her consciousness.

'No, no, is big moment,' said Rahm. 'You is must come. We is late.'

Meiji was too depleted to resist. She wrapped her sheet around herself as securely as she could, tucking it in at the waist to give it a bit of shape. She followed Rahm out, paying no attention to her surroundings or to what the other girl told her about what they were likely to see. They went up two floors, then turned along corridors that led towards the outer cells of the structure. They ducked into an entrance that was intentionally dark and narrow, and Meiji found herself in a dim-lit chamber with curving, maroon walls.

All the available floor space was taken up by others. They were sitting on cushions. At the farther end of the room was a low stage that was tilted sharply from back to front. In the centre of the stage, and rising out of it at an angle surrounded by filigree screens, was a curious throne. It was heavily cushioned, covered in black satin or patent leather and decorated in tiny, winking diamantes. It had a tall back and sturdy arms, but its seat was shaped like a horseshoe. Hanging from the ceiling directly above the throne were two thick cords, gold and black, their brightly coloured bead-tassels dangling on either side of the ornate seat.

Every possible surface aside from the screens and the polished mahogany floor was covered with silk-brocade drapery. The air was warm and scented. Music was playing: a breathy reed, as moody and formless as a sharp sea-breeze whistling through limestone caves.

As they entered the space, someone standing at the entrance leaned towards Rahm and whispered, 'Go on – go ahead – there are two cushions right in front.'

Rahm caught Meiji's hand and drew her forward, both stumbling as they went, until they saw the spaces that had apparently been kept for them.

Meiji did not look at the other figures seated around them. She was not interested in anything but her own thoughts. But Rahm leaned towards her as they sat down. She whispered, 'It is important thing. Other teams is here, many much. Maybe even six teams. All together.'

'Okay,' said Meiji. She had sat down with her feet tucked under her bum, her knees together, her hands on her thighs. She had no intention of engaging with whatever she had been brought to see or listen to. She wanted to be alone.

There was a rustling sound on the stage and Rahm gave her a hard shove with her right elbow, forcing her to look up.

In the centre of the sloping platform, there now stood an extremely pale-skinned woman with her silver-white hair drawn up to form a sharp spike at the top of her head. She was flanked by two attendants, one on either side.

The pale woman was dressed in a loose, glittering gown of fine gold lace. It had a central slit edged with red glass beads that began just above her midriff and extended all the way down to the floor. The attendants were dressed in black silk tunics with red pajamas underneath, their hair tied back in tight buns.

At the time that Meiji looked up, the gown was drawn closed. In the next instant, however, the attendants had parted the slit, drawing the sheer material back to reveal that the woman's belly, beneath the gown, was enormously swollen. The pale skin had been decorated with a swirling pattern in deep orange mehendi, centred on the woman's navel. The gathered spectators gave soft whoops of approval and anticipation.

'Welcome, Candidates!' she said now. 'I am Mentor Maia. I have invited you here to witness the true miracle of life: the birth of a human soul.'

2

Meiji felt her face growing hot. She wanted to cover her eyes and squirm away. Sitting where she was, hemmed in by strangers, she was absolutely trapped. The woman at the centre of the stage was staring directly at her.

'Our bodies,' began Maia, 'the bodies of female beings, are the source of immense power: the power to give birth. We are the Earth, we are the Universe, we are the Sun and all the stars combined, for within our bodies the mystery of life remains coiled and dormant …'

The white-haired woman spoke in a voice like an iron spear, heavy with portent.

Meiji felt it was aimed directly at her. After her first glance towards the stage, she had not dared to raise her face again, but sat instead with her gaze directed downwards at the outer edge of the cushion upon which she sat, memorizing its contours.

'In the past, the use of this power was available to anyone who had the physical equipment. But in recent years, better sense has prevailed. Now it is only the rare few amongst us who are endowed with this Immortal Trust. I am one of these. A Sacred Bearer. We bear life on behalf of all those who are not fit for this high calling.

'Today, in front of your eyes, I will bring forth New Life.'

All around her, Meiji could feel the other Candidates in the room stirring and whispering. She wondered if they had seen this before.

'In ages past, women were powerless and wretched. Their

mystic energy was trapped by the powers of men, who sought to control them and therefore to control the force of life itself. It suited these base and ignorant beings to ensure that birth was a horrifying ordeal of pain and bloodshed. Untold millions of women in the past lost their lives in the agony of the Child Bed. Countless generations of us have grown to adulthood believing our bodies to be our adversaries, seething with uncontrollable forces.

'Truly, we have advanced since those days.'

There was a flourish of trumpets. Meiji heard the murmurs around her swell into a chorus of gasps. She raised her head.

The Mentor was no longer standing. She had seated herself on the throne, bracing herself on the two hanging cords, with her knees parted. A spotlight was directed towards what looked like an enormous crimson blossom that sprouted from between her legs. It looked nothing like any human organ Meiji had ever seen, even though she had seen plenty in the past few days on the Island. The Mentor's posture was also remarkable. Her feet were planted apart at an extremely wide angle, apparently with no strain at all.

'As you can all see,' said Maia, 'my body has been radically altered. For me, and others of my profession, birth is the glory it was always meant to be. My hips have been surgically widened. The mouth of my birth canal looks like a lotus flower in full bloom. The passage itself is lubricated with fragrant oils that my own body has been trained to produce and its muscular walls are as broad as they are strong. The child who has grown within me for these past six months is in my absolute control as she waits to pass from pre-existence into life.'

Maia's breathing was thickening in a rhythm.

'Because I am not in pain, I am calm. Because I am calm, so is my unborn child. I can feel her at the brink of my birth canal, huge and hot with life, waiting serenely to be born.'

Images were flashing through Meiji's mind. Not of people, but of animals being born. Cows. Pigs. Horses. She could remember them with piercing clarity, as if the heavy curtain across her memory had made an exception of these tableaux, complete with sound and scent.

The pungent tumult of the small stalls, the straw on the floor, the labouring beasts, groaning aloud and tossing their heads, the hours of waiting. Then! With no warning, the slithering torrent from the rear end. The liquid jumble of limbs and hooves that flowed out. Solidifying in the very next instant, to become twitching ears and knobbly knees.

Weak. Struggling. Miraculous.

'Breathe with me now!'

The two attendants on either side of Maia led a fluting push-pull of sound, *Ha!-HUM! Ha!-HUM!*, which was taken up by the Candidates in the room. The whole chamber became a single tide of shushing sound, the reed music building on the tempo, higher and higher, louder and louder until with a jolt of invisible energy such that the air and walls and floor itself shuddered and bounced, out popped a small red head from the blossom between Maia's legs.

A moment later, there she was, alive and whole in the hands of the two attendants: a tiny being, scarlet and squirming, bound in electric blue cords.

The whole room reverberated with ululating cries.

But Meiji had stopped watching long before the head appeared. Her gaze was turned inwards, towards the visions within her memory. She had sensed a presence beside her as she watched the animals in the pictures in her mind. A person whom she knew and loved had been there with her. Who was this person? *Who?*

Not even Rahm's sharp elbow digging into her side could shake her loose from her urgent reverie.

Maia, glancing up from the stage, saw the girl sitting with her eyes averted. For that instant she felt a curtain of fury fall over her reason. Then her newborn child cried, and all other thoughts and concerns were erased from her mind.

3

After the show ended, the gathered Candidates shuffled out, passing in single file through the narrow passage that led back to the corridor.

Rahm and Meiji were amongst the last to leave. Meiji avoided looking up towards her companion for as long as possible. 'Come on!' insisted the big-haired girl, finally. 'You is not impress?'

Meiji twitched her shoulders and shook her head. She wished she could just get *away*.

'You is maximum rude feem,' said Rahm now. She was whispering, her mouth close to Meiji's left ear, the great halo of her hair feeling like a heated powder-puff against Meiji's bare scalp. 'Mentor Maia is all-the-time look at you. And you is not look up, nothing.'

'I didn't want to be present. I didn't want to see.'

'Even now everyone is look at you.'

It was true. Meiji could sense from the corner of her eye that the remaining girls and women in the room were turning in her direction, staring. She had deliberately avoided looking at them when she had first entered the audience chamber, because even in the dim light she had seen that many of them were half-unclothed, their bare limbs and plump, jiggling, tattooed bodies open to view. She had not yet grown accustomed to these sights. Now, surrounded by these others, it was all she could do to avoid holding her hands up to her face, shielding her gaze.

'It's not my fault,' Meiji whispered in return. 'I'm not doing anything.'

'Yes, you IS,' insisted Rahm. 'You is not watch Mentor. You is not make breath-chant, you is not scream and clap. You is every time being different. From all, everyone else.'

'It's not my fault,' repeated Meiji.

'It is rude. It is stupid,' said Rahm. 'And also, it is danger.'

'Danger?'

'To be not-same is danger. To you.' Rahm's voice dropped down to a barely audible hiss. 'See up. See at others. They is all look at you.'

Perhaps thirty girls were left in the darkened room, moving towards the exit. Raising her head, Meiji looked around. They were darker than her, these other Candidates, their skin-colours ranging from Rahm's shining indigo hue to bronzes and mahoganies. She felt like an insubstantial wraith surrounded by beings more solid than herself. Every one of them wore piercings that gave off glittering twinkles and sparkles, a type of visual twittering. One or two of them had shimmering white tattooes like Rahm's. Many of them wore their hair in mounds and peaks, spikes and knobs.

They were turning and whispering, raking her with their eyes, then whispering again.

Meiji tightened her lips and drew her sheet more tightly around herself. 'I don't care,' she whispered to Rahm.

'You is must care,' Rahm whispered back. Then she stiffened.

One of the others had turned and was addressing Meiji directly.

'So,' she began, her full mouth curling in a sneer. '*You're* the famous one? Such a little shrimp?'

Rahm bristled at once. 'You is shut it, Jeesa!' she hissed.

The other girl was lithe and straight, like a dark string bean. She had a line of pale green rings down the middle of her forehead, each one pulsing light. The upper portion of her body was bare, and a skirt of shifting beads was slung around her hips.

Glancing at Rahm, she said, 'Oh-oh-oh, is that you Rahmato'u? Still on the Island all these months and not yet learnt to speak?'

Around her, the cohort of the girl's friends began to snuffle and snigger.

Jeesa returned her focus on Meiji. 'We hear you have something Very Special between your legs ...'

There were more snickers from the other girls.

'I said, you is SHUT IT, Jeesa!' said Rahm. 'Midji is quiet feem, not barking dog like you!'

'And you're not her guard-baboon neither,' Jeesa snarled.

A voice shot an arrow towards Meiji, 'Hey, little Boy-Girl! A peek, a peek! Give us a peek!'

Another voice elaborated, 'A peek of your pee-pee, Boy-Girl!'

More voices chorused, 'Yes! Yes! We want to play with it!'

They closed in now, these others, even as the group as a whole continued to press towards the exit. Meiji felt her gorge rising. The desire to run was prickling out of her skin, like thorns on a cactus. Hands were reaching out, plucking at her thin white sheet.

Rahm placed her arm tight around Meiji. 'Enough! You is not touch her—'

Instead of feeling comforted, Meiji felt strangled by the other girl's protection. Her breath was being squeezed out of her. With a despairing gasp, she pushed with all her strength against her team leader. As the other girl lost her balance, Meiji wriggled free of the swaddling sheet and darted forward, towards the dark exit passage.

It was only a couple of metres deep. She rammed her way past the three girls who were still inside, her lack of piercings and the advantage of surprise making it relatively easy for her to burst out of the mouth of the passage without being caught.

Standing in the outer corridor were two other girls. Meiji heard one of them say, 'Hey, hey! No running—' but she had already swung away from them in the opposite direction, her feet digging into the floor in exactly the way she knew was forbidden. She wasn't sure where she was, no idea where she was going. She just knew that she was *off*.

A moment later she had crashed into a hard, muscular wall. A green wall. Two hands like steel vices gripped her by the arms and a voice spoke to her in a calm, commanding voice. 'Meiji. Stop. That's enough now. No running in the corridors.'

With her breath pumping in and out of her chest, Meiji reared back, ready to jump at the throat of whoever had dared to stop her. What she saw was an impossibility: a face made up entirely of leaves, with two pale grey eyes staring out at her, lit from within.

'I am Mentor Folia,' said the leafy face.

Meiji felt like a bird has flown into a block of liquid ice, frozen in midflight.

'It's all right,' said Folia. 'You're safe now. You're with me.'

4

They were in Folia's green and leafy apartment, Meiji, Rahm and the Mentor. Meiji was kneeling on a cushion, on the floor, her hands over her eyes. 'I want to be AWAY,' she said. 'Away. Away.'

'Repetition doesn't make a thing happen,' said Folia. She was seated on the floor, with her feet in a shallow pool of water. Rahm was near her, facing Meiji, sitting cross-legged in the attitude of an observer. She had brought the sheet that Meiji had left behind and was sitting with it wrapped around her own shoulders.

'Then what *does* ... make things happen?' asked Meiji, not looking up. Folia had given her a light kimono with a pattern of golden bamboo printed on it to wear.

'Maybe nothing,' said Folia. 'Maybe accepting reality for what it is.'

There was a pause.

'Meiji, what do you want?' asked Folia.

'To be in some other place,' said Meiji at once.

'Maybe there *is* no other place,' said Folia.

'There has to be,' said Meiji. She raised her head to look into Folia's bizarrely decorated face. 'Everyone here has some place that they came from. Everyone here has others who look a bit like themselves. Even if they don't remember their pasts, they can see from their *bodies* and their *decorations* that they came from some other place where there are others like themselves.'

Rahm jerked forward as if to interject, but Folia stopped her.

'All right. Suppose the thing you want isn't possible? Suppose the place you want to go to, or where you think you came from, can no longer be returned to?'

Meiji stared at Folia. Then she tapped her head, 'In *here*. It's not just a different *place*. It's a different way of being. I don't know how to explain myself. I can feel it! But I can't see it around me. And no one knows what I'm talking about.' She flicked her eyes away. She could feel tears prickling under her lids, but she was determined not to cry.

There was a silence.

'All right,' said Folia. 'Let us imagine you're right. What would you say if there's nothing to be done about it … ?'

'No,' said Meiji. She made a sideways-chopping motion with her head. 'I won't accept that.'

Rahm looked at Folia with a 'you-see?' expression.

Meiji raised her eyes to Folia's. 'And even if it's true? Even if there is *no* place I can go back to? I want my memories back.' She stated this flatly, as a demand. 'I must have them. I don't care what they are—'

'No! Past is full of poisons!' cried Rahm. 'Memories is burn and bite you!'

'I don't *care*!' exclaimed Meiji in a matching tone. She flung her gaze at Folia once more. 'Mentor Vane said it was possible. She told me I could have my memories in exchange for doing … something. A challenge. I don't know what she meant exactly. I didn't ask and I don't care: I'll do it. Whatever it is. Anything. I want to know.'

'Oh?' said Folia. 'Anything?'

'*Anything!*'

'Including settling down? Being calm? And patient?'

Meiji clutched her head again. She leapt to her feet as if intending to pace up and down. As she did, her kimono fell open and it was only then, when she looked down, that she realized that a casualty had occurred as she had rushed out of the auditorium.

Rahm saw it too. 'Ho,' she said. 'Look! Your … *thing*. Is torn.'

Meiji tilted her hips up, trying to assess the extent of the damage. The flaccid tube that had dangled between her legs for three years now was hanging askew. It wasn't quite torn but had been stretched beyond capacity.

She sucked in her breath, frowning.

In the next moment, she dug her thumbs into the waistband of the prosthesis and tore it off her skin. It made a sharp, ripping sound. Then she was stepping out of it, reducing it to a mangled twist of skin-brown rubber in her hands. She threw it down onto Folia's smooth black floor and whipped her head up, defiant.

'There,' she said. 'It's gone. Why did it matter so much? All of you – Rahm, Mentor Vane and … and … all the other girls – everyone looks lumpy and twisted to *me*! Everyone. Yet I am the one that all of you point at! I am treated like the only one who is different, who is a … *freak* … ' Her voice had begun to falter.

Then she stopped speaking altogether, though her mouth remained open.

A memory had sprung, full-formed, out of the locked room in her mind. It took the shape of a huge person, a man as tall as he was wide, who towered over her, instructing her to step into the stretchy prosthetic device for the first time. The image was as vivid as if he were standing in front of her. She was shrunken in size, reaching up no higher than his waist, panicked and afraid. Yet the fear was not directed at him. Not really. He was someone she knew and trusted as much as the sweet-scented grasses tickling her calves.

An *uncle*.

She had three uncles. He was one of them.

He and she were standing in a field of grass that stretched from the night behind them, to the edge of dawn in front of them.

The sky was pearly mauve and there was a scent, a perfume, that enfolded the uncle like a cloak. It reached out to her as well, holding her in its comforting embrace.

Then the memory snapped off, as abruptly as it had begun.

Meiji returned to her present with a jerk. She snapped her mouth shut, unable to recall what she had been talking about before.

Folia, looking at her, saw the girl's energy shift from defeat to strength in the space of an eye-blink. A hand had reached out from her past and supported her in the moment of her need. She had staggered but did not fall.

Meiji glanced up. 'Even now,' she said, her voice subdued, 'you're both still giving me that look.' The edge of pain was gone from her voice. The cloak of invulnerability that her memory had flung over her, as insubstantial as the phantom scent she could not name, nevertheless protected her.

Rahm shrugged as she said, 'Midji, you is always feel too much about no-anythings. Just now I is only looks at you, with no any bad-bad. Because I is surprise, is all.' Then she knelt up so that she could pat her own crotch. 'See! Before you is got little pipe-thing, but now you is got *hair*! Is very surprise. Is no one else here have, because we is all perma-shave it off. So even now you is still different from all-everyone.'

Meiji twitched her shoulders. She didn't know how to respond to this observation. When she glanced at Folia, she saw the leaves of the Mentor's face were arranged in a sly smile.

'You don't realize it, Meiji,' said the Mentor, 'but you've already changed since you first came here.' She didn't wait for the girl to respond. 'Remember the Welcome Field? Remember how you resisted being asked to remove your clothes?'

It was true: Meiji hadn't even noticed that she was for all practical purposes naked in full view of two others. 'Too much has happened,' she said. 'I … I don't … it doesn't …'

Rahm grinned and said, 'Mentor Folia is say true. You is change, Midji! You is not care so much no more about your clothes.'

5

The two girls returned to their quarters, saying very little along the way. Folia had told them that they would be shifting residence very soon. She had explained that the Island was emptying out. Rahm nodded, knowing what this meant: they would feel the structure rocking and bouncing around them as they moved around it, because of changes in weight on each floor.

Meiji staggered like a drunk, her arms outstretched, touching the walls on either side to keep herself from tipping over. She remembered what had happened on her way back from her encounter with Vane. She had tucked it away without mentioning it to anyone. Just one more mystery.

Rahm was ahead of her, stepping as carefully as a cat crossing a wet lawn. The muffled thumps, booms and clicks which characterized the Island had increased in frequency and the sound of water pouring in and out of hidden crevices all through the structure was louder than ever before.

'Why is it happening?' she asked, but Rahm had turned around with a finger to her mouth.

Meiji shrugged. She was distracted by the lightness of spirit she felt within herself. Something had shifted during their visit to Folia. Just the knowledge that in her past there had been a place of safety and comfort had been enough to help her overcome the chaos of her present.

There were no other teammates in their room. 'They is go to other Islands,' said Rahm. 'Only you and me is stay. For next challenge.'

'Oh!' said Meiji. 'Do you know what it is?'

Rahm nodded. 'Is creature-challenge.' She shuddered and looked away. Clearly, it was not something she was looking forward to.

Meiji frowned. She didn't think she would be allowed onto another whale so soon after what had happened with Noor.

'Not whale,' said Rahm guessing the direction of Meiji's thoughts. 'Other creature.' She bit her lip. 'I is not like this one.' She glanced up at Meiji. 'Is because you is want memory-recall. Mentor Folia is told me. Is hard challenge. I is think you is not ready.' Her tone was not accusing so much as resigned. 'But you is make big noise. So. Now we will both go for this one.'

'Why? I don't understand—'

They were sitting at the hexagonal table, not quite facing one another, with one seat vacant between them.

Rahm tightened the corners of her generous mouth, as if preparing to make a difficult admission. 'Mentor Folia is asked me to look out for you, Midji.' She raised her eyebrows and shrugged. 'Is happen when you is arrive in Island. Mentor Vane is asking Mentor Folia and for me: *Will you look out for special case feem?* So of course I is say *Yes!* Is good for me to have the protection experiences. Is good for my credits.'

She paused, waiting to see if Meiji was following.

'We is get credits for trainings. More is difficult training means more is credits. Credit score is decide where we is go.'

'Go?' asked Meiji, wrinkling her forehead.

Rahm clicked her tongue. 'I is tell you before once already: after Island training is complete, Mentors is decide what kind of workers we is become. Credit score is help decide.' She shrugged. 'Some feems is even go back to Zone, because they is not liking to work for Mentors. They is not want to spend all life with only feems, no mans.'

Meiji asked, 'And you?'

'I is train for to be Mentor. And that is long-long path. Needing many-much credits.' She bent her head to one side. 'But you is not only special case, Midji! You is *hard* case! I is not know that before I is say *yes*.'

Meiji wondered if she should feel surprised or embarrassed. 'I … I'm sorry,' she said, though she did not feel in the least apologetic. She would have been stupid not to notice that the other girl was protective towards her. Nor did it surprise her to hear that she needed special attention. It merely confirmed her certainty that she was, after all, different from all the rest of the inmates on the Island. 'Maybe I can ask Mentor Vane to let you go?'

'No, no,' said Rahm tiredly. 'That is not the way on Island. We is must be brave and strong. Maybe tomorrow is worst-hard case than you! And maybe that day I is Mentor! Then I is got nowhere to run. So I is must face the challenge. Same to you.'

Rahm's words blew wind into her own sails and she drew herself upright. 'Come. Time is go fast. First I is must take you to see Mentor Tasha, then we is come back to eat and prepare for challenge.'

'Wait, wait,' said Meiji. 'Who is Mentor Tasha?'

'She is Restorer,' said Rahm. 'For memories.'

Meiji jumped to her feet in her excitement. 'I'll go there first? Before the creature challenge?'

Rahm made a huffing sound, midway between a laugh and snort. 'Heh. You is not be so happy when you is come back! That much I is sure.'

'You are *wrong*,' said Meiji. 'When we were with Mentor Folia, a tiny memory came back to me—'

'Midji, I is see five … no, *six* feems, who is got memory-restore,' said Rahm. 'Four is ask to perma-rase.' She paused for effect. 'Number five is *suicide*.' She lifted her upper lip, exposing its pink underside. 'You is not know all-everything. The past is sad-max place. I is know for real. I is that sixth feem. I is also ask for restore.' She looked away.

'REALLY!' said Meiji, astonished. 'But you always said ...'

'I is have to do it, because I is want Mentor-path.' The big-haired girl continued to look away to the side, as if watching a screen that only she could see. 'So I is not allowed perma-rase. Instead I is get restore. So I is know all-everything about my past.'

She brought her eyes back to Meiji.

'I is born to sex-circus family. You is know what is that? No, you is not know. Is mean living in Zone, performing the sex for teams. My mother is train me. Or maybe is my sister. I is not know which. When I is one year old, she is give me to her Big Man to use and he is use me three ways, then he is pass me around to his friends. From then is start, every day, every night. My mother is feed me the drugs instead of milk.

'Because I is not have any other life so I's think this is best life. I's happy. When I am twelve years, already I am have every-all sickness. I is give suck to dogs. To pigs. On stage. To make laugh to Zone teams. Then we is get food for whole family.'

She stopped. Tears were welling out of her eyes and washing down her cheeks. 'I is not really crying, Midji. But my eyes is make water when I is look at that past. I is say I was happy? Yes. Because I is not know what is "happy" mean.' She leaned forward on her elbows, speaking as earnestly as she could, 'Midji, you is happy now. Stay happy. Don't look to yesterday. Be happy for today.'

Meiji knew that she needed to be sympathetic to the other girl's story. But within her mind the warm aura of her nameless uncle's protection wrapped itself around her shoulders once more, like an invisible shawl. She felt sure that her experiences would be different. She had to know more.

Rahm stood up, her face in shadow. 'Come. I is know you will not listen to Rahm. Let us go.'

6

'We shall eat shark tomorrow for lunch,' said the General. He spoke in a soft, measured tone, but Aila already knew this was a false front. She didn't know exactly what had transpired between him and Yasmine via their radio link, but something had clearly gone wrong. Maybe Yasmine had refused to do what he had been told. Or been unable to do it.

Whatever the case, the General was in a state of rage. He would try to control it, but it would get the better of him and eventually he would take it out on her. At this moment, he was allowing himself to be entertained by torturing the two creatures that had earlier consumed the unfortunate drone.

Both sharks were currently tethered to the boat by hooks through their tails. They could not live for long in this condition. Being dragged backward meant that very little water passed over their open, forward-facing gill-slits. In effect, they were drowning, slowly and agonizingly. They were still thrashing strenuously enough so that Aila could feel the disturbance as she sat on the fore deck.

Aila was dressed in gauzy black strips that covered her from neck to ankle, secured in a few strategic places with flimsy diamante-encrusted ties that sparkled in the midday sun. She wore a broad-rimmed hat. She was staring at her hands, saying nothing.

'I wanted to allow them to digest their last supper, you see,' said the General. 'So that when we eat their meat we too will get the benefit of our late crew-member's proteins and fats without the tedium of being cannibals. I call that efficient. What do you call it, Algebra?'

When she didn't answer, the General, who had been jogging back and forth on the deck in his usual manner, suddenly reached for her chair and pulled it away from under her. She had heard his footsteps and had anticipated his actions, so she was able to time her fall to make it seem as if he had succeeded in surprising her.

The polished wood was burning hot under her cheek, but she lay still, breathing carefully. Her eyes were shut but her hat had fallen off. She felt the General's shadow as it fell over her. 'I asked you a question,' he said, bending low over her. His breath was sour under her nose. 'You didn't answer.'

'I call it cruel,' said Aila.

He laughed. 'Efficiency often is!'

He picked her off the floor, then forced his attentions on her, front and back, for half an hour. She denied him the satisfaction of letting him know that he was hurting or offending her. She knew he would find her resistance infuriating. Eventually, he began punching her shoulders as she lay face forward with the upper half of her body draped over the wooden table.

When she continued to offer no reaction, he withdrew with a snarl, leaving her where she lay, exposed and bruised. She waited a short while, without moving. When the movements of the boat told her that he had gone below decks, she straightened up. The skin of her back smarted and her limbs were covered in the General's slime. Still. She felt a smile developing within herself.

Nothing had changed: the General had only retreated for the moment. Her sense of accomplishment was as empty as a soap bubble. And yet, like a bubble, a film of iridescent light defined her mood. Why? There was no one to whom she could explain or who would understand her if she tried. Perhaps even Yasmine would not understand.

It was that she had gone beyond her earlier need to please. And it wasn't just the General. It was the need altogether.

Her entire life so far had taken place in a room the size of the interior of her skull. Within that room, her only imperative was to please all those who existed outside that room. It didn't matter what they asked of her or who they were, or how harshly they behaved towards her.

All that mattered was pleasing them because, otherwise, the space of her tiny mental room filled up with pain. Their pain. It was as if she had been born to receive and process the anger, unhappiness and frustration of all those she came in contact with. Her only tools were the parts of her body that she could make available in order to help others achieve their fleeting squirts. Their pain was so relentless, so without end, that the pauses between sessions were fleeting. Even so, they gave her relief and allowed her to believe that her existence had meaning.

Meeting the General had been a revelation.

His need went beyond anything she had known. Where other men were like storage tanks that could be emptied, this man was like an inexhaustible well. His need was not based on pain or anger. In truth, she could not fathom it. He spewed words to describe the ways in which he and his brothers were exceptional, but his words didn't have counterparts in her understanding of other men.

He was like an electronic device that needed continuous recharging. The sex-act was a form of nourishment, but he obviously needed something more, because he was insatiable. Perhaps, when he was within range of his clone-brothers, they provided one another with whatever it was, that other kind of nourishment, that charging. Perhaps everyone needed charging in that way, through contact with like-minded people. All she could say for certain was that she had done her best to meet his demands, and she had fallen short.

Another thing she could now say about herself that she had not known before was that there was a limit to her ability to sacrifice herself on the altar of a man's need. It had happened at the time of the drone-killing. When the General had tried forcing her to enjoy his cruel sport, she had felt something break inside. She lost the desire to please him. For the first time, or so it seemed to her, she could separate her own feelings from another person's need to be pleasured. That, for her, was a type of liberation.

She stood upright now and looked around.

There were no drones in sight. She rearranged her dress and went sternwards. That was where they were, clustered together. Five small figures were clinging to the rails and looking down into the water. At the still-thrashing, dying sharks trailing in the ships wake.

She wondered if they understood that these creatures had eaten their brother-drone. Was that why they were watching the death throes? Because they sensed that the energy of one of them was experiencing an afterlife in the flailing fins, tails and snapping jaws of the fish? Or were they simply enjoying the spectacle of suffering, the purity and helplessness of another creature's death throes, for its own sake?

There was no way of knowing.

7

Youngest may have dozed off or been sedated, he could not tell. Vane hadn't said how long she would be away.

He awoke to find Vane's assistant at his side. She had a plug of what looked like putty in her hands. She proceeded to place it in his mouth, moulding it onto his back teeth. It tasted foul. The material was dense and heavy, but malleable enough that he could bite down into it. It hardened quickly.

Vane had returned and was standing by his side, studying a flat black disk that she held against the right side of his face, by his jaw. 'For the moment, your receiver-transmitter's frequency has been cancelled.' She held the disk up so that he could also see its display window. 'The original signal shows up as a wavering red line. Then it fades out.'

Youngest was sitting upright on the raised platform, with a sheet wrapped around himself. The unnamed assistant who had heard the clicking in his mouth and reported it to Vane was standing on his left.

'No signal,' he said, barely able to believe his own words. He was free of the General. He could of course still hear the loop of recorded sound from the chip within his teeth, but that was nothing compared to the living broadcasts. And the mind-altering pain.

He was free. No longer leashed to the General.

His mind flew to Meiji.

Where was she? How would he find her?

He wasn't able to ask. He was an exploding volcano of

questions, with no vents.

'Good,' said Vane. She glanced up at the assistant and gestured to her to come around. To Youngest she said, 'There is much that I want to know and need to ask. But time is not on our side. Right now I need you to ... ah. Your foot. Can you walk?' The assistant positioned herself at his side to help him get down from the platform.

Youngest had not thought about his foot for a while. His mind was still struggling to believe he was untethered from the radio.

'We need to move in, away from the exterior walls,' said Vane.

'I don't understand,' said Youngest, trying not to pant. At any moment he expected to feel the blinding, thought-cancelling surge of pain in his jaw. He began to turn himself around. 'I mean, about the exterior walls?' he asked as he put down the injured foot.

There was no sensation in the foot. Instead, he felt as if a leaden weight had been attached to the end of his right leg. The mass of pain-relieving grey jelly had shrunk around his foot, so that it looked now like a translucent sock. No doubt it would soon vanish altogether.

The attendant offered her arm for him to lean on. The pent-up frustration within him was growing uncontainable. He wanted to run, he wanted to bellow and sing out, he wanted to crash through walls and charge through doors. Instead of which, he had to speak in a soft, measured voice, behaving with the grovelling humility of a prisoner at the mercy of his captors.

'It's to do with the Island,' said Vane watching his maneouvres. 'We're in the midst of a dismantling. My staff have to clear and secure my living spaces.'

'I'm sorry. In the midst of a ... what?' Youngest looked up as he hobbled forward.

'I'll explain later,' said Vane. 'For the moment all you need to know is that the Island is being dismantled. It will disintegrate. Vanish.' She turned from him and began to move away.

Youngest hopped after Vane, like a giant, one-legged frog. His thoughts were whirling, as he struggled to keep his focus clear. The attendant tried to follow him, but got left behind. She did not persevere.

'Wait, please,' he said, 'wait. The man with whom I was communicating – he'll know, when he can't get through, that the frequency is blocked. His next move will be to force his way in—'

'Into the *Island*?' said the Mentor, turning slightly as she lifted one shoulder in a shrug. 'And then what? I mean, there's only *one* of him, am I right? What can one man ever do? Even assuming he could get in, that is.'

'Yes, but—'

'In any case, he won't be able to. This Island will have scattered by the time he tries to board us. There won't be anything for him to force his way into.'

'I'm sorry,' said Youngest. 'I'm finding it hard to believe that a solid structure can just … disintegrate!' How could it possibly happen fast enough to prevent the General from boarding? And Meiji! Where was she?

'I mentioned it earlier. About the dismantling.'

'Yes – but—' said Youngest.

Vane turned, impatience inflating her voice. 'This Island is not a solid structure. It's made of detachable parts – look around – can you see that there's a modularity? Look at where the struts join floor to ceiling – if you train yourself to see the joints, you'll notice that there's a regularity to the jointing. So. The entire Island, or all of it except the sunken undersea docks, is made up of separate units. Separate cells. Each cell is about the size of a one-person room. When the cells join up, they can form larger rooms. Like this one, for instance.' She paused, waiting for his comprehension to catch up with the clues she was feeding him.

Youngest looked around, struggling to remain focused on the conversation. Inside his head, urgent questions were bumping about like ping-pong balls. Had he shaken off the General only to lose Meiji?

'I … I see,' he said, though he didn't really. 'So how are the separate units fitted together? What kind of sealants are flexible and strong enough to … to …'

At no point in his plans for escaping from the clutches of the General had he allowed himself the luxury of plotting the consequences of success. All his thinking had been done before he committed himself to the path. Once committed, he had been forced to compress his own personality down to the size of a mustard seed, in order to permit the General's personality, via the radio link and the tooth-embedded recording, to strut about within his skull.

Vane was shaking her head in response to his questions. 'No, no – they're not simple prefabricated blocks! How could they be? We don't have access to factories. We needed flexibility and durability, both. Don't you get it?'

Youngest looked around, mystified. He shook his head.

'Oh come on – stretch your mind a bit, Yasmine! Or whatever your real name is – which materials are infinitely self-renewing, given ideal conditions?'

He stared at her.

Then he looked around again.

He sucked in his breath, recalling all the little clues – the irregular joints, the elastic membranes, the sentient elevator cars, the uncanny intimacy of the toilet seat – suddenly pointing, like lighted arrows, in a single direction.

'*Organic materials*,' he breathed out, impressed in spite of himself.

It had to be the answer.

The Island was a cluster of highly modified living creatures.

'Crabs, specifically,' said Vane. 'They proved extremely versatile. We hybridized them, grossly altered their physical dimensions and created a strain that lives symbiotically with us. So long as we maintain their food supply, they can function indefinitely.'

Youngest looked around again.

'Their nervous systems provide us with whatever we need in the way of power. Nervous energy *is* a form of electricity, after all. It's transmitted via nerves instead of copper wires. The marine world has produced versions of everything we use in electronics. There are electric eels, shape-shifting octopi and spectacular forms of bio-luminescence, all produced by the complex nervous systems of creatures in the natural world. We have merely synthesized and repurposed what was already there.'

Youngest pursed his mouth in appreciation. 'Amazing,' he said.

'There's one more piece to the puzzle, though,' said Vane. Her expression was odd, like someone on the brink of telling a joke. 'It's a rather crucial piece. In order for you to understand, you need to submit to a ... procedure. Come. The others are waiting.'

8

A group of five Mentors was seated on the floor perhaps twenty paces ahead of where Youngest and Vane were. It was hard to tell whether they had been there all along or screened from view till just now.

The apartment was circular, with its curving wall of windows providing a 360-degree view from the top floor of the Island. The platform on which he had been resting was near the windows, whereas the Mentors were seated closer to the centre of the apartment, near the elevator shaft through which he and Bella had entered earlier.

'I … I must speak to you,' said Youngest to Vane. He saw, with a sense of unease, that the others were seated around a shallow trough. They were looking expectantly towards Vane and himself. The trough was perhaps a hand's width deep, with smooth curving sides, its interior creamy-smooth, golden ivory in colour. It was long enough to accommodate a broad, tall person.

'It will have to wait,' said Vane. She introduced the Mentors. 'Brahi, Asma, Emmi and Kesh,' she said, pointing to the four women kneeling on cushions, arranged symmetrically on either side of the depression in the floor. 'And finally, Cha.' Cha was at the farther end. 'Mentors, this is … Yasmine.'

Youngest turned to Vane, trying to make eye-contact with her. 'Mentor Vane, I *must speak—*'

He had already considered the possibility of making a rush for the windows. But even if he succeeded, even if he could break through without being stopped, what then? He could not survive in the jellyfish-infested waters. He had no means of locating the General's yacht. And he would lose any chance he ever had of locating Meiji.

'No,' said Vane. 'There's something I need you to do right now.' She pointed to the trough. 'I need you to lie down in that shallow depression. As you can see, it's just enough to contain your height.'

Youngest bit his lips, frowning. He had no choice.

She told him to remove the sheet he had wrapped around himself. When he was on his back, she told him to stretch his arms by his sides. 'You must force yourself to relax. When you're ready, close your eyes.'

Youngest felt angry, helpless, ridiculous. *Meiji, Meiji, Meiji,* he thought to himself, *this is for you. Only you. You had better be here. On this Island.* He tried to make her name his mantra. But it made him tense up all the more. Supposing she wasn't here? Supposing it was already much too late?

He flexed his neck, held his arms stiffly along his sides and shrugged his shoulders a couple of times. Above him, on the ceiling, the virtual palm fronds swayed against the blinding whiteness of the fake sky. He shut his eyes. Reverse images of the palm fronds flashed on his retina.

Then he gasped and recoiled: a cool wet mask was placed over his eyes, covering them completely, eclipsing the light. Simultaneously, he felt hands upon him.

'You must try to relax,' repeated Vane. Her voice came from behind his head. 'Pay attention to my voice. We are going to take you through a process which, as I've already told you, will be crucial for what lies ahead for you.'

'No … I …' stammered Youngest wanting at once to leap up and away from the trough. But they women had slipped restraints on him, around his upper arms and wrists. Five pairs of hands were holding him down, two at his shoulders, two each at his thighs, one at his feet.

'You have to trust me, Yasmine,' said Vane. 'Do not resist.'

'I can't!' said Youngest. 'You've placed restraints on me!' He deliberately allowed his voice to slip into his masculine register. 'And look, I can guess what you're going to do – and I can tell you, it won't work. You don't understand.' He tried to raise his head, but there was a pair of hands there too, combing fingers through his hair and drawing it away from under his head. He guessed they were Vane's hands.

'*You* are the one who does not understand,' said Vane. 'We're not going to harm you. You have to trust us. You're going to like this.'

No, I will not, thought Youngest. *You'll find that out for yourself soon enough.*

'Relax your hands,' said Vane once more. 'Release your breath.'

He snorted his breath out forcefully, feeling like a chained dragon. His teeth were clenched tight. If he wanted, he could keep himself in this taut, furious state for hours.

But the voices were maddeningly unresponsive and calm.

'Relax your hands,' they repeated, now in unison. 'Release. Your. Breath.'

Relax. Release. Breathe. *Relax. Release. Breathe.* Relax. Release. Breathe.

He felt a source of heat above his belly, then he smelt a rich earthy scent, fresh rain on fertile soil. *Vetiver*. It was a fragrance he knew and loved. His skin pores loosened and shivered open. His breath grew calm without any conscious effort.

'We begin with aromatic oil,' said a new voice, speaking in a low murmur. It may have been the Mentor he had recognized from the hold, Brahi. 'It is heated. I will begin pouring above your navel.' A point of scalding heat bloomed on the skin of his belly, quickly trickling sideways in molten rivulets. Immediately, two pairs of hands, one on either side of him, began to spread the oil in smooth, unhurried strokes, using just the tips of the fingers.

Two more streams of oil began in the middle of his chest and on his forehead.

It was not a massage in the sense that Youngest was used to, but a formal caress, rhythmic and platonic, applied by six separate people. He guessed that the focus would eventually shift south of his navel, whereupon there would be a tedious repeat of the encounter with Anita. But as the minutes ticked by, the gently swirling fingers, went on and on, with mesmeric, unvarying regularity. They made no distinction between his shoulders and his breasts, his face and his lower abdomen. On and on they went, on and on, until the boundary between the moving fingers and Youngest's skin slipped away, enveloping him in a delicate cocoon of perfumed heat.

He did not recall being asked to part his legs or raise his knees.

This time, it was Vane who spoke. 'The oil, again.'

He felt the point of heat upon the cleft between his legs. He wanted to object. He wanted to warn her that it would be futile to offer him any sexual release. He opened his mouth but the hands at his head immediately swirled down and closed it.

Then, against all reason, his nerves began to tingle and sway. He felt a bloom of expectation in a place that had not existed till then.

He could not make sense of this. He was not equipped to support erotic feelings in his female organs. Yet … fingers were plucking at the ghost-wires strung across the instrument of his body. Making it sing.

He heard his breathing change.

His back arched up of its own accord.

His consciousness melted away.

Cries emerged from his throat in a voice he had never heard before.

A tumult lifted his mind away altogether.

9

'It's done then,' said the General. Aila and he were on the foredeck of the yacht, looking towards the still-invisible Island. Knowing precisely where to look allowed them to notice, now, the slight anomalies in light that hinted at its outlines: a shape similar to a loaf of bread, long and low, that extended perhaps 200 metres from edge to edge. They knew it was cylindrical. The General had pointed to the water, tracing unexplained irregularities that hinted at a hidden presence.

'What is done?' asked Aila mechanically.

'Yasmine,' said the General. 'He's crossed over to the other side.'

For a moment Aila thought this meant Yasmine had died.

The General continued, 'My radio connection is live, but I cannot hear him. I'm guessing he can't hear me. Or if he can, he chooses not to talk back to me. Which means he has broken loose. Cut his link. Defected.' He paused. 'No matter.'

He was turned away from Aila and could not see her face stiffen as if she expected momentarily to be slapped or punched or told to bend over double, gripping her ankles. It would be normal, for him to vent his fury at a moment like this. She was wearing a halter-necked red satin shift extending down to her ankles. It fluttered now in the breeze.

Instead, he did nothing. He seemed, if possible, given the limits of his personality and temperament, to be in a good mood. 'This late afternoon, we will change our location. Make towards the mainland. If Yasmine attempts to look for us, he'll think we've given up and gone away.'

'But …' said Aila. She shaded her eyes, looking towards the emptiness that nevertheless included a hidden island. 'We is just leave him?'

Now he slapped her. 'What have I told you? No baby talk!'

'I'm sorry,' she said, her voice contrite. 'I … I was worried, that's all.'

'About Yasmine? Don't bother. He's all right. He has a way of looking after himself. No, I'm not worried at all. In fact, this plan will work out even better than the old one.'

Over the course of the afternoon he described how he had spent the past two days studying the Island. Initially, he was frustrated by his inability to see it and to gain access to it. Then it occurred to him that the shields would most likely not extend underwater. When he turned on his underwater scopes with the night-vision on, a world of secret activity sprang into view. Not only could he see the enormous mass of the structure in the water, but he also saw that it appeared to be disintegrating. Substantial chunks kept tipping over its sides and falling away.

He had wondered whether it was imploding, perhaps because of some internal catastrophe caused by 'Yasmine'. But he soon saw that the chunks were not moving randomly. Indeed, they gave every appearance of moving under their own power. As if they were separate, automated units. As if the whole Island, instead of being a solid structure were instead made up of discrete cells, each one capable of mobility.

'It is all very, very interesting, Alhambra,' said the General. 'An entirely unfamiliar technology. The Brotherland will enjoy acquiring it. All in good time, of course. Right now, our priority is to see where all the activity is leading. Not that it's a mystery. I already have a good idea.'

He had been able to observe that the automated cells were scrambling away from the mother-structure in an orderly fashion, not merely tumbling into the murk of the ocean floor and scattering. None of them, for instance, moved towards the ship, in the direction that he would call East. Instead, the majority went South, following a very precise path. They vanished from the underwater scope's view, but each one had tail lights and these remained visible for a while. It was as if the units were beads threaded along a fixed number of strands. While the majority headed South, a handful could be seen heading off in an alternative direction, due North and tending West.

'That's the direction I am interested in, too, you see,' said the General. 'We shall wait until dark and follow the lights.'

Aila was chewing on her index finger, her brow knotted. 'But ...Yasmine?'

The General leapt to his feet and returned to his pacing. He spat responses at her as he trotted back and forth across the deck. 'I am no longer interested in him! I don't need him any more!' He panted slightly as he whipped this way and that. 'I have you in his place, after all. Which is perhaps the reason he agreed to bring you along.'

Aila had not considered this idea before and her distress registered sharply on her plain, angular face.

'What!' sneered the General as he passed her. 'Are you amazed to hear he thought only of his own convenience, not yours?' He bared his teeth. 'He's as worthless and as selfish as everyone else. He's forgotten about you just as he's forgotten about me. His only thoughts are of that filthy Vermin squirt of his. His thoughts circle around her like a vulture guarding its last meal.' Now he laughed. 'Little does he know!'

Aila stared at the General, trying to recover the equilibrium of the day before. She did not succeed. 'What do you mean?' she asked, her voice tight.

'You don't need to know either,' he said, his expression coldly exultant.

10

Some hours later, Youngest was newly showered, and appeared with a fresh wrap tied around himself, his hair combed down his back. Vane had suggested he watch the disassembly of her apartments while she took care of some business elsewhere on the Island.

I could make a dash now, he thought.

There was no one watching over him. His foot was almost healed. But he didn't so much as twitch. The central thread of his being had come undone. The General's recorded voice purring its way through his brain was the most familiar thing about him at that moment. It forced him to keep in mind that he was someone other than the jellified mush he had become following the *procedure*. Or whatever it had been.

If there's such a thing as a pleasurable rape, that's what they performed, thought Youngest. He could not understand how such an experience could be necessary to being on the Island.

The usable space of Vane's apartment had already shrunk to a fifth of its original size. He could see now that the vertical columns through which the elevator cells travelled were like central vanes from which the rest of the apartment's cells grew outward. Two assistants worked methodically, sealing off each individual unit from its neighbours. They applied manual pressure along the seams that defined the boundaries of each cell to release the shuttering mechanism. Some cells had four walls, some had five or more. There were gaps between adjacent pairs of walls.

The apartment had been created in four concentric rings. The outermost had one transparent wall, forming the continuous shield of viewing windows. As each outer ring of cells was sealed, the next ring inward acquired its own window-membrane, oriented outwards. One assistant went clockwise and the other anti-clockwise until they ended together in a single cell, from which they withdrew at the same time, before bringing down the final shutter of the outermost ring.

Forced orgasm, mused Youngest. *Is it fair to satisfy someone against their will? Should I feel glad to know that I can still feel pleasure?*

Once the now-shuttered cells had been locked down and made separate from one another, they began, one by one, to shake themselves loose, revealing themselves for the first time as enormous crustaceans, separate and individual. It was a surreal, disturbing sight. Rising up on multiple jointed limbs, each creature with its room-shaped hump upon its back, hesitated for a few moments with front claws upraised, and pairs of telescoping feelers unfurled. Then, turning with ponderous deliberation sideways to its original orientation, each one began to move slowly and thoughtfully seaward, until it reached the edge of the storey beneath. There it would perch, twiddling feelers once more before abruptly tipping over the edge and vanishing out of sight.

Youngest could not remember ever having been so disengaged before. He watched the extraordinary proceedings in front of him without feeling the need to analyse what he saw. He noticed that the creatures disappearing out of view had grass growing along the upper surfaces of the chamber they carried upon their backs. Beneath them, they trailed pipes and tubes. They had more limbs than ordinary crabs. Yet, to all these observations he felt no stirring of curiosity. He did not pursue the question of how they dealt with flotation when they were underwater;

or what happened to the contents of the rooms they carried around; or how they would be coerced into re-grouping once more.

He breathed slowly in and out, his mind refusing to tick. He wondered if mental flaccidity was the normal outcome of sexual satisfaction. Was there a difference between a woman's aftermath and a man's? In a rash moment, he tried to recall what he'd felt, as a man, after a night of love. But his mind braked hard right there, at the threshold of those distant memories, refusing to let him in.

The corners of his mouth lifted slightly. He smiled at himself. *Prude!* he thought.

11

Vane came for Youngest when the apartment had been reduced to a few clusters of core-cells. She took him up a flight of stairs to the Welcome Field.

Youngest drank in the raw sea air in big gulps as he followed Vane. The last time he had been in the open had been on the deck of the General's yacht. He had not noticed how much he missed the scent and sensation of open spaces.

'I thought you might enjoy the sight of our grass,' said Vane, as she rubbed her bare feet in it. With the reduction of Vane's apartment beneath it, the Field had shrunk to the size of a circular, medium-size lawn. Being raised several metres above sea-level and surrounded by the open ocean produced the effect of standing in the centre of a grass-lined dinner plate on a giant's table.

A humming cloud of shutterflies rose out of the grass to greet them. The afternoon had advanced to that point where the sun, though undiminished, was preparing for its curtain call. The only sounds were of the wind hushing past them and the ocean murmuring two storeys down from where they stood.

Youngest swung his arms, walking towards the edge but remaining a respectful distance from it. He was facing in the direction from which he had approached the Island, away from the setting sun. He wondered if he would be able to spot the General's yacht. It was camouflaged so he did not expect to see it in clear view. He might be able to guess its location from reflections of light in the water, however.

Vane was standing behind him. He could see her shadow on the grass as it lay towards his right. She allowed a pause of silence to pass.

'Tell me now,' she said. 'What you wanted to tell me earlier, downstairs. Before the Procedure.'

Youngest opened his mouth. The urgency had gone out of him. He felt like a gas balloon that had lost its string. He was free, yes, but with no propulsive force of his own. He remained silent, with his back to the Mentor.

'It was about the girl, I suppose?'

A bolt of anger shot through Youngest. *So. She's known all along!*

He felt hollow and ridiculous. Like an adolescent: with all the urges of an adult but none of the entitlement. He turned his body slightly, without changing the position of his feet and said, 'Yes.'

'I thought so.' The shadow on the grass nodded. 'In which case, you're going to be disappointed.' She paused. 'She's not here, you know.'

Youngest continued looking in the direction he called East. *You're lying, of course,* he thought.

'We don't keep our girls for very long. That's the point of these Islands. We rehabilitate them and send them on.'

Meiji's locator had brought him here. Vane certainly knew that. So why bother with this lie? It was pointless. It was mean-spirited.

'But even if she were here,' continued the Mentor, 'I wouldn't permit a meeting. There would be no point.'

'Why?'

'You'd be a stranger to her.'

Youngest felt a fierce tingling in his arms, his shoulders, his hands: the urge to swivel and hit. He swallowed hard, to keep his reactions in check. He didn't trust himself to speak.

'She wouldn't recognize you to begin with,' said Vane, 'and if you insisted on jogging her memory, it could damage her mind. We've put a lot of work into helping her settle down to her new life. One incident like that could set her back completely.'

Is it because I look like a woman, wondered Youngest. He wanted to cut Vane some slack. He wanted to like her. He was beholden to her. *But no, that could not be it.* Vane could not know for sure whether or not Meiji had last seen him before or after his transformation. He turned around now to face the Mentor. 'I don't understand what you're telling me,' he said.

The westering sun was behind Vane, though it was not yet low enough to obscure her face.

'We erase their memories,' she said. 'The Candidates' memories. If they had a choice, they would ask us to do it. The majority of them come here like rag-dolls with their stuffing torn out of them. They spend days and sometimes weeks in the vats of regenerative solution, just to get their bodies working again. The surgical scars, piercings and tattoos from their previous lives remain on their bodies as evidence of that life. But if the memories of their history and degradation were still with them, they would never be able to face the rest of their lives. Erasing their memories is a kindness.'

If the white-haired Mentor had been hoping to see some reaction on Youngest's face, he did not oblige her.

He said, 'That makes sense.' Paused. 'For the others.'

He kept his behaviour calm and reasonable, making no sudden moves. 'But for *my* girl ...' He trailed off. Surely the most obvious thing about her was that she had NOT been physically damaged?

'Ah, yes. No doubt you'd prefer special treatment? For your special little princess?' asked Vane, raising her eyebrows. She shook her head. 'The Island is not a health spa, Yasmine. We're not doing cosmetic surgery here. The direct opposite. The girls who arrive here have faced the worst and most horrific forms of disfigurement, torture and assault. Our aim is to return them to something like normalcy. That includes healing their physical and mental wounds, yes, of course, but it especially involves instilling a sense of what we call Equal Dignity. Or else we risk creating a hierarchy of injury. The most damaged girls would become disability-queens. Misfortune would be their primary identity. They would become their injuries.'

She drew in a breath. Perhaps she expected him to speak. He did not.

'By the standards of what we've seen here, your girl certainly wasn't highest on the scale of need. But she wasn't lowest either.' Vane paused. 'Even so, there were many amongst us – my own Mentors, here on the Island – who criticized me bitterly for bringing her here, for the price I paid for her and most especially for her unmarked, unblemished body. They felt she did not belong amongst the rest of the Candidates because she is pristine, uncut, unmarked. It's reverse discrimination, yes, and I fought for her. I'm glad we have her. But erasing her memories was as much to protect her as to protect her fellow Candidates on the Island. And if you will allow me the foresight of experience, I can assure you that what we're doing *is* right for her.'

Vane stopped, waiting for Youngest to respond.

He stood with his arms crossed, his face turned to one side, not meeting Vane's gaze. He was controlling his breath, by counting slowly, five in and five out, in order to avoid revealing the build-up of heat within his throat. 'I see,' was all he said.

'If we had left her memories intact, she would know that in addition to being physically different to the others, her personal history is so unique and so bizarre that she'd never be able to go beyond it. Her scars would become her identity. Whatever slender chance she had of settling in and adjusting to the new realities of her life – well, it would be lost forever.'

Youngest didn't want Vane to realize that he was growing angry. He knew he had to be patient. He was still entirely within her power. But the open spaces around them, the fact that she was both older than him, and inevitably weaker, was causing the dark energy to build within him, the boiling fury that had both served and hampered him all through his life.

Violent mental images flickered through his mind in split-second fragments: of him picking Vane up and bodily flinging her over the edge of the Field; of him squeezing Vane's face between his hands; of him scraping the cloak of smug control off her person and replacing it with the chain-mail of fear and desperation he had lived with for the past four years.

Give me my girl, he wanted to bellow. *My life's breath. My heart's desire.*

He did none of these things.

Instead he bowed his head and said, 'I'm sure you're right.'

'Your tone and posture tell me that I've not succeeded in convincing you,' said Vane.

He looked up, meeting her gaze. 'That is correct. You have not.' Then he drew himself up taller. 'Nevertheless, I'm not going to fight you over it, Mentor Vane. I am in your debt, after all. You could have cut me down and fed me to the … the … crabs the moment I arrived. And in all the moments after I arrived, too.

'Instead… You healed my wounds. You fed and clothed me. You showed me great hospitality. Where I come from, that puts me in your debt. I am honour-bound to repay that debt.

'And besides: I have much to learn. So if you will continue to accept the burden of my presence, I will continue to be advised by you.'

He stopped himself from adding, *For the time being.*

Vane lifted her chin in a reverse nod and said, 'Yes. That's the best we can hope for at this time, I suppose.' She turned to go.

'Come. We must quit the Island. You will come with me.'

Youngest clenched his teeth. He wanted to stay. Meiji was here. He was sure of it. He wanted to remain close to her. But he followed Vane. 'By what means will we travel?'

Vane glanced over her shoulder and surprised him with a broad grin. 'We're taking a TravelCrab!' she said. Then she stepped down through the open skylight. 'Stopping in the Zone.'

12

The rest of the day had gone badly. The General had spent the afternoon with his charts and his calculations. Aila never asked him what he was occupied with. She had showered and changed into fresh clothes. She wore a white lace shift that draped in graceful folds down to her calves, with cut-away patches at her chest and crotch.

Then she had gone into the galley to discover what the drones were preparing for the evening meal. She had taken to overseeing their efforts and they responded in small ways. She had, for instance, demonstrated the method for making an omelette out of turtle eggs and they had been able to mimic her actions. Granted, their omelettes were flat, like pancakes, with strips of seaweed layered above and below. Still, they were an improvement over plain soft-boiled fish-flavoured eggs. She had set them up with a plan for making crab soup served with a mound of dried jellyfish crackers and had then gone above-deck.

The General was standing at the bow, staring out to sea and doing sit-ups as he stood. He did not turn when she drew back the cane chair that was placed beside the tea table, though he must have heard her.

When he swivelled, it was with the whiplash speed that signalled fury. He came straight towards her, his face dark with rage. There was no explanation, no warning. He began to slap her with the flat of his palms, first with one hand, then the other, moving with mechanical precision. His eyes were opaque and unseeing. He might have been flogging an unruly animal. As in the morning, she did nothing to resist him. She neither cried out nor did anything to protect herself from his blows. This passivity infuriated him, as she knew it would. He wanted her to ask him why he was hitting her, but she would not give him that satisfaction, so he continued, unable to stop in the grip of his own compulsion. He was grimacing with the pain from his own hands, but he could not stop.

'Tell me to stop,' he commanded her, 'beg me. Come on. BEG ME!'

Aila began to laugh.

A witness to the scene may have interpreted the laughter as hysteria. But if Aila had been asked why she was laughing, she would have said it was because she found it profoundly funny that a man was so rigid in his ways that he was unable to spare himself the pain of hitting someone else unless he received the triggering request.

She didn't realize that she had passed out until she returned to consciousness. Perhaps half an hour had passed. Maybe longer. The sky was trending towards twilight. She was looking straight up towards it and realized only belatedly that she was flat on her back.

She had been tied down onto the rear deck, spread-eagled, with her wrists and ankles secured by ropes to the hooks on either side of the deck. Naked, of course.

The polished wood beneath her skin was slippery with sweat. She felt no fear or real concern. She believed the General needed her enough to not let her die. He wanted her to suffer but not to become incapacitated. On the other hand, he may have lost his mind. In which case he would not be able to help himself.

Either way, she was not concerned.

She might have been a neutral observer to her own fate, a window-shopper at a store too exclusive to enter. She felt thirsty, her skin was itchy from exposure to the sun, she was hungry.

Her wrists and ankles hurt. Her shoulders ached. But these were mere physical discomforts. In her mind and in her heart, there was nothing to fear, nothing to regret. She had lived a particular life, it had been without any visible meaning and now, perhaps, she was within some hours of dying. At all other times of her life, she would have struggled against her fate, railed against the General, screamed, howled, cried for mercy, for another chance.

Not today.

She shut her eyes. As the day's heat loosened up from dusk to night, she was grateful for the slight breeze, the softer temperatures. She could feel and hear the General's movements about the boat as well as the soft padding of the drones as they passed around her. Twice, she heard the General instruct them to pour sea-water onto her, which they did.

To her surprise, they also poured drinking water into her mouth.

This happened late at night, after the General had gone below stairs. It appeared to be their own initiative. One of them did the pouring, using the glass measuring cup which had a spout, while two of the others held a bottle of water for refilling the cup. The one who knelt by her head to pour the water patted the top of her head and only began to pour when she opened her eyes. She had to raise her head in order to avoid being drowned, and turned away when she didn't want more.

It was too dark to see the drone's face as it controlled the flow of water into her mouth. But she was grateful.

A short while after giving her water and scurrying away, all five drones returned. Acting together, without discussion, they each knelt on either side of her and began to lick her skin. Three started near her shoulders, one for each arm and one down her trunk, from just below her collarbone. The remaining two began on either side of her hips. They scoured her with their small and somewhat dry tongues, working with methodical precision. It was impossible to know what their aim was. They paid no special attention to the obviously erogenous regions of her body. Instead, when the four who were on limb-detail reached her hands and feet, they lavished their attention upon these extremities, while the fifth concentrated on her navel.

Having taken perhaps a full hour to complete their task, they got to their feet, poured another couple of buckets of seawater onto her and departed.

Aila didn't know whether to feel disgusted or touched.

13

'Are you sure you want to do this?' asked the woman who had introduced herself as Mentor Tasha. She spoke in a rasping whisper and wore her grey hair like a soft lacy cape that extended down to her knees.

Meiji nodded. 'Yes,' she confirmed. Her own hair had been growing out as tiny black bristles but Tasha had shaved it clean off once again.

'I must warn you that the results are very often ...' Tasha paused, as if pulling the word up from a great depth,' ... *distressing*.' She drew in a breath. 'Especially since most of those who seek to recover their memories believe they will be *relieved* of distress.'

'I still want to do it,' said Meiji. She was seated upright, in a bright room with open windows on all sides. She knew they were probably not real windows, just simulations. The seat was sturdy and padded, raised up on a pedestal and could be swivelled around in any direction. From the ceiling, a number of slender, flexible pipes similar to the tentacle-lights had been pulled down, each with a different implement at the end of it.

Tasha sat in her own seat, leaning at an angle towards Meiji. 'I am going to describe what I will do. I will give you a few cues to establish that you know when I am present and when I am not. You must not make the error of thinking that you're dreaming. That would lead to entirely the wrong results. You need to think of this exercise as one of entering a series of nested chambers that have been inaccessible to you for a little while.'

Meiji nodded.

'Your aim,' said Tasha, 'will be to enter and exit the various rooms you will find yourself in *without panic*. Do you understand me?'

'I am not sure,' said Meiji.

'Tell yourself that you are not in any actual physical danger. That whatever you see is only inside your mind. Not in the room with you.'

'But—'

'The aim is merely to become aware of what is present in your mind. NOT to interact with it. Because you can do that at your leisure later on.'

'Why do you tell me that I will be afraid?'

Tasha gave the girl a probing look. 'You misunderstood me. I am not *insisting* that you will be afraid. I am merely *warning* you that what you encounter may frighten you. If so, walk away. Do not run. And more than that, do not close any doors. The object of this exercise is to OPEN the doors that were formerly shut.'

It was hard for Meiji to continue sitting still, waiting for the formal instruction to run its course.

'The cues I give you will take the form of *sounds*. You must listen for three specific sounds.' She had a circular dial in her hand, with which she could generate audio signals. 'I'll play them now,' she said, as she selected them.

The first was the roar of waves on sand.

The second was the call of a peacock.

The third was the tinkling crash of breaking glass.

'When you hear these three sounds played one after the other, you must assume that I am sending you a signal and that I want you to look away from whatever you're doing.'

'That's all?' asked Meiji. 'Just look away?'

'Yes,' said Tasha. 'I won't know what you're experiencing so I can't be more specific. I'll only be able to tell that your stress levels are rising beyond acceptable limits. My intervention is designed to help you break away from whatever it is you're remembering, not to save you from it.' She rose from her seat. 'It's best if we begin.' Her behaviour suggested that she had deep misgivings about the whole enterprise.

She stood behind the seated girl. 'I will begin by placing two guidants against your skull,' she said. 'One will remain stationary, one will move around.'

Meiji sensed the woman's presence behind her and then the hands moving just around her head. She assumed, without actually knowing it, that the guidants, whatever they were, were amongst the implements hanging from the ceiling. 'Will I feel anything?' she asked.

'I am already touching your scalp now,' said Tasha. 'You should feel nothing. First I will locate the molecular blocks we placed within your memory then I will switch them to neutral. As I begin switching, your recall of events in your past will gradually become apparent to you. I will tell you when to begin your visualization.'

Meiji had been given the option of closing her eyes but had preferred to keep them open. Looking straight ahead she had a virtual view of the ocean from Tasha's room. Presently she heard Tasha clear her throat.

'To begin, I would like you to think of an open space,' said the Mentor.

That's easy, thought Meiji. She thought about the Welcome Field. As she thought about it, the image in front of her eyes changed from the windows through which she could see the ocean into that of a flat expanse of green that surrounded her on all sides. The open sky was its boundary.

The procedure had begun.

'Are you in an open space?' said Mentor Tasha. 'All right. Now I want you to place a building in the middle of your space.

It does not have to be elaborate. The simplest building that you can think of.'

A pale orange block appeared directly ahead of her, perhaps 20 metres away. It wasn't a building so much as a rectangular shape, punctured by windows in the centres of both the walls she could see. The height of the windows suggested that they were on the first floor. On the ground floor, there was a door, with a stoop leading up to it. Two steps up. A black iron railing. And the door was ... bright yellow.

She looked at the windows. They were white, with panes of clear glass. She could see that there was empty space behind them, with no details of interiors. As she wondered about adding a roof, a sloped roof appeared.

She wanted to tell Tasha that she was enjoying herself but didn't.

'Move towards the building. Try to keep all your movements slow and steady because that will help you return to that pace ... later ... if you need to slow down.'

It was interesting, thought Meiji, that she could hear Tasha normally, while flashing forward in quick jerks, within her visualization. For instance, she had reached the door of 'her' house in a twinkling. In another flash, she was at the top step and looking at the door. Now she realized that she'd forgotten to add a door knob.

It was not a simple matter of putting one in. Not all doors had knobs. Not all knobs were the same. Some were handles. Some were bolted. This one?

She gave it a push and it moved aside. Rather like the shrinking screens of entrances at the Island. That wasn't right, she decided. If she couldn't call up a door in memory, it meant that Tasha had not unblocked the location in her mind where such memories were stored.

She didn't wait to fix the door, but instead stepped inside

the room.

It was completely bare. Stunningly so. The bareness was impossible. She glanced up and then around. It was as if she were standing within a pale tangerine box, lit from within though lacking a visible light source. The floor wasn't even tiled, just a flat orange plane. The ceiling was high, but without the slope she had imagined from outside. There should have been windows up there, at the first-floor level, in the position she had seen them from outside. She spun around. Sure enough! No door.

Her eyes were open and when she made a conscious effort she could see Tasha's room around her. Inside her head, however, she was trapped within a pale orange box.

Don't panic, she thought, *don't panic. Be calm.*

'See if you can get inside the house,' said Tasha, her voice suggesting that she was far away. 'Do not force yourself in. Do not do anything in a hurried or desperate way. If there is a handle, turn it gently. Or better still, see if you can imagine an open archway.'

Meiji found herself smiling. She was ahead of the game. The smile helped dispel the panic that had boiled up. She decided not to bother with the door just yet. It would come.

She looked around the room once more. Obviously, her aim had to be to fill it with things. *What things?* Things that could be opened, she guessed. Cupboards. Drawers. Shelves. Chairs. *Chairs?* It wasn't possible to open a chair. Images were refusing to form with any fluency. She could think of the words, but when she tried to create them in three dimensions, they remained stubbornly unavailable. *Okay, how about a box?* Yes, there was a box on the floor now. Creamy tangerine in colour, just like the walls. She placed another box upon it and then another and another. *Excellent.* Soon she had a makeshift partition in the centre of the room, reaching up to the height of her own head, created out of identical boxes lined up in stacks.

'If you can enter the room, do so now,' she heard Tasha say.

Meiji considered the wall of boxes. She could think of them as either drawers or as cubby-holes. Either way, she needed to add knobs to them. As with the door, though, this too proved to be difficult. So then she thought of an alternative approach: a hole into which she could extend a finger. That worked. One by one, the boxes each acquired a hole the size of her right index finger. She had to look at each separate box to effect the change. She made some into drawers and others into cubbies. When she was done, she reached for the nearest one, pushed her finger in till the knuckle of the first phalange then gently drew back the little door.

Inside: nothing.

Disappointment! *Don't panic*, she thought. *Don't panic*.

She tried another and another. She tried each one. There was nothing inside any of them. Nothing. *I'm empty*, she thought. *They made a mistake. They erased everything. It's all gone, permanently*.

She was kneeling as she had these thoughts, having looked into the lowermost row of drawers. She withdrew her finger, looking at the empty rectilinear container yawning open in front of her knees. The light in the room had an unvarying, constant quality. But the drawer was darker than the surrounding space. It was filled with a shadow. *Not* her own. A man's shadow.

She felt the hair on the back of her neck prickling. In the next instant she was panting hard, as if running up a very steep hill. Her lungs were bursting. She had to stop running.

She turned and there he was. A man wearing dark robes. She knew, though she couldn't decide how, that it wasn't the same man who had loomed out of her memories in Folia's room.

No. This was a leaner man, tall, with long, tapering fingers. He was towering over her. His head against the lighted ceiling was obscured from her view. She had shrunk. She was a child.

He had her face in his hands, gripping hard. She was cowering. She was shrinking.

She heard the sound of glass shattering. A peacock called. The ocean roared.

She was back in Tasha's room.

'Good!' said Tasha. 'You recovered quickly. That is what you should aim for.'

Meiji's skin was damp with sweat. Her chest was heaving. She didn't think there was anything good about what had just happened. 'If I go back now will it … will I be in the same situation?'

'I cannot direct you,' said Tasha. 'These are your memories. You have to control them.'

They began again.

The girl paused, wanting to re-enter the orange box from a different angle, but found that the moment she directed her thoughts towards the room it sprang up around her full-formed exactly as it had been before.

Without the man.

What a relief.

Also, with no conscious effort on her part, there were now many more objects in the room. How enchanting. Shiny surfaces, so many shiny surfaces. Everywhere she looked, there were vistas and complexities that she had no names for. Doors, windows, terraces, platforms, stairs, columns, cushions, carpets and fountains of tinkling glass. Tinkling glass? Her ears pricked up, listening for the companion sounds, but there were none. She saw a wind-chime and realized that the sound was from it.

She returned to her reverie.

Now a stunted figure came into view, walking slowly, heavy-headed and with chalk-white skin. He or it, she couldn't be sure, moved like clockwork, walking towards her, then turning abruptly, around a tumbling cascade of rose-pink lace. She tried to follow him, but a sense of foreboding overtook her and she twitched her attention away. Through a window, now, she saw a crowded promenade, glittering figures walked this way and that, like jewelled butterflies.

All of them were – how very odd! – they were all men. Wait. No! That wasn't odd at all.

With great amazement she realized that for her *that* was familiar: being surrounded only by men. It was the all-woman environment of the Island that was strange. But only for her. These were her memories. Where she had come from there were only men.

Then, with no warning, she felt the prickling sensation again, at the back of her neck.

It was a man again but a very different one. Warm and tall. Sweet-scented.

He was holding her, turning her around, stroking her back, picking her up in his embrace, till she lay in his arms as small as a puppy, the heat from his body like that of a furnace. His presence was joyous, unbounded and infinitely loving. Gladness flooded her spirit.

She laughed out loud.

Like a peacock.

Glass shattered. The ocean roared.

She was back in Tasha's room.

Meiji was panting, her eyes bright.

'You see?' Tasha was saying in her breathy rustle. 'You see? It can be very disturbing to return to one's memories!'

Meiji didn't speak. Her heart had lifted with the knowledge of a loving attention so intense it was painful. If she opened her mouth, it would spill out and flood this room, this Island. Everyone here would drown in that scalding tide.

There would be no point telling the Mentor that what she had experienced was radiant happiness. Not fear, not pain, not loss. She knew now that she had been adored and treasured. That her past had been filled with laughter and music. Sunlit afternoons. A vast home. Echoing halls.

Three men, she knew, had been the guardians of her breath. One she had felt in Folia's apartment, one today. There was a third, but his presence had not solidified into an image. He was in some way more remote. Perhaps older. What mattered was the quality of their devotion to her. It was like a beam of golden light, touching and healing every part of her being.

Their faces were shrouded, so that she could not see them clearly. Yet she could feel their presence, smell their distinct, separate fragrances. In Folia's room, the scent had been sharp, with burnt honey at the edges. Today's was sweeter, with a touch of damp earth and rose. There was another one too, perhaps of ripening mangoes. Lichees. Clove.

She could hear the rumble of their deep voices in her heart. She guessed that she would never see any part of that life again. But it did not matter.

They were hers forever, in the vault of her mind.

They were her secret, hers alone.

14

Meiji bounced recklessly along the corridor outside Mentor Tasha's apartment. The Island was half-empty now and the two floors beneath the Mentor's apartments had been vacated. She found that if she timed her steps just right, she could make the floor into a narrow, wobbling springboard. Supporting herself with a hand on the walls, she took several bounding leaps before tumbling to her knees, laughing in breathy gasps. She was unconcerned and unafraid that she might trigger another episode of twisting corridors.

She felt as if she might explode with happiness. She was bursting to tell Rahm how wrong the girl had been to fear the past because she, Meiji, had wonderful memories. Yes, there were some murky bits. Particularly the recent years. And a great portion remained unrevealed. Mentor Tasha had said that undoing the blocks did not automatically result in doors being opened. She helped fill in some details but Meiji would have to do the work of long-term recovery herself.

Still, what she knew now was enough to make her feel like a helium-filled balloon. Tasha told Meiji that she had been born in a distant land. Then something terrible had happened. Tasha said she didn't have details. All she knew was that there had been a group of extremely cruel and powerful men. And they had destroyed all the women and all the girls of Meiji's country.

Except one. Except herself.

This was an absolutely thrilling idea, made all the more so by her realization that the anguish and displacement she had felt were absolutely justified! Why – she was unique! No wonder there was no one on the Island who understood her, no wonder no one else's life mirrored hers in any small detail. Unlike all the other girls here, her past was not tainted by horror.

Her cheeks were aching from smiling.

It was only now, while returning to her Team Room, that she understood why there were few written symbols of any kind on the Island. She knew now that these skills were unknown in her current location though she had remembered that she could read and write.

By the time she had scraped on the room's entrance panel, she was in a thoughtful mood.

'Rahm?' she called out as she entered the cell. 'Are you here?'

The panel snicked shut behind her. The room was dim.

'Yes,' said Rahm, sitting up in her sleep-cradle. 'I is not asleep. I is come out.' She slipped down at once. 'How it was? You is okay? You is not too …' Her whole face radiated concern. 'Too sad?'

Meiji drew a breath and was about to spill out her pleasure and relief when a competing idea arose in her mind. She could choose to keep the knowledge of her happy past to herself. It was dark enough that Rahm may not have noticed the glow in her eyes.

She lowered the tone of her voice. 'It was like you said,' she told the other girl. 'Bad things happened. But I … I … think I will be able to manage.' She kept her eyes lowered. She had not told any actual lies.

Rahm put one slender muscular arm around Meiji's shoulders. 'Is will be okay,' she whispered, her voice husky with sympathetic tears. She touched the tangerine halo of her hair to Meiji's smooth scalp. 'You is stronger than you is know. You will smile again.'

Meiji felt an unfamiliar sweetness sweep through herself: she had given away a moment of triumph in order to protect the feelings of the girl who had become her friend.

It didn't feel wrong or dishonest.

Awkwardly, she bent her arm around the other girl and accepted the hug.

15

Aila remained out on the deck for most of the night, dozing between bouts of intolerable discomfort. Now and then, she hummed softly to herself. The stars reeled overhead. An hour before dawn, while it was still dark, the General came above and had the drones cut her loose. He helped her to her feet, placed a robe around her shoulders and supported her as she staggered, stiff and groggy, down the stairs and to his bed. He did not attempt to use her, but instead left her to sleep. Which she did.

She woke late, showered and dressed. She wore a soft, pearl-pink dress that left her shoulders bare. She was still so stiff that climbing up the stairs was an ordeal. But in the sun, sitting at the breakfast table, where the General had already finished eating his turtle-egg omelette, her muscles began to relax. She could almost hear them, as they twanged and straightened out.

No words were exchanged until after she had finished eating.

Now the General glanced in her direction and said, 'Not bad. You survived the night.'

Aila nodded. 'I am surprised too.' She didn't smile, but she didn't frown or cry either.

'It was a test, of course. I wanted to see what your breaking point was. But you didn't break. Which was disappointing, in a way. I need to know what the limits of your endurance are. Because what lies ahead will require strength of will. In every sense of the word. I doubt that you possess it. Never mind. Today we will move forward with our plans.'

Aila frowned. 'Meaning what?'

'Meaning, we will skip forward to the final part of our plan and pretend for the moment that the middle portion, which should have been completed by your friend Yasmine, is in fact complete.'

The General was remarkably calm. No twitching, no pacing. He remained seated in his deck chair, smoking a cheroot. Looking towards the empty horizon. He always dressed with fastidious care, shaving his head and face every day, wearing freshly pressed and laundered clothes. Today he had taken special care over his style of dress. He wore white socks and black sandals, his blinding-white bush-shirt was crisp, his shorts had hard creases.

Aila waited.

'The penultimate part of this plan involves the Zone,' said the General. 'Yasmine always thought that capturing an Island was the final part of the plan. That he would lead me to an Island by placing his Vermin-spawn child within one and then, if he succeeded, I would set him and the girl free. Well yes, it's true that I wanted to capture an Island so that I could establish a base here. But he was wrong to think it was the final part of the plan. It was not. Never was. The final part involves returning to the Brotherland. That's what this entire campaign is about.'

Aila blinked, frowning. 'Huh?' She couldn't imagine in what way the General could connect with anything relating to the Zone. He had no Team affiliation, no trophies and he had shown no interest whatsoever in the games. 'You are interested in … in … the *games*?'

'The Zone conflicts are of interest to us Brothers, of course,' said the General, his voice beginning to bristle with sharp points. 'How could they not be?' He seemed to think that she would naturally understand the focus of his interest. 'We, the Brotherland, have a stake in altering the balance of power in the world that has ignored us. We want to topple the existing order.

So that the playing field will tilt. So that the players and more importantly their backers will be forced out of their … out of their …'

He leapt to his feet and paced back and forth for several minutes.

When he came back, his face was red and he was panting. Leaning on the table he said, speaking into Aila's face so that she could smell his egg-flavoured breath, 'Will be forced out of their delusions regarding a safe and stable world.'

16

Vane and Youngest descended three floors and walked along several corridors before entering a cell with a viewing window. The Island had been emptying itself out all day. As the structure lost mass, it had begun swaying and shifting underfoot, and became steadily more buoyant. The corridors down which they walked were empty. They heard muted booming, mechanical thudding and the continuous click-scissoring of crab-claws as they zippered and unzippered the structures that depended on them for suspension.

Vane had explained that any of the cells could be used for transport, but some were customized for that purpose. She had chosen an eight-sided cell. Two tendril lights deployed as soon as Vane crossed the threshold. The entrance snicked shut behind Youngest.

There was no one else in the room. The floor was covered with pale grey fur. The window, which was directly across from the entrance, showed the water-line as a white, frothing demarcation about half a metre down from its upper margin. Above the white line was the sky. Below it was the iron grey of the ocean. Phantom blobs bobbed and danced in the murk, as the jellyfish cohort pursued their placid, venomous lives.

'A little later I will show you what I do to control the crab,' said Vane. 'For the moment, please just fold out a wall-seat. Strap yourself in.'

She did not glance up to see whether Youngest was following her instructions, but instead went directly to a spot in front of the window, bending her knees one at a time until she was kneeling. When she was comfortably established she leant over in the attitude of a weeding gardener, poking her fingers into the floor. When a matched pair of ridges appeared beneath her fingers, she reversed her movements with careful deliberation in order to stand up once more. Her age showed itself in these moments, with the time she took to move.

'Straps?' asked Youngest, frowning. 'Are we expecting turbulence?' He stared at the wall he had been asked to probe, not wishing to fumble but feeling certain that he was going to, nevertheless. He did not feel any more confident about the mechanical features of the Island now that he knew they were partially conscious.

Vane glanced around. 'Come now! Don't you know what to do? Stroke the surface lightly, using the backs of two fingers.' She used the tone of someone speaking to a rustic who had not yet encountered electricity. She returned to pulling up her command console. It was an altogether more elaborate affair and needed her attention before all its features unfolded.

Youngest followed her instructions. Once the padded semi-recliner had fully unfolded, he lowered himself into it. The belts and straps made themselves immediately apparent to him. It was extremely comfortable and he found himself relaxing. The thought came to him that until this moment he had felt every action of his met with resistance whereas now the reverse was true. The merest touch here and there produced desirable results.

When he leaned his head back, for instance, the headrest accommodated itself to the shape of his head. When he tapped the armrest, a palm-sized tablet folded out of it, within which he could see the coiled shape of a drinking-water spout.

He wondered if it was Vane's presence that made the difference.

'Ready?' Vane turned again to look at him. She had created a blocky shape around herself. It had elements of an armchair fused with that of a pilot's cockpit. Instead of a console in front of her, the controls were within reach of her hands.

'Ready,' confirmed Youngest.

'You see this?' she asked. Beneath her right hand was a softly glowing sphere. 'In a moment I am going to press down on it. There's one under my left hand too. When they're both depressed the crab will begin to shake itself loose.' Saying which, she pressed down with both her palms.

A tremor wriggled under and through the entire cabin. It was as if until that instant the room had been asleep. Now it was awake and the entire space of it, not merely the walls, floor and ceiling but the air within the chamber as well, began to throb with a *presence*. Even though this chamber was only an air-filled structure that did not directly impact the life of the creature supporting it, somehow its character invaded even this inanimate part of its shell.

'What are you doing?' asked Youngest. 'Are you communicating with it?'

'I'm using a type of communication,' said Vane, speaking over her shoulder, 'but it's entirely physical – or, maybe I should say, sensory. These spherical structures under my hands are part of the crab's nervous system. They're similar to eyes or ears, so they're extremely sensitive. They're equipped to interpret input directly through the touch of our skin.' She paused. 'In fact I can't talk right now – do you notice it's stopped moving? – I have to think about what I want it to do while manipulating the spheres.'

She turned away.

Within minutes the vibration began anew, now accompanied by a furious scrabbling, creaking and squelching. The *glop-glop-glop* of the sea outside was augmented by the thrashing movements of the living vehicle's limbs.

Youngest felt his skin rippling with a combination of distaste and amazement. Being a tenant within the body of another living thing was surely something he had never hoped to be. A parasite! He tried to tell himself it was only a variation of riding a horse or an elephant, but found it difficult to rid his mind of the thought that he was inside this creature, not merely riding it.

Glancing at the window, Youngest felt his stomach flip over as the water-line shifted drunkenly, tilting first one way and then the other as the chamber lurched from left to right. He remembered what he had seen while standing in Vane's apartment. The creature was rising up on its claws, testing its weight.

Then, with no warning, it hiccupped forward, moving in fast jerks. Youngest felt his entire body lift against the straps, bouncing straight up before being flung from side to side. Abruptly, the water-line slipped up the window before vanishing altogether.

They had careened forward and over the side of the Island, down into the steely murk.

17

The General unlocked the hatch in the floor of the larder and took Aila down through to the hidden lower deck. 'You see this?' he said, spreading his arms wide. 'This is what the entire trip is about. Not me, not Yasmine, not his brat and certainly not you. It's *this*.'

He had brought a torch with him, and had turned it on, playing its spot of light around the room. Shelves lined the walls. Cartons were stacked from floor to ceiling. Sealed kegs were nested in boxes lined with wood-shavings. Rows of longer items, swaddled in protective padding, were arranged in neat piles along the floor, leaving just enough space for manoeuvering around them. On the shelves were hundreds of smaller cartons, each one in its own plain brown wrapping. Oil cloth, wood and plastic made up the materials used in the packaging and all the colours were drab: brown, grey, black. There were no labels, but names and numbers were neatly lettered on each parcel.

Aila looked around wonderingly. 'What is it?' she asked. 'I can only see many packages, things carefully packed. Very plain.'

The General took a couple of steps, stopped by a pillar of wire-sided cartons, gave her the torch to hold and pried an object out of one of the cartons. When he had retrieved the torch, he held up the object in his hand and shone the torch onto it. 'Have you seen anything like this before?'

It was an oval, fist-sized object, dark grey or perhaps even black, its surface etched by a grid of small squares. The General held it so that its top could be clearly seen, a hard round cap, with a short handle that lay alongside the curved surface of its body.

Aila extended her hand towards the object, saying 'No, I've never seen that before. Is it a … fruit? Something to eat?' She was still thinking of this deck as an extension of the larder above.

The General's teeth glistened in the backwash of the torch's light, as he snatched the object out of her reach. 'Ha. Fruit! Not exactly. Not at all.'

He replaced the thing carefully.

'It's called a "grenade". And it's no surprise that you haven't seen one before. Your world has abolished such things, hasn't it? At least as far as the Zone is concerned. Not elsewhere. Only in the Zone.'

'I don't understand … ' said Aila.

The General began to move forward through the room, pointing as he went along. 'Firearms,' said the General. 'Guns. Missiles. Gunpowder. All of these items are missing from your world. Just like written scripts. And paper.'

He stopped to point at different packaged objects, stabbing through the darkness with his torch. 'But that's what we've got around us. An armoury of exploding devices. Magazines of bullets. Hand guns. Laser-guided rifles. Landmines. Nail bombs. Mortar shells. Acid bombs.'

He turned the torch on Aila's face, so that she flinched and shielded her eyes from its harsh glare. 'And this is only what I've got on this small ship. Back in the Brotherland, we've got enough weapons to arm all the teams of the Zone. Not that we would, of course. The plan is to arm only the strongest teams.' He turned now and passed between the shelves to reveal a further door.

'But …'

'Don't ask questions. Your ignorance annoys me. It'll make sense in a day or two.'

He passed into the other room. This one was the same size

as the room they had just left but with overhead lighting and no shelves or packages. Fluorescent bulbs flickered to life, revealing two bulky shapes, each one the size and shape of a crouching elephant swathed in tarpaulin. They were both securely tethered onto two separate platforms.

The General walked between the two shrouded shapes, then turned a corner to his right. Two white cabinets stood, braced securely to the floor and reaching up to the ceiling. The cabinets were identical, with dark viewing panels a quarter of the way down from their tops. The General touched the surface of one of these panels, generating a line of pale blue blinking lights. There was a low peep and the blue blinks speeded up. Lower down on the cabinet, a panel slid back to reveal a manual keypad with numbers as well as letters.

Aila watched, mystified, as the General entered a code consisting of dozens of keystrokes into the pad. When he was done, there was a further peep, the keypad retreated and the blue lights stopped blinking.

He turned to face Aila and said, 'It will take some minutes. We can remove the covers from these Rovers in the meantime.' His voice was unusually subdued.

The coverings were fastened with straps that had to be unbuckled one by one and the stiff, heavy material gradually pulled back panel by panel to reveal a stubby, heavy-bodied, open-top vehicle beneath it, raised up on blocks. It had the huge, bulbous tires of an all-terrain vehicle. In its rear, instead of passenger seats, it had metal lattices, straps and cross-struts for holding and securing cargo.

When they were done, the General stood back and said, 'Is it starting to make sense now?'

Aila nodded uncertainly. 'It's a transport, for carrying the … the things in the other room?'

'Delivering armaments to the Zone,' said the General. 'We

are going to deliver long-distance explosive devices to a conflict that has so far used only impact weapons such as swords, axes, maces, spears, flaming arrows and so on. Naturally, the team that gets to use our explosive weapons will triumph. Whereupon we will offer to supply them with yet more. The result will be that the Zone and the prissy little world-order which depends upon it will collapse within a pool of its own lily-livered piss.'

He looked up with his thin lips stretched in a smile that made him look reptilian. For a moment, Aila imagined she saw a forked tongue flickering out, and she instinctively jerked her head away though she knew it was an illusion.

'It doesn't matter what happens to me in the short run. Maybe I will be eliminated in the course of making my delivery. Maybe the losing team will refuse to fight or insist on a rematch. *Whatever happens*, the Whole World Union will be forced to take notice of us. Take notice of the Brotherland. We, the rabid dog they tried to starve out of existence, will rise up from the ashes and bite the world in the one place they protect so passionately: their belief in themselves.'

From around the corner, there came a loud, steady tone.

The General whipped around. The white cabinet was rimmed with blue light. Tendrils of thick white smoke were curling out from behind the rims. In two strides he stood before it.

Aila remained where she was.

The front of the cabinet snapped aside and amidst the white coils seething out, the figure of a man appeared. At first sight he appeared to be a head taller than the General, but when he stepped down and out of the recess within which he had been contained, it was clear that the two men were identical. Not just in height but in every other way. Except that one was clothed and the other was not.

Aila watched the two clones standing face to face, the clothed General and the unclothed, their forearms held out to one another, hands gripping each other's elbows. They stood together thus, their gaze locked for several minutes. Then, without saying a word, each man lifted his hands to the face of the other, drew together and joined their mouths in a deep and passionate kiss.

Aila felt her heart convulse with a complex pain.

It wasn't that she knew intuitively that her presence had immediately slipped into non-relevance by this unexpected appearance. It wasn't the fear of knowing that now, most likely, both men would use her body with the same dispassionate violence as one had done, on his own. It wasn't even the realization that she was going to be a party to a plot that would plunge the fragile world to which she belonged back into another pit of the same kind from which it had crawled out with such difficulty.

No, the thing that hurt her was to see one man kiss another in a way that she, despite her warm and loving nature, despite her willingness to give of herself and to spare herself no pain or effort to provide what another might want, had never known.

Not once, in her entire life.

18

The Crab had no headlights. Visibility from the lighted cabin's window extended for less than a metre in front of it. But it did not need to find its way across the ocean. Submerged cables functioned as highways between the Island networks.

Once Vane had guided the creature towards the path she wanted it to take, it ran towards its destination without requiring further guidance. Its movement was jerky, with pauses for feeding, excretion and occasional attempts to escape bondage. But while it was in motion, it fairly galloped along.

According to Vane, the giant crustaceans were capable of being frisky and unpredictable once they were unhinged from one another. 'But we created them with an addiction to having these sensory globes stimulated,' she said. 'It's a form of pleasure for them. And we're the only ones who can deliver it. So they accept our control and we fulfil our part of the bargain by providing them with regular stimulation.

'That's what we're doing when we stroke their control points on the Island, to make them deploy a piece of furniture, extend the corridors or move the travelling cells. We're stimulating their pleasure receptors, whereupon they reciprocate by extending or retracting the feature that we want to use.'

Youngest shifted his head to one side. 'Isn't that just a little …' He paused before saying, 'manipulative?'

Vane snorted a laugh. 'Really? You think so? But attraction-repulsion systems are at the heart of all reality! The physical world depends on infinitesimal affinities, the minute attractions that keep electrons orbiting protons, protons bonded with their neutrons, atoms clustered into molecules—'

Youngest shrugged. He was not in the mood for an argument. The idea of customizing a creature to be hooked and dependent on pleasure-stimulation in return for its labour felt cynical. Even as the thought entered his mind, he knew that it was he who was being either sentimental or unrealistic or both. He said, 'Maybe I don't know enough to have an opinion.'

'Physicists speak of "attraction" and "positive charge",' said Vane. 'But could we not just as well regard these fundamental interactions as expressions of …' she glanced around '… *love*?'

Youngest looked away.

He felt uncomfortable and outpaced by the conversation. He didn't want to say what came to the forefront of his mind: that he hadn't enjoyed being stroked into compliance. It made him feel he was a variation upon a modified crab. 'I don't know,' he said, carefully. 'I think I prefer a less prosaic definition of that word.'

'Or maybe you need to update your notion of prosaic,' said Vane. 'You may have noticed that your interactions with Island appliances have become smoother and more predictable since the procedure?'

'I have,' said Youngest.

'That's because your entire nervous system got a re-haul,' said Vane, her voice matter-of-fact. She might have been discussing financial accounts. 'The Anita who was your initial room companion tried to interest you in a sexual encounter but she wasn't successful. You can't have realized it at the time, but on our Islands being pleasure neutral is not an option. If you are to become part of our community, learning to think of sexual pleasure as a routine part of life – indeed, as a *necessary* feature of our work – would be one of the adjustments you'd have to make.'

Youngest did not know what to say. It made him acutely uncomfortable to think of private pleasure as public property. 'I don't know,' he repeated. 'I'm not used to thinking of sexual pleasure as a … a … social obligation.'

Vane smiled in a pitying way. 'Well. That may be part of your masculine legacy. A man's sexual pleasure is so brief and transitory. A lonely mechanical spasm no different to a sneeze! But you're a woman now. What we tried to show you through our procedure was a fraction of what you could achieve if you allowed yourself to be wired for pleasure. You could become part of the covenant we share on these Islands, you could choose to hitch your potential to something greater than your private little self.'

Youngest listened, nodding now and then, saying in the end, 'It's all very new to me. I will have to think it through.' Privately, to himself, he thought, *Never in a million years.*

19

They made landfall within the drowned remains of what had once been a carpark under what must have been a cliff-side apartment complex, three levels down. It had been built after the cement-rot disease had reduced whole cities to dust and rubble, out of plastene and petro-wood, so it had not crumbled into dust. Its rectangular outlines were still recognizable as man-made structures, but the rising oceans had engulfed the building above it. The Crab scrambled through the ruins, finding its way up the piles of rubble, thickets of swaying seaweed and explosions of tiny, startled fish. Now and then it would pause to pick up a snack or two from amidst the abundance of colourful prey scattering in all directions.

It had extruded two of its interior tendril lights so that it could see where it was going. Making its way towards a ramp, it scraped and slipped, using its multiple claws to find purchase in the slippery surfaces underfoot. It jettisoned the water it had filled into its swim bladders and with regained buoyancy managed to rise all the way up until it could go no further. A tunnel of yellow plastene braces, tall and wide enough to allow the passage of the travelling cell, led away in a direction Youngest would call northwesterly. The TravelCrab took it without being prompted by Vane but it was careless of its boundaries, resulting in bumps and scrapes for its human passengers. Twice, Vane had to halt its progress in order to force it to re-fill its swim-bladders, to make it sink closer to the floor of the channel.

When the rubble gave way to rock, the walls of the tunnel

smoothed out and became gradually broader and taller. The Crab sensed it was nearing the end of its journey and sped along with no more pauses. Two hours from the time they entered the ruined structure, they rose into a lighted, air-filled cave.

Vane turned the Crab around, backing it into a horseshoe-shaped bay. The crab's entrance pane opened directly onto a wooden pier. 'Watch your step,' she said, as Youngest emerged. He was groggy and stumbling from having slept through the final one-third of the journey. 'Welcome to Base Vane. We name the mainland bases for ourselves rather than with numbers. We want to avoid suggesting a hierarchy or indeed to reveal how many there might be.'

Youngest stretched his arms and arched his back, feeling as if he had emerged from deep hibernation.

'I don't understand,' he said. 'I thought we were going to be on dry land? In the Zone?' When he turned to look at the Crab in which he had travelled, he saw a rounded and irregular shape, creamy yellow in colour, bobbing on the surface of an immense pool of black water. There were five other bays, similar to the one at which this Crab had docked. Two others were currently occupied. Overhead, the height of the cave was obscured in shadows. Huge fish-bowl lights were suspended from girders that stretched right across the length and width of the space, though only a handful were lit. They were conventional electric lights, Youngest noticed, with ordinary incandescent bulbs within them.

'This *is* dry land,' said Vane, ambling forward in her unhurried way. 'And we *are* officially within the Zone. But our presence is masked by several thousand tons of rock. It's all real and solid, an ancient volcanic mountain range.'

The pool was rimmed by a gently sloping sandy bank, grey-white in colour. Where the bank met the sides of the cavern, there were sections of wooded panelling, storage shelves, racks of rubber suits and other dockside paraphernalia.

Youngest saw now that there were two other figures in the cavern, one of whom had only just come in through a shuttered doorway. Both figures were dressed in cotton overalls. They were bare-armed, with their long hair secured in neat ponytails. Their bodies were muscular, but they were clearly women, perhaps in their early thirties. One had shiny black skin, while the other was mottled brown. Up close, it became clear that the mottling was the result of pink freckles distributed unevenly here and there, as if she had been spattered by a careless house-painter.

'They're Deenas,' said Vane to Youngest, as she waved. 'Though they'll give you their real names too if you ask.' She glanced at him, saying, 'Names on the Island double as designations, you know.'

Youngest nodded, 'Yes, Anita told me.' To himself he wondered, *And me? What is my 'official name'?*

'Well, you'll meet a number of new designations here,' said Vane.

Then they were being introduced and were ushered away from the pier. One of the Deenas came with them, while the one with pink spatters went over to the Crab with a bag of food.

20

Vane took Youngest on a tour of the base. She introduced him as 'Yasmine, a trainee, no designation yet'. They visited laboratories where zoöbiotic models were in development. There was a TravelCrab in production that could seat five travellers at a time. She showed him the power-emitting cells called 'creature-batteries' that were based on animals such as the electric eel. They provided all the power used by the facility. Some were connected in relays to electrify conventional gadgets such as incandescent light bulbs. Others were coupled directly to animal gadgets, such as fans made from giant modified dragonfly wings and cold-light fittings synthesized from fireflies.

'We feed them liquid shrimp-concentrate but they're not alive or sentient,' said Vane. 'The nervous systems of the original creatures were cloned, synthesized and repurposed until we could form them into functioning organic machines. They don't have individual consciousness.'

Or so you say, thought Youngest.

For lunch they had shark meat, greens and wheat bread. According to Vane, wheat was a delicacy available only in the old-north areas of the Zone. Then she took him to where fruit and vegetables were grown in tiered beds of artificial soil, housed in a tall, cylindrical shaft. Water, light and air had to be pumped in. The plants were tended to by agricultural workers called Floras.

Finally, they were standing in a space that Vane referred to as the Media Room. They were on the upper level, facing a virtual window that extended from floor to ceiling, two storeys tall and half as wide. At floor level there were seats arranged facing the window. The room was only half-full. The young women working there were called Tinzins. They were skilled technicians. The seats were equipped with lighted screens. There were tentacled tools coiled in readiness near each individual work-station.

Through the window, a boulder-strewn vista was visible. It extended perhaps 10 metres from the window's lower edge, giving the impression that if one of the Tinzins were to walk forward through the window, she would find herself in a clearing, open to the sky.

Youngest assumed that the source of the image had no connection to the room that he and Vane and the Tinzins were in. Nevertheless, the illusion was very persuasive. Even though he knew there was a rock wall behind the window's frame, it was hard to convince himself that the scene was not right outside this virtual window. A single cloud was visible in the bleached-blue sky, appearing to be painted into place. Only the dreamlike motion of distant birds, soaring like paired eyebrows on invisible updrafts of heat, betrayed the fact that the image was live.

Beyond the clearing was a rolling plain, lemon yellow and shimmering with heat-haze.

Youngest stared out for several moments.

Then, without turning his head, he said, 'Mentor Vane, what exactly is your plan for me?'

He could see out of the corner of his eye Vane's head bend and nod. 'That depends on you, Yasmine,' she said. The answer came out pat, as if it had been rehearsed. 'We do not force our will on those who come to us. We show the way and …'

She stopped, then altered her tone. 'No, let me say this differently. I will not pretend that we have ever been in this situation before. That is, our Island has never been boarded by an intruder before. So in every sense, the path ahead of you is for you to shape.'

He gave an ironic laugh. 'For me "to shape"! Really? You'd let me leave?'

'Ah – no! I meant, your willingness to become integrated into our community is your choice. After all, as an intruder, you have no rights. We could have fed you to the crabs immediately, as you said, and no one would have been the wiser. Had you fought us, or brought weapons on board, I can assure you, you would no longer be breathing. Even though I recognized you from the Collectory and I was already intrigued on account of the girl, I wouldn't have risked the Island's security. But you conducted yourself with dignity, even while attempting to storm your way out of your room. Your response to the pleasure ritual was quite positive. That was unexpected. Especially in someone who was once a man.'

Youngest sucked in his breath, embarrassed. 'Not that you gave me a choice.'

'That's true,' said Vane. 'Your conscious mind played no part in that event. Your body allowed itself to submit to our attentions and relaxed its boundaries. That was daring on its part. Very unusual.' She paused. 'Then again, maybe it was only practical? Perhaps your belief in your agenda is so fixed and so desperate that you have trained your nervous system to accept anything, to *be* anything, so long as the path towards your ultimate goal remains available to you?'

Youngest said nothing. He sensed the white-haired Mentor turn towards him. He could feel her attention acutely upon him, as if probing his skull.

'Of course, you realize,' she continued, 'if I discover that's all it is, just your private selfish response to overcome adversity, it will be rather disappointing. I will be forced to treat you like any other new recruit.'

'Which is?' Youngest did not turn his head.

'We would wipe your memory and set about training you to

one of the standard skill sets. It wouldn't be a bad life, though it would surely be dull compared to what you've known so far. I suspect you have a number of interesting stories to tell us, Yasmine. I would be sorry to lose them.'

Youngest breathed in and out, in and out, to a count of ten. Hostility was starting to build within him once more. He didn't want Vane to see it. He knew that she was being as friendly as she could be, under the circumstances. Yet the condescension implicit in her remarks grated upon him.

He had once been a man of property, with lands and factories to his name. Even the General's worst humiliations were played out against the backdrop of Youngest's true identity, which the General knew.

By contrast, Vane treated him with friendly indifference. She neither knew nor cared what he used to be. She saw in front of her a woman who had once been a man and she responded to him as a powerful woman responds to an inferior one. She couldn't help it. And neither could he, for resenting her.

He knew he had no choice but to dance to the Mentor's tune until he could find a way to smash his path out of the mountain surrounding him. It wasn't just the rock. It was also the continuous, suffocating surveillance. The hive of protection and co-dependence that both sustained and imprisoned all who dwelt within.

After which he would need to find his girl.

Then take her away from Vane and the Islanders.

How? He had no idea.

And where to?

He had no idea.

He straightened up. 'Mentor Vane, I realize that my choices are extremely limited. I should be satisfied to know that I can find a home amongst your community. Nevertheless. I have to pick my way through a maze of poisoned thorns. I cannot afford to make the wrong move. Nor can I afford to go back.'

He was about to turn to look at her but a movement caught his eye, out on the blistering plain revealed through the window.

Vane had already stepped forward and called down to the Tinzins, 'Come! It is beginning.'

The girls had already seen the figures moving onto the plain. With jarring suddenness, the scene blurred and jerked forward. The camera that was providing the visuals was zooming in. The effect was as if the whole room were being made to hurtle forward hundreds of metres in lurching increments. Youngest clutched the railing on the platform instinctively then glanced sideways to see whether Vane had noticed his reaction. She hadn't.

Within seconds, they had been brought to the edge of the great stone arena. The point of view had shifted several metres up in the air. Two groups of extravagantly costumed men were amassing on either side of a flat, stony field. Both sides had marching bands pacing alongside the teams.

One of the Tinzins called up from the pit, 'Commencing audio feed.'

A brassy cacophony swelled into the Media Room while on the screen, two men stepped forward, one from either side. They began to strut and twirl. They each wore tall headdresses, facemasks and flashing armour. Both wielded glittering maces. They were physically enormous, with bulging calves and rippling biceps. Some distance from them was an unadorned stone block, perhaps a metre high.

Vane indicated the block. 'See that? It's the Trophy Platform. Each team has its own, and they're all made to conform to a single standard shape and size – in order that it can always be recognized for what it is. I'm assuming you've not seen any of this before? An actual Zone Match in progress?'

Youngest shook his head.

'This is just the tune-up. The two leading champions from

either side will display and then fight. Usually to the death. Whoever's left standing chooses the trophy and it'll be placed on the Platform, where it will remain on view for a fixed period of time. Generally not more than half a day, but the teams are allowed till sunrise the next day. The Display usually takes twenty minutes so let me give you a little background while it's going on.'

She turned around and, going up to the blank wall behind them, touched a broad screen into existence. 'It won't be possible to appreciate the match unless you understand something of the underlying politics.'

21

The screen revealed a long grey diagram that extended across most of the wall. It took the shape of a crude hammer lying on its side: the handle extending left, bulging at the top, its lower boundary jagged.

'This is a schematic of the Zone,' said Vane. 'Have you seen one before? It expresses the physical land area of the continent as a pattern of team boundaries.'

Youngest shook his head. 'The only maps I've seen were on the Ascensor,' he said, 'on my way to the Suspended City.' Aeons had passed since then. 'I had barely heard about the Zone at the time, so I didn't know what to look for.' He still didn't.

'Ah. Well. What do you know about the game? Anything?'

'Just the basics.' Aila had struggled to describe the many levels of strategy and intrigue to him. 'I gather it's got elements of the ancient game of Buzkhashi, but with strategy. A kind of chess, but with physical battles and no board …'

Vane nodded and shrugged. 'Yes, and also no. The teams can choose what item they will use as the trophy – I mean, instead of a dead calf's body they might use, say, a totem-item belonging to the opposing team. Or a sacred goat. Not something symbolic, in other words, but an item that has actual value for the pursuit-team. Then there are the rules for forming associations which can result in blocs and enclaves deep within one team's territory – more Go than chess. And then, of course, there are the geo-political implications of victories and defeats. The fact that victories and defeats are translated into gains and losses on the stock exchanges of the player nations.' She was looking at his face, gauging his comprehension. 'You were aware of that, yes? The game is also a type of highly contrived war?'

Youngest nodded. He was trying to understand the purpose behind this lecture. It was not merely to broaden his general knowledge. The Mentor was not one to waste her time.

Using a light-pointer that she held in her hand, Vane began to tap the schematic, causing patches of colour to spring up from the grey. 'The teams are identified by colours. So you can see, as I go along, which areas belong to which teams – and then, of course, the alliances, which are identified by combinations of colours. Do you know the names?'

Youngest said, 'I ... well, there's the Dzingi –'

Vane immediately shook her head, 'No, no – that's just the Mod¡Kung word meaning "red". The four dominant teams are named Zhen, Ning, Chi and Bay – faint back-reference to the old Mongol game of mah-jong – corresponding to the colours blue, red, black and green.'

As she lit the screen, it was becoming clear that the balance of colours was shifting to red. Just as Aila had told him. Youngest could not rid himself of the image of the continent of Africa, now lying horizontally on its eastern coast, gradually being painted a dull red. Patches of green, blue and black were spread unevenly across the entire surface. There was a concentration of blues where they were currently located, in the mountains once known as the Roof of Africa.

Youngest said, 'I'm told that the ... Ning, represented by the coloured? ... The Ning have been doing very well of late. Too well. Apparently their success represents a problem for the Zone?'

Vane glanced at him.

'Obviously, your informant was an opposition supporter. A Zhen, perhaps? Well, of course, then! The Zhens and Nings are mortal enemies. Each one claims that the other team practices cannibalism and black magic.' She shrugged. 'At the moment, all three opponents have formed alliances against the Nings because the Nings have won a number of their strategic contests. And yes, that represents a problem. Then again …' She trailed off as she continued filling in spaces on the map.

Youngest wondered what the trailing thought was.

She had finished tapping out the final areas in the South of the map. Now she pointed to the mountainous area along the East flank of the spur that defined the lower reaches of the land mass as it was now depicted. 'As you have perhaps guessed, we are currently located in this region.' She glanced over her shoulder at him. 'Near an ancient caldera. As with everything else, it has been renamed and is now known as the Heart Basin, because of its shape. You can see it here, this elliptical patch?'

'Yes,' he confirmed. 'Tell me Mentor, that word "caldera" … doesn't that mean that the range we are in, this mountain in which your base has been excavated, is volcanic?'

'We made use of old vents and ancient pathways while building our retreat,' said Vane. 'It helped us that the sea has risen to bring the coast practically to the foot of the range.'

The region Vane was indicating was one of the bigger patches of blue on the map. The caldera was to the North of the patch.

'That's what you can see in the virtual window,' she was saying now. 'The primary battlefield of the Zhens. That's been their stronghold from the earliest years of the Zone. What we're about to see is the Nings challenging them here, in their heartland. It's certain to be an extremely bitter fight. Bloody and savage. As Islanders, we are not supposed to take sides in Zone conflicts, we do not support one team or another. But it's hard. And growing harder. The Nings have a reputation for extreme brutality. Today we shall see it on full display. This will be a decisive battle.'

Youngest was silent for a beat. Then he turned to look at the white-haired woman by his side. 'Mentor Vane,' he said. 'I will ask you again: where exactly is this conversation leading? And what are we doing here?'

The drumming and screeching twangs from the screen behind them had been growing louder at a steady pace. Vane's face creased in the preamble to a smile. 'Yes, I know you are curious. But I will keep you in suspense for a little while longer,' she said. 'Let us return to our ringside seat at the arena.'

22

The two Generals and Aila travelled through the night, arriving at the ruined coast-line while it was still dark.

They followed the taillights on one of the TravelCrabs going in that direction. When the mobile unit disappeared into a pile of rubble, the original General, the one Aila thought of as "her" General, donned a wetsuit and slipped into the water.

Aila, sitting on the rear deck with the other man, wondered what he was thinking, this newly minted person, as he watched his clone-brother vanishing into a lightless tunnel on the underwater scope.

He had not looked at her, this new being, nor had he addressed a single word to her. He wore the same clothes as his clone-brother, though he favoured small variations – in his choice of socks, for instance, and the colour of the handkerchief in the front pocket of his T-shirt. He had the same shaven head and the tattoo across his forehead in the place of his eyebrows. But at the corner of his temple, instead of the scissors, he had a flat rectangular object that Aila took a few moments to recognize as a tiny cleaver.

The drones responded to his presence with the same mute deference that they showed to his brother, appearing in attendance at all times and focusing their attention like hunting dogs upon their targets.

The original General had eventually introduced him to her, saying, 'Brother, this is one of our helpers.' And that was all he said before returning to the sub-audible conversations he had been having with his clone. They spoke rapidly and all the time, barely moving their lips. She could not tell whether they were linked by radio in that internal way that Yasmine had described to her while they were perched above the Chasm in what seemed to be another age.

Her mouth flexed in a wan smile in the darkness of the deck. It seemed to her that just as soon as she thought she had adjusted to one set of circumstances, the world would tilt, and she would once more be full of fear and self-doubt.

The night was moonless. From all around them came the clop-clop-clopping murmur of the sea as it slopped in and out of the remains of the coastal town poking up out of the water. What had once been a beachside resort was now a jagged forest of broken roofs, fallen towers, spars, spurs, rusting hoops of iron and mounds of debris. The boat moved in a slow circle, as tight as it could manage in order to remain roughly stationary. The black waters were spangled with phosphorescence. Beyond the up-thrusting jumble in the water reared the ridges of the ancient mountains that rimmed this coast.

It was an area that Aila knew from news footage as the stronghold of the Blues. She had never travelled to it herself but she remembered stories of her childhood, told by her mother, about trips to the beach in the Time Before.

She feared the plan outlined by the General.

She wondered what he would expect of her.

She asked herself if she'd have the will power to resist him. She doubted it. There was nothing for her to do but wait.

It was near dawn before the original General returned. The brother-General hurried below decks to receive him. Aila fell asleep where she was, in a deck chair, out in the open. It was afternoon the next day by the time she awoke. One of the drones jogged her elbow. It had brought a cup of hot crab soup for her and was now pointing to the front deck.

The boat was moving forward again. The brothers were standing at the table, looking at the glowing surface of an interactive map, tapping it and talking.

Aila drew close.

The map showed the region they were in, though it had been turned the wrong way, according to her understanding of maps. She did not mention this, of course.

It was also covered with the squiggling patterns that she knew were called 'script'. Her father could read such things. So could these men. The map was on a pane of flexible material called glazz. By flicking their fingers on the surface of the glazz, the Generals could change the size of the view. It was satellite-linked and could be made to zoom in or out on any given point.

'Finally,' said the original General, looking up at her. 'What took you so long? We need you to tell us what we're looking at here.' As he spoke, his brother began to increase magnification on a particular spot on the map.

The point of view was straight down, a still picture, in daylight. As soon as individual figures could be seen, Aila said, 'Oh it's a … it's the Display. Opposing teams decide which one will run with the trophy.'

She could see at once that the two teams were the Reds and Blues. It was no surprise. Events had been building towards this confrontation for months. The picture had been taken at a moment before the duel between two champions had begun. Nevertheless, the two warriors had taken up their positions. She could tell which one was which and assumed that the Generals could as well.

Then she glanced up and realized they could not: there was no audio feed from the satellite. They had no idea of the names of the teams. She lowered her eyes again and said, pointing to the image on the map, 'This one is the Ning Champion and this one here is the Zhen. They will fight and then …' She gave them a brief description of the opening moves of the game, using the official names. She told them which team was in the ascendant.

Her General interrupted her. 'Those names,' he said. 'Do they having meanings?'

'Blue and Red,' she said. 'The colours of their helmets.' She had switched the names, however. When she pointed at Red, she used the name 'Zhen', and 'Ning' in reference to the Blue. It was a very small gesture, she knew.

Still.

It might result in the General destroying the Reds with his special weapons rather than the Blues. His scheme for 'tilting the playing field' by supporting the winning team would be thwarted at least until he realized that she'd tricked him. No doubt she would be mercilessly punished. She didn't care. She'd like to think that in however tiny and insignificant a way, she too had pushed back against a cruel, invincible force.

23

The floor of the Media Room had filled up with Tinzins.

On the screen now, the two strutting and posturing warriors had bleeding cuts and their costumes were hanging slightly askew. They had just come out of a clench and were standing at a short distance from one another, panting. Neither was carrying his mace any longer. Each had a pair of seconds, two young men with oiled and glistening bodies, hovering close at hand and wearing uniforms that consisted wholly of knives, swords and hatchets in a range of sizes.

The musical accompaniment had turned into a wall of tooth-rattling noise, with no discernible form or content.

The image was not static, but swooped in close, cutting and swerving, to get multiple perspectives and angles. It could zoom right up close to the sweat-beaded foreheads of individual spectators on either side of the duel and it could pull out and look down directly from above to show the teams massed on either side.

It was possible to see that of the pair at the centre the man whose helmet-crest had once risen blue and proud like a fountain of flame, was now bare-headed. His teeth, which were shielded with steel plates, were bared, and blood flowed freely from the empty socket of his left eye. His partner was by no means unscathed. His right arm was gashed from shoulder to elbow and there was a dagger lodged in his side. But his helmet remained in place, a smooth scarlet dome with spikes poking out sideways in all directions. He already bore the smirk of a victor.

Youngest leaned towards Vane to ask, 'The cameras that record this scene – where exactly *are* they?'

Vane looked surprised as she said, 'Oh, I thought you would be familiar with this technology because of the fly-viewer you had on your wrist. It's the same concept, except our "flies" here are bigger. We call them shutterbees. They have longer range and greater resolution, plus we have more control over them. That's what the Tinzins are doing here in the Media Room—'

She pointed to the women at their consoles at ground level. 'They're editing the raw footage from shutterbees, before directing it to the virtual window for us to see.

'If you look along the edges of the screen, you'll see insets. They're from the even bigger cameras patrolling the area. Some of them are about the size of sparrows. They're owned by the commercial news networks covering the Zone. Their images are what you can see streaming live when you're in the Suspended City – *ahh*!'

She broke off to gasp.

On the screen, the Ning champion had sprung high in the air, then straightened out his thick-muscled legs so that he was briefly horizontal as he struck the Zhen full in the chest, with both his leather-bound feet. It was a decisive blow. The Blue man tottered back. Both his seconds sprang to his side, to keep him upright. The Ning had judged his angle perfectly, however. In the next moment, he was standing right on the barrelled chest of his opponent, bearing down with his full weight.

He bounced up and down with his head thrown back in a shrieking bellow of triumph, his steel-clad teeth flashing in the sun. From the teams on either side came ululating roars.

His seconds were already beside him.

Before the opposing seconds could anticipate the Ning's movements, he had reached for the great two-handed axe that one of his seconds held ready for him. Then he jumped down to the bloodied earth beside his fallen opponent, lifted the axe and slammed it down. The force of his blow caused the other man's head and body to jerk up from the ground on either side of the giant blade.

In the next instant, the seconds had snatched up the severed head, holding it by its ears – its single eye still open, its eyebrows raised up in horror – and thrown it down, dripping gore, onto the trophy platform.

Vane's hands covered her mouth. '*Ah,*' she gasped. 'That is *unprecedented.* The Champion's head as trophy.' The white mane of her hair was vibrating with disapproval, as she shook her head. 'Ah. This is wrong. Wrong!'

24

The match was adjourned till dawn the next day. Youngest and Vane ate a communal meal with the other members of the base, then retreated to Vane's private chambers.

It had a low ceiling and was carved out of porous volcanic rock. Amenities were minimal: a meditation pool and a virtual window that filled one wall showing the night sky. Instead of beds or chairs there were mats rolled in the corner and throw cushions on the rush-mat floor. Tentacles that extended down from the ceiling pointed enquiring fingers of light here and there. Youngest saw that each light was a single organism. When turned off, it looked like a circular maroon patch clinging to the ceiling with a nipple-like digit protruding from it. If the digit was tweaked, the tip lit up and unraveled downward, allowing itself to be positioned.

Steam rose off the surface of the perfumed water in the mediation pool. Youngest could not identify the scent. It had an elusive richness, as if at full strength it might be a powerful intoxicant. The pool extended downwards into the surrounding rock. It had sloped sides and narrow ledges to afford perching surfaces.

Vane invited Youngest to sit in the meditation pool with her. They sat in silence for several minutes. Vane's eyes were shut, her head leaning back, towel folded beneath it. Youngest tried to enjoy the sensation of being immersed up to his shoulders in the pool, but he could not suppress the thoughts continuously wriggling like spiky worms on the surface of his mind.

How will I leave?

Where is Meiji?

What will I do after I find her?

What are the plumbing arrangements here?

Sewage pipes were likely to be the most reliable exit from a rock-bound fortress. Locating them would at least give him some ideas about possible avenues of escape. Whether he got an opportunity to use them or not was another matter.

Vane began to speak. Her voice was becalmed to the level of a murmur by the heat of the pool. 'The question you need to ask yourself, Yasmine,' she said drowsily, 'is not "What is the quickest exit from this rat's nest?" but "What can I contribute to this world I have entered?"'

Youngest's scalp prickled. The Mentor had an uncanny ability to guess his thoughts. He opened his mouth to speak, but she pre-empted him.

'While I do have electronic instruments for reading minds, I have not used one on you so far. It's just a habit of knowledge. About other people. About motivations.

'You, for instance. I've been studying your responses during the short time I've known you. Only a mad woman would have attempted what you did. So it isn't difficult for me to guess that the single focus of your life for the past ten or twelve years has been your child.

'Naturally enough. No one can fault you on that.

'Your aim would have been to bring her to "safety". But how could you know that no such place exists in our world? You could not. Besides, any chance is better than no chance. So you took the chance. And at one level you succeeded. You got her out of her toxic birthplace.

'Or maybe not.

'Maybe you have failed. Because here you are, listening to a white-haired crone, babbling about motivations. Meanwhile, *your child, your child, your child.* Your child is all you can think of.'

Youngest was gazing down as he listened. He could see the two plump drupes of his breasts floating in the water and the familiar rounded expanse of his belly below. He was keenly aware of the Mentor's presence, hovering like a pale pink mass on the periphery of his vision but his inhibitions kept him from looking directly at her. Regardless of her sagging body, he could not delink his knowledge of himself as a man and her as a woman. Would she have been less willing to share a pool with him, he wondered, had she known that he continued to regard himself as a man?

He raised his head. 'Mentor Vane, I feel you should know that I don't think of myself as "Yasmine". My real name is "Youngest".' He said the name in his own language first, pressing on the translator disk at his throat before repeating its Unida formulation. He was still not looking in her direction.

'Yes, all right,' said Vane. 'I am glad to know that. It explains why you avoid looking directly at me as we sit here.' She waited for him to turn his head, reluctantly, in her direction, so that he could see her smile. 'Thank you. But as you perhaps realize, it makes no difference to me, what you believe yourself to be "on the inside".'

She had lifted her head off the towel and was gazing at him with her pale blue eyes that could, at times, imitate twin beams of sapphire light. 'What matters to me now is what you *are*, not what you *were*.'

Youngest frowned and shook his head slightly.

'Your past is over. That's what we teach our Candidates. We tell them to let it go. I would say the same to you. Let your past *go*.

'Like a seed that bears the energy required to grow a tree, or a sunflower, or a weed, we each have potential. But so many of us are trapped in private fixations over past wrongs and past calamities, past loves and past obsessions, that we allow the years to fly by until eventually our potential rots in the ground.

'Forget "Youngest". Embrace "Yasmine". That's my advice to you. With your broad mind, powerful body and deep intelligence you could add so much to the broken, wounded world we live in. If only you would give yourself the chance.'

Youngest's gaze dropped away from her face.

He heard her sigh.

'Fine. You don't want a lecture. Okay then. I'll go straight to the matter that interests me. It's very simple: I want you to help us join the conflict.'

'What?' Youngest was genuinely startled.

'Yasmine, listen to me. For twenty years – twenty-two to be exact – we Island communities have kept our commitment to neutrality. Based on that promise we were permitted to build our ringside positions. We fought to remain where we were at the time that the Whole World Union was setting up the Zone. Women and girls had been professional victims even in the years before the Cataclysm. We anticipated that their plight would only get worse under the new rules of engagement. We were right. There were some who suggested that the teams could be mixed-gender or that an all-women's team would automatically solve the problem. But there was never enough funding for those ideas.

'That's what it comes down to in the end, right? Funding. Even a seedling needs its start-up capital of water and air to sprout. There was never enough funding for a Women's Team or even a TransGender Team. Once it was clear that there would only ever be all-men's teams, the whole shameful exploitation of women who live in the Zone – as booty, as trophies, as entertainment, whatever – became the established norm.

'When the Suspended City became an economic powerhouse and the Collectory was created, the women who designed that facility threw off the yoke of the Union. They became the sole benefactors of the Islands and granted us full autonomy, with no oversight from the WWU.

'Similarly in the Zone: there are no referees or umpires here. The teams live and die based on the illusion of the Three Freedoms: Entertainment, Warfare, Commerce – the holy trinity. What the teams earn for their owners, the owners pump back into the teams. The approval ratings from viewers, the provision of arms, the calculation of odds, the betting on outcomes, even the quality of food supplements to Champions, have all become part of the Zone's essential ecology.

'So, yes. It is a complex system. And it works, in a fashion. But what has been the result? Over the years, a continuous erosion of every value that we would call "human". What you saw today was just one more symptom of this disease. In the short term, shock and horror will be expressed. The other teams will rally. They'll throw their weight behind the Zhens. If you look at the schematic now you'll find that in local contests all through the Zone there have been reversals and upsets for the Nings. But in the long term, the trend has only ever been downwards. Today, a Champion's head became the trophy for the first time. Everyone is horrified. A couple of months from now? It'll be routine.

'And I am sick of it. Sick to my heart. I believe the time for neutrality is over.'

'What do you mean?' asked Youngest. 'Surely you don't want the Islands to join forces and create warrior teams?'

'No,' said Vane. 'The girls who come to us have already experienced terrible violence. We don't plan to expose them yet again.' She leaned her head back and closed her eyes.

'I don't understand,' said Youngest. 'What other option is there?' *Where do I fit within this picture*, he wanted to ask. *And what happens to me if I don't want to fit?*

'We have been working in secret,' said Vane, 'on a bold

initiative. Perhaps tomorrow we will see the first example of it. Until then, and until you've given yourself time to think through your options, Yasmine, my request to you is to take no decisions.'

With her right hand, she tapped her chest, causing ripples in the water. 'Even here, inside: don't harden your heart.' She paused. 'Listen to me, Yasmine. I am old and I am wise. I know more than you can ever guess about loss and heartache. I had children too. And I lost them. One to the separation of the world into exclusive Enclaves and one to the Zone. So I understand the intensity of your fixation. I know what it means to feel that hammer-blow to the soul, when we discover the loss is final.'

Which I've not felt yet, old woman, thought Youngest. *Do not include me in your "we"*.

'Yet I also know that we can get over these private sorrows. We can find rewards in a higher calling. We can live in a way that will not leave us bereaved.'

Youngest remained silent.

'Will you at least give me an assurance that you will think about it? Overnight? Before you do anything rash?'

Youngest nodded. 'All right,' he said. One night. He owed her that much. 'I do have a question, though.'

'What is it?'

'I am curious about the plumbing.'

Vane raised her head. '*Plumbing*?'

'I can't understand how this pool is supplied with water or what its outlet is. Or indeed how all the rest of the sanitation is achieved … ?'

The Mentor stared at him.

Then a half-smile formed on her face. 'Ah, Yasmine. There's *no outlet*. No viaduct of sewage leading out of the fortress. No escape.'

Youngest shook his head from side to side. 'No, no, Mentor! You don't understand. Ever since we came to this base, I've been distracted by this question. It's my private obsession, if you want to call it that. My need to know about underlying structures is like an itch that must be scratched.'

Vane smiled as she shrugged. She leaned her head back once more, closing her eyes. 'I've told you already: organic interfaces. Just like on the Island.'

'So … this pool we're sitting in is actually some kind of organism?'

'Only the inner surface,' said Vane. Her voice was starting to curl around the edges. 'Look, I'll have to explain some other time. It's not really complicated.'

Then she was asleep.

25

Vane woke Youngest before dawn. They returned to the Media Room and its viewing gallery. A low buzz of activity rose from the lower floor. The window showed only a night-time view of the clearing and the distant field.

Youngest leaned towards Vane and said, 'The image on the window now is from a still camera, not a shutterbee, right? I was wondering where the camera is positioned relative to the Media Room.' He was wondering how near or far they were from the playing field.

'What we're looking at now is a loop,' said Vane. 'It's not live. Our shutterbees will only begin streaming in full daylight. Can't function without the sun.'

'Oh,' said Youngest. But she had not quite answered his question.

They were no longer alone. Four other Mentors joined them on the platform. Brahi, from the fresh-catch hold, Asma, Tasha and Emmi. Youngest couldn't be sure whether or not they were amongst the five who had assisted in his 'procedure' in Vane's apartment. It seemed to him they had each responded to him with special warmth.

He was feeling acutely ill at ease. He tried to tell himself that his embarrassment was compounded by the lack of suitable clothes. On the Island, he had worn loose shifts paired with calf-length pajamas. They had been light and well cut, so it did not matter that they hadn't been made specifically for his dimensions.

But this morning, Vane had handed him overalls that looked as if they had been designed for an orangutan. She had apologized, saying that she would find more suitable clothes for him later in the day. She couldn't know that for Youngest, who even as a man had always been a highly selective dresser, to be so ill-clothed was a torment.

He stepped back, wanting to absent himself from the company. He noticed that each of the mentors wore a wristband equipped with a flat black panels. Shutterbee viewers. His own viewer was in Vane's room.

He asked to be excused to go fetch his wristband.

The rooms had been created in spiral arrangements around a central core, perhaps reflecting the positions of old volcanic stems leading towards craters and vents.

When he got to Vane's room, he located his viewer, snapped it around his wrist and prepared to leave. Then he paused, looking once more at the meditation pool. He felt he was missing something. Something obvious was staring him in the face, yet he was unable to see it.

He went over to the pool. It had a cover over it. But when he bent to remove it, he realized, to his surprise, that it wasn't a cover. It was the pool itself. The water had become a solid mass, with a leathery overlay that curved up from the rim of the pool, giving it the appearance of a pale green lid.

He knelt beside the rim, wondering whether the leathery surface would respond to his touch. He put out a finger and gave the lid a tentative tap. When it produced no result, he tried again, in different locations. It was quite rigid, he found, and smooth to the touch. It didn't give in to pressure, nor did it show any sign of being elastic, springy or in any way other way flexible.

He paused, trying to think his way toward the correct solution. On the Island, doors opened and furniture folded out of walls based on lightly scraping nails against panels. Maybe the same was true here? He turned the palm of his right hand up and traced a light arc across the rigid surface of the pond with the nail of the index finger.

Immediately, the entire surface trembled, as if made of jelly. Then it went still again.

Youngest gave a nervous chuckle, feeling like a child experimenting with adult toys. He reached again, and this time he caressed the surface using the nails of all four fingers.

No response. The surface was obstinately solid once more.

He knocked. He tapped. He swiped his whole palm across it.

Nothing.

It was only when he used one finger again that he got a jiggle in response.

So. It had something to do with single fingers.

He tried each one in turn, and got only jiggles. He tried switching hands. He tried just his thumbs. Each time, he either got no response or only the jiggle.

Then he used the index fingers of both his hands, and that the lid, as if relieved of the task of being rigid, gave an audible sigh and began to liquefy. It grew translucent as it melted and the surface sank below the lip of the pond. In a few minutes, there at his feet was the pool of steaming, fragrant liquid he had seen the previous evening.

Youngest stood back, amused and amazed. The water was real, but there was an organism lining the pool that could stiffen itself, giving the appearance and feel of a hard surface. A sentient gel perhaps? Something that could absorb water or release it, depending on the type of stimulation it got?

He smiled to himself, enveloped in the pleasant scent from the pool. So all right, sewage was not being piped out of the fortress, just as Vane had said. The answer to the puzzle of waste disposal was that the fortress employed organisms to consume organic wastes, some of which they would convert into useful by-products. Such as water. And air. Maybe even some foods.

But there had to be ways and means of exiting the fortress other than the underwater route! A facility of this size had to have several exits and entrances, just as a safety precaution if nothing else.

He had repeatedly been shown that design solutions tended to be neat and economical, rather than convoluted. So: what he was looking for would most likely be hidden in plain view. It would be something he had seen but not recognized for what it was.

26

Sounds from the sports arena were audible as Youngest returned to the viewing platform above the Media Room. The discordant booming of the orchestra was limited to just one team today as the players took their positions facing across from one another, separated by a broad strip of open ground, with the Trophy Platform at its centre.

Vane and the other Mentors were watching the window while talking amongst themselves. The sky was light but dawn was still some minutes away.

Youngest had fashioned a belt for himself by ripping a two-inch strip off the lower edge of his garment. Tying the strip around his waist gave him a bit of a shape even though it left him with a ragged hemline. In his view, anything was better than masquerading as a potato wearing a gunnysack caftan.

Feeling slightly more secure about his appearance, he ventured towards the tall Mentor called Brahi. She nodded at him, smiling. 'I hardly recognize you,' she said, 'without your fish-tail and scales!'

He smiled back, bending his neck sociably, his hands clasped in front of him. An idea had occurred to him.

The fact that Vane had not given him a straight answer regarding the relative location of the sports arena nagged at him. If it were of no consequence she could have simply told him: *It's two kilometres away. It's a week's march away. It's unreachable.*

She could even have lied.

Instead, she had avoided answering.

That could mean she believed the information might help him in some way: help him to plot his escape for instance. Help him to think he had options.

Which meant he needed to find out for himself. Perhaps from one of the other Mentors.

Pointing to the viewer on Brahi's wrist he said, 'I've been wondering: do these things work inside this fortress?' He guessed that her device would have a greater range than his own.

'Oh, yes,' said Brahi at once, switching it on as she extended her arm. The little black screen was bigger than the one on his wrist. 'It can pick up transmissions from a range of zoöbots – flies, bees and even those fancy news-media cameras.'

As the screen warmed to life, images careened across it, jinking and twitching as it streamed dozens of sources within range. The device had a far clearer picture than the one on his wrist. Coordinates flickering in its upper left hand corner represented source-positions in three dimensions, recorded in hundredths of a second. He bent over, squinting at the tiny picture, hoping that the Mentor would tune it quickly to one of the streams. It didn't matter very much which one it was so long as it showed the playing field and displayed its coordinates.

He could sense that Vane was keeping her eye on him. She did not trust him. But she knew what his options were, whereas he didn't.

'It's still a bit early in the day,' said Brahi, tapping her wrist. 'The bees need strong sunlight to power-up.'

Images of boulders appeared and then disappeared. Patches of sky. More rock.

Then … a movement.

'Hmmm,' said Youngest. 'I think I saw something.' Whatever it was had shifted away. 'Can you … that is, does your viewer track-and-follow?'

'Of course,' said Brahi. 'Give me a moment?' She moved her

wrist in order to see the screen clearly.

'My viewer is very simple,' said Youngest. 'Really just a toy.'

'There we are,' said the Mentor. She was about to hold her arm out again for Youngest but frowned instead, holding the screen closer to her face. 'That's *odd*. Is that a … sort of … *child*? No … it's … it's a very short man.'

She held her wrist out now. 'Do you see?'

Youngest gasped.

'What?' asked Brahi.

'It's a *drone*,' said Youngest. He didn't have time to explain what he meant. 'I don't understand … where would this image be streaming from?'

He began to cast around, his head swinging this way and that as if he expected at any moment to see the little manling strutting about inside the Media Room.

'If it's on your viewer, the source of the image has got to be close at hand, yes? It can't be far away?' The question was directed towards Brahi but Vane and the others had jerked around at the urgency in his voice.

'The little … uh … person can't function on its own.' His mind was racing. 'It can only mean that there are others around, too.'

'You're gabbling,' said Vane, striding up to him. 'Stop it. Speak clearly – what's going on?'

'The General,' said Youngest, unsure whether his words made sense to the others around him. 'The man who was controlling me, who had my coordinates earlier – he must have tracked me after all. This manling is one of his servants—'

'I'm sharing coordinates,' said Brahi, as the other Mentors turned theirs on. 'He seems to be alone, your little whatever-you-called-it, Yasmine. Just walking around.'

Vane, who did not wear a viewer, was beside Brahi now, addressing Youngest. 'I don't understand. What can this

"General" hope to do here? Unless he's … I mean, has he got a task force following him?'

'No, no – well, in the sense that he's got a few drones and …' And Aila.

'Yes, but he's not a tourist!' said Vane. 'So what's he doing *here—*'

'Look!' This was Emmi. 'I've got them on a sparrow. Higher up.' She beamed coordinates. 'One grown person, a woman – and at least three little ones. Carrying heavy equipment.'

'See! They're above this ridge,' said Brahi. 'Directly above our position – I can see one of the hidden vents—'

'Do us all a favour and stream it to the wall-screen behind us, for pity's sake!' exclaimed Vane. 'I can't see a thing on these ridiculous pin-head viewers!'

But there was a swelling roar from the virtual window. The sun had risen. The cameras were focused on the playing field.

The Nings had begun their attack. The Zhens had counter-attacked. Within seconds, six pairs of metal-clad warriors were locked in struggling formations around the Trophy Platform. Behind them, on either side, their teamsters were pounding on their shields, with the flats of their swords, ululating at top volume.

On either side, expert stealth troops had already lowered themselves to the ground wearing mirror-sheaths and vision helmets, preparing to find openings between the wrestling metal-backs in order to get through to the grisly trophy.

Then, with no warning sound, there was a flash.

All the screens, big and small, went black.

The sudden black-out was followed by a boom so loud that it knocked Youngest sideways. He landed against someone else. There was a sound like dozens of whistles being blown simultaneously: the young women on the lower floor were shrieking in high-pitched unison.

Huge clouds of white smoke were billowing in from somewhere.

Vane's voice cut through the confusion. 'The … SCREEN! The screen has been breached! Evacuate – evacuate at once. Everyone down, go down one level, DOWN.' She turned, intending to use the stairs.

Youngest picked himself up from the floor.

He didn't give himself time to think. Swinging forward, he vaulted over the balcony. His head was still ringing like a bell from the explosion and he could see lights popping in front of his eyes, but his only thought was: *Vane didn't want to tell me we were close to the arena because I might realize that the screen doesn't just look like a giant window. It IS one. It's an exit.*

He had been looking at his way out all along.

It was a short drop to the floor. Smoke was pouring in through the shattered screen-window. He dashed towards it. In another couple of moments, he was through.

Out in the open air.

Free.

PART V

MEIJI

1

Meiji, Rahm and four girls from other teams left the Island in three TravelCrabs, two girls in each.

Rahm showed Meiji how to strap herself in and settle down. 'We is must have sleep-teach,' said Rahm, as she snapped herself into her seat. 'We is go straight to new training.' They were fully dressed, both of them, in tight-fitting black slick-suits.

At the controls of the Crab was a similarly dressed woman. She had introduced herself as Juno and said she was a Wrangler.

Meiji did not know what the designation meant. There was so much she didn't understand and wanted to know more about. But there was no time.

She was seated opposite Rahm, on the other side of the cramped TravelCrabs, their knees almost touching. Juno's seat had formed up around her, its back close enough for Meiji to lean her arm on.

Her head was bursting with questions. It was impossible to believe that the Island was generated from organic parts. Not just organic: actually *alive*. There had been plenty of indications. The tentacle lights in particular: the way they flinched away if they did not want to be turned on. The way that entrances and exits yawned open or snapped shut, as if anticipating the touch of inhabitants.

But the idea that the rooms themselves were supported on the backs of giant crustaceans ... which lived in linked clusters ... then came apart, in order to function as mobile units? *That* was beyond conception. Even though she could see the proof all around her, she could not wrap her mind around the reality of it. It was as if the memory retrieval exercise had shaken her grip on reality: she found herself anticipating that any moment she would hear the call of a peacock, or glass shattering, and wake up.

Instead, what she heard was the sound of water continuously shifting around her. The continuous *glop-glop* sloshing that she had noticed in the very beginning of her awakening from deep stasis was still apparent though the clicking and scissoring had faded away.

Tremors were starting up in the wall behind her, and through the floor, as the creature they were in began to shake itself loose in preparation for lifting itself up on its multiple-jointed legs. She didn't know whether to feel horrified or delighted. The idea of being a tenant within the body of a living organism was repugnant to her. Like being a louse or a tick. She wished she could understand more about how the animals were created and trained. Whether they understood that they were being used. Whether they minded that use.

She hadn't realized that she was straining forward in her seat, tense and fretful until she saw that Juno had turned around and was speaking to her.

'I said, it's going to be a bumpy ride,' repeated Juno. 'You need to settle back in your seat and relax. I'll turn on the sleep-teach right away.'

'Oh, but I—' Meiji had not intended to asleep. She wanted to see where they were going. She wanted to ask questions about the route and how the crabs found their way and why they needed to leave the Island at all—

'Is not choice,' said Rahm. Her voice was cold and abrupt. It wasn't from unfriendliness but anxiety. 'Is long distance and I is already say, we is need much to learn.'

Meiji clicked her tongue in irritation as she prepared to lean back. Just then the crab beneath them gave an enormous jerk forward and she was thrown towards Juno. In the next moment the crab jerked the other way. But the straps that held her in place were well padded: she felt the movement without being bruised by the restraints.

She glanced towards Rahm, wanting to say that maybe it was a good thing they would be semi-conscious. But the other girl had shut her eyes.

So Meiji looked towards Juno instead.

'I'm ready,' she said, resignedly.

2

Many hours later, all six Candidates were standing in a cramped, semi-circular underground cave hewn out of black rock. It was lit by electric lamps that hung down from the ceiling on wires. A stream of cool air circulated through the space from overhead vents. One wall of the room was flat, with a monitor built into it and a low platform in front of it. The single entrance into the room, with no door to seal it off from the corridor beyond it, was also cut into this wall. Folding chairs were stacked against the curving surface that faced the monitor and the entrance. Underfoot, the floor was smooth and reflective, like black glass.

The girls had eaten a hot meal, been shown to their shared sleep-chamber and allowed to wash up using basins of salty water before being brought to this briefing room.

'Welcome to the Lair,' said the woman who had introduced herself as Wrangler Dane. 'Gola, Rahmato'u, Perine, Licha, Meiji, Naïm. Welcome and congratulations. You are the first team of Candidates to be considered for training at this facility.'

Her face had a natural smiling expression. She was lithe and wiry, with salt-and-pepper hair cropped short. Her skin was matt brown, like tea brewed in milk. Traces of old tattoos remained down one side of her face. She wore the same type of black slick-suit that the girls were dressed in and stood on the platform to make her introductory presentation.

'As you know from what you learned during your journey here, we are going to introduce you to a mount that will be very different to any you have met so far.'

She paused, looking at each of the girls in turn, as if assessing each one's personality. 'All of you have ridden whales. That experience and your performance with the whales is what made you eligible to come to this facility today. But you need to understand clearly that even we Wranglers have not had enough time to work with these animals. They are wholly unlike any of the creatures we have trained with so far. They are harder to control, harder to like and definitely more dangerous.

'So, yes, there is an increased risk. We will only be able to guide you up to a point: beyond that point, you will be guiding *us*. Your experiences will become the ones on which future Candidates will build their learning templates.

'And, yes, we're not expecting that all of you will make it past the training. We will not expose you beyond what we think you can handle. We'll hold you back if we think you're exposing yourselves to too much harm. In any case, we will be able to take only two of you forward towards the challenge we hope to use as a launch-pad for a – what shall I call it? – a bold new initiative in the Island's history. A new direction.

'If none of you is ready for the challenge then … so be it. We'll accept that our facility is not ready and will delay our launch to some future date. Is it clear? Just being here is going to test your physical and emotional stability to the maximum. Yes, emotional: you will soon see what I mean by that. So do not push yourselves to fulfil the task if you know you can't make it. This is not a life-test, but a *training*. Whatever you fail at today, tomorrow and the days that follow, you will have chances to recover your position and to try again. If at any time you feel this particular challenge is not for you then you will leave the training, with no loss of work credits.'

She paused again, giving the girls time to absorb what she had said. 'All right. Before I go any further, any questions?'

The girls shifted and murmured.

Perine, fair-haired, with muscular shoulders and a prosthetic arm, raised a hand. 'Wrangler Dane,' she said. 'You mentioned that we are being initiated into something completely new: different to anything that the Islands have attempted before. But it is to be on *land.* Is that right? Does that mean we're ... we're ... *in the Zone*?'

Even before the query was complete, Wrangler Dane had turned to stroke the monitor behind her to life. When it did not light up at once, she glanced towards the girls again, saying, 'You may find that our technology here is quite a bit slower than on the Island. We use ordinary electricity to power our gadgets, not organicals.' She blinked, before adding, 'Organic machines. Like you have on the Islands.'

Behind her, the panel now showed a map.

Meiji jerked forward, frowning.

She could see that it was a representation of the world's landmasses but there was something seriously wrong with it. Right in the middle, spread all the way across it, was a long, misshapen lump that resembled no continent she could identify. Around this lump were a number of other shapes that looked vaguely familiar, but so stretched and distorted that it was hard to be sure whether this was the whole world or just a part of it or ... What was this?

She turned her head reflexively towards Rahm, but the other girl merely glanced back and shrugged, not showing any special concern. Meiji had to assume she found the map normal. So, apparently, did the other girls. None of them seemed surprised in any way. She decided therefore to keep her mouth shut until she could understand why she was the only one who thought it looked odd.

Wrangler Dane tapped the monitor and spread her fingers to zoom in on the image. 'As all of you know, Vane Island was situated along the southern boundary of the Zone,' she said. 'Here.'

The map had resized itself multiple times in quick succession until all that was visible was the dark ochre representing land filling the upper portion of the monitor. Below the land was a blue mass representing the sea. Towards the right of the map, a thick wedge of the sea extended northwards. A small red glow marked the position of the Island that Dane pointed to with her finger.

Now she expanded the map some more whilst also shifting it, so that the focus moved north and east of the red marker, along the blue wedge.

'When you left Vane Island, your crabs travelled underwater, following cables on the seabed. You notice this greyish-blue area, all of this? It represents where there used to be dry land before the rising of the seas. Ports and cities. Everything is drowned underwater now. But your crabs by-passed all of that to arrive at this area *here*—'

Her finger traced a path that led from the blue wedge directly into the ochre. As her finger traced along the map, a trail of dots lit up. 'This is only a rough approximation of the path the crabs took. The tunnels they used were what we excavated in the rock many years ago, at the time we built this facility. If I pull back out—' she reduced the scale of the map once more '—you'll see that we were tunnelling into the relatively soft rock of an ancient caldera.' She glanced over her shoulder. 'A volcanic crater.'

The dots under her finger had traced a soft arc tending towards the west along an immense elliptical feature. Its lowest point was in the east, representing the vent of a long-extinct volcano. A loose ring-shaped ridge represented the extent of the crater once created by that dead mouth.

Dane looked towards Perine. 'So ... the answer to your question is *yes*. The rock into which we have burrowed does indeed belong to the Zone. And *yes*, though you haven't asked about it, our presence here is illegal. We Islanders were permitted to maintain off-shore facilities, nothing more. We were never supposed to have access to any part of the mainland. Everything we do here has been in secret, without support or approval or funds from the Whole World Union. They never dreamt we would have ambitions beyond our stated humanitarian goals.' Her face creased into a smile. 'Yet we did. So we went ahead and burrowed. And here we have been, ever since.'

Two more hands went up. Naïm wanted to know how long the training would take. Gola asked about credits. Dane nodded to both of them but said, 'Please! Before I say anything else, I think you need to see something.' She drew a remote control from her slick-suit and pointed it towards the floor. 'The water followed us in wherever we tunnelled. So we had a series of underground water-bodies already in place.'

Lights beneath the floor began to come on, revealing that the floor of the room was in effect the top of a gigantic cavern, swarming with fish. All six Candidates gasped, clutching one another and lifting their feet in an instinctive reflex, though there was no question of falling through the sturdy plate-glass. 'That proved to be very useful once we began work on our current project.'

The lights did not penetrate all the way to the floor of the cavern. Nevertheless, it was possible to see that, there below, in the green-grey murk was an enormous, pale and sinuous shape. Its body had a long neck and an even longer tail. At the end of the neck was a narrow, triangular head, but it was hard to see any details. The creature was ducking away from the light, moving deeper down.

Meiji heard a stifled cry from Rahm. She turned towards her friend, putting an arm around her shoulders. The other girl was trembling violently, the great halo of her hair shuddering. 'I is not able to do this,' she said, her voice hoarse and gasping.

'*Not*. NOT.'

But Meiji, straining to see more clearly, felt her heart quickening with excitement. She knew she would go forward into the challenge. She just *knew* it.

3

Two days later, Meiji was shivering in the damp gloom of the Lair's Deep Dock. Her mount was in its watery paddock, its back exposed to the air. She had spent most of the previous day in its company, and was no longer so thrilled about being one of the two girls going forward into the challenge.

It was a giant hybrid reptile, created from the DNA of a tiny tropical lizard belonging to the genus Draco. Whereas the original animal was not even a foot in length, this one and its artificially created sisters were the size of two horses end-to-end, not including its tail. It was massive, it was agile and, when it spread the membranes between its front and rear limbs, it could fly.

The water in its trough was chilled. The lizard was cold-blooded. That meant, when it was in the trough it was only partially alive, because unlike warm-blooded animals, it could not maintain its own body heat. Without body-heat, it could not move. Which was why she could afford to sit near it.

Waiting to be strapped on to its back.

From where she sat, she could see only one of its lemon-yellow eyes glowing up from the dark water. Its slitted pupil was trained upon her. Tracking her movements. Unblinking. It had a clear membrane, like flexible glass, that swiped across its eyes every five seconds. It was awake, aware and hungry – but immobilized by its own blood-chemistry.

The mood was hushed in the dock. Rahm had dropped out of training shortly after that first sight of the creature in the briefing room observatory. The only other girl who had qualified was Gola. She had two prosthetic feet and pink scar tissue all the way down her back. She was quiet but purposeful. On the way to the Dock she had told Meiji that she came from a tribe of snake-charmers. 'This is only another kind of snake,' she said. 'Just bigger and with legs. Not even poisonous.'

Meiji returned the creature's gaze. She had been told to think of a name for it. But it inspired no positive feelings in her. She wasn't afraid of it and yet, because it was not in any sense friendly or companionable, naming it seemed to be a waste of energy. The coldness of its metabolism was part of its personality. It sought out warm-blooded prey. No matter that the prey may have been riding on its back a moment earlier, directing its actions, providing it with movement-sustaining warmth – if it got a chance, it would gulp down its rider without a moment's hesitation.

There was a boom as the elevator door opened. Mentor Kesh stepped out, followed by Folia. 'Ah, Meiji!' she called. 'Glad to see you're getting acquainted.' She meant with the creature.

'It's staring at me,' said Meiji. 'It wants to eat me.'

'They don't know how else to be,' said Folia. 'That's how we designed them. Have you found a name for it yet? Or "her", rather.'

'No. I can't.' The yellow eye shifted for a split second, to look up at Folia, before returning to Meiji. 'I can't name something that thinks of me as food.'

'Oh, I wouldn't be so rigid about it,' said Folia. 'Everyone's got to live.' She held out her hand to Meiji, pulling her upright. 'Come on. A few warm-up exercises.' She meant this quite literally. They had to bring their blood-heat up to the surface of their skins.

The lizards could accommodate two riders. Meiji stripped down, then she and Folia stepped into their open-fronted suits.

They had Wranglers to help with the helmets, breathing gear and neuro-circuitry. Gel-pads placed on their shaven scalps conducted their brain waves to processors in the helmets. The processors created an interface through which the riders had control over the brains of the lizards.

There was no question of sharing air with these animals. Their brain functions, however, were malleable. They thought in simple patterns, with short decision-trees. The challenge for the riders lay in maintaining control over the animal's brain without losing sight of their own mission. That was why there were two riders. The Primary controlled the lizard, while the Backer controlled the Primary.

Meiji had ridden as Backer the previous two days, behind Folia. They had circled the water in the dock, allowing her to get a sense of how the lizard moved, the combination of liquid grace and sideways jerks, the elastic power in its limbs and the balancing weight of its tail. Folia kept up a continuous commentary of how she was dealing with the sensory input she got via the helmet. It was hard to get a sense of what this was like. As Backer, Meiji was also wired into the nervous system of the rear limbs and tail, but it was more like learning to use a mechanical extension of her arms or legs. Not difficult.

Her heart was pounding. Which was good. It meant that her skin would make hot contact with the creature's naked back-patch. But she was frightened, too. Today she would control the front limbs, the flight ribs and the head.

The head.

That meant she'd have input from the lizard's eyes, nose and ears. She would sense its mouth and know the flickering movements of its long black tongue. She would also acquire an additional sense unknown to humans – of heat-imaging.

'Ready?' said Folia. 'You go first. It will be a full six minutes before our friend warms up enough to start struggling, so you have that window of time – oh!' She stopped herself from locking down her helmet. 'Choose a name! It'll matter to you, even though the lizard doesn't care either way.'

'Okay,' said Meiji, her voice muffled by the helmet. 'I'll call it "Smaug".' That was the name of a dragon she had read about, in a famous children's book. A translation.

'Smoke?'

'No, S-M-A-U-G,' said Meiji. 'From a story I read a long time ago.'

Folia smiled and nodded. 'Ah, *The Hobbit*. I keep forgetting you can read!' Her tone was approving. 'All right, except …' She paused.

Meiji looked at her through the helmet's visor, worried.

But Folia was smiling. 'Nothing major! Just that, if I remember correctly, Smaug was male. Right? Intelligent, fire-breathing, gold-hungry, etcetera, etcetera! Your mount is female. Not mythical, not magical. Not very bright either. Just a wee little tropical reptile blown up to a thousand times its natural size, with only one thing on her mind: FOOD. It's important to keep the distinction in mind.'

Meiji flexed her mouth in an *I get it!* grimace.

'Come on,' said Folia. 'Time to go.'

4

With Wranglers to assist her on either side, Meiji was harnessed and hoisted up, her body arranged so that she was horizontal in the air above the creature's back. Then she would be lowered onto the exposed patch of skin, free of scales, on its back. She could see it below her, a tender pink area shaped a bit like a star. The skin was practically translucent: she could see a tracery of bones beneath the dark maroon of its muscles.

When she was lowered onto it, she felt that it was cold to the touch and damp, but not slimy.

'Down,' she heard one Wrangler say, while on either side of her hands quickly strapped her into place. The leather body-saddle fitted all the way around the lizard's chest, forming a tight bond. The whole front of her body, naked from neck to crotch, was plastered down along the creature's bare skin.

Two sets of wranglers worked together now, connecting up the helmet. They had to move fast because she had to gain control over the creature's nervous system before it warmed up enough to move. Or else it would start flailing, its limbs striking against the sides of the trough it was in, potentially damaging itself. Its mental agitation could also wash back into the rider, whereupon the ride would have to be aborted.

As Folia was also lowered into position, Meiji felt the lizard's body sink lower in the water with the added weight. She remembered her childhood book and smiled. The image came into her mind of the great dragon lying within his cave of gold coins, covered in them, luxuriating in them.

Sounds from outside the helmet were muffled. She felt a hand tapping her shoulder. One of the Wranglers was asking her to lift her head in order to position the hose for her air supply. When she obliged, the Wrangler held the back of the helmet steady, while shifting the nose-piece into place through the space on the front of the visor. It was an unpleasant sensation: a pair of sentient probes entered her nostrils and, like the Trak, locked themselves into place inside her nose. A moment later, when the air started to flow, the discomfort melted away.

There was a crackle as Mentor Folia's voice came in through the helmet's ear-phones. 'Meiji? Can you hear me?'

'Yes,' said Meiji. 'Loud and clear.' She had been given a series of stock phrases as responses. 'Loud and clear' was one of them.

'Try and relax,' came Folia's voice in her ears. 'If you are tense, Smaug will pick that up from you and become tense, too.'

The Wrangler's hand tapped again on her right shoulder.

This was the signal for being linked to the lizard's senses. Less than a minute had passed but she could already feel the muscles of its back twitching beneath her.

Meiji lifted her right hand with the thumb turned up. The Wrangler gripped that hand, to reassure her as the other two Wranglers began coupling the wires. She felt a powerful jerk, as the animal beneath her registered her presence within its brain. Then with a fluttering shiver, sensations began to pour into her mind.

Abruptly, her vision split into two separate streams, each one extremely sharp, as she began receiving input from the eyes on either side of Smaug's head.

She could see individual hairs on the arms of the Wranglers standing around the trough; the shoe-laces on their shoes wriggling like worms; light bouncing off the water, haloed with rainbows.

The creature's nose came online. Scents as sharp as arrows

pierced her consciousness, pouring in from every surface. She could not begin to trace the source of these ribbons of sensation, each one as distinct as a spice, that wafted in from the floor, from the air, from separate strands of cloth.

And then the mouth.

There was the metallic flavour of the water, the grainy saltiness of it, rippling with the afterlife of thousands of sea-creatures. Alongside the tongue, the interior of the mouth bristled with two rows of saw-edged teeth. Behind the tongue and plunging deep into the gut, was a burning sensation, like a furnace. A furnace of pure, white-hot hunger.

And, finally, there was the shapely heat, pouring in and out of focus, of every person in the dock. These were portraits as round and full with the promise of nourishment as a 3D video of steaming food. Yet it wasn't an impression of physical shape; it was of their three-dimensional *heat*. She could sense the delicate pulsing of hearts – so many red, beating hearts! – accompanied by the warm mush of their brains and the bright fire of their eyes. They were all engorged with that life-sustaining heat that she, Smaug, did not possess.

They were standing around her, these glowing, fragrant packets of pure energy, standing within easy, easy reach … Meanwhile her limbs were still locked in torpor, sluggish and frozen.

'Meiji!' called Folia in her ears. 'Keep track of yourself.' The voice creaked at the edges, the words clicking and rustling like dry leaves, stripped of meaning. 'Locate and isolate your own sensory stream!'

As if at a great distance, Meiji felt another self struggling to raise its voice above the cataracts of sensation flooding into her from the lizard. Her own body was calling to her, sending out signals of distress and need. The sensory information flooded her conscious, pushing her attention this way and that, from the lizard and from her body. They were like powerful magnetic currents vying for control over the single iron filing of her attention.

Folia spoke again, 'Meiji? Answer me! Do you copy?'

And she was able to stammer, 'Y-yes! Mentor Folia. Yes. I copy. Yes. Meiji here.'

Beneath her the great beast was now bucking and trembling, all its muscles straining to move its wooden limbs. She could feel the power coursing through it and from it into her. It was like her arms and legs had been flexed outwards, lengthened and jointed in unfamiliar ways, urgent with power. It was like lying astride an engine made of bone and muscle, the whole of it vibrating with the need to jerk forward. The sinuous train of the lizard's back was powering up, its neck swaying from side to side, the jaws opening and clacking.

'Mentor Folia,' gasped Meiji, 'permission to move! I can't hold it – *her!* – much longer. Are you ready?'

'I am ready,' said Folia.

5

They circled the dock three times, moving along a channel that forced the lizard to swim rather than walk. Gola was close behind, on her mount, with Mentor Kesh as the Backer. The two lizards did not seem to notice one another, or if they did were too hungry to acknowledge the other's presence. The Wranglers were ready with small chunks of seal meat to slip into the water at regular intervals in order to keep the creatures moving.

But it was clear to Meiji that these treats were less than meaningless. They were like cruel taunts to one whose stomach was ablaze with need. 'We need more,' she said to Folia. 'There's just not enough. We're ravenous. We need something *hot*—'

Folia chuckled. 'Yes, yes, I know!'

It was time to leave the dock.

A ramp led up and out of the dock. In order to reach it Meiji would have to guide Smaug to pass beneath a solid iron grille before reaching the ramp. There was incentive in the form of a larger-than-usual portion of seal in the water, but just as she got to it the meat disappeared out of sight.

Meiji–Smaug immediately ducked her head under the water. Her clear eyelids were like goggles and she could see perfectly well. The water was murky and the lizard had to turn her head from side to side before sighting the meat. There it was, in the water, on the floor of the channel. She raised her head to get a big gulp of air, then dove down in a smooth, swooping movement, towards the meat.

Folia said, 'Well done. Steady now. Don't grab the meat too

quickly … and remember that *you* still have to breathe!'

Meiji–Smaug did not reply. She was concentrating on remaining crouched down on the slippery stone floor, with her shoulders low, elbows bent up high, higher even than her ears. Never letting the meat out of her sight.

It was moving away, dragged along the floor, scraping a path through the green slime on the stones. Her belly was scraping the floor now, as she slithered along. She could keep her nostrils shut tight and could hold her breath under water for at least ten minutes, but the icy temperature slowed her down. The meat was in front of her, just out of reach. She crept after it as it began to slide up an incline, eventually re-emerging from the water. Then it was on dry floor. She could see the clamp attached to a mechanical arm extending down from the ceiling. The arm was attached to an overhead track. The snack kept moving out of reach.

Meiji–Smaug's feet were inclined to slip but she had talons. They found purchase in the cracks and joints of the floor. She was still too cold to move quickly. She could *smell* the meat right in front of her nose, but it just kept moving further away!

Meiji–Smaug stopped, raised her head and let out a frustrated bellow. It sounded like a short, sharp yap, with fluting undertones, like an angry trumpet. Then she shook herself hard, thousands of scales rattling, to remove the water caught in the folds and joints along her long body.

'Stop that!' complained Folia in her scratchy human voice. 'Or at least give me some warning before you shake, Meiji. I almost bit my tongue. *Keep moving.* We've got to release the meat hook, so that Gola can follow behind us. It's not very far. Just keep moving forward. *Meiji!* Do you copy?'

The girl recovered her own voice and said, 'Yes! Yes, Mentor Folia. I copy. Sorry. We got a little distracted.'

'I know, I know – just keep moving!'

The meat had moved out of sight, but its scent was vivid in Meiji–Smaug's nose: raw, salty, chewy, with a smooth blanket of fat and a hint of fur. Just around the corner.

She chased after it, moving at a lithe, loping pace, her head extended forward at full stretch, her jaws open and salivating, moving in a spiralling path, up, up and …

Out. They were in the open air.

The meat had been flung forward and beyond the archway at the top of the ramp, on to a stretch of bare rock, open to the sky. The clamp that had held it snapped open, before being whipped up and away, returning the way it had come.

Meiji–Smaug sprinted forward and pounced on the red meat. She picked it up and flung her head back in the same movement in order to gulp it down whole, her whole body shuddering with pleasure and need. She was standing almost upright now, balanced on her tail.

There was a distant squawking in Meiji's ears.

Folia's voice came sharply again. 'STOP THAT! You have to take control of your mount. Stop her from standing upright. It's very uncomfortable for me.'

Meiji–Smaug stood still, paying no attention to the voice. She was looking around. This was amazing. The view. The sun was low in the east, but the air was toasty hot, out here in the open. Above them was the brilliant, burning sky. The rock underfoot had not warmed up yet. And there was no food within sight or scent.

She extended her neck this way and that, crouching forward once more. Warmth from the air around them was rippling across her skin like molten joy. She could feel fingers of heat rimming each of her scales. It was much warmer here than anything she had experienced before, underground.

She was quivering with energy. And still very hungry. In a moment, she felt a pressure near her anus. *Pop!* She had flicked her tail up and loosed a pile of slimy boluses of pungent dung.

'Aaarggghhh!' groaned Folia. 'You could warn your Backer before letting fly?'

Meiji struggled to maintain her perspective.

She knew what was required of her and Smaug. They had to move forward to the edge of a cliff. She had seen pictures, she knew what to expect. But everything she'd seen had been through her own eyes. Not Smaug's.

Now, the world was miraculous with bright colour and fresh experiences. There was no brake on the lizard's responses. She experienced reality in violent sensory streams, each one as urgent as the next. From moment to moment, Meiji had to rein herself in, clamp down on Smaug and hope they could both do what Folia wanted of them.

Gingerly, with her talons flexed upwards in order to avoid clicking on the rock, she began to walk forward. The ridge they were on was part of a curving cliff, dropping to a basin that continued as an endless rolling plain.

As she approached the edge of the cliff, she began to hear a continuous jarring disturbance on the air. She turned her head this way and that, waiting for meanings to reveal themselves. The wind whipped around the curving walls of the vast caldera, delivering sounds in intermittent bursts.

Folia said, 'See if you can lean her head down over the side. She needs to see the floor of the clearing at the foot of the cliffs.'

Meiji–Smaug crept forward, the boisterous air currents ruffling the edges of the scales on her face, making her uncomfortable. She kept wanting to snap at what felt like tendrils of possible food touching her face.

Meiji could feel the lateral vanes along the sides of the lizard's body twitching nervously, as if preparing for flight. The elastic membranes between the slender ribs rippled with air, causing momentary weightlessness.

She had her rear end high, elbows flexed up and head down, and was about to bend her neck over the edge of the cliff when a powerful flash from the other side of the caldera lit up the scene below.

Following the flash came a sound like ten thunderbolts striking at the same moment.

Smaug bounced up in the air with shock.

The huge semi-circular gliders on either side of her body billowed outwards and went rigid. With a suddenness that knocked the air out of both riders' lungs, the animal sailed up off the cliff. It rose straight up in the air, its huge limbs outflung, carried upon a violent updraft. It immediately wriggled sideways, pure instinct leading it to find the angle at which it could sustain a glide. Within seconds, it had righted itself, adjusting the small flaps on its neck and using its tail as a rudder to keep itself airborne. It planed away from the cliff, but in a curving arc that would bring it around to the place from which the flash had come.

In her ears, Meiji could hear Folia. She was cawing about something, her voice charged with urgency. 'Meiji,' she shrilled, 'Meiji – bring her back – bring her around – there's something weird going on. We can't—'

But it was hopeless. Meiji could not focus long enough to hear whole words.

Smaug's head was tilted earthwards, her nostrils flared wide open. Along with the flash and the terrifying sound, there had come a scent of harsh, unnatural chemicals as well as that other scent. The one filled with infinite heat and the promise of replenishment.

Live prey.

Dozens of them.

Scattered like beads of pure contentment on the plain below.

6

'Meiji?' called Folia, 'Meiji! Answer me! Do you copy?' Her voice sounded hoarse. Meiji raised her head, or tried to. There was something holding it down. Air pressure. 'Meiji! Come in Meiji! Answer me, please—'

'Yes,' said Meiji, her voice unsteady. 'Mentor Folia, I …' She couldn't complete the formula of words because of the distractions flooding her brain.

They were high in the air, descending fast. The wind shearing off the edges of her scales was like dozens of high-pitched whistles screeching in her ears. The air was flowing so fast over her head that she was pinned down to Smaug's neck just as surely as if a pair of phantom hands were holding her down.

Simultaneously, below, she could see two-legged shapes scattering. They appeared both as visual images and also as heat-impressions. She knew, with her human mind, that they were men and that they were running away from someone or something. With Smaug's mind, however, all she knew was the roar inside her belly. The bellowing of her hunger drowned out every other thought and impulse.

They landed lightly on the hard earth, with the air still wrapped under the membranous wings, giving them lift as they sprinted forward.

Meiji's mind shut down completely. She was aware only that there were wriggling parcels of live red heat all around her. With her gaping mouth and lunging neck, she began to snap at those that came within her reach.

It all happened very fast. She could feel small cuts and blows aimed at her, but they were like dull thumps bouncing off the shiny chain mail of her hard scales. With economical jerks, she dispatched the two-legged prey. Her methods were simple: first she caught their heads in her jaws and gave the body a quick shake to end the wriggling. Then she held the legs down with one foot while she tore off the head. It came away with a satisfying pop and a gush of bright scarlet. She swallowed it whole before turning her attention to the glorious viscera, soft and steaming, succulent beyond her wildest imaginings.

Now and then she might stop to throw her head back and give out a joyous bugling call, red gore streaming down the sides of her face. In the great distance, she could hear harsh fluting shrieks that made little or no sense to her just now.

There were also certain hard, brassy sounds that hurt her ears, preceded by bright flashes. Meiji–Smaug discovered she could shut down her hearing selectively, like blinking her eyes. She did so. Sparing her sensitive ears.

Now and then there were unexpectedly hard thumps upon her body. Initially, she paid no attention to these, since she had no idea what they were. But as the frequency of the thumps and the sounds continued to build and the violence of her hunger began to abate, she paused to take stock of the situation.

She had landed in the middle of the flattest part of the low area surrounded by cliffs. She had been running forward as she gorged herself and was now at the base of the rock-face. The blood-stained earth around her was littered with limbs and entrails. Behind her, she could hear crunching, squelching and occasional bugling. She recognized these as being from the other lizard that had accompanied her on this mission.

Directly in front of her, however, and standing at a slight height, was one of the wrigglers.

Something about this one distinguished it from all those she had dispatched so far. For one, it smelt different. Instead of salt and blood like all the rest, this one's scent contained stinging elements, hurtful to the nose. It had hard, oily edges, reminiscent of the ugly flashes.

Unnatural. Distasteful.

It looked different, too. Not only was it thinner and lighter in colour but, most importantly, it was not running away.

It was standing still.

It was shaking one of its upper limbs in the air. At the end of that limb was something small, round and black.

Meiji's mind stirred too.

This man.

There was something powerfully familiar about him. His pale skin and the deliberate movements, his self-possession. Where had she seen him before?

Her skin prickled with fear. There was a memory of childhood terror, buried very deep, about a dangerous, powerful man. Someone from whom she always had to be hidden. She wanted to cry out, to warn Smaug to back away from him. But it was too late. The lizard was hypnotized by the man's movements. Through Smaug's eyes, she saw him draw back his arm. She saw the small black thing, aimed squarely at them arcing through the air.

Smaug, becalmed from a surfeit of food, recognized it for what it was: a fly.

What else could such a thing be?

Without a second's reflection, she gave a half-hop and caught the small object between the tips of her pointed jaws.

In the next moment she recoiled: it tasted utterly vile. Acrid, harsh and cold. It smelled of the flashing thunder she had seen from high up on the cliff.

With a hasty snort, she spat it right out again, well-coated with gobs of bloody spittle, in the direction from which it had come. Straight at the wriggler that had thrown it at her.

Whereupon, to her amazement, the black object burst in a ball of blinding light.

Smaug reared back in fright, her wings flaring on either side.

Meiji heard an angry exclamation from Folia. 'Will you never control your mount? We'll both die of concussion before the morning's out. What the hell was that sound?'

The scent of charred meat smote the lizard's sensitive nose. She blinked her eyes against the smoke and fragments of blackened skin drifting in the air. Nevertheless she was curious. Meat is meat, after all, charred or uncharred. She poked her head forward once more, to see what it might be.

The wriggler was still moving, though only its upper portion was intact. The lower limbs had been blown away. Smaug turned her head this way and that, looking first with one eye then the other. It was still a wriggler and still rich with fat and juice. She turned her hearing back on and noticed that the thing was certainly producing a fair amount of sound, despite having lost two-thirds of itself.

An irritating, grating, bothersome sound.

Not worth listening to.

Leaning down, the lizard placed one foot on the wriggler's torso, opened her jaws and casually snapped off its head. The neck spurted just as satisfyingly as all the others, with the added benefit of bringing on a welcome silence. Nuzzling the remains of the body, she ripped away its light outer membranes, then buried her nose in the hot squish of its abdomen, siphoning up the entrails with lazy slurps.

A vast torpor was bringing the curtain down on her senses. She had gorged herself to the limit. Never in her short life had she felt so full. Meanwhile, the sun's heat had increased dangerously and would soon threaten her with heat stroke.

She needed to seek shade and a cool, quiet lair in which to recover from the feast.

It had been a good day.

7

The sun had gone down, leaving the sky a burnt orange and bright marigold. Meiji was seated in the open, facing towards the direction she called 'West', at the brow of the cliff that overlooked the morning's carnage. Mentor Folia, Mentor Vane and three others from the Island had their backs to the sunset. Gola had remained inside the rock fortress, wanting to sleep. Across from Meiji there was a tall, angular being, introduced as Aila. Her presence had not been explained. She had a fairly attractive face though her nose was rather long and she spoke in that childish way, like Rahm.

There was also one Other Person. He had introduced himself as her Uncle Youngest though he was actually her father. But was he a man or a woman? It was hard to tell. While all the others in the group and she herself had changed into loose caftans, he wore a strange sack-like outfit that covered him from neck to ankle, with a belt tied at the waist.

Meiji was sitting with her knees bent up and her arms folded across the tops of them. The Other Person was sitting just behind her. His voice was deep and manly. It was what she remembered of him and she loved him for it. But his face had changed. It was softer and more rounded. The hair, which had always been long was now tied in a knot at the nape of his neck. Like a woman. The body within the overalls was also clearly that of a woman. There were two fleshy lumps on his chest, jiggling inside the cloth.

So, no. She could not look at him just yet.

The group was sitting on rugs and cushions. Someone had brought flasks of hot food.

Folia was talking about the experience of being a Backer. 'I couldn't see! All the action was in the front. I just kept the tail lashing from side to side, hoping that it would be enough to sweep attackers aside.'

Kesh spoke about the struggle she'd had, keeping her Primary from losing focus. Brahi wondered whether there was any point attempting to control the lizards' blood lust. 'After all,' she said, 'if anyone stops to consider what we are doing – what *the lizards* are doing – we could not condone it.'

Vane was smiling and nodding, not saying much.

Asma, the mentor with the big halo of hair turned now and addressed the Other Person directly. 'Well? And what do you think, now that you know what our plan is?'

From behind Meiji, the rich contralto voice rumbled out, reassuring and warm. 'It is bold. Creative. I like that about it.'

Vane said, '—not enough to keep you with us.' It was not a question.

There was a slight pause. 'Forgive me, Mentor Vane,' said the Other Person, 'but no.' He paused. 'I need time – we *both* need time, Meiji included – to enjoy the pleasure of making our own decisions before we sign up for anything.'

Meiji could feel the pressure of attention focusing on her. She bent her neck so that her forehead rested on her forearms.

Kesh said, 'I suppose you realize there's nowhere for you to go aside from the Zone? Or the Suspended City? Movement between the Enclaves is not possible.'

'Not permitted or not possible?' asked the Other Person.

'Certainly not possible,' said Vane, 'because the means for long distance travel no longer exist. But forbidden? I don't think any of us knows. The question of trying to return to distant Enclaves has never arisen.'

Brahi said, 'What about your homeland? Is no part of it safe for you?'

'Not so long as the Generals remain in power,' said the Other Person.

Aila said, 'Then maybe we is go back to the Suspended City? Is a good life there. We is both have much money. Is can be good.'

'We'? thought Meiji.

'No!' said the Other Person. 'I found it suffocating. I need the open air. Emptiness and silence. The luxury of boredom.'

'Not many options in that case,' said Folia, with a dry chuckle. 'Boredom is a precious commodity in our world.'

'Even in the Zone?'

'Especially in the Zone,' said Brahi. 'There are no neutral areas. Every village is aligned with this or that team. Alliances shift on a weekly basis.'

'Surely there are nomads?' ventured the Other Person. 'People who drift outside the ebb and flow of the games?'

'If there are hidden populations,' said Brahi, 'they've done a good job of remaining hidden. We know of mercenaries and hunters, whom you must have met in the Suspended City. They're not nomadic. Just unattached.' Her voice trailed off. 'It would be a precarious life.'

'You'd be safe with us,' said Vane.

'Hardly!' exclaimed Asma. 'Now that our Base has been exposed …'

'Ah, yes,' Vane sighed. 'That's true. The Whole World Union has already sent furious messages demanding explanations. The player nations are bellowing.' She shrugged. 'Still: firearms were used and no one else knows how or why. The Forbidden Country has suddenly risen out of the mists but we're the only ones who know that. Knowledge is power.' She paused, drawing in a deep breath. 'We'll have to make the best possible use of it.'

Brahi said, to the Other Person. 'How is it you cannot return to your homeland even though the man … did you call him a General? … is dead?'

'Because Clone Brother is not die,' cut in Aila, in pidgin. 'He is stay on ship.'

'Hmm,' said Vane.

Aila said, 'Three drones is also stay. And maybe there is one more Clone Brother, still inside box. I is not sure. When they is go back, they is tell other brothers. Then all can come back to Zone. With more guns. With many ships. That is their plan.'

Meiji raised her head.

Vane was looking away. 'How ironic that we have joined this field of battle at the very point when a new force has entered the fray. What a shame.' Her voice was sober. 'What a waste of lives.'

Asma held out her wrist with the media-viewer on it. 'The news networks have been trying to report the story with almost no images to support their speculations. Most of the media-birds were knocked out by the very first blast.'

'None of the player nations has issued a coherent statement about what lies ahead,' said Brahi. 'The situation is unprecedented.'

Vane looked towards Meiji and the Other Person. 'So. You need to make decisions soon. Both of you.'

Meiji felt a warm hand on her shoulder. She did not turn her head around, but she didn't shake the hand away either.

'Where is Smaug?' she asked. It was the first thing she had said for several hours.

'Sleeping off her feast,' said Folia. 'She and the other beast. We sealed off the space they're in and flooded it with water. They'll be too cold to move once they wake up.'

Meiji looked at Vane. 'I want to stay with Smaug.' She paused. 'Please.'

Folia shook her head, 'She's not a pet, Meiji. You won't be

able to control her on your own.'

Meiji half-turned towards the Other Person. 'Maybe if … ?' She had not yet looked him in the eye or spoken directly to him.

Vane said, 'He'll need training.' She wasn't smiling but there was a glimmer in her eyes. 'And he will *owe* me for that training. With both time and information.'

'—a *lot* of training!' said Folia. 'These creatures are hard task-masters.'

'What about you, Aila?' asked Vane, turning towards the angular-faced person. Her voice softened. 'I believe you have known great suffering. It would not be hard for us to include you in our midst.' She paused. 'Either here at the Base or on the Island.'

Aila's face was strongly etched with shadows, lit on one side by the fading sky. She seemed bewildered for an instant. Then a slow crease appeared on either side of her mouth. 'You … you is ask me to stay?'

Vane nodded.

The hand on Meiji's shoulder felt warm and heavy. It was lightly massaging the back of her neck in a way that made her want to purr. In a short while, she believed she might lean back and accept an embrace. Maybe.

Vane turned towards the two of them once more. 'There seems to me little choice but to invite both of you to remain with us, for a while,' she said. 'We can offer hospitality, training and the freedom to come and go as you please. In exchange we want information. Everything you can tell us. About the Generals. About the Forbidden Lands. Whatever you know and whatever might help us in the conflicts that lie ahead. We can draw up an agreement.'

'You are kind, Mentor Vane,' said the Other Person. His voice sounded deeper than usual. 'I … *we* … accept your offer. With thanks.'

Without turning around, Meiji reached for her father's hands.

She drew his arms around her till he surrounded her, like a warm, breathing cloak. They sat thus, listening to the soft voices of the others as the dusk waned into night.

Acknowledgements

I want to thank my friends and family, in particular Geeta, Surya and Ethan, for having supported me with their patience, time and money for the five years it took me to write this book. I exiled myself to a tiny flat in Rhode Island (USA), living alone for the duration. Since I do not discuss work in progress with anyone, they had to take it on faith that I was actually writing something rather than just watching movies on Netflix all day long.

Thanks are also due to Thomas Abraham, my publisher. He believed in this book long before it was written and long after I had ceased to believe in it myself. There were many times when the only reason I didn't give up was the knowledge that there was a contract and that I had to honor it at least to the extent of producing a finished manuscript.

Thanks especially to my editor, Poulomi Chatterjee, for her belief in the book once I was finally able to e-mail the files to her. She has been the best of editors: friendly, tough and methodical – but friendly most of all. We had some great lunches.

ALSO AVAILABLE FROM HACHETTE INDIA

Escape

Manjula Padmanabhan

In the country she inhabits, Meiji is unique. The only surviving female in a land where women have been exterminated, she has been brought up in secret, cloistered and protected, by three men she knows as her uncles – Eldest, Middle and Youngest. Now, as she approaches adolescence, her guardians must ensure that the despotic clone-Generals who rule their homeland never get to know of her existence, and it falls to Youngest to escort Meiji on a long and treacherous journey through ravaged landscapes to the very edge of the world known to them.

An adventure story like no other, a tale of love and self-discovery in several unexpected layers, *Escape* is as unsettling as it is unputdownable. In its captivating portrayal of tender relationships blooming and thriving in a vicious, forbidding landscape, it bears out Manjula Padmanabhan's genius as a creator of compelling alternative worlds.